The UNSTOPPABLE Ramona AND BEEZUS

Beverly Cleary

OXFORD
UNIVERSITY PRESS

OXFORD

UNIVERSITY PRESS

Great Clarendon Street, Oxford OX2 6DP

Oxford University Press is a department of the University of Oxford.
It furthers the University's objective of excellence in research, scholarship,
and education by publishing worldwide in

Oxford   New York

Auckland   Cape Town   Dar es Salaam   Hong Kong   Karachi
Kuala Lumpur   Madrid   Melbourne   Mexico City   Nairobi
New Delhi   Shanghai   Taipei   Toronto

With offices in

Argentina   Austria   Brazil   Chile   Czech Republic   France   Greece
Guatemala   Hungary   Italy   Japan   Poland   Portugal   Singapore
South Korea   Switzerland   Thailand   Turkey   Ukraine   Vietnam

Oxford is a registered trade mark of Oxford University Press
in the UK and in certain other countries

Ramona and Her Mother first published 1978
Ramona Quimby, Age 8 first published 1981
Ramona Forever first published 1984
Ramona's World first published 1999

First published in this edition 2010 by arrangement with
HarperCollins Publishers Inc., New York, USA

British Library Cataloguing in Publication Data

Data available

ISBN: 978-0-19-278997-6

5 7 9 10 8 6 4

Printed in Great Britain

Paper used in the production of this book is a natural,
recyclable product made from wood grown in sustainable forests.
The manufacturing process conforms to the environmental
regulations of the country of origin

CONTENTS

Contents

RaMoNa aND HeR MoTHeR

CONTENTS

Contents

I

A PRESENT FOR WILLA JEAN

'When will they be here?' asked Ramona Quimby, who was supposed to be dusting the living room but instead was twirling around trying to make herself dizzy. She was much too excited to dust.

'In half an hour,' cried her mother from the kitchen, where she and Ramona's big sister Beatrice were opening and closing the refrigerator and oven doors, bumping into one another, forgetting where they had laid the pot holders, finding them and losing the measuring spoons.

The Quimbys were about to entertain their neighbours at a New Year's Day brunch to celebrate Mr Quimby's finding a job at the Shop-Rite Market after being out of work for several months. Ramona liked the word *brunch*, half breakfast and half lunch, and secretly felt the family had cheated because they had eaten their real breakfast earlier. They needed their strength to get ready for the party.

'And Ramona,' said Mrs Quimby as she hastily

laid out silverware on the dining-room table, 'be nice to Willa Jean, will you? Try to keep her out of everyone's hair.'

'Ramona, watch what you're doing!' said Mr Quimby, who was laying a fire in the fireplace. 'You almost knocked over the lamp.'

Ramona stopped twirling, staggered from dizziness, and made a face. Willa Jean, the messy little sister of her friend Howie Kemp, was sticky, crumby, into everything, and always had to have her own way.

'And behave yourself,' said Mr Quimby. 'Willa Jean is company.'

Not my company, thought Ramona, who saw quite enough of Willa Jean when she played at Howie's house. 'If Howie can't come to the brunch because he has a cold, why can't Willa Jean stay home with their grandmother, too?' Ramona asked.

'I really don't know,' said Ramona's mother. 'That isn't the way things worked out. When the Kemps asked if they could bring Willa Jean, I could hardly say no.'

I could, thought Ramona, deciding that since Willa Jean, welcome or not, was coming to the brunch, she had better prepare to defend her possessions. She went to her room, where she swept her best crayons and drawing paper into

6

a drawer and covered them with her pyjamas. Her Christmas roller skates and favourite toys, battered stuffed animals that she rarely played with but still loved, went into the corner of her closet. There she hid them under her bathrobe and shut the door tight.

But what could she find to amuse Willa Jean? If Willa Jean did not have something to play with, she would run tattling to the grown-ups. 'Ramona hid her toys!' Ramona laid a stuffed snake on her bed, then doubted if even Willa Jean could love a stuffed snake.

What Ramona needed was a present for Willa Jean, a present wrapped and tied with a good hard knot, a present that would take a long time to unwrap. Next to receiving presents, Ramona liked to give presents, and if she gave Willa Jean a present today, she would not only have the fun of giving, but of knowing the grown-ups would think, Isn't Ramona kind, isn't she generous to give Willa Jean a present? And so soon after Christmas, too. They would look at Ramona in her new red-and-green-plaid slacks and red turtleneck sweater and say, Ramona is one of Santa's helpers, a regular little Christmas elf.

Ramona smiled at herself in the mirror and was pleased. Two of her most important teeth were only halfway in, which made her look like a

7

jack-o'-lantern, but she did not mind. If she had grown-up teeth, the rest of her face would catch up someday.

Over her shoulder she saw reflected in the mirror a half-empty box of Kleenex on the floor beside her bed. Kleenex! That was the answer to a present for Willa Jean. She ran into the kitchen, where Beezus was beating muffin batter while her father fried sausages and her mother struggled to unmould a large gelatine salad onto a plate covered with lettuce.

'A present is a good idea,' agreed Mrs Quimby when Ramona asked permission, 'but a box of Kleenex doesn't seem like much of a present.' She shook the mould. The salad refused to slide out. Her face was flushed and she glanced at the clock on the stove.

Ramona was insistent. 'Willa Jean would like it. I know she would.' There was no time for explaining what Willa Jean was to do with the Kleenex.

Mrs Quimby was having her problems with the stubborn salad. 'All right,' she consented. 'There's an extra box in the bathroom cupboard.' The salad slid slowly from the mould and rested, green and shimmering, on the lettuce.

By the time Ramona had wrapped a large box of Kleenex in leftover Christmas paper, the guests had begun to arrive. First came the Hugginses and McCarthys and little Mrs Swink in a bright-green pants suit. Umbrellas were leaned outside the front door, coats taken into the bedroom, and the usual grown-up remarks exchanged. 'Happy New Year!' 'Good to see you!' 'We thought we would have to swim over, it's raining so hard.' 'Do you think this rain will ever stop?' 'Who says it's raining?' 'This is good old Oregon sunshine!' Ramona felt she had heard that joke one million times, and she was only in the second grade.

Then Mr Huggins said to Ramona's father, 'Congratulations! I hear you have a new job.'

'That's right,' said Mr Quimby. 'Starts tomorrow.'

'Great,' said Mr Huggins, and Ramona silently agreed. Having a father without a job had been hard on the whole family.

Then Mrs Swink smiled at Ramona and said, 'My, Juanita, you're getting to be a big girl. How old are you? I can't keep track.'

Should Ramona tell Mrs Swink her name was not Juanita? No, Mrs Swink was very old and should be treated with courtesy. Last year Ramona would have spoken up and said, My name is not Juanita, it's Ramona. Not this year. The room fell silent as Ramona answered, 'I'm seven and a half right now.' She was proud of herself for speaking so politely.

There was soft laughter from the grown-ups,

which embarrassed Ramona. Why did they have to laugh? She *was* seven and a half right now. She would not be seven and a half for ever.

Then the Grumbies arrived, followed by Howie's mother and father, the Kemps, and of course Willa Jean. Although Willa Jean was perfectly capable of walking, her father was carrying her so she would not get her little white shoes and socks wet. Willa Jean in turn was carrying a big stuffed bear. When Mr Kemp set his daughter down, her mother peeled off her coat, one arm at a time so Willa Jean would not have to let go of her bear.

There stood usually messy Willa Jean in a pink dress with tiny flowers embroidered on the collar. Her curly blonde hair, freshly washed, stood out like a halo. Her blue eyes were the colour of the plastic handle on Ramona's toothbrush. When she smiled, she showed her pearly little baby teeth. Willa Jean was not messy at all.

Ramona in her corduroy slacks and turtleneck sweater suddenly felt big and awkward beside her little guest and embarrassed to have jack-o'-lantern teeth.

And the things those grown-ups said to Willa Jean! 'Why, hello there, sweetheart!' 'My, don't you look like a little angel!' 'Bless your little heart. Did Santa bring you the great big bear?' Willa Jean smiled and hugged her bear. Ramona noticed she had lace ruffles sewn to the seat of her underpants.

'What is your bear's name, dear?' asked Mrs Swink.

'Woger,' answered Willa Jean.

Mrs Kemp smiled as if Willa Jean had said something clever and explained, 'She named her bear Roger after the milkman.'

Mrs Quimby said with amusement, 'I remember when Ramona named one of her dolls Chevrolet after the car.' Everyone laughed.

She didn't have to go and tell that, thought Ramona, feeling that her mother had betrayed her by telling, as if it were funny, something she had done a long time ago. She still thought Chevrolet was a beautiful name, even though she was old enough to know that dolls were not usually named after cars.

'See my bear?' Willa Jean held Woger up for Ramona to admire. Because everyone was watching, Ramona said politely, 'He's a nice bear.' And he was a nice bear, the nicest bear Ramona had ever seen. He was big and soft with a kindly look on his furry face and—this was the best part— each of his four big paws had five furry toes. You could count them, five on each paw. Even though Ramona felt she should be outgrowing bears, she longed to hold that bear, to put her arms around him, hug him close and love him. 'Would you like me to hold the bear for you?' she asked.

'No,' said Willa Jean.

'Ramona,' whispered Mrs Quimby, 'take Willa Jean into the kitchen and sit her at the table so she won't spill orange juice on the carpet.' Ramona gave her mother a baulky look, which was returned with her mother's you-do-it-or-you'll-catch-it look. Mrs Quimby was not at her best when about to serve a meal to a living room full of guests.

In the kitchen Willa Jean set Woger carefully on the chair before she climbed up beside him, displaying her ruffled underpants, and grasped her orange juice with both hands, dribbling some down the front of her fresh pink dress.

Mrs Quimby, assisted by Beezus, set out a platter of scrambled eggs and another of bacon and sausage beside the gelatine salad. Hastily she snatched two small plates from the cupboard and dished out two servings of brunch, which she set in front of Ramona and Willa Jean. Beezus, acting like a grown-up, filled a basket with muffins and carried it into the dining room. Guests took plates from the stack at the end of the table and began to serve themselves.

Ramona scowled. If Beezus got to eat in the living room with the grown-ups, why couldn't she? She was no baby. She would not spill.

'Be a good girl!' whispered Mrs Quimby, who had forgotten the marmalade.

I'm trying, thought Ramona, but her mother was too flurried to notice her efforts. Willa Jean took one bite of scrambled eggs and then went to work, patting the rest flat on her plate with the back of her spoon.

Ramona watched her charge give her egg a final pat with the back of her spoon, pick up her bear, and trot off to the living room, leaving Ramona alone to nibble a muffin, think, and look at her artwork, arithmetic papers, and some cartoons her father had drawn, which had been taped to the refrigerator door for the family to admire. Nobody missed Ramona, all alone out there in the kitchen. Conversation from the living room was boring, all about high prices and who would be the next president, with no mention of children or anything interesting until someone said, 'Oops. Careful, Willa Jean.'

Then Mrs Kemp said, 'No-no, Willa Jean. Mustn't put your fingers in Mr Grumbie's marmalade. It's sticky.'

Mrs Quimby slipped into the kitchen to see if the coffee was ready. 'Ramona, it's time to take Willa Jean to your room and give her your present,' she whispered.

'I changed my mind,' said Ramona.

Mr Quimby, refilling the muffin basket, overheard. 'Do as your mother says,' he ordered in a whisper, 'so that kid will give us a little peace.'

Ramona considered. Should she make a fuss? What would a fuss accomplish? On the other hand, if she gave Willa Jean her present, maybe she would have a chance to hold that lovable bear for a little while.

'OK,' Ramona agreed without enthusiasm.

Mrs Quimby followed Ramona into the living room. 'Willa Jean,' she said. 'Ramona has a present for you. In her room.'

Willa Jean's attention was caught.

'Go with Ramona,' Mrs Quimby said firmly.

Willa Jean, still clutching her bear, went.

'Here.' Ramona thrust the package at Willa Jean, and when her guest set her bear on the bed, Ramona started to pick him up.

Willa Jean dropped the package. 'Woger's my bear,' she said, and ran off to the living room with him. In a moment she returned bearless to pull and yank and tear the wrapping from the package. 'That's not a present.' Willa Jean looked cross. 'That's Kleenex.'

'But it's your very own,' said Ramona. 'Sit down and I'll show you what to do.' She broke the perforation in the top of the box and pulled out one pink sheet and then another. 'See. You can sit here and pull out all you want because it's your very own. You can pull out the whole box if you want.' She did not bother telling Willa Jean that she had always wanted to pull out a whole box of Kleenex, one sheet after another.

Willa Jean looked interested. Slowly she pulled out one sheet and then a second. And another and another. She began to pull faster. Soon she was pulling out sheet after sheet and having such a good time that Ramona wanted to join the fun.

'It's mine,' said Willa Jean when Ramona reached for a tissue. Willa Jean got to her feet and, pulling and flinging, ran down the hall to the living room. Ramona followed.

'See me!' Willa Jean ordered the grown-ups as she ran around pulling and flinging Kleenex all over the room. Guests grabbed their coffee mugs and held them high for safety.

'No-no, Willa Jean,' said Mrs Kemp. 'Mrs Quimby won't like you wasting her Kleenex.'

'It's mine!' Willa Jean was carried away by the joy of wasting Kleenex and being the centre of attention at the same time. 'Ramona gave it to me.'

Ramona looked around for the bear, which was sitting on Mr Grumbie's lap. 'Would you like me to hold Roger?' Ramona asked, careful not to say Woger.

'No.' The bear's owner saw through Ramona's scheme. 'Woger wants to sit *there*.' Mr Grumbie did not look particularly pleased.

Willa Jean's parents made no effort to stop their daughter's spree of pull and fling. Ramona watched, feeling much older than she had earlier in the day. She also felt awkward while Beezus moved around the living room, dodging Willa Jean and pouring coffee as if she were a grown-up herself.

At first guests were amused by Willa Jean. But amusement faded as coffee mugs had to be rescued every time Willa Jean passed by. Pink Kleenex littered the room. Ramona heard Mr Huggins whisper, 'How much Kleenex in a box anyway?'

Mrs McCarthy answered, 'Two hundred and fifty sheets.'

'That's a lot of Kleenex,' said Mr Huggins.

When Willa Jean came to the last piece of Kleenex, she climbed on the couch and carefully laid it on Mr Grumbie's bald head. 'Now you have a hat,' she said.

Conversation died, and the party died, too. No one called Willa Jean an angel now or blessed her little heart.

The Grumbies were first to leave. Mr Grumbie handed the bear to Willa Jean's mother as Willa

Jean filled her arms with pink tissues and tossed them into the air. 'Whee!' she cried, and scooped up another armful. 'Whee!'

Their departure seemed to be a signal for everyone to leave. 'Don't you want to take the Kleenex with you?' Mrs Quimby asked Willa Jean's mother. 'We can put it in a bag.'

'That's all right. Willa Jean has had her fun.' Mrs Kemp was helping Willa Jean into her coat.

'Bye-bye,' said Willa Jean prettily as her father carried her and Woger out of the door.

Other guests were telling Mr and Mrs Quimby how much they had enjoyed the brunch. Beezus was standing beside them as if it had been her party, too. Mrs McCarthy smiled. 'I can see you are your mother's girl,' she said.

'I couldn't get along without her,' Mrs Quimby replied generously.

'Goodbye, Juanita,' said little Mrs Swink.

'Goodbye, Mrs Swink,' answered Ramona, polite to the end.

She tossed an armful of Kleenex into the air so that her mother might notice her, too. Somehow tossing someone else's pulled-out Kleenex was not much fun, and Mrs Quimby was so busy saying goodbye to other guests she did not pay attention.

At last the door was closed, and from the porch where the neighbours were opening umbrellas,

Ramona's sharp ears caught her name. 'Willa Jean certainly reminds me of Ramona when she was Willa Jean's age,' someone said.

And someone else answered, 'She's Ramona all over again, all right.'

Ramona was filled with indignation. Willa Jean is *not* me all over again, she thought fiercely. I was never such a pest.

'Whew!' said Mr Quimby. 'That's over. What's the matter with those people, letting the kid show off like that?'

'Too much grandmother, I suppose,' answered Mrs Quimby. 'Or maybe it's easier for them to ignore her behaviour.'

'Come on, let's all pitch in and clean up this place,' said Mr Quimby. 'Ramona, you find a bag and pick up all the Kleenex.'

'Kleenex is made of trees,' said Beezus, already helping her mother collect coffee mugs from the living room. 'We shouldn't waste it.' Lately Beezus had become a friend of trees.

'Put the bag of Kleenex in the cupboard in the bathroom,' said Mrs Quimby, 'and let's all remember to use it.'

I never was as awful as Willa Jean, Ramona told herself as she went to work collecting two hundred and fifty pieces of scattered pink Kleenex. I just know I wasn't. She followed the trail of Kleenex back to her bedroom, and when the two hundred and fiftieth piece was stuffed in the bag, she leaned against her dresser to study herself in the mirror.

How come nobody ever calls me my mother's girl? Ramona thought. How come mother never says she couldn't get along without me?

2

SLACKS FOR ELLA FUNT

The day Ramona's father went to work at the check-out counter of the Shop-Rite Market, life in the Quimby household changed. Sometimes Mr Quimby worked all day; sometimes he worked afternoons and evenings. Sometimes he took the car to work while Mrs Quimby took the bus to her job in Dr Hobson's office. Sometimes she drove the car while he took the bus, or one would drop the other off at work.

Life was different for Ramona, too. She now went home with Howie Kemp after school. The Quimbys paid Howie's grandmother to look after Ramona until one of her parents could come for her after work. Mrs Quimby said she could not hold a job unless she knew where Ramona was. Every single minute. Beezus also went to the Kemps' house after school unless she telephoned her mother for permission to go to a friend's house. Ramona had no choice.

One rainy Saturday morning, when Mr Quimby had worked at the market for several weeks,

Ramona asked her mother, 'Where do you have to go today?' Mr Quimby always worked on Saturday, the busiest day at the market, which meant Mrs Quimby had the use of the car to run errands. Ramona was concerned about her mother's errands because she always had to go with her, or as she thought of it, be dragged along. Most of them were of no interest to her.

Mrs Quimby thought a moment before she said in surprise, 'Well, what do you know? No place. We have groceries in the cupboard. No one needs to go shopping for shoes. No one needs a present to take to a birthday party. I can stay home.'

'Then what are you going to do?' asked Ramona. She hoped her mother would not decide to clean the house.

'Sew,' answered Mrs Quimby. 'I've been trying to finish a blouse for weeks.'

Sewing seemed like a cosy way to spend a rainy morning. Ramona watched her mother get out the portable sewing machine and set it on the dining-room table along with a pattern and bundle of fabric.

'I'm going to wash my hair,' announced Beezus.

'Again?' enquired Mrs Quimby. 'You washed it only the day before yesterday.'

'But it's so oily,' complained Beezus.

'Don't worry, it's just your age,' reassured Mrs Quimby. 'You'll outgrow it.'

'Yes,' said Beezus gloomily. 'In about a million years when I'm too old to care.'

'You'll never be that old,' said Mrs Quimby. 'I promise.'

Ramona, bored with her sister's daily complaints about oily hair, leaned on the dining-room table to watch her mother.

'I like it when you stay home,' she remarked, thinking of the days before her mother had gone to work when the house had smelled of baking cookies or homemade bread on Saturday morning. 'Can I sew, too?' she asked, picturing a companionable morning close to her mother. She imagined a neighbour dropping in and saying, Ramona is her mother's girl, as the two of them stitched away together. Yes, her mother would answer, I can't get along without Ramona.

'Of course you may sew. You know where the scrap bag is,' answered her mother with a smile. 'What would you like to make?'

'I'll have to think,' Ramona said. She went to her room and in a moment returned with a tired-looking stuffed elephant and a large piece of red-and-white checked cloth left over from a dress her mother had made for her when she was in kindergarten. Ramona had liked that dress

23

because it matched the red plastic hat the firemen gave her when the kindergarten class visited the fire department.

Mrs Quimby looked up from the sewing machine. 'I haven't seen Ella Funt for a long time,' she remarked as Ramona stood the elephant on its four feet on the table.

'I'm going to make her some slacks,' said Ramona as she spread out the fabric. 'All my other animals have clothes. Except that snake.'

Mrs Quimby considered. 'Slacks for an elephant won't be easy. Why not make slacks for Chevrolet?'

'She's too beat up,' said Ramona critically.

'If I were you, I would—' began Mrs Quimby as Ramona studied the checked cloth.

'I can *do* it,' interrupted Ramona, who was impatient with instructions. Mrs Quimby said no more. The sewing machine began to hum. Ramona picked up her mother's pinking shears and began to cut. There was something satisfying about using pinking shears and watching fabric part in such a neat zigzag line. Working quietly at the table with her mother was even more satisfying. Even the grouchy old cat, Picky-picky, sitting on a corner of the dining-room carpet washing his paws, was behaving like a satisfactory pet.

This morning was a time for sharing confidences.

'Mother, did I used to be like Willa Jean?' Ramona asked the question that had worried her since the brunch.

Mrs Quimby answered when she came to the end of her seam. 'You were a lively little girl with a lot of imagination. And you still are.'

Ramona was reassured by her mother's words. 'I would never throw Kleenex all over the living room when someone had a party,' she said virtuously.

If only every Saturday could be like this one: no errands to run, and the two of them sewing and talking together. 'Are you going to stop working now that Daddy has a job?' Ramona asked as Beezus, her hair wet but combed, came into the dining room with a paper bag in her hand.

Mrs Quimby looked up from the collar she was pinning to her blouse. 'Why, no,' she answered as if she were surprised by the question.

'Why not?' demanded Ramona as Beezus pulled some sewing out of the bag.

'Because we got behind on our bills when Daddy was out of work,' explained Mrs Quimby, 'and because we have plenty of ways to use money. Beezus will be ready for college in five years, and in a few more years you will be ready, too.'

College, to Ramona, was a faraway school for young grown-ups. When they went to college, their mothers worried about them and mailed them boxes of cookies that they called Care Packages. She had learned this from listening to some of the neighbours talk to her mother. Ramona was surprised to learn that she and her sister would be expected to go to such a school someday.

'Besides,' continued Mrs Quimby, 'I like my job. The people are interesting, and Dr Hobson is pleasant to work for.'

'I wish Daddy liked his job.' Beezus's head was bent over the skirt she was basting together.

Ramona understood what Beezus meant, because she felt sad, too, and her stomach felt tight when her father came home tired and discouraged after a day in the check-out line. People were in a hurry, many were cross because the line was long, and some customers acted as if he were to blame because prices were so high.

'So do I wish he liked his job.' There was a hint of sadness in Mrs Quimby's voice. 'But maybe when he has worked at Shop-Rite longer he will like it better. New jobs take getting used to.'

Ramona held up the two pieces of cloth she had cut out for the front and back of the slacks. Both were the same. Until now she had fastened together whatever she was making with Scotch tape or a stapler. Now Ramona felt the time had come for her to advance. Beezus had been using the sewing machine for several years. 'Can I sew on the machine?' she asked.

'If you're careful.' Mrs Quimby demonstrated the use of the machine. Even though Ramona had to stand up to stitch, she found the machine easier to use than she had expected. She followed her mother's instructions carefully and watched the needle move up and down, leaving behind a trail of tiny, even stitches. Ramona was filled with pleasure at the sight. The sewing machine was much more satisfactory than the stapler, which often stuck or ran out of staples. All sorts of uses for the sewing machine began to fly through Ramona's imagination. Maybe she could even sew paper and make a book. Quickly, but still carefully, she finished the seams of Ella Funt's slacks.

'See? I can use the sewing machine, too,' Ramona bragged to Beezus.

Beezus did not bother to answer. She was busy pulling on her skirt while Mrs Quimby stood by to see how it fit.

Ramona picked up her grey-flannel elephant and shoved its hind legs into the legs of the slacks.

Mrs Quimby pinned the waistband for Beezus and stood back to look at the skirt. 'It fits nicely,' she said. 'You can go ahead and stitch it.' Pleased, Beezus went off to the bedroom to admire her work in the mirror.

Ramona tugged and tugged at Ella Funt's slacks, but no matter how hard she tugged she could not make them come up to the elephant's waist, or to what she guessed was the elephant's waist. Ella Funt's bottom was too big, or the slacks were too small. At the same time, the front of the slacks seemed way too big. They bunched under Ella Funt's paunch. Ramona scowled.

Beezus twirled into the living room to make her skirt stand out. Anyone could see she was pleased with what she had accomplished.

Ramona scowled harder, but no one noticed. No one even cared. The sewing machine hummed. Beezus slipped out of her skirt. Ramona heaved a gusty sigh. The sewing machine stopped humming.

'Having problems, Ramona?' enquired Mrs Quimby.

'These slacks look terrible.' Ramona glowered. 'They look awful!'

Mrs Quimby considered Ella Funt and her slacks. 'Well,' she said, after a moment, 'maybe you could find something easier to sew. Slacks for an elephant are very hard to make. I'm sure I couldn't do it.'

Ramona could not scowl any harder. 'I *like* to do hard things.'

'I know you do, and I admire you for it,'

answered Ramona's mother, 'but sometimes it's better to start with something easy and work up.'

'Why don't you make a skirt?' suggested Beezus. 'Ella Funt is a girl elephant.'

'I don't want to make a skirt!' Ramona's voice was rising. 'I want to make pants!' She looked at her mother and sister, so calm and happy with their sewing. Why couldn't her sewing turn out right the way theirs did? Ramona felt shut out from something she longed to share. Picky-picky stopped washing, gave Ramona a long stare, and slowly and disdainfully left the room.

'Now, Ramona,' said Mrs Quimby gently, 'I know you are disappointed, but life is full of little disappointments. You'll get over it. Why don't you try something else? A skirt the way Beezus suggested.'

'I won't either get over it!' Nobody had to tell Ramona that life was full of disappointments. She already knew. She was disappointed almost every evening because she had to go to bed at eight-thirty and never got to see the end of the eight o'clock movie on television. She had seen many beginnings but no endings. And even though she had outgrown her tricycle, she was still disappointed because she never could find a tricycle licence plate with her name printed on it. Didn't the people who made those licence plates care about little girls named Ramona? And then there was that time she had gone to the Easter egg hunt in the park with a big paper bag and had found only two little candy eggs, one of which had been stepped on. Nobody had to tell Ramona about disappointment.

The disappointment of Ella Funt's slacks was not one of life's little disappointments to Ramona. It was a big disappointment because she had failed at something she wanted to do and because she no longer felt she was sharing with her mother. Beezus was doing so instead. 'I don't want to do something easier!' yelled Ramona, and hurled poor old Ella Funt and her slacks across the room. As the elephant bounced off the wall, a thought flashed through Ramona's mind. Her mother had not actually said she was not like Willa Jean.

Mrs Quimby spoke sharply. 'That's enough, Ramona. Calm down.'

'I won't calm down!' shouted Ramona, bursting into tears. She fled to that haven of anyone in the family who had tears to shed, the bathroom, where she sat on the edge of the tub sniffling miserably. Nothing was fair. Her mother was always saying everyone must be patient with Beezus when she was cross because Beezus had reached a difficult age, but what about Ramona? Her age was difficult, too—not old enough to sit down with her mother and sew something she wanted to sew and too old to go pulling out a whole box of Kleenex and flinging it all over the house like Willa Jean. People should not think being seven and a half years old was easy, because it wasn't.

As Ramona sat on the hard edge of the tub, feeling sorry for herself and trying to sort out her thoughts, she noticed a brand-new red-white-and-blue tube of toothpaste lying beside the washbasin. How smooth and shiny it looked with only one little dent where someone had squeezed it once. That tube was as good as new, and it was the large economy size.

Ramona was suddenly filled with longing. All her life she had wanted to squeeze toothpaste, really squeeze it, not just one little squirt on her toothbrush but a whole tube, a large economy size tube, all at one time just as she had longed to pull out a whole box of Kleenex.

I'll give it one little squeeze, thought Ramona. Just one teeny squeeze to make me feel better. She seized the tube. How fat and smooth it felt in her hand. She unscrewed the cap and laid it on the counter. Then she squeezed that tube the way she had been told she must never squeeze it, right in the middle. White paste shot out faster than she had expected.

That squirt really did make Ramona feel

better. She squeezed again. Another satisfying squirt. She felt even better. This was more fun than finger painting or modelling turtles out of clay. Suddenly Ramona no longer cared what anyone thought. She squeezed and squirted, squeezed and squirted. She forgot about Ella Funt's slacks, she forgot about her mother and Beezus, she forgot that no one ever called her her mother's girl. The paste coiled and swirled and mounded in the washbasin. Ramona decorated the mound with toothpaste roses as if it were a toothpaste birthday cake. When the tube was almost empty, she rolled it properly from the bottom and squeezed some more. Tighter and tighter she rolled it until not another speck of toothpaste could be squeezed out.

There, thought Ramona with pleasure and satisfaction, which unfortunately lasted only a moment. With the rolled-up tube in her hand Ramona stood looking at the white mound. What would her mother say? What could she do with it? Wash it down the drain? It might foam all over the bathroom. Or it might stop up the sink. Then she really would be in trouble.

Of course just at that moment Beezus came down the hall towards the bathroom. Ramona started to slam the door, but Beezus blocked it with her foot.

Ramona tried to hide the toothpaste by standing tall in front of the washbasin. Unfortunately, she was not tall enough.

Beezus looked over her shoulder. 'Is that *toothpaste*?' she asked in disbelief.

Ramona scowled because she did not know what else to do.

'Mother!' Beezus had seen the rolled-up squeezed-out tube. 'Ramona has wasted a whole tube of toothpaste!' Now apparently Beezus was not only a friend of trees, she was a friend of toothpaste as well.

'You keep quiet!' ordered Ramona. 'I'll pick it up.'

'How?' asked Beezus. 'How can you pick up toothpaste?'

'With a spoon. I can put it in a plastic bag with a spoon,' said Ramona. 'We can dip our toothbrushes in the bag.'

'Yuck,' said Beezus rudely. 'Everybody's germs will get mixed up.'

'Picky,' said Ramona.

'Girls!' Mrs Quimby came to see what the argument was about. 'Ramona, what on earth got into you?' she asked in exasperation when she saw the toothpaste birthday cake.

The whole thing was much too difficult to explain. Really impossible, so Ramona said cockily,

33

like the funny man on television, 'The devil made me do it.'

'That's not funny, Ramona.' Mrs Quimby meant what she said.

Ramona did not understand. Everyone laughed when the man on television said the devil made him do something. Why wasn't the remark funny when she said it? Because she was seven and a half (right now!). That was why. Grown-ups could get away with anything. It wasn't fair.

'Get a spoon and a jar from the kitchen,' directed Mrs Quimby, 'and scoop up the toothpaste.' Then she said to Beezus, 'She can use it herself, and the rest of us can use a fresh tube.'

Somehow Ramona felt sad knowing she was to be excluded from the family tube of toothpaste for a long time. And she wished her mother would not speak about her to Beezus as if she were not in the room.

'Ramona,' said her mother, 'don't you ever let me catch you squeezing out a whole tube of toothpaste again.'

'I won't,' promised Ramona, and as she went off to the kitchen for a jar and a spoon she felt unexpectedly cheerful. She had done something she had always wanted to do. *Of course* she would never squeeze out a whole tube of toothpaste again. She had done it once. She did not need to do it again.

3

NOBODY LIKES RAMONA

In February there came a day for Ramona when everything went wrong, one thing after another, like a row of dominoes falling over. Ramona's mother set it off. 'By the way, Ramona,' said Mrs Quimby after breakfast as she hastily tossed potatoes, carrots, and stew meat into the Crock-Pot to simmer while the family was away all day. 'Please don't run in the hall in your socks. You might slip and fall.'

Ramona's father was next. 'And Ramona,' he said, pulling strings off celery before slicing it and adding it to the stew, 'when you wash your hands, don't leave the dirt on the cake of soap.'

Then Beezus. 'Or wipe it on the towel.'

'I haven't had time to get dirty,' said Ramona, who had finished her breakfast. 'And I have my shoes on.'

'We are talking about yesterday,' said her father.

Ramona thought yesterday was a long time ago, hardly worth mentioning. 'Everybody picks on me,' she said.

'Poor kid.' Mr Quimby kissed his wife on the cheek and each daughter on the top of her head. Then he said, singing the first few words, 'Hi-ho, hi-ho, it's off to work I go and at least forty-six changes in produce prices to remember.'

Ramona knew her father dreaded Wednesdays, the day prices were changed on fruits and vegetables.

'Maybe things will be easier when you are more used to the job,' said Mrs Quimby. After her husband left to catch the bus, she kissed the girls as if she were thinking about something else and handed Ramona her lunch box and Beezus the brown paper bag that held her sandwich. Seventh-graders thought lunch boxes were babyish. 'Scoot along,' Mrs Quimby said. 'I have to leave early to take the car for brake adjustment, and then I have to take the bus to work.'

'I wish Daddy would get used to his job,' remarked Beezus as the sisters plodded towards Glenwood School. Clouds hung low, and the wind was cold. For days the sidewalks had been too wet for roller skating.

'Me, too,' said Ramona, who wanted her parents to be happy so their children could be happy, too. 'Why doesn't he find another job?'

'Jobs aren't that easy to get,' Beezus explained.

'Remember how long he was out of work before he found a job at the market.'

Ramona did remember. She remembered how discouraged her father had been after a day of job-hunting and how he had disliked standing in line to collect unemployment insurance.

'It might be easier if he had finished college,' said Beezus.

'Why didn't he?' asked Ramona.

'Because he and mother got married,' Beezus explained. 'And then they had me.' Beezus sounded smug, as if being the first born made her more important to her parents than Ramona.

But I'm the baby, thought Ramona. She was glad when school started; maybe her day would improve in school. Ramona liked Mrs Rudge, her new teacher, who had taken over the second grade when the former teacher left after Christmas to have a baby. She *thought* Mrs Rudge liked her, as she liked all the children, but she was not sure exactly where she stood with her. The classroom buzzed softly and busily with the sound of children learning about Indians and joined-up writing.

When the morning was half over, Ramona finished her work sheet and was busy filling all the double *oo*'s she could find with crossed eyes and frowns:

book

Mrs Rudge paused beside her desk. Ramona did not have time to hide the frowning *oo*'s.

Mrs Rudge glanced over Ramona's work sheet. 'Why don't you look again?' she suggested. 'Is *like* spelled *l-i-c-k?*'

'I can't spell,' said Ramona. 'I'm terrible at spelling.' That's what her family said whenever Ramona wrote a note. They always laughed and said, 'Ramona is no speller. See how she spells *much m-u-c-k.*' They behaved as if she had done something clever.

Ramona learned right there that Mrs Rudge was a teacher who did not accept excuses. 'There is no such word as *can't*,' she said, and went on to inspect Becky's work sheet.

How can there be no such word as *can't*? Ramona wondered. Mrs Rudge had just said *can't*. If there was no such word as *can't*, Mrs Rudge could not have said there was no such word as *can't*. Therefore, what Mrs Rudge had said could not be true. Ramona was left with a vague feeling that Mrs Rudge did not like her because she did not offer to give Ramona extra help in spelling.

At lunchtime when Ramona went into the

multipurpose room with her lunch box, she found that she had a leftover-pot-roast sandwich in her lunch. She did not like a leftover-pot-roast sandwich because the meat slid out in big pieces when she bit into it. After chewing awhile she thought, I won't eat it, and she stuffed the rest of her sandwich into the hole in her milk carton and threw it into the trash can. She sat there arguing with herself about how there had to be a word *can't* because she had just thought it. This was not a good day.

After school at the Kemps' house, Ramona and Howie drank the same old apple juice and ate the same old graham crackers that Mrs Kemp always set out for them. Sticky Willa Jean, holding Woger by one paw, stood and watched. She was wearing a T-shirt with *Grandma Loves Me* printed on the front. The shirt had shrunk so much it showed her navel—tummy button, Mrs Kemp called it.

Then Howie got out the checkerboard, which he placed on the carpet. Kneeling, he and Ramona began to divide the red and black checkers.

'I want to play.' Willa Jean plunked herself down on the carpet, sitting on Woger as if he were a cushion, which was no way to treat a bear, especially a bear like Woger.

'Aw, Willa Jean—' protested Howie, who had his problems with his little sister.

'Now, Howie,' said Mrs Kemp, busy with her endless knitting, 'play nicely with your sister. She's little, you know.'

Howie knew all right.

Willa Jean, pleased to have her grandmother on her side, set a red checker on top of a black checker. 'Your turn,' she said to Ramona as if she were being generous.

Ramona and Howie shared one hopeless look. They were familiar with Willa Jean's original rules for checkers. Ramona set a black checker on top of Willa Jean's red checker. Howie added red and so on in turn until the tower of checkers grew high and crooked. At last, when Willa Jean set a checker on top, the tower tumbled.

'I won!' crowed Willa Jean as Howie tried to prevent scattered checkers from rolling under the couch. 'Grandma, I beat Howie and Wamona!'

'Smart girl!' Mrs Kemp paused in her knitting to smile down upon her granddaughter.

The situation was hopeless. 'Let's go down in the basement and see if we can think of something to build,' said Howie, and Ramona agreed. They would be undisturbed in the basement. Willa Jean was afraid of the furnace.

Safe from interruption, Howie and Ramona decided to build a boat of the scrap lumber Mr Kemp collected for Howie to work with. They had already built a dog, a cat, and a duck decoy that Mr Kemp said would never fool a real live duck. Now they sawed and pounded until they had a boat with two decks. They were so good at nailing by now they did not even pound their fingers. Next they found a dowel and sawed off two pieces for smokestacks, which Howie studied. 'It's going to be hard to nail them to our boat,' he said.

'We could use Scotch tape,' said Ramona, who felt that almost anything could be accomplished with Scotch tape.

'I don't think it's strong enough for wood,' was Howie's objection. 'Glue might be better.'

'Scotch tape would work if we use lots of it.' Ramona was an experienced user of Scotch tape.

In the end, glue won out because Howie thought a boat should look neat. Very, very carefully they spread glue on the ends of the dowels and pressed them in place. They put the top back on the tube of glue, and each held a dowel in place, waiting for the glue to dry. They had not spilled a drop. Fortunately, the glue was quick drying.

'Let's see if our boat will float,' said Howie. He pressed the plug of the laundry tub in place and turned on the tap.

'Howie, what are you two doing down there?' Mrs Kemp called from the top of the stairs.

'Just seeing if our boat will float,' he answered.

'All right,' said Mrs Kemp. 'Just don't let the tub overflow.'

'We won't,' promised Howie.

The boat floated. Howie and Ramona stirred up a storm at sea to make things interesting and watched their boat ride the waves. As it bobbed up and down, Ramona happened to glance up at a shelf above the laundry tub. There she spotted a blue plastic bottle with the picture of a nice old-fashioned lady's face on the label. Bluing!

Ramona knew all about bluing because her mother had used it to make white washing look whiter back in the days before she had gone to work. 'If we could get that bottle, we could turn the water blue like a real ocean,' she suggested. 'It only takes a little bit.'

Howie was enthusiastic, but how were they to reach a bottle on such a high shelf? For some reason, Mrs Rudge's words, there's no such word as *can't*, ran through Ramona's mind. Of course they could get that bottle of bluing.

Ramona managed to balance on her stomach on the edge of the tub. Then she got one knee up and with a boost from Howie was able to climb up onto the edge of the tub. She stood teetering on the narrow edge clinging to the front of the shelf with one hand while she managed to grasp the bottle with the other and hand it down to Howie. As she did so, the top flew off. Bluing splashed over Howie, who tried to catch the top only to have the bottle slip from his fingers into the tub of water, where it poured forth swirls of beautiful deep blue. Ramona was so startled she lost her balance and landed standing up to her knees in blue water.

'Boy, Ramona, see what you've done.' Howie looked down at his shirt and jeans, now streaked with blue.

Ramona felt Howie was being most unfair. She did not spill the bluing on purpose. Besides, why wasn't the top of the bottle screwed on tight? Because some grown-up had not screwed it on, that's why. Children weren't the only people who did things wrong. She fumbled through the blue water, now much bluer than any ocean, and pulled the plug. As the water drained out, she and Howie looked at one another. Now what should they do?

Mrs Kemp called down the stairway. 'It's awfully quiet down there. What are you two up to?'

'We had—sort of an accident,' confessed Howie.

Mrs Kemp came running down the stairs. 'Oh, my land!' she cried. 'Oh, my goodness!'

Willa Jean began to howl at the top of the stairs.

'Grandma won't let the furnace get you, darling,' said Mrs Kemp. Willa Jean sat down at the top of the stairs and wept.

Mrs Kemp lifted dripping Ramona out of the tub. Then, right there in front of Howie, she pulled off Ramona's socks, slacks, and blouse and dumped them in the washing machine. Then she pulled off Howie's socks, shirt, and jeans and dumped those in the washing machine, too. Ramona and Howie did not know where to look, they were so embarrassed to be standing there in their underwear. Two years ago they would not have minded, but now that they were in the second grade, they felt that underwear was private.

Mrs Kemp filled the tub with a few inches of clear water and lifted Ramona back in. Without a word she began to scrub Ramona's feet with a bar of yellow soap. When it was plain that Ramona's feet were going to stay blue, she lifted Ramona out again, pulled a towel out of the dryer, and handed it to her. Then Mrs Kemp went to work on Howie's blue hands.

When Ramona's blue feet were dry, she asked politely, 'What will I wear?' Of course she could not go around in her underwear.

'We'll find something.' Mrs Kemp, rinsing Ramona's shoes, sounded grim. She held up the shoes, now a strange greenish brown, to let the water drain off them before she leaned them against the furnace to dry.

Suddenly Mrs Kemp missed Willa Jean. 'Oh, my goodness!' she cried, and dashed up the stairs. Ramona and Howie, careful not to look at one another, followed. What Ramona saw made tears come to her eyes. There sat Willa Jean under the dining-room table holding a pair of scissors, sharp scissors, and Woger, who now had only one leg. Willa Jean had cut off Woger's leg! That lovable bear. How could Willa Jean do such a terrible thing? Ramona felt like crying, she loved Woger so.

'Give Grandma the scissors,' coaxed Mrs Kemp. 'We don't want the scissors to hurt Willa Jean.'

'Boy, Willa Jean.' Howie was disgusted. 'What did you have to go and do a dumb thing like that for?'

Willa Jean looked as if her brother had said something unkind. 'I wanted to see if Woger had bones,' she said.

'He is so soft you should know he doesn't have bones,' said Howie. 'You didn't have to wreck him.'

Willa Jean looked at the stuffing coming out of her bear's wounds and began to cry.

'Never mind, darling,' said Mrs Kemp. 'Grandma will sew Woger's leg back on after she finds some clothes for Howie and Ramona.'

Ramona was soon bundled into Howie's old shirt and jeans and a pair of ragged sneakers much too big for her. She sat on one end of the couch while Howie sat on the other.

Ramona was cross because she did not like wearing Howie's old clothes. Howie was cross because Ramona had thought of dying the water blue. Both were cross with Willa Jean for spoiling the checker game. Mrs Kemp, who was sewing Woger's leg back on, was cross with Ramona and Howie, but of course she was not cross with Willa Jean. Only Willa Jean, lying on her back under the coffee table and sucking her thumb, was happy.

This afternoon was not the first time Ramona had been in trouble at the Kemps' house. There was that day she and Howie found Mrs Kemp's pinking shears. Ramona had been pinking Howie's hair when Mrs Kemp discovered what they were up to. Ramona had thought she was unreasonably displeased, because Howie's hair was so curly the pinking did not show.

Now Ramona worried. If she got into any more trouble, maybe Mrs Kemp would not want to look after her. Then her mother could no longer work in Dr Hobson's office and would have to stay home. Ramona quickly squashed a deep-down thought that she would like to have her mother stay home again. She waited anxiously for Beezus to come. She waited and waited. No Beezus.

Howie looked at a sporting-goods catalogue turning the pages with blue hands. Boots, quilted jackets with many pockets, and those tents that folded into tiny packages interested Howie. He did not offer to share the catalogue with Ramona, even though he knew she liked pictures of duck decoys.

Ramona heaved a gusty sigh. She wished she had brought her Betsy book with her. She enjoyed reading about Betsy because everyone in the book was so nice to her.

When Woger's wounds were mended, Mrs Kemp started supper. The fragrance of pork chops floated from the kitchen. The younger Mrs Kemp, Howie's mother, came home with packages and bags of groceries. 'Why, hello, Ramona,' she said. 'I didn't know you were still here.'

Mr Kemp came home from work. 'Hello there,' he said. 'Are you still here?'

Ramona did not know how to answer such a question. She felt embarrassed, in the way, unwanted. Where was Beezus? What had happened to her parents? Her ears strained for familiar footsteps or the sound of the Quimby car.

'Your mother and father are late today,' remarked Howie's mother as she set the table.

Once more Ramona did not know how to answer. Cars were now driving with their lights on. Why didn't someone come? What if her mother and father had been in an accident? Who would take care of Ramona? It seemed as if she might have to sit here on the couch in Howie's old clothes for ever.

Ramona began to feel hungry. How good a pork chop would taste! She knew she would not be asked to share the Kemps' supper. With the price of meat these days there would not be an extra chop. Ramona's mouth watered so much she had to swallow. She thought of the pot-roast sandwich she had not finished at lunchtime.

'Ramona, could I fix you some peanut butter and crackers?' asked Howie's mother.

'No, thank you.' Ramona pictured a brown chop with mashed potatoes and pool of gravy.

The Kemps sat down at the table with Willa Jean perched on two cushions beside her grandmother, who began to cut her meat for her. And she won't even eat a whole chop, thought Ramona, who felt like a stranger, an intruder in the lives of others. The Kemps said little as they ate. Perhaps they did not want to talk in front of an outsider. Ramona listened to the clink of knives and forks against plates as the Kemps ate their pork chops. She was profoundly embarrassed.

'Willa Jean, darlin', we don't chew with our mouth open,' said Willa Jean's grandmother.

At last, when Ramona was blinking back tears because she was sure her parents would never come, the old familiar car turned into the driveway.

'Goodbye!' cried Ramona, pulling on her car coat as she ran out of the door.

Mr Quimby was driving, Mrs Quimby sat next to him, and Beezus was in the back seat. She must have been picked up at a friend's house. 'You were late,' Ramona informed her family, her voice stern. 'You kept me waiting.'

'I'm sorry.' Mrs Quimby sounded tired. 'It was one of those days. After work when I went to catch a bus to the garage to pick up the car, the bus was late, and when I finally got to the garage, the mechanics hadn't finished the job and I had to wait some more. And I had to keep your father waiting, too.'

'What a day!' said Mr Quimby. 'Price changes to remember, and I worked the express line besides.' Ramona knew her father disliked the express line in which customers were not supposed to have more than nine items in each basket. Many people tried to slip through with ten or eleven items. Everyone in line was in a hurry and counted the items in one another's baskets. There were arguments. All this unpleasantness took a lot out of Mr Quimby.

Please, please like your job, prayed Ramona, forgetting her own troubles for a moment.

Mrs Quimby turned in the front seat to look at her daughters. Of course she noticed Ramona was wearing Howie's old clothes.

'Ramona, why are you wearing . . . ?' Mrs Quimby seemed too tired to finish the question.

'Howie and I sort of spilled some stuff and Mrs Kemp washed our clothes and they aren't dry yet,' explained Ramona. Her mother could discover her blue feet later. 'It was Willa Jean's fault. She wrecked our checker game so we had to go down in the basement to get away from her.'

'Sounds like you,' said Beezus. 'I can remember when you used to bump the coffee table with your tricycle when I was playing checkers with a friend.'

'I did not!' Ramona was indignant.

'You did, too,' said Beezus. 'You just can't remember.'

'Girls!' said Mrs Quimby. 'It doesn't really matter who wrecked whose checker game or where or when.'

Rain slanted through the beams of the car lights, the windshield wipers *splip-splopped*, the family was silent. Ramona, huddled in the corner of the back seat, wondered if she really had been as awful as Willa Jean. Nobody loved Ramona— well, maybe her father a little bit sometimes. If her mother really loved her, she would say to Beezus that Ramona was never anything like Willa Jean.

Ramona not only felt unloved, she was so hungry her stomach growled. As Mr Quimby turned their car into the driveway, she thought of the stew that had been simmering away in the Crock-Pot all day. How good it would smell when they opened the door! The Crock-Pot always gave out a warm and welcoming fragrance as if Ramona's mother had been home all day preparing supper to greet them. One whiff of stew, Ramona was sure, and everything would be all right again. Her mother would forget her troubles with the car, her father would begin to make jokes again, she and Beezus would set the table, and they would all sit down to a nice warm dinner.

4

The Quarrel

As soon as Ramona stepped through the back door, she knew something was wrong. There was a chill about the house, and it had the faint mustiness of a place that had been closed and unoccupied all day. There was no welcoming fragrance of simmering meat and vegetables. The tiny light on the Crock-Pot was dark, the pot cold.

'Oh, no!' cried Mrs Quimby, noticing.

'What's wrong?' asked Mr Quimby, coming in from the hall where he had gone to turn up the thermostat of the furnace.

'Wrong!' Mrs Quimby lifted the lid of the electric casserole on the kitchen counter. 'Someone forgot to plug in the Crock-Pot this morning, that's what's wrong.'

The family gathered to peer in at the cold vegetables and raw meat.

'I'm starving!' wailed Beezus.

'Me, too,' said Ramona.

'I thought you turned it on,' said Mrs Quimby to her husband as she shoved the plug into the socket. The stew could cook overnight and be warmed up for the next evening.

'Don't look at me,' said Mr Quimby to his wife. 'I thought you turned it on.' There was an edge to his voice.

For some reason his remark annoyed Mrs Quimby. 'I suppose you think turning on a Crock-Pot is woman's work.' The edge in her voice matched the edge in his.

'Not exactly,' said Mr Quimby, 'but now that you mention it—'

'Don't forget the time you forgot to fork the potatoes you put in to bake and they exploded,' his wife reminded him.

Ramona stifled a laugh at that memory. Her father had looked so surprised the evening the potatoes exploded—*poof !*—when he had opened the oven door.

Mr Quimby was not going to be drawn into a discussion of past baked potatoes. 'Why not just throw the stuff into the frying pan and cook it?' he asked. His idea of cooking was to toss everything into a pan and stir until done. Sometimes he invented interesting dishes with ground meat and eggs, zucchini and cheese. Other times the family tried to be good sports at dinner.

'Because you can't fry stew meat.' Mrs Quimby

sounded annoyed as she looked into the cupboard and the refrigerator. 'It's too tough. You know that. Did you bring groceries?'

'No. I thought we were having stew for dinner,' answered Mr Quimby. Crossly, Ramona thought. 'I didn't see anything on the grocery list.'

Picky-picky, the cat, rubbed against Mrs Quimby's legs, telling her how hungry he was. 'Scat,' said Mrs Quimby.

Picky-picky went to Beezus, not Ramona. He did not like Ramona, had never liked her because she was too noisy.

'I'm practically dying of hunger,' said Beezus as she picked up the old cat and rubbed her cheek against him.

'Me, too,' said Ramona.

'You girls are no help,' Mrs Quimby told her daughters. 'We have a couple of eggs, not enough for an omelette, two strips of bacon, three carrots, and some tired old lettuce. That's it.' She looked at her husband. 'We don't have to let the cupboard get completely bare before we buy groceries.'

This remark gave Ramona a cue. 'Old Mother Hubbard went to the cupboard—' she began, but she did not finish the rhyme because she could see no one was listening.

'Anytime we are low on groceries, just make

a list,' said Mr Quimby. 'That's all you have to do.'

'I could make carrot salad,' suggested Beezus, as if carrot salad might smooth things over.

'We could have pancakes,' said Mr Quimby, 'with half a strip of bacon apiece.'

'Not a very nutritious meal,' said Mrs Quimby, 'but better than starvation.' She reached for a mixing bowl while Beezus, who had dropped Picky-picky and washed her hands, began to grate carrots onto a sheet of waxed paper. Ramona leaned against the counter to watch. She wanted to make sure her sister did not grate her fingers into the salad.

'Ramona, don't just stand there,' said Mr Quimby as he laid the bacon in a frying pan. 'Get busy and set the table. As my grandmother used to say, "Every kettle must rest on its own bottom," so do your part.'

Ramona made a face as she reached for the place mats. 'Daddy, I bet your grandmother didn't really say all the things you say she said.'

'If she did, she must have been a dreadful bore,' said Mrs Quimby, who was beating batter as if she were angry with it.

Mr Quimby looked hurt. 'You didn't know my grandmother.'

'If she went around spouting wisdom all the

time, I can't say I'm sorry.' Mrs Quimby was on her knees, dragging the griddle from behind the pots and pans in the bottom of the cupboard.

Ramona paused in laying the silverware to make sure there was no blood on the carrots. She felt the muscles of her stomach tighten as they always tightened when her mother was cross with her father.

'My grandmother was a wonderful woman,' said Mr Quimby. 'She had a hard life out there in the country, but she was good to us kids and we learned a lot from her.'

'Well, my grandmother wasn't so bad herself.' With an angry sounding crash the griddle knocked over two pans and a double boiler as Mrs Quimby yanked it from the cupboard. 'And I learned a lot from her.'

Ramona and Beezus exchanged an anxious look.

'Just what did you learn from your grandmother?' asked Mr Quimby. 'As far as I could see, all she ever did was gad around and play bridge.'

Ramona and Beezus exchanged another look. Were their parents quarrelling? Really quarrelling? Yes, the sisters' eyes agreed. Both girls were worried.

Mrs Quimby set the griddle on the stove with more noise than necessary. She was plainly trying to think what she had learned from her grandmother. Finally she said, 'My grandmother taught me to pick flowers with long stems and to pick a few leaves to put in with them.'

'Very useful,' said Mr Quimby.

The hint of sarcasm in his voice must have annoyed Mrs Quimby because she said, 'My grandmother didn't have much money, but she had a sense of beauty.' The drop of water she flicked on the griddle refused to dance.

'No matter how much my grandmother had to scrimp and pinch to make ends meet,' said Mr Quimby, 'she always managed to find money to buy paper for me to draw on.'

Scrimp and pinch to make ends meet, thought Ramona, liking the sound of the words. She would remember them. The smell of bacon sizzling made her feel better. It also made her hungrier.

'My grandmother taught me useful things, too.' Mrs Quimby had had time to think. 'She taught me that a dab of spit would stop a run in a stocking.' She flicked another drop of water on the griddle. This one danced. The griddle was hot.

'Some grandmother,' said Mr Quimby, 'spitting on her stockings.'

'You're both being silly,' Beezus burst out. 'Just plain silly!'

'Young lady, you keep out of this,' ordered Mr Quimby.

Beezus glared at her father. 'Well, you are,' she muttered.

Mrs Quimby silently poured four puddles of batter on the griddle. Ramona prayed that the quarrel, whatever it was about, was over.

Beezus stirred mayonnaise into the blood-free carrots, which she then divided on four limp lettuce leaves on four salad plates. Mr Quimby turned the bacon. Mrs Quimby flipped the pancakes. Ramona's stomach relaxed. In a moment her mother would slide the pancakes onto a platter and start another four cooking. Ramona could hardly wait, she was so hungry.

'Are you sure those pancakes are done?' asked Mr Quimby as his wife slid the pancake turner under them. 'They don't look done to me.'

'They bubbled in the middle before I turned them,' said Mrs Quimby, 'and they look done to me.'

Mr Quimby took the pancake turner from his wife. Using it as a weapon, he slashed each pancake in the centre. Ramona and Beezus exchanged a shocked look. Their father had slashed their mother's pancakes! He had gone too far. Frightened, they watched raw batter ooze from four gashes in the pancakes. Their father was right. The cakes were not done. Now what would their mother do?

Mrs Quimby was furious. She snatched back the pancake turner, scooped up the oozing cakes, and tossed them into the garbage.

'You didn't need to do that.' Mr Quimby looked amused. He had won. 'You could have turned them again and let them finish cooking.'

'And I suppose your grandmother made absolutely perfect pancakes,' said Mrs Quimby in a voice stiff with anger.

Mr Quimby looked calm and even more amused. 'As a matter of fact, she did,' he said. 'Brown and lacy, cooked all the way through, and with crisp edges.'

'The best pancakes you ever ate,' stated Mrs Quimby in a voice that made Ramona silently pray. Mother, be nice again. Please, please be nice again.

'Right,' said Mr Quimby. 'Light enough to melt in your mouth.'

Be quiet, Daddy, prayed Ramona. You'll make things worse.

'Oh—you!' Mrs Quimby gave Mr Quimby a swat on the seat of his pants with the pancake turner before she threw it on the counter. 'Bake them yourself since you learned so much from that noble grandmother of yours!'

Ramona and Beezus stood frozen with shock. Their mother had hit their father with a pancake turner. Ramona wanted to fly at her mother, to strike her and cry out, You hit my daddy! She dared not.

Mr Quimby tucked a dish towel in his belt for an apron and calmly ladled batter onto the griddle while his wife stalked into the living room and sat down with the newspaper. If only he wouldn't whistle so cheerfully as he deftly turned the cakes and drained the bacon.

'Dinner is served,' Mr Quimby announced as he set a platter of hot cakes and bacon on the table and pulled the dish towel from his belt. Silently Mrs Quimby joined the family.

Even though her mother was usually a much better cook than her father, Ramona had to admit her father made excellent pancakes. Unfortunately, she was no longer very hungry. She felt all churned up inside, as if she didn't know whether to cry or to burst out of the house shouting, My mother and father had a fight!

'Please pass the butter.' Mrs Quimby might have been speaking to a stranger.

'May I please have the syrup?' Mr Quimby asked politely.

'The funniest thing happened at school,' said Beezus, and Ramona understood that her sister was anxious to start a conversation that would smooth things over and make their parents forget their quarrel, perhaps make them laugh.

After a moment of silence Mrs Quimby said, 'Tell me.'

'You'll never guess how a boy spelled *relief* in a spelling test,' said Beezus.

'How?' asked Ramona to help the conversation along. Mr Quimby silently served himself two more hot cakes.

'He spelled it *r-o-l-a-i-d-s*,' said Beezus, looking anxiously at her parents, who actually smiled.

Ramona did not smile. 'But the man on television spells *relief* that way. He said *r-o-l-a-i-d-s* spells *relief*. I've heard him.'

'Silly,' said Beezus, but this time she spoke with affection. 'That's just a slogan. *Relief* is *r-e-l-i-e-f*.'

'Oh.' Ramona was glad to know. Tabletalk sank back into silence while Ramona thought about spelling. Spelling was full of traps—blends and silent letters and letters that sounded one way in one word and a different way in another—and having a man stand there on television fooling children was no help. She was glad she had a big sister who understood those things.

The evening was quiet. Mr Quimby dozed in front of the television set. Mrs Quimby took a shower and went to bed to read. Beezus did her homework in her room. Ramona tried to draw a monster eating a mouthful of people, but she could not make the picture on paper match the one in her imagination. Her monster looked as if he were eating paper dolls instead of real people. The house was unnaturally quiet. The television droned on. Both girls went to bed without being told.

Unhappy thoughts kept Ramona awake. What if her mother and father did not love one another any more? What if they decided to get a divorce like her friend Davy's parents? What would happen to her? Who would take care of her? Beezus was closer to being a grown-up but what about Ramona? She wanted to cry but could not. She felt too tight inside to cry. Tears teetered on her eyelashes but would not give her the relief of falling.

Finally Ramona could stand her fear and loneliness no longer. She slipped out of bed and tiptoed into her sister's room.

'Ramona?' Beezus too was awake.

'I can't go to sleep,' whispered Ramona.

'Neither can I,' said Beezus. 'Come on, get in bed with me.'

This invitation was what Ramona had been hoping for. Gratefully she slipped beneath the covers and snuggled against her sister. 'Do you think they'll get a divorce?' she whispered. 'They won't talk to each other.'

'Of course not,' said Beezus. 'At least I don't think so.'

'Who would take care of me if they did?' Ramona felt she had to have the answer from someone. 'I'm still little.' Beezus, of course, was her mother's girl, but what about Ramona?

Beezus seemed to be considering the question. 'I'll try,' she said at last.

'You aren't grown up enough,' said Ramona, nevertheless comforted. Beezus cared.

'I know,' admitted Beezus. 'I read a book about a girl who took care of her brothers and sisters when their father died, but that was off in the mountains someplace where they all picked herbs and things. It wouldn't work in the city.'

'Mother and Daddy won't be dead.' Ramona was consoled by this knowledge.

Beezus was silent awhile. 'They could have been joking,' she said. 'Sort of.'

'But mother hit Daddy,' Ramona pointed out. 'On the seat of his pants with a pancake turner.'

'I don't think that's the same as if she had hit him with something hard,' said Beezus. 'After all, she didn't really hurt him.'

Ramona tried to find a bright side. 'And he didn't hit her back,' she said. 'But if they loved us, they wouldn't fight.' She silently said her prayers, ending with, 'Please, please don't let mother and Daddy fight.'

From the kitchen came a whiff of the stew that would simmer through the night for their supper the next evening. Soothed by the homey fragrance, the sisters fell asleep.

In the morning, a few seconds after she awoke and found herself in her sister's bed, a dull, unhappy feeling settled over Ramona. Her parents had quarrelled. She dreaded facing them at breakfast. She did not know what to say to them. Beezus looked unhappy, too. Getting dressed took longer than usual, and when they finally went into the kitchen, they were surprised to see their parents sharing the morning paper as they ate breakfast together.

'Good morning, girls,' said Mr Quimby with his usual cheerfulness.

'There is oatmeal on the stove.' Mrs Quimby smiled fondly at her daughters. 'Did you sleep well?'

Beezus was suddenly angry. 'No, we didn't!'

'No, we didn't,' echoed Ramona, encouraged by her sister's anger. How could her mother expect them to sleep well when they were so worried?

Startled, both parents laid down the newspaper.

'And it's all your fault,' Beezus informed them.

'What on earth are you talking about?' asked Mrs Quimby.

Beezus was near tears. 'Your big fight, that's what.'

Ramona blinked back tears, too. 'You wouldn't even talk to each other. And you hit Daddy!'

'Of course we were speaking,' said Mrs Quimby. 'Where did you get the idea we weren't? We were just tired is all. We had one of those days when everything seemed to go wrong.'

So did I, thought Ramona.

'I went to bed and read,' continued Mrs Quimby, 'and your father watched television. That was all there was to it.'

Ramona felt almost limp with relief. At the same time she was angry with her parents for causing so much worry. 'Grown-ups aren't supposed to fight,' she informed them.

'Oh, for heaven's sake,' said Mrs Quimby. 'Why not?'

Ramona was stern. 'Grown-ups are supposed to be perfect.'

Both her parents laughed. 'Well, they are,' Ramona insisted, annoyed by their laughter.

'Name one perfect grown-up,' challenged Mr Quimby. 'You can't do it.'

'Haven't you noticed grown-ups aren't perfect?' asked Mrs Quimby. 'Especially when they're tired.'

'Then how come you expect us kids to be so perfect all the time?' demanded Ramona.

'Good question,' said Mr Quimby. 'I'll have to think of an answer.'

'We want you to be perfect so you won't grow up to bicker about your grandmothers and their pancakes,' said Mrs Quimby. Both parents thought her reply was funny.

Ramona felt the way Picky-picky looked when someone rumpled his fur. Maybe grown-ups weren't perfect, but they should be, her parents most of all. They should be cheerful, patient, loving, never sick and never tired. And fun, too.

'You kids fight,' said Mr Quimby. 'Why shouldn't we?'

'It isn't dignified,' said Beezus, giving Ramona another word to add to her list. 'Especially when you hit someone with a pancake turner.'

'Oh, you silly little girls,' said Mrs Quimby with amusement and affection.

'Why should we let you kids have all the fun?' asked Mr Quimby.

67

'We don't quarrel for fun,' Ramona informed her father.

'You could fool me,' said Mr Quimby.

Ramona refused to smile. 'Don't you ever do it again,' she ordered her parents in her sternest voice.

'Yes, ma'am,' answered Mrs Quimby with mock meekness, as if she were poking a little fun at Ramona.

'Yes, *ma'am*!' said her father, and saluted as if she were somebody important.

This time Ramona had to laugh.

5

THE GREAT HAIR ARGUMENT

'Ramona, stand on both feet and hold still,' said Mrs Quimby one Saturday morning. 'I can't cut your bangs straight when you wiggle.'

'I'm trying,' said Ramona. Bits of falling hair made her nose tickle. She blew upwards, fanning out her bangs from her forehead, to rid herself of the tickle.

'Now see what you've done.' Mrs Quimby recombed the bangs.

Ramona stood perfectly still in an agony of itching, twitching her nose to get rid of snips of falling hair, until her mother finally said, 'There, little rabbit, we're finished.' She removed the towel from Ramona's shoulders and shook it over the kitchen wastebasket. Ramona, who liked being called a little rabbit, continued to twitch her nose and think of the warm and cosy picture books about bears and rabbits her mother used to read to her at bedtime before she kissed her goodnight. She had loved those books. They made her feel safe. During the daytime she had preferred books about steam shovels, the noisier the better, but at night—bears, nice bears, and bunnies.

'Next!' Mrs Quimby called out to Beezus, who had just washed her hair. These days Beezus spent a lot of time locked in the bathroom with a bottle of shampoo.

'Beezus, don't keep me waiting,' said Mrs Quimby. 'I have a lot to do this morning.' The washing machine had broken down, and because no one had been able to stay home during the week to admit a repairman, Mrs Quimby had to drive to a laundromat with three loads of washing. Repairmen did not work on Saturdays.

'I'm waiting,' repeated Mrs Quimby.

Beezus, rubbing her hair with a towel, appeared in the doorway. 'Mother, I don't want you to cut my hair,' she announced.

Ramona, about to leave the kitchen, decided to stay. She sensed an interesting argument.

'But, Beezus, you're so shaggy,' protested Mrs Quimby. 'You look untidy.'

'I don't want to look tidy,' said Beezus. 'I want to look nice.'

'You look nice when you're neat.' Mrs Quimby's voice told Ramona her mother's patience was stretched thin. 'And don't forget, how you look is not as important as how you behave.'

'Mother, you're so old-fashioned,' said Beezus.

Mrs Quimby looked both annoyed and amused. 'That's news to me.'

Beezus plainly resented her mother's amusement. 'Well you *are*.'

'All right. I'm old-fashioned,' said Mrs Quimby in a way that told Ramona she did not mean what she was saying. 'But what are we going to do about your shaggy hair?'

'I am not a sheep dog,' said Beezus. 'You make me sound like one.'

Mrs Quimby chose silence while Ramona, fascinated, waited to see what would happen next. Deep down she was pleased, and guilty because she was pleased, that her mother was annoyed with Beezus. At the same time, their disagreement worried her. She wanted her family to be happy.

'I want to get my hair cut in a beauty shop,' said Beezus. 'Like all the other girls.'

'Why, Beezus, you know we can't afford a luxury like that,' said Mrs Quimby. 'Your hair is sensible and easy to care for.'

'I'm practically the only girl in my whole class who gets a home haircut,' persisted Beezus, ignoring her mother's little speech.

'Now you're exaggerating.' Mrs Quimby looked tired.

Ramona did not like to see her mother look tired so she tried to help. 'Karen in my room at school says her mother cuts her hair and her sister's too, and her sister is in your class.'

Beezus turned on her sister. 'You keep out of this!'

'Let's not get all worked up,' said Mrs Quimby.

'I'm not worked up,' said Beezus. 'I just don't want to have a home haircut, and I'm not going to have one.'

'Be sensible,' said Mrs Quimby.

Beezus scowled. 'I've been good old sensible Beezus all my life, and I'm tired of being sensible.' She underlined this announcement by adding, 'Ramona can get away with anything, but not me. No. I always have to be good old sensible Beezus.'

'That's not so.' Ramona was indignant. 'I never get away with anything.'

After a thoughtful moment, Mrs Quimby spoke. 'So am I tired of being sensible all the time.'

Both sisters were surprised, Ramona most of all. Mothers were supposed to be sensible. That was what mothers were for.

Mrs Quimby continued. 'Once in a while I would like to do something that isn't sensible.'

'Like what?' asked Beezus.

'Oh—I don't know.' Mrs Quimby looked at the breakfast dishes in the sink and at the rain spattering against the windows. 'Sit on a cushion

72

in the sunshine, I guess, and blow the fluff off dandelions.'

Beezus looked as if she did not quite believe her mother. 'Weeds don't bloom this time of year,' she pointed out.

Ramona felt suddenly close to her mother and a little shy. 'I would like to sit on a cushion and blow dandelion fluff with you,' she confided, thinking what fun it would be, just the two of them, sitting in warm sunshine, blowing on the yellow blossoms, sending dandelion down dancing off into the sunlight. She leaned against her mother, who put her arm around her and gave her a little hug. Ramona twitched her nose with pleasure.

'But, mother,' said Beezus, 'you always said we shouldn't blow on dandelions because we would scatter seeds and they would get started in the lawn and are hard to dig out.'

'I know,' admitted Mrs Quimby, her moment of fantasy at an end. 'Very sensible of me.'

Beezus was silenced for the time being.

'I like your hair, mother,' said Ramona, and she did. Her mother's short hair was straight, parted on one side and usually tucked behind her left ear. It always smelled good and looked, Ramona felt, the way a mother's hair should look, at least the way her mother's hair should look. 'I think your hair looks nice,' she said, 'and I don't mind when you cut my hair.' In the interest of truth she added, 'Except when my nose tickles.'

Beezus flared up once more. 'Well, goody-goody for you, you little twerp,' she said, and flounced out of the kitchen. In a moment the door of her room slammed.

Ramona's feelings were hurt. 'I'm not a little twerp, am I?' she asked, wondering if her mother agreed.

Mrs Quimby reached for the broom to sweep bits of hair from the kitchen floor. 'Of course not,' she said. 'I don't bring up my daughters to be twerps.'

Ramona twitched her nose like a rabbit.

Afterwards neither Mrs Quimby nor Beezus mentioned hair. Beezus's hair grew shaggier and Ramona decided that if her sister did not look like a sheep dog yet, she soon would. She also sensed that, as much as her mother wanted to say something about Beezus's hair, she was determined not to.

Beezus, on the other hand, looked defiant. She sat at the dinner table with a you-can't-make-me-if-I-don't-want-to look on her face.

Ramona discovered that the tiny part of herself, deep down inside, that had been pleased because her mother was angry with her sister was no longer pleased. Anger over one person's hair was not worth upsetting the family.

'Women,' muttered Mr Quimby every evening at supper. He also remarked, as if he had hair on his mind, that he thought he was getting a little thin on top and maybe he should massage his scalp.

Conversation was strained. Beezus avoided speaking to her mother. Mrs Quimby tried to look as if nothing had happened. She said calmly, 'Beezus, when the shampoo bottle is almost empty, don't forget to add shampoo to the grocery list. We use it, too, you know.'

'Yes, mother,' said Beezus.

Ramona felt like yelling, Stop it, both of you! She tried to think of interesting things to talk about at the dinner table to make her family forget about hair.

One evening, to distract her family from hair, Ramona was telling how her teacher had explained that the class should not be afraid of big words because big words were often made up of little words: *dishcloth* meant a cloth for washing dishes and *pancake* meant a cake cooked in a pan.

'But I bake cakes in pans—or used to—and this does not make them pancakes,' Mrs Quimby pointed out. 'If I bake an angelfood cake in a pan, it is not a pancake.'

'I know,' said Ramona. 'I don't understand it because *carpet* does not mean a pet that rides in a car. Picky-picky is not a carpet when we take him to the vet.' At this example her parents laughed, which pleased Ramona until she noticed that Beezus was neither laughing nor listening.

Beezus took a deep breath. 'Mother,' she said in a determined way that told Ramona her sister was about to say something her mother might not like. The words came out in a rush. 'Some of the girls at school get their hair cut at Robert's School of Hair Design. People who are learning to cut hair do the work, but a teacher watches to see that they do it right. It doesn't cost as much as a regular beauty shop. I've saved my allowance, and there's this lady named Dawna who is really good and can cut hair so it looks like that girl who ice skates on TV. You know, the one with the hair that sort of floats when she twirls around and then falls in place when she stops. Please, mother, I have enough money saved.' When Beezus had finished this speech she sat back in her chair with an anxious, pleading expression on her face.

Mrs Quimby, who had looked tense when Beezus first began to speak, relaxed. 'That seems reasonable. Where is Robert's School of Hair Design?'

'In that new shopping centre on the other side

of town.' Beezus explained. 'Please, mother, I'll do anything you want if you'll let me go.'

Ramona did not take this promise seriously.

In the interests of family peace, Mrs Quimby relented. 'All right,' she said with a small sigh. 'But I'll have to drive you over. If you can hold out until Saturday, we'll go see what Dawna can do about your hair after I drive your father to work.'

'Oh, thank you, mother!' Beezus looked happier than she had since the beginning of the great hair argument.

Ramona was pleased, too, even though she knew she would have to be dragged along. Peace in the family was worth a boring morning.

Saturday turned out to be cold, raw, and wet. Ramona despaired of ever using her roller skates. The Quimbys hurried through breakfast, stacked the dishes in the sink, piled into the car and drove off, windshield wipers flopping furiously, to deliver Mr Quimby to the Shop-Rite Market. Ramona, resigned to a tiresome morning, could feel Beezus's excitement and see how tightly she clutched her allowance in the drawstring bag she had crocheted.

When Mr Quimby had been dropped off at the market, Beezus joined her mother in the front seat. She always gets to sit in the front seat, thought Ramona.

Mrs Quimby started up the on-ramp to the freeway that cut the city in two. 'Beezus, watch for the signs. I have to keep my eyes on my driving,' she directed.

Ramona thought, I can read, too, if the words aren't too long.

Mrs Quimby looked back over her shoulder for a space in which to merge with the heavy morning traffic. A space came down the freeway, and Mrs Quimby managed to fit the car into it. In no time they were crossing the river, which looked cold and grey between the black girders of the bridge. Green signs spanned the freeway.

'Do I turn left?' asked Mrs Quimby, uncertain of the way to the shopping centre.

'Right,' said Beezus.

Mrs Quimby turned right onto the off-ramp.

'Mother,' cried Beezus. 'You were supposed to turn left.'

'Then why did you tell me to turn right?' Mrs Quimby sounded angry.

'You asked if you should turn left,' said Beezus, 'and I meant, "Right, you should turn left".'

'After this, use your head,' said Mrs Quimby. 'Now how do I get back on the freeway?' She drove through a maze of unfamiliar one-way streets looking for an on-ramp sign. Finally she asked for directions from a man at a service

78

station. He looked disagreeable because he had to come out in the rain.

Ramona sighed. The whole world seemed grey and cross, and it was most unfair that she should have to be dragged along on a dreary ride just because Beezus wanted her hair cut by Dawna. Her mother would never go to all this trouble for Ramona's hair. Huddled in the back seat, she began to feel car-sick. The Quimby car, which they had bought from someone who had owned a large dog, began to smell like a dog. 'Oh-h,' moaned Ramona, feeling sick. She thought about the oatmeal she had eaten for breakfast and quickly tried not to think about it.

Mrs Quimby glanced in the rear-view mirror. 'Are you all right, Ramona?' Her voice was anxious.

Ramona did not answer. She was afraid to open her mouth.

'I think she's going to upchuck,' said Beezus, who, since she was in the seventh grade, said *upchuck* instead of *throw up*. She felt the new word was more sophisticated.

'Hang on, Ramona!' said Mrs Quimby. 'I can't stop on the freeway, and there's no way to get off.'

'Mother!' cried Beezus. 'She's turning green!'

'Ramona, open the window and hang on!' ordered Mrs Quimby.

Ramona was too miserable to move. Beezus understood. She unbuckled her seat belt, which buzzed angrily. 'Oh, shut up,' she said to her seat belt as she leaned over and lowered a window for Ramona.

Cold air swept away the doggy smell, and drops of rain against her face made Ramona feel better, but she kept her mouth shut and did not move. Hanging on was not easy.

'How did I ever get into this?' Mrs Quimby wondered aloud as she turned onto the off-ramp that led from the freeway.

When the haircut expedition finally reached the shopping centre and parked near Robert's School of Hair Design, the three Quimbys splashed through the rain. Ramona, who had quickly recovered when the car stopped, found a certain grim pleasure in stomping in puddles with her boots.

After the cold, the air inside the beauty school seemed too warm and too fragrant. Pee-you, thought Ramona as she listened to running water, snipping scissors, and the hushed roar of hair dryers.

A man, probably Robert himself, asked, 'What can I do to help you ladies?' as perspiring Ramona began to wiggle out of her car coat.

Beezus was suddenly shy. 'I—I would like Dawna to cut my hair,' she said in almost a whisper.

'Dawna graduated last week,' said Robert, glancing behind the screen that hid the activity of the school, 'but Lester can take you.'

'Go ahead,' said Mrs Quimby, answering Beezus's questioning eyes. 'You want your hair cut.'

When Robert asked for payment in advance, Beezus pulled open her crocheted bag and unfolded the bills she had saved. As Robert led her behind the screen, Mrs Quimby sank with a little sigh into one of the plastic chairs and picked up a shabby magazine. Ramona tried to amuse herself by drawing pictures with her toe in the damp and muddy spots their boots had left on the linoleum.

'Ramona, please don't do that,' said Mrs Quimby, glancing up from her magazine.

Ramona flopped back in a chair and sighed. Her booted feet were beginning to feel hot. To pass the time, she studied pictures of hair styles mounted on the wall. 'Is Beezus going to look like *that*?' she whispered.

Mrs Quimby glanced up again. 'I hope not,' she whispered back.

Ramona peeked behind the screen and reported to her mother. 'A man is washing Beezus's hair, and she's lying back with her head in a sink. He's using gobs of shampoo. He's wasting it.'

'Mm-mm.' Mrs Quimby did not raise her eyes

from the magazine. Ramona twisted her head to see what her mother found so interesting. Recipes.

Ramona returned for another look. 'He's rubbing her hair with a towel,' she reported.

'Mm-mm.' Ramona disliked her mother's mm-mming. She walked quietly behind the screen to watch. Lester was studying Beezus's hair, one lock at a time, while a woman, probably a teacher, watched.

'Ramona, come back here,' Mrs Quimby whispered from the edge of the screen.

Once more Ramona flopped down in the plastic chair and swung her legs back and forth. How nice it would be if she could have her hair shampooed, too. She raised her eyebrows as high as she could to make her bangs look longer and thought of her quarter, two nickels, and eight pennies at home in a Q-tip box.

'Little girl, would you like to have your hair cut?' asked Robert, as if he had read her mind—or was tired of watching her swing her legs.

Ramona stopped swinging her legs and answered politely, 'No, thank you. We are scrimping and pinching to make ends meet.' Using 'scrimping and pinching' made her feel grown-up.

An exasperated sigh escaped Mrs Quimby. She glanced at her watch. Beezus's haircut was taking longer than she had planned.

'Haircuts for children under ten are half price,' said Robert, 'and no waiting. We aren't very busy on a wet morning like this.'

Mrs Quimby studied Ramona's hair while Ramona tried to push her eyebrows still higher. 'All right, Ramona,' she said. 'Your hair does need cutting again, and it will help to have one more Saturday chore out of the way.'

In a moment Ramona found herself draped with a poodle-printed plastic sheet and lying back with her hair buried under mounds of lather while a young woman named Denise rubbed her scalp. Such bliss! Washing hair at home was never like this. No soap in her eyes, no having to complain that the water was too hot or too cold, no bumping her head on the kitchen tap while her knees ached from kneeling on a chair, no one telling her to stop wiggling, no water dribbling down her neck. The shampoo was over much too soon. Denise rubbed Ramona's hair with a towel and guided her to a chair in front of a mirror. On the other side of the row of mirrors, she could hear Beezus's hair being snipped with long pauses between snips.

'She's definitely the pixie type,' said the teacher to Denise.

Me? thought Ramona, surprised and pleased. Ramona the pixie sounded much nicer than

Ramona the pest as she had so often been called by Beezus and her friends.

'A little off the bangs,' said the teacher, 'and the ends tapered.'

Denise went to work. Her scissors flashed and snipped. Unlike Lester on the other side of the mirror, Denise was sure of what she was doing. Perhaps she had studied longer.

Ramona closed her eyes. *Snip-snip-snip* went her bangs. When she opened her eyes she was surprised to discover they were a tiny bit longer in the centre of her forehead. Like the top of a heart, thought Ramona, like a valentine.

Denise lifted locks of wet hair between her fingers and snipped with flying scissors. Lift and snip, all the way around Ramona's head. Flicks of a comb, and Denise aimed a handheld hair dryer at Ramona's head with one hand while she guided Ramona's hair into place with a brush held in the other. In no time Ramona's hair was dry. More flicks of the comb, the plastic sheet was whisked away, and there sat Ramona with shining hair neatly shaped to her head.

'Excellent,' said the teacher to Denise. 'She looks adorable.'

Students who had no customers gathered around. Ramona could not believe the words she was hearing. 'Darling.' 'Cute as a bug.' 'A real little pixie.' The dryer was humming on the other side of the mirror.

Ramona felt light and happy when she returned to her mother.

'Why, Ramona!' said Mrs Quimby, laying aside her magazine. 'Your hair looks lovely. So neat and shiny.'

Ramona couldn't stop smiling, she was so happy. She twitched her nose with joy.

But something made the smile on Mrs Quimby's face fade. Ramona turned and stared at Beezus standing beside the screen. Her sister's hair had been teased and sprayed until it stood up three inches above her face. Her bangs were plastered in a curve across her forehead. Beezus did not look like an ice skater on television. She looked like an unhappy seventh-grade girl with forty-year-old hair.

Ramona did not know what to say. No one knew what to say except Robert. 'You look lovely, dear,' he said, but no one answered. Beezus's face looked stiff as her hair.

Ramona thought of the allowance Beezus had saved and wanted to shout at Robert, 'She does not look lovely! My sister looks terrible!' For once she kept still. She felt sorry for her sister and sad about the allowance she had saved for so long, but deep inside, where she was ashamed of her feeling, she felt a tiny triumph. Ramona looked nicer than Beezus.

Ramona walked carefully to the car, not wanting to disturb her hair by running and hopping. Beezus walked in stony silence. When all three had buckled their seat belts, Beezus could no longer hold back her feelings. 'Well, go ahead and say it!' she burst out in anger and in tears. 'Tell me my hair looks terrible. Tell me my hair looks stiff and horrible, like a wig. A *cheap* wig!'

'Now, Beezus.' Mrs Quimby spoke gently.

'Well, it *does*! You know it does,' Beezus went on. 'I tried to tell the man I didn't want my hair to stand up, but he said I would be pleased when he finished, and now I've wasted your whole morning and all my allowance. I look terrible and can't go to school because everyone will laugh at me.' She began to sob.

'Dear girl—' Mrs Quimby took Beezus in her arms and let her weep against her shoulder.

Tears came into Ramona's eyes. She felt she could not bear her sister's unhappiness even if she did look nicer than Beezus. That awful stiff hair, the wasted allowance . . . Ramona no longer triumphed in looking nicer. She did not want to look nicer. She wanted them to look the same so people would say, there goes that nice looking Beatrice Quimby and her nice-looking little sister.

'I j-just wanted to look nice.' Beezus's voice was muffled by her mother's coat. 'I know th-that what I do is more important than how I look, but I just wanted to look nice.'

'Of course you do,' soothed Mrs Quimby. 'No matter what we say, we all want to look nice.'

Ramona sniffed, she felt so sad.

'And you will look nice,' Mrs Quimby continued, 'once you wash out all that hair spray and comb your hair. Don't forget Lester cut your hair, and that's what counts.'

Beezus raised her soggy tear-stained face. 'Do you really think it will look all right when it's washed?'

'Yes, I do,' said Mrs Quimby. 'It just needs to be washed and combed.'

Beezus sat up and let out an exhausted sigh.

Mother and daughter had forgotten their adorable pixie buckled down in the corner of the back seat. Ramona hoped she could make it home without upchucking. She did not want to muss her hair.

6

Ramona's New Pyjamas

As Mrs Quimby had predicted, once Beezus washed her hair she looked like Beezus again. Because they were so glad to see her looking like a seventh-grader, Ramona and her mother did not point out that her new haircut did not look much different from the cuts her mother had given her.

As for Ramona, for a few days grown-ups said, 'Why, how nice your hair looks,' as if they were surprised that her hair could look nice.

Children asked, 'How come your bangs are longer in the middle?'

'Because I'm a pixie,' Ramona answered, or sometimes, 'because I'm a valentine.' In a few days everyone forgot about her hair, including Ramona.

Clearly Ramona's parents had something more important on their minds. At first Ramona did not know what it was. She heard long, serious conversations coming from their bedroom, and when she knelt by the furnace outlet to try to catch what they were saying, she could make out only a few words. 'I don't . . . school . . . why don't . . . we could . . . teacher . . . school.' They sounded as if they might be arguing.

'I told you not to fight any more!' Ramona yelled through the furnace pipes. There was a startled silence, then laughter from the bedroom. Afterwards Ramona could hear only whispers.

Ramona decided her parents must be talking about her. What could they say about Beezus and school? Nothing. What could they say about Ramona and school? To begin with, there was her spelling . . .

For a while Ramona expected her parents to have one of those little talks with her about really working at her spelling or being a better girl. When they did not, she put their conversations out of her mind and went back to twitching her nose, pretending she was her mother's little rabbit, warm and snug and loved like little bears and bunnies in the books her mother read to her at bedtime when she was little.

One evening, when Ramona had turned from a pixie into a rabbit, she held her feet close together and, twitching her nose, went hopping down the hall. *Thud. Thud. Thud.*

'Ramona, do you have to do that?' asked her mother, who was watching the evening news on television while she let down a hem on a dress for Beezus.

Ramona stopped being her mother's little rabbit, but she did not answer. Of course she did not have to hop. She wanted to. Her mother should know that.

Mrs Quimby glanced up from her sewing. 'Why, Ramona,' she remarked, 'those pyjamas are way too small for you.'

And so they were. Ramona, who had been outgrowing clothes all her life, discovered that the sleeves reached only halfway to her wrists, the legs halfway to her ankles, and the seat was too tight. Her pyjamas had been washed so often that the fuzz had worn off the flannel.

'I have another pair put away for you,' said Mrs Quimby. 'I'll get them and you can change.'

'Did Beezus outgrow them?' Ramona was all too familiar with her mother's habit of putting away for Ramona the clothes that Beezus had outgrown several years before.

Mrs Quimby went to the linen closet. 'Not this time. I bought them on sale.' She handed Ramona a pair of white pyjamas printed with coloured balloons. They were so new they were still folded and pinned together.

Ramona quickly pulled out the pins and changed from too-small pyjamas into too-big pyjamas. The sleeves covered her hands, the legs rumpled around her ankles, and the seat bagged, but oh, how soft and warm and cosy they felt, like the fur of a baby rabbit.

'Just fold up the bottoms so you won't trip,' said Mrs Quimby. 'They'll shrink when they're washed, and you'll grow into them before you know it.'

Ramona did as she was told and discovered that, now that her pyjamas were no longer tight, she could stoop lower and jump higher. Twitching her nose, she became a rabbit once more and *thump, thump, thumped* down the hall to bed, where she snuggled down, warm and cosy as a little rabbit in a nest, in the pyjamas that had never been worn by her sister.

The next morning she awoke still feeling warm and cosy. She lay in bed, not wanting to take off the pyjamas, they felt so good.

'Ramona, come along and eat your oatmeal while it's still hot,' her mother called to her.

Reluctantly Ramona got out of bed, dabbed a damp washcloth in the middle of her face, and, still in her pyjamas, went to breakfast.

'Why, Ramona, you aren't even dressed.' Mrs Quimby, having finished her breakfast, was rinsing her dishes. Mr Quimby and Beezus were carrying theirs to the sink.

'Don't worry, mother,' said Ramona. 'I'm not going to school in my pyjamas.' As soon as she had spoken Ramona thought how pleasant it would be if she could go to school in her pyjamas and feel the soft fuzz against her skin all day.

'Don't dawdle.' Mr Quimby kissed the top of Ramona's head and left for work. Ramona twitched her nose.

Ramona quickly ate her oatmeal—this was easy because oatmeal did not require much chewing—and as she ate she thought about wearing her pyjamas to school. Suddenly she recalled seeing the kindergarten class in their red plastic fire hats trooping back from a visit to the fire station, which made her think of her own visit to the firehouse when she was in kindergarten and how she had loved her fire hat. For days afterwards, whenever she found even two newspapers piled together, she had called her parents' attention to a fire hazard. She also recalled how astonished she had been to learn that firemen slept in their underwear so that they could jump out of bed and into their clothes if they were called out in the night. Of course, Ramona did not sleep in her underwear, but if she put her clothes on over her pyjamas she could pretend to be a fireman anyway.

As Ramona rinsed her dishes she stopped being a rabbit and became a fireman. She raced down the hall and pulled her slacks on over her pyjama bottoms. Fortunately, she was not really on her way to fight a fire because she had a hard time stuffing the folded-up legs into her slacks. Then she jerked on her turtleneck sweater over the pyjama top. The knitted neck and wristbands hid the flannel nicely. Ramona felt stuffed, but cosy and warm. She remembered to brush her teeth and was ready for school. Like a fireman she pulled on her boots, grabbed her raincoat and hat, and raced into the kitchen for her lunch box.

'Bye, mother,' she called out as she ran out of the back door.

'Where's the fire?' her mother called after her.

How did she guess? Ramona wondered as she ran towards school. Then she decided her mother had not really guessed because she often asked where the fire was when Ramona was in a hurry.

A warm, misty spring rain was falling. Bits of green tipped the black branches of trees. Ramona slowed down to investigate crocus buds like tiny yellow and blue Easter eggs that were pushing up through a neighbour's lawn. Then she ran on as fast as she could in her stuffed condition, her mouth open, wailing like a fire engine, her boots clomping on the sidewalk. She paid no attention to the people walking to the bus stop who looked at her in surprise. Firemen must get awfully hot, thought Ramona, when she arrived panting and sweating at Glenwood School.

Ramona was glad to sit down on the floor of the cloakroom and pull off her boots. At least her feet felt cooler. She flopped down at her desk. Her face was flushed, and her pyjamas no longer felt as soft as a baby rabbit. They were damp with sweat. Maybe pretending to be a fireman wasn't such a good idea after all, thought Ramona, and wondered if anyone would think she looked different. As it turned out, only Davy noticed because Davy always kept an eye on Ramona, who had been chasing him ever since kindergarten. 'You look fat,' he said.

'I ate a big breakfast,' answered Ramona. Then she added. 'Davy-in-the-gravy' to keep Davy quiet. She knew he did not like to be called Davy-in-the-gravy.

The classroom seemed unbearably hot, and her clothes felt as tight as the skin on a sausage. As Ramona stood for the flag salute, she wished she had something to unbutton. Later, as she bent over her workbook, she could not help trying to squirm inside her damp clothes.

Mrs Rudge walked slowly up and down between the desks, looking over shoulders at workbooks. Ramona, finding it difficult to think about her work when she was so uncomfortable, noticed that Davy crooked his arm around his page and bent his head low to hide his work while Becky sat up straight so Mrs Rudge would be sure to see how perfect her work was. 'I like the way Davy keeps his eyes on his own work,' said Mrs Rudge. Davy's ears turned pink with pleasure.

Ramona quickly lowered her eyes to her workbook and remembered that her parents had had more serious talks in their bedroom about school. What was wrong? she wondered again. Mrs Rudge paused beside her desk to look, not at Ramona's workbook, but at Ramona whose pyjamas felt so damp she thought they might be shrinking.

'Ramona, how do you feel this morning?' whispered Mrs Rudge.

'Fine,' answered Ramona, trying to sound as if she spoke the truth.

'Your cheeks are very pink,' said Mrs Rudge. 'I think you had better go to the office and ask Mrs Miller to take your temperature.'

'Now?' asked Ramona.

'Yes,' said Mrs Rudge. 'Run along.'

Ramona laid down her pencil and tried to look thin as she walked out of the room to a rustle of whispers from the class. What was the matter with Ramona? Was she sick? Would she have to be sent home?

Once in the hall she grasped her sweater and pyjama top and pulled them up an instant to feel the relief of cool air against her sweaty skin. Then she took hold of both her elastic waistbands and pulled them out and in several times to fan a little cool air inside her slacks.

In the office Mrs Miller, the school secretary, had Ramona sit on a chair and poked a thermometer under her tongue. 'Be sure to keep your lips closed,' she said. 'We don't want any thermometers falling on the floor and breaking.'

Ramona sat still while Mrs Miller answered the telephone and carried on a long conversation with a mother who was worried about her child's schoolwork and was anxious to talk to the principal. She sat still while a sixth-grade boy came in to use the telephone to call his mother to tell her he had forgotten his lunch money. She sat still while a mother came in to deliver a lunch to a fourth grader who had gone off without it.

Ramona sat and sat. She thought of the long day ahead, of recess and of lunchtime, and began to wish she really were sick. Maybe she was. Maybe she had a fever, a fever so high Mrs Miller would telephone her mother at work, and her mother would come and take her home and put her to bed between cool white sheets. They would be alone in the house, just the two of them. Her mother would lay her hand on Ramona's hot forehead and give her little treats—ice cream between meals and cold orange juice, not fresh-frozen orange juice but fresh-fresh orange juice squeezed out of real oranges and not dumped out of a can and thinned with water. Her mother would read aloud stories from library books and would find in the bookcase the books Ramona had loved so much when she was little, especially the one about the little bear whose mother looked so soft and kind and loving in her long white apron and the book about the bunny snug in bed who said goodnight to everything, mittens, a mouse, the moon, and the stars. Later, when Ramona was feeling better, her mother would tuck her up on the couch in the living room so she could watch television and even get to see the ends of old movies.

Pursing her lips tight around the thermometer, Ramona sighed through her nose. Mrs Miller, her back turned, was busy with the ditto machine.

Finally, when Ramona could not sit still another second, she made a sort of angry humming noise. 'M-m-m! M-m-m!'

'Oh, my goodness, Ramona,' said Mrs Miller. 'You were so quiet I forgot all about you. Thank you for buzzing like a little bee to remind me.' She pulled the thermometer from Ramona's mouth, turned it until she found the silver line that told the temperature, and then said, 'Run along back to your room, and tell Mrs Rudge you're just fine. OK?'

'OK.' Ramona was disappointed. Now there would be no rescuing telephone call to her mother, only a long, sweaty day. Oh, well, she knew she would not really have been rescued by her mother, who could not leave her work. Howie's grandmother, accompanied by Willa Jean and probably Woger, would have come for her.

Ramona paused at the drinking fountain for a long, cool drink of water and fanned more air under her clothes before she returned to Room 2.

'What did Mrs Miller say?' said Mrs Rudge.

'She says I'm fine,' said Ramona.

Minutes dragged. The seconds between each click of the electric clock seemed to stretch longer and longer. Ramona felt so sleepy she wanted to put her head down on her arms and take a nap.

When the recess bell finally rang, Mrs Rudge said, 'Ramona, would you please come here a minute?'

Reluctantly Ramona walked to Mrs Rudge's desk.

'Is there something you would like to tell me?' asked the teacher.

Ramona looked up into Mrs Rudge's brown eyes, then down at the floor, shook her head, and looked up at Mrs Rudge once more. Her teacher seemed so kind, so soft and plump, that Ramona longed to lean against her and tell her all her troubles, how hot she was and how no one ever said she was her mother's girl and how she wanted her mother to love her like a little rabbit and how somehow all these feelings had led to pretending to be a fireman.

'I can keep a secret,' said Mrs Rudge. 'I promise.'

This encouragement was all Ramona needed. 'I—I'm too warm,' she confessed. 'I've got my pyjamas on.' Please, please, Mrs Rudge, don't make me tell why, she prayed, because now that she had confessed she felt that wearing pyjamas to school was a silly thing to do. A second-grader pretending to be a fireman—it was the dumbest thing she had ever imagined.

'Why, that's no problem,' said Mrs Rudge. 'Just go to the girls' bathroom and take off your pyjamas.' She reached into a drawer and pulled out a paper bag. 'Roll up your pyjamas and put them in this bag and hide them in your desk.'

Ramona shook her head. 'I can't.' As soon as she had spoken, she realized she had chosen the wrong words. Now Mrs Rudge would say, There's no such word as *can't*, and Ramona would argue with herself all over again. How could there not be such a word as *can't*? Mrs Rudge had just said *can't* so *can't* had to be a word.

To Ramona's relief, Mrs Rudge merely said, 'Why not?'

'I don't have any underwear on,' confessed Ramona. Was there amusement in Mrs Rudge's warm brown eyes? There better not be. No, it was all right. Mrs Rudge was not laughing at her.

'I see,' said the teacher. 'That *is* a problem, but I don't think you need to worry about it. Your slacks and sweater are warm enough on a day like this.'

'You mean go without any underwear?' Ramona was a little shocked at the suggestion. In summer she did not wear an undershirt, but she had always worn underpants, even in the hottest weather.

'Why not?' asked Mrs Rudge with a wave of her hand, as if she were waving away underwear as unimportant. Underwear—pooh!

'Well . . .' said Ramona, halfway agreeing. 'But . . . promise you won't tell my mother what I did?'

'I promise,' said Mrs Rudge with a big smile. 'Now run along before you melt into a puddle right here on the floor.'

Ramona did as she was told, and, oh, the relief she felt in the girls' bathroom when she shut herself in a cubicle and peeled off those damp pyjamas, which, to her surprise, had not shrunk at all. She quickly pulled on her clothes and rolled up the pyjamas as tight as she could and hid them in the paper bag. Even though skipping in the halls was forbidden, Ramona skipped. The halls were empty, recess was over, and she was late, but still she skipped because she felt as light and as cool as a spring breeze. And who would know she was not wearing underwear? Nobody, that's who. Maybe wearing underwear wasn't so important after all. Maybe after today Ramona would skip underwear—at least in summer when she was wearing slacks.

Back in Room 2, Ramona lifted the lid of her desk and hid her package way at the back behind her books. She pretended not to notice the curious stares of the boys and girls, who were wondering why Mrs Rudge said nothing about Ramona's being late. Instead she looked at Mrs Rudge, who gave her a tiny smile that said quite plainly, We have a secret, just the two of us.

Ramona's heart was warm with love for her teacher. She smiled back and twitched her nose like a bunny.

7

THE TELEPHONE CALL

By the time school was over Ramona had forgotten about the pyjamas in her desk, and that evening she was so busy practising her name in joined-up writing that they remained forgotten. No more babyish printing for Ramona. Mrs Rudge had taught her to write in what Ramona used to call 'that rumply stuff'. And write she did.

Ramona Quimby

She wrote in pencil, ballpoint pen, and crayon on any paper she could find—paper bags, old envelopes, the backs of arithmetic papers, around the edge of the newspaper. She wrote her name with her finger in steam on the bathroom mirror when her father had taken a shower after work. Before supper she wrote her name in dust on the top of the television set. After supper she went outside where, beneath the porch light, she wrote Ramona Quimby in chalk on each of the front steps. When she came back into the house, she found her mother and Beezus on the couch studying pictures in a paperback book.

'Let me see, too,' said Ramona, wiping her chalky fingers on the seat of her slacks and twitching her nose.

'It's just a book on how to cut hair that I ran across,' said Mrs Quimby. 'I thought I would try to learn to cut Beezus's hair so it would look like the ice skater on television.'

'See, mother,' said Beezus. 'First you twist the top hair up out of the way and cut the bottom hair first.'

'I see,' said Mrs Quimby. 'That doesn't look so difficult.'

Ramona felt left out. Somehow that trip to the beauty school had brought her mother and Beezus closer together. They were friends again, close friends.

'Bedtime, Ramona,' said Mrs Quimby, still studying the book.

A terrible thought crossed Ramona's mind. Her new pyjamas! She had left them rolled up in her desk at school. Then Ramona had an even worse thought. This was Friday. She could not bring her pyjamas home until Monday. How could she explain if her family found out?

Ramona made up her mind right then and there

that neither her parents nor Beezus would find out because she was going to keep those pyjamas a secret. Without waiting for a second reminder Ramona was in and out of the bathtub in no time. She could not locate the old pyjamas she had taken off the night before, but she did come across another too-small pair in a drawer. She put them on, turned off the light, hopped into bed, and pulled the covers up tight around her ears. But what if she fell asleep before her parents came in to kiss her goodnight?

Ramona took no chances. 'Come and kiss me goodnight,' she sang out while hanging on tight to the sheet and blankets.

Mr Quimby was first. 'What's got into you, Ramona?' he asked after he had kissed her. 'You forgot to beg to stay up just a little longer to watch TV or finish drawing a picture or read another chapter. You forgot to remind us you don't have to go to school tomorrow. Don't you feel good?'

Ramona giggled. 'Daddy, you're so silly. I feel fine.' She was pleased that her father had noticed she now read books with chapters.

Mrs Quimby was next. Ramona pulled the covers tight around her ears when she heard her mother coming down the hall. Mrs Quimby kissed Ramona and then looked at her in the dim light from the hall. 'Are you cold?' she asked.

'No,' answered Ramona.

'If you are, I can get another blanket from the linen closet,' said Mrs Quimby. Then she added, 'Nighty-night. Sweet dreams.'

That was close, thought Ramona with a twitch of her nose. When she said her prayers, she added a request at the end. Please, God, do not let anyone find out I wore my pyjamas to school. She felt that although God was probably too busy to think about her pyjamas, asking would not hurt and might even help.

Saturday morning she dressed in the closet and hid the too-small pyjamas in her bottom drawer. She was happy to discover that her father was home for the morning, even though he would have to work at the Shop-Rite Market Saturday afternoon and evening. Today was going to be a good day. The sun was shining, the sidewalk dry, and her father could watch her skate.

That is, she was happy until Mr Quimby looked around the living room and said, 'This is a home, not a base camp.' He had recently watched a television programme on mountain climbing. 'Let's all pitch in and clean this place up. Ramona, pick up all the newspapers and magazines and dust the living room. Beezus, you can run the vacuum cleaner. Then both of you tackle your rooms. Change the sheets and straighten up.

Every kettle must rest on its own bottom around here.' He did not mention that this was one of his grandmother's sayings.

Except for washing the egg beater in sudsy water so she could beat up a lot of suds, Ramona did not care much for housework, and this morning she longed to be outside racing up and down the sidewalk on her roller skates. However, she carried the old newspapers out to the garage without complaining and hastily flicked a dustcloth around the living room while Beezus plugged in the vacuum cleaner and made it growl back and forth across the carpet. Mr Quimby went off to clean the bathroom while Mrs Quimby was busy in the kitchen.

In a playful mood Beezus pushed the vacuum cleaner right up to Ramona's shoes. Ramona squealed as if she expected the vacuum cleaner to nibble her toes. Beezus pursued her with the vacuum cleaner. Around the carpet they went until Ramona said, 'Ha-ha, you can't catch me!' and crawled behind the couch. Beezus returned to running the vacuum cleaner properly, back and forth in straight lines, the way their father mowed the lawn.

Ramona sat hugging her knees behind the couch. She was in no hurry, as her father put it, to tackle her room.

Ramona sat there behind the couch, a kettle resting on its bottom, thinking. She thought how embarrassed she would be if her family found out she had worn her pyjamas to school. She thought about her mother and Beezus and what good friends they had become, almost as if they were the same age.

As Ramona sat letting these thoughts slide through her mind, the telephone rang in the kitchen. Above the growl of the vacuum cleaner, she heard her mother say, 'Why hel*lo*!' as if she were surprised to hear from the person calling.

Who had surprised her mother? Ramona listened hard. Beezus must have been curious, too, for she turned off the vacuum cleaner, which made eavesdropping easier for Ramona.

'Oh . . . ? Yes . . . Yes . . . Oh, does she?' Mrs Quimby went on in a friendly polite voice quite different from the friendly voice she used when she talked to her sister, the girls' Aunt Beatrice.

Who does what? Ramona wondered, alert since she was usually the one who had done something. Her mother laughed. Ramona felt indignant without knowing why. She could not think of anything she had done that anyone would telephone her mother about.

Mrs Quimby continued for some time, but Ramona could make no sense out of the conversation. Finally her mother said, 'Thank you for telling me, Mrs Rudge.' Then she hung up.

The sound of her teacher's name gave Ramona a strange feeling, as if she were in an elevator that had suddenly gone down when she expected it to go up. When she stopped feeling as if the floor had dropped beneath her, she was furious. So that was why her mother had laughed. Mrs Rudge had told! She had telephoned her mother and tattled. And her mother thought it was funny! Ramona would never forgive either of them. Never, never, *never.*

Beezus turned on the vacuum cleaner again. Ramona crawled on her hands and knees from behind the couch and was surprised to see that her mother had come into the living room. 'What have you been doing back there?' asked Mrs Quimby.

'Resting on my bottom,' said Ramona with a scowl.

Beezus switched off the vacuum cleaner again. Her turn had come to foresee an interesting argument.

Ramona faced her mother. 'Mrs Rudge told!' she shouted. 'And she promised she would never tell. And then you had to go and laugh!'

'Now calm down.' Mrs Quimby plucked a fluff of dust from Ramona's sleeve.

'I *won't* calm down!' yelled Ramona so loud her father came down the hall to see what was going on. 'I *hate* Mrs Rudge! She's a tattle-tale. She doesn't love me and she tells fibs!' Ramona saw her mother and father exchange a familiar look that said, Which of us is going to handle this one?

'*Hate* is a strong word, Ramona,' said Mrs Quimby quietly.

'Not strong enough,' said Ramona.

'This looks like nine on the Richter scale,' said Mr Quimby, as if Ramona were an earthquake.

'And you and Daddy talk about me in your room at night,' Ramona stormed at her mother.

'Someday, Ramona,' said her father, 'you are going to have to learn that the world does not revolve around you.'

'I don't care what Mrs Rudge says,' shouted Ramona. 'I didn't leave my pyjamas at school on purpose, I forgot.'

Mrs Quimby looked astonished. 'Left your pyjamas—What on earth are your pyjamas doing at school?' She was plainly trying to stifle a laugh.

Ramona was both surprised and bewildered. If her mother did not know about her pyjamas, what could Mrs Rudge have said?

'What on earth are your pyjamas doing at school?' Ramona's mother asked again.

The whole story—her feeling that the flannel was as soft as bunny fur and how she pretended to be a fireman so she wouldn't have to take her pyjamas off—flashed through Ramona's mind and embarrassed her. 'I won't tell,' she said, folding her arms defiantly.

'She probably took them for Show and Tell,' volunteered Beezus.

Ramona gave her sister a look of contempt. Second graders in Mrs Rudge's room did not have Show and Tell every day, only when someone had something really important and educational to bring such as a butterfly that had hatched out of a cocoon in a jar. And Beezus should know that no second grader would take pyjamas to school for Show and Tell. That would be too babyish even for kindergarten. Beezus knew these things. She had been through them all. She was just trying to make Ramona look babyish.

Ramona was about to shout, I did not! but decided this would be unwise. Beezus had supplied a reason, a very weak reason, why she might have taken her pyjamas to school.

Apparently Mrs Quimby did not accept Beezus's explanation either, for she said, 'Your pyjamas did not get out of bed and run along beside you to school. Oh, well, I don't suppose it matters.'

Ramona scowled. Her mother need not think

she could win her over by being funny. She was mad and she was going to stay mad. She was mad at Beezus for always being her mother's girl. She was mad at her teacher for telling her mother something (*what?*). She was mad at her parents for not being upset because she was mad. She was mad at herself for letting it out that she had left her pyjamas at school.

'Nobody likes me. Nobody in the whole world,' said Ramona, warming to her subject as the cat walked disdainfully through the room on his way to peace on Beezus's bed. 'Not even my own mother and father. Not even the cat. Beezus gets all the attention around here. Even Picky-picky likes Beezus more than he likes me!' She was pleased that her father stayed in the living room and she didn't lose any of her audience. 'You'll be sorry someday when I'm rich and famous.'

'I didn't know you were planning to be rich and famous,' said Mr Quimby.

Neither had Ramona until that moment.

'What do you mean, I get all the attention around here?' demanded Beezus. 'Nobody tapes my schoolwork to the refrigerator door. We can hardly find the refrigerator, it is so buried under all your drawings and junk!'

Both parents looked at Beezus in surprise.

'Why, Beezus,' said Mrs Quimby, 'I had no idea you minded.'

'Well, I do,' said Beezus crossly. 'And Ramona always gets out of things like washing dishes because she is too little. She'll probably still be too little when she's eighty.'

'See?' said Ramona. 'Beezus doesn't like me because my artwork is stuck to the refrigerator.' Her parents weren't supposed to feel sorry for Beezus. They were supposed to feel sorry for Ramona.

'I'm always in the way,' said Ramona. 'You have to park me with Howie's grandmother so you can go to work, and Howie's grandmother doesn't like me. She thinks I'm so terrible she probably won't want me around any more, and then there won't be anybody to look after me and you can't go to work. So there!' Ramona flopped down on the couch, waiting for someone to tell her she was wrong.

Ramona's mother and father said nothing.

'Everybody picks on me all the time,' said Ramona. Maybe she really would be so bad Mrs Kemp would say, I simply cannot put up with Ramona another day.

Silence.

Ramona made up her mind to shock her parents, really shock them. 'I am going to run away,' she announced.

'I'm sorry to hear that,' said Mr Quimby as if running away were a perfectly natural thing to do.

'When are you leaving?' enquired Ramona's mother politely. The question was almost more than Ramona could bear. Her mother was supposed to say, Oh, Ramona, please, please don't leave me!

'Today,' Ramona managed to say with quivering lips. 'This morning.'

'She just wants you to feel sorry for her,' said heartless Beezus. 'She wants you to stop her.'

Ramona waited for her mother or father to say something, but neither spoke. Finally there was nothing for Ramona to do but get up from the couch. 'I guess I'll go pack,' she said, and started slowly towards her room.

No one tried to prevent her. When she reached her room, tears began to fall. She got out her Q-tip box with all her money, forty-three cents, in it. Still no one came to beg her not to leave. She looked around for something in which to pack, but all she could find was an old doll's nursing kit. Ramona unzipped it and placed her Q-tip box inside. She added her best box of crayons and a pair of clean socks. Outside she heard the cheerful *ching-chong, ching-chong* of roller skates on cement. Some children were happy.

If nobody stopped her, where would she run to? Not Howie's house, even though Howie was no longer mad at her. His grandmother was not paid to look after her on Saturday. She could take the bus to Aunt Beatrice's apartment house, but Aunt Beatrice would bring her back home. Maybe she could live in the park and sleep under the bushes in the cold. Poor little Ramona, all alone in the park, shivering in the dark. Well, at least it was not raining. That was something. And there were no big wild animals, just chipmunks.

She heard her mother coming down the hall. Tears stopped. Ramona was about to be rescued. Now her mother would say, Please don't run away. We love you and want you to stay.

Instead Mrs Quimby walked into the bedroom with a suitcase in one hand and two bananas in the other. 'You will need something to pack in,' she told Ramona. 'Let me help.' She opened the suitcase on the unmade bed and placed the bananas inside. 'In case you get hungry,' she explained.

Ramona was too shocked to say anything. Mothers weren't supposed to help their children run away. 'You'll need your roller skates in case you want to travel fast,' said Mrs Quimby. 'Where are they?'

As if she were walking in her sleep, Ramona pulled her roller skates from a jumble of toys in the bottom of her closet and handed them to her mother, who placed them at the bottom of the suitcase. How could her mother not love a little girl like Ramona?

'Always pack heavy things at the bottom,' advised Mrs Quimby. 'Now where are your boots in case it rains?' She looked around the room. 'And don't forget your Betsy book. And your little box of baby teeth. You wouldn't want to leave your teeth behind.'

Ramona felt she could run away without her old baby teeth, and she was hurt that her mother did not want to keep them to remember her by. She stood watching while her mother packed briskly and efficiently.

'You will want Ella Funt in case you get lonely,' said Mrs Quimby.

When Ramona said her mother did not love her, she had no idea her mother would do a terrible thing like this. And her father. Didn't he care either? Apparently not. He was too busy scrubbing the bathroom to care that Ramona was in despair. And what about Beezus? She was probably secretly glad Ramona was going to run away because she could have her parents all to herself. Even Picky-picky would be glad to see the last of her.

As Ramona watched her mother fold underwear

for her to take away, she began to understand that deep down inside in the place where her secret thoughts were hidden, she had never really doubted her mother's love for her. Not until now . . . She thought of all the things her mother had done for her, the way she had sat up most of the night when Ramona had an earache, the birthday cake she had made in the shape of a cowboy boot all frosted with chocolate with lines of white icing that looked like stitching. That was the year she was four and had wanted cowboy boots more than anything, and her parents had given her real ones as well. She thought of the way her mother reminded her to brush her teeth. Her mother would not do that unless she cared about her teeth, would she? She thought of the time her mother let her get her hair cut at the beauty school, even though they had to scrimp and pinch. She thought of the gentle books about bears and bunnies her mother had read at bedtime when she was little.

'There.' Mrs Quimby closed the suitcase, snapped the latches, and set it on the floor. 'Now you are all packed.' She sat down on the bed.

Ramona pulled her car coat out of the closet and slowly put it on, one arm and then the other. She looked at her mother with sad eyes as she grasped the handle of her suitcase and lifted.

The suitcase would not budge. Ramona grasped it with both hands. Still she could not lift it.

Hope flowed into Ramona's heart. Had her mother made her suitcase too heavy on purpose? She looked closely at her mother, who was watching her. She saw—didn't she?—a tiny smile in her mother's eyes.

'You tricked me!' cried Ramona. 'You made the suitcase too heavy on purpose. You don't want me to run away!'

'I couldn't get along without my Ramona,' said Ramona's mother. She held out her arms. Ramona ran into them. Her mother had said the words she had longed to hear. Her mother could not get along without her. She felt warm and safe and comforted and oh, how good her mother smelled, so clean and sweet like flowers. Better than any mother in the whole world. Ramona's tears dampened her mother's blouse. After a moment Mrs Quimby handed Ramona a Kleenex. When Ramona had wiped her eyes and nose, she was surprised to discover that her mother had tears in her eyes, too.

'Mama,' said Ramona, using a word she had given up as babyish, 'why did you do that?'

'Because I could see I couldn't get anyplace arguing with you,' answered her mother. 'You wouldn't listen.'

The truth made Ramona uncomfortable. 'Why did Mrs Rudge phone?' she asked, to change the subject.

Mrs Quimby looked concerned. 'She called to say that she had noticed you twitching your nose a lot—Daddy and I have noticed it, too—and she wondered if something was making you nervous. She wondered if you perhaps needed a shorter day in school.'

And a longer day with Howie's grandmother? What a terrible idea. 'School is easy,' said Ramona, not mentioning spelling, which, after all, might be easy if she paid more attention to it.

'Have you any idea what makes you twitch your nose?' asked Mrs Quimby gently. 'I noticed you twitch it three times during breakfast.'

Ramona was surprised. Maybe she had twitched so much she could twitch without knowing it. 'Of course I know why,' she said. 'I was pretending I was a rabbit, a baby rabbit, because you call me a little rabbit sometimes.'

This time Ramona did not mind when her mother laughed. She laughed a bit, too, to show that she now thought pretending to be a baby rabbit seemed silly, as if it were something she had done a long time ago when she was little.

'Rabbits are nice,' said Mrs Quimby, 'but I prefer a little girl. My little girl.'

'Really?' said Ramona, even though she knew her mother spoke the truth.

'I am glad to know you were a little rabbit,' said Ramona's mother. 'I was afraid my working full time might be too much for you, and just when we have decided Daddy will quit his job at the market and go back to school.'

Ramona was astonished. 'School! You mean do homework and stuff like that? Daddy?'

'I expect so,' answered Mrs Quimby.

'Why does he want to go and do a thing like that?' Ramona could not understand.

'To finish college,' her mother explained. 'So he can get a better job, he hopes. One that he likes.'

So this was what her parents had been talking about at night in their room. 'Will he have to go away?' asked Ramona.

'No. He can go to Portland State right here in town,' explained Mrs Quimby. 'But I will have to go on working full time, which I want to do anyway because I like my job. Do you think you can manage to get along with Mrs Kemp?'

Ramona thought how much happier her family would be if her father never came home tired from working in the express line again. 'Of course I can,' she agreed with courage. 'I've gotten along—sort of—so far.' After this she would stay away from pinking shears and bluing. As for Willa

Jean—maybe she would go to nursery school and learn to shape up. Yes, Ramona could manage. 'And I guess we'll have to scrimp and pinch some more,' she said.

'That's right. Scrimp and pinch and save as much money as we can while Daddy is studying, even though he hopes to find part-time work after school starts,' said Mrs Quimby. 'And by the way, you don't have to tell me if you don't want to, but I am curious. Why are your pyjamas at school?'

'Oh.' Ramona made a face; it all seemed so ridiculous now. She gave her mother the shortest possible explanation.

Mrs Quimby did not seem upset. She merely said, 'What next?' and laughed.

'Did Mrs Rudge say anything about my spelling?' Ramona hesitated to ask the question, but she did want to know the answer.

'Why, no,' said Mrs Quimby. 'She didn't even mention spelling, but she did say you were one of her little sparklers who made teaching interesting.' And with that Ramona's mother left the room.

A little sparkler! Ramona liked that. She thought of the last Fourth of July when she had twirled through the dusk, a sparkler fizzing and spitting in each hand and leaving circles of light and figure eights as she had spun across the front yard until she had fallen to the grass with dizziness. And now she was one of Mrs Rudge's little sparklers!

Ramona held out her arms and twirled across the room, pretending she was holding sparklers. Then she seized a pencil and paper that were lying on her bureau and wrote her name in good, bold joined-up writing:

Ramona Quimby

There. A girl who was a sparkler needed a name that looked like a sparkler. And that was the way Ramona Quimby was going to write her name.

Ching-chong, ching-chong went the roller skates out on the sidewalk. Ramona opened the suitcase and pulled out her skates.

RaMoNa
QuiMBY,
Age 8

CONTENTS

Contents

1

THE FiRST DaY OF SCHOOL

Ramona Quimby hoped her parents would forget to give her a little talking-to. She did not want anything to spoil this exciting day.

'Ha-ha, I get to ride the bus to school all by myself,' Ramona bragged to her big sister, Beatrice, at breakfast. Her stomach felt quivery with excitement at the day ahead, a day that would begin with a bus ride just the right length to make her feel a long way from home but not long enough—she hoped—to make her feel car-sick. Ramona was going to ride the bus, because changes had been made in the schools in the Quimbys' part of the city during the summer. Glenwood, the girls' old school, had become an intermediate school, which meant Ramona had to go to Cedarhurst Primary School.

'Ha-ha yourself.' Beezus was too excited to be annoyed with her little sister. 'Today I start high school.'

'*Junior* high school,' corrected Ramona, who

was not going to let her sister get away with acting older than she really was. 'Rosemont Junior High School is not the same as high school, and besides you have to walk.'

Ramona had reached the age of demanding accuracy from everyone, even herself. All summer, whenever a grown-up asked what grade she was in, she felt as if she were fibbing when she answered, 'third', because she had not actually started the third grade. Still, she could not say she was in the second grade since she had finished that grade last June. Grown-ups did not understand that summers were free from grades.

'Ha-ha to both of you,' said Mr Quimby, as he carried his breakfast dishes into the kitchen. 'You're not the only ones going to school today.' Yesterday had been his last day working at the check-out counter of the Shop-Rite Market. Today he was returning to college to become what he called 'a real, live school teacher'. He was also going to work one day a week in the frozen-food warehouse of the chain of Shop-Rite Markets to help the family 'squeak by', as the grown-ups put it, until he finished his schooling.

'Ha-ha to all of you if you don't hurry up,' said Mrs Quimby, as she swished the suds in the dishpan. She stood back from the sink so she would not spatter the white uniform she wore in the doctor's office where she worked as a receptionist.

'Daddy, will you have to do homework?' Ramona wiped off her milk moustache and gathered up her dishes.

'That's right.' Mr Quimby flicked a dish towel at Ramona as she passed him. She giggled and dodged, happy because he was happy. Never again would he stand all day at a cash register, ringing up groceries for a long line of people who were always in a hurry.

Ramona slid her plate into the dishwater. 'And will mother have to sign your progress reports?'

Mrs Quimby laughed. 'I hope so.'

Beezus was last to bring her dishes into the kitchen. 'Daddy, what do you have to study to learn to be a teacher?' she asked.

Ramona had been wondering the same thing. Her father knew how to read and do arithmetic. He also knew about Oregon pioneers and about two pints making one quart.

Mr Quimby wiped a plate and stacked it in the cupboard. 'I'm taking an art course, because I want to teach art. And I'll study child development—'

Ramona interrupted. 'What's child development?'

'How kids grow,' answered her father.

Why does anyone have to go to school to study

a thing like that? wondered Ramona. All her life she had been told that the way to grow was to eat good food, usually food she did not like, and get plenty of sleep, usually when she had more interesting things to do than go to bed.

Mrs Quimby hung up the dishcloth, scooped up Picky-picky, the Quimbys' old yellow cat, and dropped him at the top of the basement steps. 'Scat, all of you,' she said, 'or you'll be late for school.'

After the family's rush to brush teeth, Mr Quimby said to his daughters, 'Hold out your hands,' and into each waiting pair he dropped a new pink eraser. 'Just for luck,' he said, 'not because I expect you to make mistakes.'

'Thank you,' said the girls. Even a small present was appreciated, because presents of any kind had been scarce while the family tried to save money so Mr Quimby could return to school. Ramona, who liked to draw as much as her father, especially treasured the new eraser, smooth, pearly pink, smelling softly of rubber, and just right for erasing pencil lines.

Mrs Quimby handed each member of her family a lunch, two in paper bags and one in a lunch box for Ramona. 'Now, Ramona—' she began.

Ramona sighed. Here it was, that little talking-to she always dreaded.

'Please remember,' said her mother, 'you really must be nice to Willa Jean.'

Ramona made a face. 'I try, but it's awfully hard.'

Being nice to Willa Jean was the part of Ramona's life that was not changing, the part she wished would change. Every day after school she had to go to her friend Howie Kemp's house, where her parents paid Howie's grandmother to look after her until one of them could come for her. Both of Howie's parents, too, went off to work each day. She liked Howie, but after spending most of the summer, except for swimming lessons in the park, at the Kemps' house, she was tired of having to play with four-year-old Willa Jean. She was also tired of apple juice and graham crackers for a snack every single day.

'No matter what Willa Jean does,' complained Ramona, 'her grandmother thinks it's my fault because I'm bigger. Like the time Willa Jean wore her flippers when she ran under the sprinkler, pretending she was the mermaid on the tuna-fish can, and then left big wet footprints on the kitchen floor. Mrs Kemp said I should have stopped her because Willa Jean didn't know any better!'

Mrs Quimby gave Ramona a quick hug. 'I know it isn't easy, but keep trying.'

When Ramona sighed, her father hugged her and said, 'Remember, kid, we're counting on you.' Then he began to sing, 'We've got high hopes, try hopes, buy cherry pie-in-July hopes—'

Ramona enjoyed her father's making up new words for the song about the little old ant moving the rubber tree plant, and she liked being big enough to be counted on, but sometimes when she went to the Kemps' she felt as if everything depended on her. If Howie's grandmother did not look after her, her mother could not work full time. If her mother did not work full time, her father could not go to school. If her father did not go to school, he might have to go back to being a checker, the work that made him tired and cross.

Still, Ramona had too many interesting things to think about to let her responsibility worry her as she walked through the autumn sunshine towards her school bus stop, her new eraser in hand, new sandals on her feet, that quivery feeling of excitement in her stomach, and the song about high hopes running through her head.

She thought about her father's new part-time job zipping around in a warehouse on a fork-lift truck, filling orders for orange juice, peas, fish sticks, and all the other frozen items the markets carried. He called himself Santa's Little Helper, because the temperature of the warehouse was way below zero, and he would have to wear heavy padded clothing to keep from freezing. The job sounded like fun to Ramona. She wondered how she was going to feel about her father's teaching art to other people's children and decided not to think about that for a while.

Instead, Ramona thought about Beezus going off to another school, where she would get to take a cooking class and where she could not come to the rescue if her little sister got into trouble. As Ramona approached her bus stop, she thought about one of the best parts of her new school: none of her teachers in her new school would know she was Beatrice's little sister. Teachers always liked Beezus; she was so prompt and neat. When both girls had gone to Glenwood School, Ramona often felt as if teachers were thinking, I wonder why Ramona Quimby isn't more like her big sister.

When Ramona reached the bus stop, she found Howie Kemp already waiting with his grandmother and Willa Jean, who had come to wave goodbye.

Howie looked up from his lunch box, which he had opened to see what he was going to have for lunch, and said to Ramona, 'Those new sandals make your feet look awfully big.'

'Why, Howie,' said his grandmother, 'that's not a nice thing to say.'

Ramona studied her feet. Howie was right, but why shouldn't her new sandals make her feet look big? Her feet had grown since her last pair. She was not offended.

'Today, I'm going to *kidnergarten*,' boasted Willa Jean, who was wearing new coveralls and T-shirt and a pair of her mother's old earrings. Willa Jean was convinced she was beautiful, because her grandmother said so. Ramona's mother said Mrs Kemp was right. Willa Jean was beautiful when she was clean, because she was a healthy child. Willa Jean did not feel she was beautiful like a healthy child. She felt she was beautiful like a grown-up lady on TV.

Ramona tried to act kindly towards little Willa Jean. After all, her family was depending on her. 'Not *kidnergarten*, Willa Jean,' she said. 'You mean nursery school.'

Willa Jean gave Ramona a cross, stubborn look that Ramona knew too well. 'I am too going to *kid*nergarten,' she said. '*Kid*nergarten is where the kids are.'

'Bless her little heart,' said her grandmother, admiring as always.

The bus, the little yellow school bus Ramona had waited all summer to ride, pulled up at the kerb. Ramona and Howie climbed aboard as if they were used to getting on buses by themselves. I did it just like a grown-up, thought Ramona.

'Good morning. I am Mrs Hanna, your bus aide,' said a woman sitting behind the driver. 'Take the first empty seats towards the back.' Ramona and Howie took window seats on opposite sides of the bus, which had a reassuring new smell. Ramona always dreaded the people-and-fumes smell of the big city buses.

'Bye-byee,' called Mrs Kemp and Willa Jean, waving as if Ramona and Howie were going on a long, long journey. 'Bye-byee.' Howie pretended not to know them.

As soon as the bus pulled away from the kerb, Ramona felt someone kick the back of her seat. She turned and faced a sturdy boy wearing a baseball cap with the visor turned up and a white T-shirt with a long word printed across the front. She studied the word to see if she could find short words in it, as she had learned to do in second grade. *Earth. Quakes. Earthquakes.* Some kind of team. Yes, he looked like the sort of boy whose father would take him to ball games. He did not have a lunch box, which meant he was going to buy his lunch in the cafeteria.

A grown-up would not call him a purple cootie. Ramona faced front without speaking. This boy was not going to spoil her first day in the third grade.

Thump, thump, thump against the back of Ramona's seat. The bus stopped for other children, some excited and some anxious. Still the kicking continued. Ramona ignored it as the bus passed her former school. Good old Glenwood, thought Ramona, as if she had gone there a long, long time ago.

'All right, Danny,' said the bus aide to the kicking boy. 'As long as I'm riding shotgun on this bus, we won't have anyone kicking the seats. Understand?'

Ramona smiled to herself as she heard Danny mutter an answer. How funny—the bus aide saying she was riding shotgun as if she were guarding a shipment of gold on a stagecoach instead of making children behave on a little yellow school bus.

Ramona pretended she was riding a stagecoach pursued by robbers until she discovered her eraser, her beautiful pink eraser, was missing. 'Did you see my eraser?' she asked a second-grade girl, who had taken the seat beside her. The two searched the seat and the floor. No eraser.

Ramona felt a tap on her shoulder and turned. 'Was it a pink eraser?' asked the boy in the baseball cap.

'Yes.' Ramona was ready to forgive him for kicking her seat. 'Have you seen it?'

'Nope.' The boy grinned as he jerked down the visor of his baseball cap.

That grin was too much for Ramona. 'Liar!' she said with her most ferocious glare, and faced front once more, angry at the loss of her new eraser, angry with herself for dropping it so the boy could find it. Purple cootie, she thought, and hoped the cafeteria would serve him fish portions and those canned green beans with the strings left on. And apple wedges, the soft mushy kind with tough skins, for dessert.

The bus stopped at Cedarhurst, Ramona's new school, a two-storey red-brick building very much like her old school. As the children hopped out of the bus, Ramona felt a little thrill of triumph. She had not been car-sick. She now discovered she felt as if she had grown even more than her feet. Third-graders were the biggest people— except teachers, of course—at this school. All the little first- and second-graders running around the playground, looking so young, made Ramona feel tall, grown-up, and sort of . . . well, wise in the ways of the world.

Danny shoved ahead of her. 'Catch!' he yelled to another boy. Something small and pink flew through the air and into the second boy's cupped hands. The boy wound up as if he were pitching a baseball, and the eraser flew back to Danny.

'You gimme back my eraser!' Encumbered by her lunch box, Ramona chased Danny, who ran, ducking and dodging, among the first- and second-graders. When she was about to catch him, he tossed her eraser to the other boy. If her lunch box had not banged against her knees, Ramona might have been able to grab him. Unfortunately, the bell rang first.

'Yard apes!' yelled Ramona, her name for the sort of boys who always got the best balls, who were always first on the playground, and who chased their soccer balls through other people's hopscotch games. She saw her pink eraser fly back into Danny's hands. 'Yard apes!' she yelled again, tears of anger in her eyes. 'Yucky yard apes!' The boys, of course, paid no attention.

Still fuming, Ramona entered her new school and climbed the stairs to find her assigned classroom, which she discovered looked out over roofs and treetops to Mount Hood in the distance. I wish it would erupt, she thought, because she felt like exploding with anger.

Ramona's new room was filled with excitement and confusion. She saw some people she had known at her old school. Others were strangers. Everyone was talking at once, shouting greetings to old friends or looking over those who would soon become new friends, rivals, or enemies. Ramona missed Howie, who had been assigned to another room, but wouldn't you know? That yard ape, Danny, was sitting at a desk, still wearing his baseball cap and tossing Ramona's new eraser from one hand to another. Ramona was too frustrated to speak. She wanted to hit him. How dare he spoil her day?

'All right, you guys, quiet down,' said the teacher.

Ramona was startled to hear her class called 'you guys'. Most teachers she had known would say something like, 'I feel I am talking very loud. Is it because the room is noisy?' She chose a chair at a table at the front of the room and studied her new teacher, a strong-looking woman with short hair and a deep tan. Like my swimming teacher, thought Ramona.

'My name is Mrs Whaley,' said the teacher, as she printed her name on the blackboard. '*W-h-a-l-e-y*. I'm a whale with a *y* for a tail.' She laughed and so did her class. Then the whale with a *y* for a tail handed Ramona some slips of paper. 'Please pass these out,' she directed. 'We need some name tags until I get to know you.'

Ramona did as she was told, and as she walked among the desks she discovered her new sandals squeaked. *Squeak, creak, squeak*. Ramona giggled, and so did the rest of the class. *Squeak, creak, squeak*. Ramona went up one aisle and down the other. The last person she gave a slip to was the boy from the bus, who was still wearing his baseball cap. 'You give me back my eraser, you yard ape!' she whispered.

'Try and get it, Bigfoot,' he whispered back with a grin.

Ramona stared at her feet. Bigfoot? Bigfoot was a hairy creature ten feet tall, who was supposed to leave huge footprints in the mountain snows of southern Oregon. Some people thought they had seen Bigfoot slipping through the forests, but no one had ever been able to prove he really existed.

Bigfoot indeed! Ramona's feet had grown, but they were not huge. She was not going to let him get away with this insult. 'Superfoot to you, Yard Ape,' she said right out loud, realizing too late that she had given herself a new nickname.

To her astonishment, Yard Ape pulled her eraser out of his pocket and handed it to her with a grin. Well! With her nose in the air, Ramona squeaked back to her seat. She felt so triumphant that she returned the longest way around and bent her feet as much as she could to make the loudest possible squeaks. She had done the right thing! She had not let Yard Ape upset her by calling her

Bigfoot, and now she had her eraser in her hand. He would probably call her Superfoot forever, but she did not care. Superfoot was a name she had given herself. That made all the difference. She had won.

Ramona became aware that she was squeaking in the midst of an unusual silence. She stopped midsqueak when she saw her new teacher watching her with a little smile. The class was watching the teacher.

'We all know you have musical shoes,' said Mrs Whaley. Of course the class laughed.

By walking with stiff legs and not bending her feet, Ramona reached her seat without squeaking at all. She did not know what to think. At first she thought Mrs Whaley's remark was a reprimand, but then maybe her teacher was just trying to be funny. She couldn't tell about grown-ups sometimes. Ramona finally decided that any teacher who would let Yard Ape wear his baseball cap in the classroom wasn't really fussy about squeaking shoes.

Ramona bent over her paper and wrote slowly and carefully in joined-up writing, Ramona Quimby, age 8. She admired the look of what she had written, and she was happy. She liked feeling tall in her new school. She liked—or was pretty sure she liked—her nonfussy teacher.

Yard Ape—Well, he was a problem, but so far she had not let him get the best of her for keeps. Besides, although she might never admit it to anyone, now that she had her eraser back she liked him—sort of. Maybe she enjoyed a challenge.

Ramona began to draw a fancy border, all scallops and curlicues, around her name. She was happy, too, because her family had been happy that morning and because she was big enough for her family to depend on.

If only she could do something about Willa Jean . . .

2

AT HOWIE'S HOUSE

'Now be nice to Willa Jean,' said Mrs Quimby, as she handed Ramona her lunch box. Grown-ups often forgot that no child likes to be ordered to be nice to another child.

Ramona made a face. 'Mother, do you have to say that every single morning?' she asked in exasperation. Deep down inside, where she hid her darkest secrets, Ramona sometimes longed to be horrid to Willa Jean.

'OK, OK, I'll try to remember,' said Mrs Quimby with a little laugh. 'I know it isn't easy.' She kissed Ramona and said, 'Cheer up and run along or you'll miss your bus.'

Being a member of the Quimby family in the third grade was harder than Ramona had expected. Her father was often tired, in a hurry, or studying on the dining-room table, which meant no one could disturb him by watching television. At school she was still not sure how she felt about Mrs Whaley. Liking a teacher was important, Ramona had discovered when she was in the first

143

grade. And even though her family understood, Ramona still dreaded that part of the day spent at Howie's house in the company of Mrs Kemp and Willa Jean.

Those were the bad parts of the third grade. There were good parts, too. Ramona enjoyed riding the bus to school, and she enjoyed keeping Yard Ape from getting the best of her. Then another good part of the third grade began the second week of school.

Just before her class was to make its weekly visit to the school library, Mrs Whaley announced, 'Today and from now on we are going to have Sustained Silent Reading every day.'

Ramona liked the sound of Sustained Silent Reading, even though she was not sure what it meant, because it sounded important.

Mrs Whaley continued. 'This means that every day after lunch we are going to sit at our desks and read silently to ourselves any book we choose in the library.'

'Even mysteries?' someone asked.

'Even mysteries,' said Mrs Whaley.

'Do we have to give book reports on what we read?' asked one suspicious member of the class.

'No book reports on your Sustained Silent Reading books,' Mrs Whaley promised the class. Then she went on, 'I don't think Sustained Silent

Reading sounds very interesting, so I think we will call it something else.' Here she printed four big letters on the blackboard, and as she pointed she read out, 'D. E. A. R. Can anyone guess what these letters stand for?'

The class thought and thought.

'Do Everything All Right,' suggested someone. A good thought, but not the right answer.

'Don't Eat A Reader,' suggested Yard Ape. Mrs Whaley laughed and told him to try again.

As Ramona thought, she stared out of the window at the blue sky, the treetops, and, in the distance, the snow-capped peak of Mount Hood looking like a giant licked ice-cream cone. *R* could stand for *Run* and *A* for And. 'Drop Everything And Run,' Ramona burst out. Mrs Whaley, who was not the sort of teacher who expected everyone to raise a hand before speaking, laughed and said, 'Almost right, Ramona, but have you forgotten we are talking about reading?'

'Drop Everything And Read!' chorused the rest of the class. Ramona felt silly. She should have thought of that herself.

Ramona decided that she preferred Sustained Silent Reading to DEAR because it sounded more grown-up. When time came for everyone to Drop Everything And Read, she sat quietly doing her Sustained Silent Reading.

How peaceful it was to be left alone in school. She could read without trying to hide her book under her desk or behind a bigger book. She was not expected to write lists of words she did not know, so she could figure them out by skipping and guessing. Mrs Whaley did not expect the class to write summaries of what they read either, so she did not have to choose easy books to make sure she would get her summary right. Now if Mrs Whaley would leave her alone to draw, too, school would be almost perfect.

Yes, Sustained Silent Reading was the best part of the day. Howie and Ramona talked it over after school and agreed as they walked from the bus to his house. There they found two of the new friends he had made at Cedarhurst School waiting with their bicycles.

Ramona sat on the Kemps' front steps, her arms clasped around her knees, her Sustained Silent Reading book of fairy tales beside her, and looked with longing at the boys' two bicycles while Howie wheeled his bicycle out of the garage.

Because Howie was kind and because Ramona was his friend, he asked, 'Ramona, would you like to ride my bicycle to the corner and back?'

Would she! Ramona jumped up, eager to take a turn.

'Just once,' said Howie.

Ramona mounted the bicycle and, while the three boys silently watched, teetered and wobbled to the corner without falling off. Having to dismount to turn the bicycle around was embarrassing, but riding back was easier— at least she didn't wobble quite so much—and she managed to dismount as if she were used to doing so. All I need is a little practice, thought Ramona, as Howie seized his bicycle and rode off with his friends, leaving her with nothing to do but pick up her book and join Willa Jean in the house.

Now that Willa Jean was going to nursery school, she was full of ideas. Dressing up was one of them. She met Ramona at the door with an old curtain wrapped around her shoulders. 'Hurry up and have your snack,' she ordered, while her grandmother sat watching television and crocheting.

The snack turned out to be pineapple juice and Rye Crisp, a pleasant change for Ramona, even though Willa Jean stood impatiently beside her, watching every swallow until she had finished.

'Now I'll be the lady and you be the dog,' directed Willa Jean.

'But I don't want to be a dog,' said Ramona.

Willa Jean's grandmother looked up from her

crocheting, reminding Ramona with a glance that Ramona's job in the Quimby family was to get along at the Kemps'. Did she have to be a dog if Willa Jean wanted her to then?

'You have to be the dog,' said Willa Jean.

'Why?' Ramona kept an eye on Mrs Kemp as she wondered how far she dared go in resisting Willa Jean's orders.

'Because I'm a beautiful rich lady and I say so,' Willa Jean informed her.

'I'm a bigger, beautifuller, richer lady,' said Ramona, who felt neither beautiful nor rich, but certainly did not want to crawl around on her hands and knees barking.

'We can't both be the lady,' said Willa Jean, 'and I said it first.'

Ramona could not argue the justice of this point. 'What kind of dog am I supposed to be?' she asked to stall for time. She glanced wistfully at her book lying on the chair, the book she was supposed to read at school, but which she was enjoying so much she brought it home.

While Willa Jean was thinking, Mrs Kemp said, 'Sweetheart, don't forget Bruce is coming over to play in a few minutes.'

'Bruce who?' asked Ramona, hoping Willa Jean and Bruce would play together and leave her alone to read.

'Bruce who doesn't wee-wee in the sandbox,' was Willa Jean's prompt answer.

'Willa Jean!' Mrs Kemp was shocked. 'What a thing to say about your little friend.'

Ramona was not shocked. She understood that there must be a second Bruce at Willa Jean's nursery school, a Bruce who did wee-wee in the sandbox.

As things turned out, Ramona was saved from being a dog by the arrival of a small boy whose mother let him out of the car and watched him reach the front door before she drove off.

Willa Jean ran to let him in and introduced him as Ramona expected, 'This is Bruce who doesn't wee-wee in the sandbox.' Bruce looked pleased with himself.

Mrs Kemp felt a need to apologize for her granddaughter. 'Willa Jean doesn't mean what she says.'

'But I don't wee-wee in the sandbox,' said Bruce. 'I wee-wee in the—'

'Never mind, Bruce,' said Mrs Kemp. 'Now what are you three going to play?'

Ramona was trapped.

'Dress up,' was Willa Jean's prompt answer. She dragged from the corner a carton piled with old clothes. Willa Jean shoved one of her father's old jackets at Bruce and handed him an old hat and her blue flippers. She unwound the curtain from her shoulders, draped it over her head, and tied it under her chin. Then she hung a piece of old sheet from her shoulders. Satisfied with herself, she handed a torn shirt to Ramona, who put it on only because Mrs Kemp was watching.

'There,' said Willa Jean, satisfied. 'I'll be Miss Mousie, the beautiful bride, and Bruce is the frog and Ramona is Uncle Rat, and now we are going to have a wedding party.'

Ramona did not want to be Uncle Rat.

'Mr Frog would a-wooing go,' sang Willa Jean. Bruce joined in, '*Hm-m, hm-m.*' Apparently this song was popular in nursery school. Ramona *hm-med* too.

'Say it,' Willa Jean ordered Bruce.

'Willa Jean, will you marry me?' sang Bruce.

Willa Jean stamped her foot. '*Not* Willa Jean! Miss Mousie.'

Bruce started over. 'Miss Mousie, will you marry me?' he sang.

'Yes, if Uncle Rat will agree,' sang Willa Jean.

'*Hm-m, hm-m.*'

'*Hm-m, hm-m,*' hummed all three.

The two nursery-school children looked to Ramona for the next line. Since she did not remember the words used by Uncle Rat to give

Mr Frog permission to marry Miss Mousie, she said, 'Sure. Go ahead.'

'OK,' said Willa Jean. 'Now we will have the wedding party.' She seized Bruce and Ramona by the hand. 'Take Bruce's other hand,' she ordered Ramona.

Ramona found Bruce's hand inside the long sleeve of the old coat. His hand was sticky.

'Now we'll dance in a circle,' directed Willa Jean.

Ramona skipped, Willa Jean pranced, and Bruce flapped. They danced in a circle, tripping on Miss Mousie's train and wedding veil and stumbling over Mr Frog's flippers until Willa Jean gave the next order. 'Now we all fall down.'

Ramona merely dropped to her knees while Willa Jean and Bruce collapsed in a heap, laughing. Above their laughter and the sound of the television, Ramona heard the shouts of the boys outside as they rode their bicycles up and down the street. She wondered how much longer she would have to wait until her mother came to rescue her. She hoped she would arrive before Howie's parents came home from work.

Willa Jean scrambled to her feet. 'Let's play it again,' she said, beaming, convinced of her beauty in her wedding veil. Over and over the three sang, danced, and fell down. As the game went on and on, Ramona grew bored and varied the words she used to give Mr Frog permission to marry Miss Mousie. Sometimes she said, 'See if I care,' and sometimes she said, 'Yes, but you'll be sorry.' Willa Jean did not notice, she was so eager to get to the party part of the game where they all fell down in a heap.

Still the game went on, over and over, with no sign of Bruce and Willa Jean's tiring. Then Beezus came in with an armload of books.

'Hi, Beezus,' said Willa Jean, flushed with laughter. 'You can play too. You can be the old tomcat in the song.'

'I'm sorry, Willa Jean,' said Beezus. 'I don't have time to be the old tomcat. I have homework I have to do.' She settled herself at the dining-room table and opened a book.

Ramona looked at Mrs Kemp, who smiled and continued crocheting. Why did Ramona have to play with Willa Jean when Beezus did not? Because she was younger. That was why. Ramona was overwhelmed by the unfairness of it all. Because she was younger, she always had to do things she did not want to do—go to bed earlier, wear Beezus's outgrown clothes that her mother saved for her, run and fetch because her legs were younger and because Beezus was always doing homework. Now she had to get along with Willa

Jean—her whole family was depending on her—
and Beezus did not.

Once more Ramona looked at her book of
fairy tales waiting on the chair beside the front
door, and as she looked at its worn cover she had
an inspiration. Maybe her idea would work, and
maybe it wouldn't. It was worth a try.

'Willa Jean, you and Bruce will have to excuse
me now,' Ramona said in her politest voice. 'I
have to do my Sustained Silent Reading.' Out of
the corner of her eye she watched Mrs Kemp.

'OK.' Willa Jean was not only impressed by
a phrase she did not understand, she had Bruce
to boss around. Mrs Kemp, who was counting
stitches, merely nodded.

Ramona picked up her book and settled herself
in the corner of the couch. Beezus caught her eye,
and the two sisters exchanged conspiratorial smiles
while Willa Jean and Bruce, now minus Uncle
Rat, raced happily around in a circle screaming
with joy and singing, 'She'll be coming round the
mountain when she comes!'

Ramona blissfully read herself off into the land
of princesses, kings, and clever youngest sons,
satisfied that the Quimbys had a clever younger
daughter who was doing her part.

3

THE HARD-BOILED EGG FAD

With all four members of the family leaving at different times in different directions, mornings were flurried in the Quimby household. On the days when Mr Quimby had an eight o'clock class, he left early in the car. Beezus left next because she walked to school and because she wanted to stop for Mary Jane on the way.

Ramona was third to leave. She enjoyed these last few minutes alone with her mother now that Mrs Quimby no longer reminded her she must be nice to Willa Jean.

'Did you remember to give me a hard-boiled egg in my lunch like I asked?' Ramona enquired one morning. This week hard-boiled eggs were popular with third-graders, a fad started by Yard Ape, who sometimes brought his lunch. Last week the fad had been individual bags of corn chips. Ramona had been left out of that fad because her mother objected to spending money on junk food. Surely her mother would not object to a nutritious hard-boiled egg.

'Yes, I remembered the hard-boiled egg, you little rabbit,' said Mrs Quimby. 'I'm glad you have finally learned to like them.'

Ramona did not feel it necessary to explain to her mother that she still did not like hard-boiled eggs, not even when they had been dyed for Easter. Neither did she like soft-boiled eggs, because she did not like slippery, slithery food. Ramona liked devilled eggs, but devilled eggs were not the fad, at least not this week.

On the bus Ramona and Susan compared lunches. Each was happy to discover that the other had a hard-boiled egg, and both were eager for lunchtime to come.

While Ramona waited for lunch period, school turned out to be unusually interesting. After the class had filled out their arithmetic workbooks, Mrs Whaley handed each child a glass jar containing about two inches of a wet blue substance—she explained that it was oatmeal dyed blue. Ramona was first to say 'Yuck.' Most people made faces, and Yard Ape made a gagging noise.

'OK, kids, quiet down,' said Mrs Whaley. When the room was quiet, she explained that for science they were going to study fruit flies. The blue oatmeal contained fruit-fly larvae. 'And why do you think the oatmeal is blue?' she asked.

Several people thought the blue dye was some sort of food for the larvae, vitamins maybe. Marsha suggested the oatmeal was dyed blue so the children wouldn't think it was good to eat. Everybody laughed at this guess. Who would ever think cold oatmeal was good to eat? Yard Ape came up with the right answer: the oatmeal was dyed blue so the larvae could be seen. And so they could—little white specks.

As the class bent over their desks making labels for their jars, Ramona wrote her name on her slip of paper and added, 'Age 8', which she always wrote after her signature. Then she drew tiny fruit flies around it before she pasted the label on her very own jar of blue oatmeal and fruit-fly larvae. Now she had a jar of pets.

'That's a really neat label, Ramona,' said Mrs Whaley. Ramona understood that her teacher did not mean tidy when she said 'neat', but extra good. Ramona decided she liked Mrs Whaley after all.

The morning was so satisfactory that it passed quickly. When lunchtime came, Ramona collected her lunch box and went off to the cafeteria where, after waiting in line for her milk, she sat at a table with Sara, Janet, Marsha, and other third-grade girls. She opened her lunch box, and there, tucked in a paper napkin, snug between her sandwich and an orange, was her hard-boiled egg, smooth and perfect, the right size to fit her hand. Because Ramona wanted to save the best for the last, she ate the centre of her sandwich—tuna fish—and poked a hole in her orange so she could suck out the juice. Third-graders did not peel their oranges. At last it was time for the egg.

There were a number of ways of cracking eggs. The most popular, and the real reason for bringing an egg to school, was knocking the egg against one's head. There were two ways of doing so, by a lot of timid little raps or by one big whack.

Sara was a rapper. Ramona, like Yard Ape, was a whacker. She took a firm hold on her egg, waited until everyone at her table was watching, and *whack*—she found herself with a handful of crumbled shell and something cool and slimy running down her face.

Everyone at Ramona's table gasped. Ramona needed a moment to realize what had happened. Her egg was raw. Her mother had not boiled her egg at all. She tried to brush the yellow yolk and slithery white out of her hair and away from her face, but she only succeeded in making her hands eggy. Her eyes filled with tears of anger, which she tried to brush away with her wrists. The gasps at her table turned into giggles. From another table, Ramona caught a glimpse of Yard Ape grinning at her.

Marsha, a tall girl who always tried to be motherly, said, 'It's all right, Ramona. I'll take you to the bathroom and help you wash off the egg.'

Ramona was not one bit grateful. 'You go away,' she said, ashamed of being so rude. She did not want this third-grade girl treating her like a baby.

The teacher who was supervising lunch period came over to see what the commotion was about. Marsha gathered up all the paper napkins from the lunch boxes at the table and handed them to the teacher, who tried to sop up the egg. Unfortunately, the napkins did not absorb egg very well. Instead, they smeared yolk and white around in Ramona's hair. Her face felt stiff as egg white began to dry.

'Take her to the office,' the teacher said to Marsha. 'Mrs Larson will help her.'

'Come on, Ramona,' said Marsha, as if Ramona were in kindergarten. She put her hand on Ramona's shoulder because Ramona's hands were too eggy to touch.

Ramona jerked away. 'I can go by myself.' With that reply, she ran out of the cafeteria. She was so angry she was able to ignore the giggles and the few sympathetic looks of the other children. Ramona was mad at herself for following a fad. She was furious with Yard Ape for grinning at her. Most of all she was angry with her mother for not boiling the egg in the first place. By the time she reached the office, Ramona's face felt as stiff as a mask.

Ramona almost ran into Mr Wittman, the principal, which would have upset her even more. He was someone Ramona always tried to avoid ever since Beezus had told her that the way to remember how to spell the kind of principal who was the principal of a school was to remember the word ended in *p-a-l*, not *p-l-e*, because the principal was her pal. Ramona did not want the principal to be her pal. She wanted him to mind his own business, aloof and important, in his office. Mr Wittman must have felt the same way because he stepped—almost jumped—quickly aside.

Mrs Larson, the school secretary, took one look at Ramona, sprang from her desk, and said, 'Well, you need a little help, don't you?'

Ramona nodded, grateful to Mrs Larson for behaving as if eggy third-graders walked into her office every day. The secretary led her into a tiny room equipped with a cot, washbasin, and toilet that adjoined the office.

'Let's see,' said Mrs Larson, 'how shall we go about this? I guess the best way is to wash your hands, then dunk your head. You've heard of egg shampoos, haven't you? They are supposed to be wonderful for the hair.'

'Yow!' yelped Ramona, when she dipped her head into the washbasin. 'The water's cold.'

'It's probably a good thing we don't have warmer water,' said Mrs Larson. 'You wouldn't want to cook the egg in your hair, would you?' She rubbed and Ramona snuffled. She rinsed and Ramona sniffed. Finally Mrs Larson said, 'That's the best I can do,' and handed Ramona a wad of paper towels. 'Dry yourself off the best you can,' she said. 'You can wash your hair when you get home.'

Ramona accepted the towels. As she sat on the cot, rubbing and blotting and seething in humiliation and anger, she listened to sounds from the office, the click of the typewriter, the ring of the telephone, Mrs Larson's voice answering.

Ramona began to calm down and feel a little better. Maybe Mrs Kemp would let her wash her hair after school. She could let Willa Jean pretend to be working in a beauty shop and not say anything about her Sustained Silent Reading. One of these days Willa Jean was sure to catch on that she was just reading a book, and Ramona wanted to postpone that time as long as possible.

Towards the end of lunch period, Ramona heard teachers drift into the office to leave papers or pick up messages from their boxes. Then Ramona made an interesting discovery. Teachers talked about their classes.

'My class has been so good today,' said one teacher. 'I can hardly believe it. They're little angels.'

'I don't know what's the matter with my class today,' said another. 'Yesterday they knew how to subtract, and today none of them seems able to remember.'

'Perhaps it's the weather,' suggested another teacher.

Ramona found all this conversation most interesting. She had blotted her hair as best she could when she heard Mrs Whaley's big cheerful voice speaking to Mrs Larson. 'Here are those tests I was supposed to hand in yesterday,' she said. 'Sorry I'm late.' Mrs Larson murmured an answer.

Then Mrs Whaley said, 'I hear my little show-off came in with egg in her hair.' She laughed and added, 'What a nuisance.'

Ramona was so stunned she did not try to hear Mrs Larson's answer. Show-off! Nuisance! Did Mrs Whaley think she had broken a raw egg into her hair on purpose to show off? And to be called a nuisance by her teacher when she was not a nuisance. Or was she? Ramona did not mean to break an egg in her hair. Her mother was to blame. Did this accident make her a nuisance?

Ramona did not see why Mrs Whaley could think she was a nuisance when Mrs Whaley was not the one to get her hands all eggy. Yet Ramona had heard her say right out loud that she was a show-off and a nuisance. That hurt, really hurt.

Ramona sat as still as she could with the damp paper towels in her hands. She did not want to risk even the softest noise by throwing them into the wastebasket. Lunch period came to an end, and still she sat. Her body felt numb and so did her heart. She could never, never face Mrs Whaley again. Never.

Mrs Larson's typewriter clicked cheerfully away. Ramona was forgotten, which was the way she wanted it. She even wanted to forget herself and her horrible hair, now drying into stiff spikes. She no longer felt like a real person.

The next voice Ramona heard was that of Yard Ape. 'Mrs Larson,' he said, as if he had been running in the hall, 'Mrs Whaley said to tell you Ramona didn't come back after lunch.'

The typing stopped. 'Oh, my goodness,' said Mrs Larson, as she appeared in the doorway. 'Why, Ramona, are you still here?'

How was Ramona supposed to answer?

'Run along back to class with Danny,' said the secretary. 'I'm sorry I forgot all about you.'

'Do I have to?' asked Ramona.

'Of course,' said Mrs Larson. 'Your hair is almost dry. You don't want to miss class.'

Ramona did want to miss class. Forever. The third grade was spoiled forever.

'Aw, come on, Ramona,' said Yard Ape, for once not teasing.

Surprised by sympathy from Yard Ape, Ramona reluctantly left the office. She expected him to go on ahead of her, but instead he walked beside her, as if they were friends instead of rivals. Ramona felt strange walking down the hall alone with a boy. As she trudged along beside him, she felt she had to tell someone the terrible news. 'Mrs Whaley doesn't like me,' she said in a flat voice.

'Don't let old Whaley get you down,' he answered. 'She likes you OK. You're a good kid.'

Ramona was a little shocked at hearing her teacher called 'old Whaley'. However, she squeezed comfort from Yard Ape's opinion. She began to like him, really like him.

When they reached their classroom, Yard Ape, perhaps thinking he had been *too* nice to Ramona, turned and said to her with his old grin, 'Egghead!'

Oh! There was nothing for Ramona to do but follow him into the room. Sustained Silent Reading, or DEAR, as Mrs Whaley called it, was over, and class was practising writing joined-up capital letters. Mrs Whaley was describing capital *M* as she wrote it on the board. 'Swoop down, swoop up, down, up again, and down.' Ramona avoided looking at her teacher as she got out paper and pencil and began to write the capital letters of the alphabet in careful, even script. She enjoyed the work, and it soothed her hurt feelings until she came to the letter Q.

Ramona sat looking at the joined-up capital Q, the first letter of her last name. Ramona had always been fond of Q, the only letter of the alphabet with a neat little tail. She enjoyed printing Q, but she did not like her written Q. She had made it right, but it looked like a big floppy 2, which Ramona felt was a dumb way to make such a nice letter.

Ramona decided right then and there that she would never again write a joined-up Q. She would write the rest of her last name, *uimby*, in joined-up, but she would always, no matter what Mrs Whaley said, print her capital Q's.

So there, Mrs Whaley, thought Ramona. You can't make me write a joined-up Q if I don't want to. She began to feel like a real person again.

4

THE QUIMBYS' QUARREL

'But Ramona,' said Mrs Quimby on Saturday, 'I've already told you that I boiled several eggs so I wouldn't have to boil an egg for you every morning. I put the boiled eggs on one shelf in the refrigerator and the raw eggs on another. In my hurry, I took an egg from the wrong shelf. I am sorry. There is nothing more I can say.'

Ramona remained silent. She felt mean and unhappy because she wanted to forgive her mother, but something in that dark, deep-down place inside her would not let her. Hearing her teacher call her a show-off and a nuisance hurt so much she could not stop being angry at almost everyone.

Mrs Quimby sighed in a tired sort of way as she gathered up sheets and towels to feed into the washing machine in the basement. Ramona stared out of the window and wished the misty rain, which fell softly and endlessly, would go away so she could go outdoors and roller-skate away her bad feelings.

Beezus was no help. She had spent the night at Mary Jane's house with several other girls, and they had stayed up late watching a horror movie on television and eating popcorn. Afterwards they stayed awake talking, too scared to go to sleep. That morning Beezus had come home tired and grouchy and had fallen asleep almost immediately.

Ramona wandered around the house looking for something to do, when she discovered her father sitting on the couch, pencil in hand, drawing pad on his knee, frowning at one bare foot.

'Daddy, what are you doing that for?' Ramona wanted to know.

'That's what I keep asking myself,' her father answered, as he wiggled his toes. 'I have to draw a picture of my foot for my art class.'

'I wish we got to do things like that in my school,' said Ramona. She found pencil and paper, pulled off one shoe and sock, and climbed on the couch beside her father. Both studied their feet and began to sketch. Ramona soon found that drawing a foot was more difficult than she had expected. Like her father, she stared, frowned, drew, erased, stared, frowned, and drew. For a little while she forgot she was cross. She was enjoying herself.

'There,' said Ramona at last. She had drawn a good, not excellent, foot. She looked at her father's paper and was disappointed in what she saw. It was the kind of picture a teacher would pin up off in the corner where no one but the artist would notice it. Her father's foot looked like a flipper. For the first time, Ramona began to doubt that her father was the best artist in the whole world. This thought made her feel sad in addition to reminding her she was cross at that world.

Mr Quimby studied Ramona's picture. 'That's not bad,' he said. 'Not bad at all.'

'My foot is easier to draw.' Ramona felt as if she should apologize for drawing a better foot than her grown-up father. 'My foot is sort of—neater,' she explained. 'Your foot is kind of bony and your toes are hairy. That makes your foot harder to draw.'

Mr Quimby crumpled his drawing and threw it into the fireplace. 'You make me sound like Bigfoot,' he said with a rueful laugh, as he threw a cushion at Ramona.

The day dragged on. By dinnertime Ramona still had not been able to forgive her mother, who looked even more tired. Mr Quimby had crumpled several more unsatisfactory drawings of his foot, and Beezus had emerged from her room sleepy-eyed and half-awake, when her mother called the family to supper.

'I wish we could have corn bread again,' Ramona said, not because she particularly liked corn bread, but because she felt so cross she wanted to complain about something. Corn bread was a pretty shade of yellow, which would have looked cheerful on a misty day. She leaned forward to sniff the plate of food set before her.

'Ramona.' Even though her father did not speak the words, his voice said, 'We do not sniff our food in this house.'

Ramona sat up. Broccoli and baked potato, both easy to eat. Pot roast. Ramona leaned closer to examine her meat. She could not find one bit of fat, and there was only a bit of gravy poured over her serving. Good. Ramona refused even the tiniest bit of fat. She did not like the slippery squishy feeling in her mouth.

'Delicious,' remarked Mr Quimby, who did not feel he had to inspect his food before eating.

'Nice and tender,' said Beezus, beginning to cheer up after her hard night.

Ramona seized her fork, speared her meat to her plate, and began to saw with her knife.

'Ramona, try to hold your fork properly,' said her father. 'Don't grip it with your fist. A fork is not a dagger.'

With a small sigh, Ramona changed her hold on her fork. Grown-ups never remembered the difficulty of cutting meat when one's elbows were so far below the tabletop. She succeeded in cutting a bite of meat the way her parents thought proper. It was unusually tender and not the least bit stringy like some pot roasts her mother had prepared. It tasted good, too. 'Yummy,' said Ramona, forgetting her anger.

The family ate in contented silence until Beezus pushed aside her gravy with the side of her fork. Gravy was fattening, and although Beezus was slender, even skinny, she was taking no chances.

'Mother!' Beezus's voice was accusing. *'This meat has a rough surface!'*

'It does?' answered Mrs Quimby innocently.

Ramona understood her mother was trying to hide something when she saw her parents exchange their secret-sharing glance. She too scraped aside her gravy. Beezus was right. One edge of her meat was covered with tiny bumps.

'This meat is tongue.' Beezus pushed her serving aside with her fork. 'I don't like tongue.'

Tongue! Like Beezus, Ramona pushed her meat aside. 'Yuck,' she said.

'Girls, stop being silly.' Mrs Quimby's voice was sharp.

'What do you mean you don't like tongue?' demanded Mr Quimby. 'You were just eating it and enjoying it.'

'But I didn't know it was tongue then,' said Beezus. 'I hate tongue.'

'Me too,' said Ramona. 'All those yucky little bumps. Why can't we have plain meat?'

Mrs Quimby was losing patience. 'Because tongue is cheaper. That's why. It's cheaper and it's nutritious.'

'You know what I think,' said Mr Quimby. 'I think this whole thing is a lot of nonsense. You liked tongue when you didn't know it was tongue, so there is no reason why you can't eat it now.'

'Yes, this whole thing is ridiculous,' said Mrs Quimby.

'Tongue is disgusting,' said Beezus. 'Picky-picky can have mine.'

'Mine, too,' echoed Ramona, knowing she should eat what was set before her, but tongue— Her parents were asking too much.

The meal continued in silence, the girls guilty but defiant, the parents unrelenting. When Mr Quimby finished his serving of tongue, he helped himself from Ramona's plate. Picky-picky, purring like a rusty motor, walked into the dining room and rubbed against legs to remind the family that he should eat too.

'I wonder,' said Mrs Quimby, 'why we named the *cat* Picky-picky.' She and Mr Quimby looked at one another and only partly suppressed their laughter. The girls exchanged sulky glances. Parents should not laugh at their children.

Beezus silently cleared the table. Mrs Quimby served apple-sauce and oatmeal cookies while Mr Quimby talked about his work as Santa's Little Helper in the frozen-food warehouse. He told how snow fell inside the warehouse door when someone opened it and let in warm air. He told about a man who had to break icicles from his moustache when he left the warehouse.

Snow indoors, icicles on a moustache—Ramona was full of questions that she would not let herself ask. Maybe working as Santa's Little Helper wasn't as much fun as she had thought.

'I'll tell you what,' said Mr Quimby to Mrs Quimby, when the last cookie crumb had been eaten. 'You need a rest. Tomorrow the girls can get dinner and you can take it easy.'

'Good idea,' said Mrs Quimby. 'Sometimes I do get tired of cooking.'

'But I'm supposed to go to Mary Jane's tomorrow,' protested Beezus.

'Call her up and tell her you can't come.' Mr Quimby was both cheerful and heartless.

'That's not fair,' said Beezus.

'Tell me why it isn't fair,' said Mr Quimby.

When Beezus had no answer, Ramona understood their plight was serious. When their father behaved this way, he never changed his mind. 'But I don't know how to cook,' Ramona protested. 'Except Jello and French toast.'

'Nonsense,' said Mrs Quimby. 'You are in the third grade, and you can read. Anyone who can read can cook.'

'What'll we cook?' Beezus had to accept the fact that she and Ramona had no way out.

'The same things I cook,' said her mother. 'Whatever I have bought on special that you can find in the refrigerator.'

'And corn bread.' Mr Quimby, his face serious but his eyes amused, looked at Ramona. 'I expect to be served corn bread.'

That evening, after the dishes had been put away, Picky-picky was polishing gravy from his whiskers and their parents were watching the evening news on television. Ramona marched into Beezus's room and shut the door. 'It's all your fault,' she informed her sister, who was lying on the bed with a book. 'Why didn't you keep still?'

'It's just as much your fault,' said Beezus. 'You and your yucks.'

Both girls recognized nothing would be gained by arguing over blame.

'But you like to cook,' said Ramona.

'And you like to make Jello and French toast,' said Beezus.

174

The sisters looked at one another. What had gone wrong? Why didn't they want to prepare dinner?

'I think they're mean,' said Ramona.

'They're punishing us,' said Beezus. 'That's what they're doing.'

The sisters scowled. They liked to cook; they did not like to be punished. They sat in silence, thinking cross thoughts about parents, especially their parents, their unfair, unkind parents who did not appreciate what nice daughters they had. Lots of parents would be happy to have nice daughters like Beezus and Ramona.

'If I ever have a little girl, I won't ever make her eat tongue,' said Ramona. 'I'll give her good things to eat. Things like stuffed olives and whipped cream.'

'Me too,' agreed Beezus. 'I wonder what there is for us to cook.'

'Let's go look in the refrigerator,' suggested Ramona.

Beezus objected. 'If they hear us open the refrigerator, Mom and Dad will think we're hungry, and we'll get a lecture on not eating our dinner.'

'But I *am* hungry,' said Ramona, although she understood the truth of Beezus's words. Oh well, she wouldn't actually starve to death before breakfast. She found herself thinking of French toast, golden with egg under a snowfall of powdered sugar.

'Maybe . . .' Beezus was thoughtful. 'Maybe if we're extra good, they'll forget about the whole thing.'

Ramona now felt sad as well as angry. Here she had worked so hard to do her part by getting along at the Kemps', and now her family was not pulling together. Something had gone wrong. Beezus was probably right. The only way to escape punishment was to try being extra good.

'OK,' Ramona agreed, but her voice was gloomy. What a dismal thought, being extra good, but it was better than allowing their parents to punish them.

Ramona went to her own room, where she curled up on her bed with a book. She wished something nice would happen to her mother and father, something that would help them forget the scene at the dinner table. She wished her father would succeed in drawing a perfect foot, the sort of foot his teacher would want to hang in the front of the room above the middle of the blackboard. Maybe a perfect foot would make him happy.

And her mother? Maybe if Ramona could

forgive her for not boiling the egg she would be happy. In her heart Ramona had forgiven her, and she was sorry she had been so cross with her mother. She longed to go tell her, but now she could not, not when she was being punished.

5

THE EXTRA-GOOD SUNDAY

Sunday morning Ramona and Beezus were still resolved to be perfect until dinner time. They got up without being called, avoided arguing over who should read Dear Abby's advice first in the paper, complimented their mother on her French toast, and went off through the drizzly rain to Sunday school neat, combed, and bravely smiling.

Later they cleaned up their rooms without being told. At lunchtime they ate without complaint the sandwiches they knew were made of ground-up tongue. A little added pickle relish did not fool them, but it did help. They dried the dishes and carefully avoided looking in the direction of the refrigerator lest their mother be reminded they were supposed to cook the evening meal.

Mr and Mrs Quimby were good-humoured. In fact, everyone was so unnaturally pleasant that Ramona almost wished someone would say something cross. By early afternoon the question was still hanging in the air. Would the girls really have to prepare dinner?

Why doesn't somebody say something? Ramona thought, weary of being so good, weary of longing to forgive her mother for the raw egg in her lunch.

'Well, back to the old foot,' said Mr Quimby, as he once more settled himself on the couch with drawing pad and pencil and pulled off his shoe and sock.

The rain finally stopped. Ramona watched for dry spots to appear on the sidewalk and thought of her roller skates in the closet. She looked into Beezus's room and found her sister reading. Ramona knew Beezus wanted to telephone Mary Jane but had decided to wait until Mary Jane called to ask why she had not come over. Mary Jane did not call. The day dragged on.

When dry spots on the concrete in front of the Quimbys' house widened until moisture remained only in the cracks of the sidewalk, Ramona pulled her skates out of her closet. To her father, who was holding a drawing of his foot at arm's length to study it, she said, 'Well, I guess I'll go out and skate.'

'Aren't you forgetting something?' he asked.

'What?' asked Ramona, knowing very well what.

'Dinner,' he said.

The question that had hung in the air all day was answered. The matter was settled.

'We're stuck,' Ramona told Beezus. 'Now we can stop being so good.'

The sisters went into the kitchen, shut the door, and opened the refrigerator.

'A package of chicken thighs,' said Beezus with a groan. 'And a package of frozen peas. And yoghurt, one carton of plain and one of banana. There must have been a special on yoghurt.' She closed the refrigerator and reached for a cookbook.

'I could make place cards,' said Ramona, as Beezus frantically flipped pages.

'We can't eat place cards,' said Beezus. 'Besides, corn bread is your job because you brought it up.' Both girls spoke in whispers. There was no need to let their parents, their mean old parents, know what was going on in the kitchen.

In her mother's recipe file, Ramona found the card for corn bread written in Mr Quimby's grandmother's shaky handwriting, which Ramona found difficult to read.

'I can't find a recipe for chicken thighs,' said Beezus, 'just whole chicken. All I know is that mother bakes thighs in the flat glass dish with some kind of sauce.'

'Mushroom soup mixed with something and

with some kind of little specks stirred in.' Ramona remembered that much from watching her mother.

Beezus opened the cupboard of canned goods. 'But there isn't any mushroom soup,' she said. 'What are we going to do?'

'Mix up something wet,' suggested Ramona. 'It would serve them right if it tasted awful.'

'Why don't we make something awful?' asked Beezus. 'So they will know how we feel when we have to eat tongue.'

'What tastes really awful?' Ramona was eager to go along with the suggestion, united with her sister against their enemy—for the moment, their parents.

Beezus, always practical, changed her mind. 'It wouldn't work. We have to eat it too, and they're so mean we'll probably have to do the dishes besides. Anyway, I guess you might say our honour is at stake, because they think we can't cook a good meal.'

Ramona was ready with another solution. 'Throw everything in one dish.'

Beezus opened the package of chicken thighs and stared at them with distaste. 'I can't stand touching raw meat,' she said, as she picked up a thigh between two forks.

'Do we have to eat the skin?' asked Ramona. 'All those yucky little bumps.'

Beezus found a pair of kitchen tongs. She tried holding down a thigh with a fork and pulling off the skin with the tongs.

'Here, let me hold it,' said Ramona, who was not squeamish about touching such things as worms or raw meat. She took a firm hold on the thigh while Beezus grasped the skin with the tongs. Both pulled, and the skin peeled away. They played tug-of-war with each thigh, leaving a sad-looking heap of skins on the counter and a layer of chicken thighs in the glass dish.

'Can't you remember what little specks mother uses?' asked Beezus. Ramona could not. The girls studied the spice shelf, unscrewed jar lids and sniffed. Nutmeg? No. Cloves? Terrible. Cinnamon? Uh-uh. Chilli powder? Well . . . Yes, that must be it. Ramona remembered that the specks were red. Beezus stirred half a teaspoon of the dark red powder into the yoghurt, which she poured over the chicken. She slid the dish into the oven set at 350 degrees, the temperature for chicken recommended by the cookbook.

From the living room came the sound of their parents' conversation, sometimes serious and sometimes highlighted by laughter. While we're slaving out here, thought Ramona, as she climbed up on the counter to reach the box of cornmeal. After she climbed down, she discovered she had to climb up again for baking powder and soda. She finally knelt on the counter to save time and asked Beezus to bring her an egg.

'It's a good thing mother can't see you up there,' remarked Beezus, as she handed Ramona an egg.

'How else am I supposed to reach things?' Ramona successfully broke the egg and tossed the shell onto the counter. 'Now I need buttermilk.'

Beezus broke the news. There was no buttermilk in the refrigerator. 'What'll I do?' whispered Ramona in a panic.

'Here. Use this.' Beezus thrust the carton of banana yoghurt at her sister. 'Yoghurt is sort of sour, so it might work.'

The kitchen door opened a crack. 'What's going on in there?' enquired Mr Quimby.

Beezus hurled herself against the door. 'You stay out!' she ordered. 'Dinner is going to be a—surprise!'

For a moment Ramona thought Beezus had been going to say a mess. She stirred egg and yoghurt together, measured flour, spilling some on the floor, and then discovered she was short of cornmeal. More panic.

'My cooking teacher says you should always check to see if you have all the ingredients before you start to cook,' said Beezus.

'Oh, shut up.' Ramona reached for a package of Cream of Wheat, because its grains were about the same size as cornmeal. She scattered only a little on the floor.

Something was needed to sop up the sauce with little red specks when the chicken was served. Rice! The spilled Cream of Wheat gritted underneath Beezus's feet as she measured rice and boiled water according to the directions on the package. When the rice was cooking, she slipped into the dining room to set the table and then remembered they had forgotten salad. Salad! Carrot sticks were quickest. Beezus began to scrape carrots into the sink.

'Yipe!' yelped Ramona from the counter. 'The rice!' The lid of the pan was chittering. Beezus snatched a larger pan from the cupboard and transferred the rice.

'Do you girls need any help?' Mrs Quimby called from the living room.

'No!' answered her daughters.

Another calamity. The corn bread should bake at 400 degrees, a higher temperature than that needed for the chicken. What was Ramona to do?

'Stick it in the oven anyway.' Beezus's face was flushed.

In went the corn bread beside the chicken.

'Dessert!' whispered Beezus. All she could

find was a can of boring pear halves. Back to the cookbook. 'Heat with a little butter and serve with jelly in each half,' she read. Jelly. Half a jar of apricot jam would have to do. The pears and butter went into the saucepan. Never mind the syrup spilled on the floor.

'Beezus!' Ramona held up the package of peas.

Beezus groaned. Out came the partially cooked chicken while she stirred the thawing peas into the yoghurt and shoved the dish back into the oven.

The rice! They had forgotten the rice, which was only beginning to stick to the pan. Quick! Take it off the burner. How did their mother manage to get everything cooked at the right time? Put the carrot sticks on a dish. Pour the milk. 'Candles!' Beezus whispered. 'Dinner might look better if we have candles.'

Ramona found two candle holders and two partly melted candles of uneven length. One of them had been used in a Hallowe'en jack o' lantern. Beezus struck the match to light them, because although Ramona was brave about touching raw meat, she was skittish about lighting matches.

Was the chicken done? The girls anxiously examined their main dish, bubbling and brown around the edges. Beezus stabbed a thigh with a fork, and when it did not bleed, she decided it

must be done. A toothpick pricked into the co
bread came out clean. The corn bread was done—
flat, but done.

Grit, grit, grit sounded under the girls' feet. It
was amazing how a tiny bit of spilled Cream of
Wheat could make the entire kitchen floor gritty.
At last their dinner was served, the dining-room
light turned off, dinner announced, and the cooks,
tense with anxiety that was hidden by candlelight,
fell into their chairs as their parents seated
themselves. Was this dinner going to be edible?

'Candles!' exclaimed Mrs Quimby. 'What a
festive meal!'

'Let's taste it before we decide,' said Mr Quimby
with his most wicked grin.

The girls watched anxiously as their father took
his first bite of chicken. He chewed thoughtfully
and said with more surprise than necessary, 'Why
this is good!'

'It really is,' agreed Mrs Quimby, and took a bit
of corn bread. 'Very good, Ramona,' she said.

Mr Quimby tasted the corn bread. 'Just like
grandmother used to make,' he pronounced.

The girls exchanged suppressed smiles. They
could not taste the banana yoghurt, and by
candlelight no one could tell that the corn bread
was a little pale. The chicken, Ramona decided,
was not as good as her parents thought—or

'nk—but she could eat it without

...axed, and Mrs Quimby said
...der was more interesting than paprika
...asked which recipe they had used for the
chicken.

Ramona answered, 'Our own,' as she exchanged
another look with Beezus. Paprika! Those little
specks in the sauce should have been paprika.

'We wanted to be creative,' said Beezus.

Conversation was more comfortable than it
had been the previous evening. Mr Quimby said
he was finally satisfied with his drawing, which
looked like a real foot. Beezus said her cooking
class was studying the food groups everyone
should eat every day. Ramona said there was
this boy at school who called her Egghead. Mr
Quimby explained that Egghead was slang for a
very smart person. Ramona began to feel better
about Yard Ape.

The meal was a success. If the chicken did not
taste as good as the girls had hoped and the corn
bread did not rise like their mother's, both were
edible. Beezus and Ramona were silently grateful
to their parents for enjoying—or pretending to
enjoy—their cooking. The whole family cheered
up. When they had finished their pears with apricot
jam, Ramona gave her mother a shy smile.

Mrs Quimby smiled back and patted Ramona's hand. Ramona felt much lighter. Without using words, she had forgiven her mother for the unfortunate egg, and her mother had understood. Ramona could be happy again.

'You cooks have worked so hard,' said Mr Quimby, 'that I'm going to wash the dishes. I'll even finish clearing the table.'

'I'll help,' volunteered Mrs Quimby.

The girls exchanged another secret smile as they excused themselves and skipped off to their rooms before their parents discovered the pile of chicken skins and the broken eggshell on the counter, the carrot scrapings in the sink, and the Cream of Wheat flour and pear syrup on the floor.

6

SUPERNUISANCE

Once more the Quimbys were comfortable with one another—or reasonably so. Yet Mr and Mrs Quimby often had long, serious discussions at night behind their closed bedroom door. The sober sound of their voices worried Ramona, who longed to hear them laugh. However, by breakfast they were usually cheerful—cheerful but hurried.

Ramona was less comfortable at school. In fact, she was most uncomfortable because she was so anxious not to be a nuisance to her teacher. She stopped volunteering answers, and except for the bus ride and Sustained Silent Reading she dreaded school.

One morning, when Ramona was wishing she could get out of going to school, she dug a hole in the middle of her oatmeal with her spoon and watched it fill with milk as she listened to the noise from the garage, the grinding growl of a car that was reluctant to start. 'Grr-rrr-rrr,' she said, imitating the sound of the motor.

'Ramona, don't dawdle.' Mrs Quimby was whisking about the living room, picking up newspapers, straightening cushions, running a dustcloth over the windowsills and coffee table. Light housekeeping, she called it. Mrs Quimby did not like to come home to an untidy house.

Ramona ate a few spoonfuls of oatmeal, but somehow her spoon felt heavy this morning.

'And drink your milk,' said her mother. 'Remember, you can't do good work in school if you don't eat a good breakfast.'

Ramona paid scant attention to this little speech that she heard almost every morning. Out of habit, she drank her milk and managed most of her toast. In the garage the car stopped growling and started to throb.

Ramona had left the table and was brushing her teeth when she heard her father call in through the back door to her mother, 'Dorothy, can you come and steer the car while I push it into the street? I can't get it to go into reverse.'

Ramona rinsed her mouth and rushed to the front window in time to see her father put all his strength into pushing the now silent car slowly down the driveway and into the street while her mother steered. At the foot of the driveway, Mrs Quimby started the motor and drove the car forward beside the kerb.

'Now try it in reverse,' Mr Quimby directed.

In a moment Mrs Quimby called out, 'It won't go.'

Ramona put on her coat, picked up her lunch box, and hurried out to see what happened when a car would go forwards but not backwards. She soon discovered her parents found nothing funny about this state of affairs.

'I'll have to take it to the mechanic.' Mr Quimby looked cross. 'And then take a bus, which means missing my first class.'

'Let me take it, and you hurry and catch a bus now,' said Mrs Quimby. 'The answering service can take the doctor's messages a few minutes longer until I get to the office.' Then, noticing Ramona standing on the sidewalk, she said, 'Run along or you'll miss your bus,' and blew Ramona a kiss.

'What if you have to back up?' asked Ramona.

'With luck I won't have to,' her mother answered. 'Hurry along now.'

'So long, Ramona,' said Mr Quimby. Ramona could see that he was more concerned with the car than with her. Perhaps this knowledge made her feet seem heavier than usual as she plodded off to her bus stop. The ride to school seemed longer than usual. When Yard Ape said, 'Hi, Egghead,' she did not bother to answer, 'Devilled Egghead to you,' as she had planned.

When school started, Ramona sat quietly filling spaces in her workbook, trying to insert the right numbers into the right spaces but not much caring if she failed. Her head felt heavy, and her fingers did not want to move. She thought of telling Mrs Whaley that she did not feel good, but her teacher was busy writing a list of words on the blackboard and would probably think anyone who interrupted was a nuisance.

Ramona propped her head on her fist, looking at twenty-six glass jars of blue oatmeal. *Oh-h-h.* She did not want to think about blue oatmeal or white oatmeal or any oatmeal at all. She sat motionless, hoping the terrible feeling would go away. She knew she should tell her teacher, but by now Ramona was too miserable even to raise her hand. If she did not move, not even her little finger or an eyelash, she might feel better.

Go away, blue oatmeal, thought Ramona, and then she knew that the most terrible, horrible, dreadful, awful thing that could happen was going to happen. Please, God, don't let me . . . Ramona prayed too late.

The terrible, horrible, dreadful, awful thing happened. Ramona threw up. She threw up right there on the floor in front of everyone. One second her breakfast was where it belonged. Then everything in her middle seemed to go into reverse, and there was her breakfast on the floor.

Ramona had never felt worse in her whole life. Tears of shame welled in her eyes as she was aware of the shock and horror of everyone around her. She heard Mrs Whaley say, 'Oh, dear—Marsha, take Ramona to the office. Danny, run and tell Mr Watts that someone threw up. Children, you may hold your noses and file into the hall until Mr Watts comes and cleans up.'

Her instructions made Ramona feel even worse. Tears streamed down her face, and she longed for Beezus, now far away in junior high school, to come and help her. She let Marsha guide her down the steps and through the hall as the rest of her class, noses pinched between thumbs and forefingers, hurried out of the classroom.

'It's all right, Ramona,' Marsha said gently, while keeping her distance as if she expected Ramona to explode.

Ramona was crying too hard to answer. Nobody, nobody in the whole world, was a bigger nuisance than someone who threw up in school. Until now she thought Mrs Whaley had been unfair when she called her a nuisance, but now—there was no escaping the truth—she really *was* a nuisance, a horrible runny-nosed nuisance with nothing to blow her nose on.

When Ramona and Marsha entered the office, Marsha was eager to break the news. 'Oh, Mrs Larson,' she said, 'Ramona threw up.' Even the principal, sitting at his desk in the inner office, heard the news. Ramona knew he would not come out and start being her pal, because nobody wanted to be a pal to someone who threw up.

Mrs Larson, seizing a Kleenex from a box on her desk, sprang from her typewriter. 'Too bad,' she said calmly, as if throwers-up came into the office every day. 'Blow,' she directed, as she held the Kleenex to Ramona's nose. Ramona blew. The principal, of course, stayed in his office where he was safe.

Mrs Larson then took Ramona into the little room off the office, the same room in which she had washed egg out of Ramona's hair. She handed Ramona a paper cup of water. 'You want to rinse your mouth, don't you?' Ramona nodded, rinsed, and felt better. Mrs Larson did not behave as if she were a nuisance.

The school secretary laid a sheet of clean paper on the pillow on the cot, motioned Ramona to lie down, and then covered her with a blanket. 'I'll phone your mother and ask her to come and take you home,' she said.

'But she's at work,' Ramona whispered, because speaking aloud might send her stomach into reverse again. 'And Daddy is at school.'

'I see,' said Mrs Larson. 'Where do you go after school?'

'To Howie Kemp's house,' said Ramona, closing her eyes and wishing she could go to sleep and not wake up until all this misery was over. She was aware that Mrs Larson dialled a number and after a few moments replaced the receiver. Howie's grandmother was not home.

Then the terrible, horrible, dreadful, awful feeling returned. 'Mrs L-Larson,' quavered Ramona. 'I'm going to throw up.'

In an instant, Mrs Larson was holding Ramona's head in front of the toilet. 'It's a good thing I have three children of my own so I'm used to this sort of thing,' she said. When Ramona had finished, she handed her another cup of water and said cheerfully, 'You must feel as if you've just thrown up your toenails.'

Ramona managed a weak and wavery smile. 'Who's going to take care of me?' she asked, as Mrs Larson covered her with the blanket once more.

'Don't worry,' said Mrs Larson. 'We'll find someone, and until we do, you rest right here.'

Ramona felt feeble, exhausted, and grateful to Mrs Larson. Closing her eyes had never felt so good, and the next thing she knew she heard her mother whispering, 'Ramona.' She lifted heavy lids to see her mother standing over her.

'Do you feel like going home?' Mrs Quimby asked gently. She was already holding Ramona's coat.

Tears filled Ramona's eyes. She was not sure her legs would stand up, and how would they get home without a car? And what was her mother doing here when she was supposed to be at work? Would she lose her job?

Mrs Quimby helped Ramona to her feet and draped her coat over her shoulders. 'I have a taxi waiting,' she said, as she guided Ramona towards the door.

Mrs Larson looked up from her typewriter. 'Bye, Ramona. We'll miss you,' she said. 'I hope you'll feel better soon.'

Ramona had forgotten what it was like to feel better. Outside a yellow taxicab was chugging at the kerb. A taxi! Ramona had never ridden in a taxicab, and now she was too sick to enjoy it. Any other time she would have felt important to be leaving school in a taxi in the middle of the morning.

As Ramona climbed in, she saw the driver look her over as if he were doubtful about something. I will not throw up in a taxi, Ramona willed herself. I will not. A taxi is too expensive to throw up in. She added silent words to God, Don't let me throw up in a taxi.

Carefully Ramona laid her head in her mother's lap and with every click of the meter thought, I will not throw up in a taxi. And she did not. She managed to wait until she was home and in the bathroom.

How good Ramona's bed felt with its clean white sheets. She let her mother wipe her face and hands with a cool washcloth and later take her temperature. Afterwards, Ramona did not care about much of anything.

Late in the afternoon she awoke when Beezus whispered, 'Hi,' from the doorway.

When Mr Quimby came home, he too paused in the doorway. 'How's my girl?' he enquired softly.

'Sick,' answered Ramona, feeling pitiful. 'How's the car?'

'Still sick,' answered her father. 'The mechanic was so busy he couldn't work on it today.'

In a while Ramona was aware that her family was eating dinner without her, but she did not care. Later Mrs Quimby took Ramona's temperature again, propped her up, and held a glass of fizzy drink to her lips, which surprised Ramona. Her mother did not approve of junk foods.

'I talked to the paediatrician,' Mrs Quimby explained, 'and she said to give you this because you need fluids.'

The drink gave Ramona a sneezy feeling in her nose. She waited anxiously. Would it stay down? Yes. She sipped again, and in a moment again.

'Good girl,' whispered her mother.

Ramona fell back and turned her face into her pillow. Remembering what had happened at school, she began to cry.

'Dear heart,' said her mother. 'Don't cry. You just have a touch of stomach flu. You'll feel better in a day or so.'

Ramona's voice was muffled. 'No, I won't.'

'Yes, you will.' Mrs Quimby patted Ramona through the bedclothes.

Ramona turned enough to look at her mother with one teary eye. 'You don't know what happened,' she said.

Mrs Quimby looked concerned. 'What happened?'

'I threw up on the floor in front of the whole class,' sobbed Ramona.

Her mother was reassuring. 'Everybody knows you didn't throw up on purpose, and you certainly aren't the first child to do so.' She thought a moment and said, 'But you should have told Mrs Whaley you didn't feel good.'

Ramona could not bring herself to admit her teacher thought she was a nuisance. She let out a long, quavery sob.

Mrs Quimby patted Ramona again and turned out the light. 'Now go to sleep,' she said, 'and you'll feel better in the morning.'

Ramona was sure that, although her stomach might feel better in the morning, the rest of her would still feel terrible. She wondered what nickname Yard Ape would give her this time and what Mrs Whaley said to the school secretary about her at lunchtime. As she fell asleep, she decided she was a supernuisance, and a sick one at that.

7

The Patient

During the night Ramona was half awakened when her mother wiped her face with a cool washcloth and lifted her head from the pillow to help her sip something cold. Later, as the shadows of the room were fading, Ramona had to hold a thermometer under her tongue for what seemed like a long time. She felt safe, knowing her mother was watching over her. Safe but sick. No sooner did she find a cool place on her pillow than it became too hot for comfort, and Ramona turned again.

As her room grew light, Ramona dozed off, faintly aware that her family was moving quietly so they would not disturb her. One tiny corner of her mind was pleased by this consideration. She heard breakfast sounds, and then she must have fallen completely asleep, because the next thing she knew she was awake and the house was silent. Had they all gone off and left her? No, someone was moving quietly in the kitchen. Howie's grandmother must have come to stay with her.

Ramona's eyes blurred. Her family had all gone off and left her when she was sick. She blinked away the tears and discovered on her bedside table a cartoon her father had drawn for her. It showed Ramona leaning against one tree and the family car leaning against another. He had drawn her with crossed eyes and a turned-down mouth. The car's headlights were crossed and its front bumper turned down like Ramona's mouth. They both looked sick. Ramona discovered she remembered how to smile. She also discovered she felt hot and sweaty instead of hot and dry. For a moment she struggled to sit up and then fell back on her pillow. Sitting up was too much work. She longed for her mother, and suddenly, as if her wish were granted, her mother was entering the bedroom with a basin of water and a towel.

'Mother!' croaked Ramona. 'Why aren't you at work?'

'Because I stayed home to take care of you,' Mrs Quimby answered, as she gently washed Ramona's face and hands. 'Feeling better?'

'Sort of.' In some ways Ramona felt better, but she also felt sweaty, weak, and worried. 'Are you going to lose your job?' she asked, remembering the time her father had been out of work.

'No. The receptionist who retired was glad to come in for a few days to take my place.' Mrs

Quimby gave Ramona a sponge bath and helped her into cool, dry pyjamas. 'There,' she said. 'How about some tea and toast?'

'Grown-up tea?' asked Ramona, relieved that her mother's job was safe so that her father wouldn't have to drop out of school.

'Grown-up tea,' answered her mother, as she propped Ramona up with an extra pillow. In a few minutes she brought a tray that held a slice of dry toast and a cup of weak tea.

Nibbling and sipping left Ramona tired and gloomy.

'Cheer up,' said Mrs Quimby, when she came to remove the tray. 'Your temperature is down, and you're going to be all right.'

Ramona did feel a little better. Her mother was right. She had not thrown up on purpose. Other children had done the same thing. There was that boy in kindergarten and the girl in first grade . . .

Ramona dozed off, and when she awoke, she was bored and cranky. She wanted butter on the toast her mother brought her and scowled when her mother said people with stomach flu should not eat butter.

Mrs Quimby smiled and said, 'I can tell you're beginning to get well when you act like a wounded tiger.'

Ramona scowled. 'I am *not* acting like a

wounded tiger,' she informed her mother. When Mrs Quimby made her a bed on the living-room couch so she could watch television, she was cross with the television set because she found daytime programmes dumb, stupid, and boring. Commercials were much more interesting than the programmes. She lay back and hoped for a cat food commercial because she liked to look at nice cats. As she waited, she brooded about her teacher.

'Of course I didn't throw up on purpose,' Ramona told herself. Mrs Whaley should know that. And deep down inside I am really a nice person, she comforted herself. Mrs Whaley should know that, too.

'Who pays teachers?' Ramona suddenly asked, when her mother came into the room.

'Why, we all do.' Mrs Quimby seemed surprised by the question. 'We pay taxes, and teachers' salaries come out of tax money.'

Ramona knew that taxes were something unpleasant that worried parents. 'I think you should stop paying taxes,' Ramona informed her mother.

Mrs Quimby looked amused. 'I wish we could— at least until we finish paying for the room we added to the house. Whatever put such an idea into your head?'

'Mrs Whaley doesn't like me,' Ramona answered. 'She is supposed to like me. It's her job to like me.'

All Mrs Quimby had to say was, 'If you're this grouchy at school, liking you could be hard work.'

Ramona was indignant. Her mother was supposed to feel sorry for her poor, weak little girl.

Picky-picky strolled into the living room and stared at Ramona as if he felt she did not belong on the couch. With an arthritic leap, he jumped up beside her on the blanket, washed himself from his ears to the tip of his tail, kneaded the blanket, and, purring, curled up beside Ramona who lay very still so he would not go away. When he was asleep, she petted him gently. Picky-picky usually avoided her because she was noisy, or so her mother said.

A funny man appeared on the television screen. He had eaten a pizza, which had given him indigestion. He groaned. 'I can't believe I ate the *whole* thing.' Ramona smiled.

The next commercial showed a cat stepping back and forth in a little dance. 'Do you think we could train Picky-picky to do that?' Ramona asked her mother.

Mrs Quimby was amused at the idea of old

Picky-picky dancing. 'I doubt it,' she said. 'That cat isn't really dancing. They just turn the film back and forth so it looks as if he's dancing.'

How disappointing. Ramona dozed while another cat-food commercial appeared. She awoke enough to watch a big yellow cat ignore several brands of cat food before he settled down to eat a bowl of dry food silently. That's funny, thought Ramona. When Picky-picky ate dry cat food, he ground and crunched so noisily she could hear him from any room in the house, but television cats never made any sound at all when they ate. The commercials lied. That's what they did. Ramona was cross with cat-food commercials. Cheaters! She was angry with the whole world.

Late that afternoon Ramona was aroused once more by the doorbell. Was it someone interesting? She hoped so, for she was bored. The visitor turned out to be Sara.

Ramona lay back on her pillow and tried to look pale and weak as her mother said, 'Why, hello, Sara. I'm glad to see you, but I don't think you should come in until Ramona is feeling better.'

'That's all right,' said Sara, 'I just brought some letters the class wrote to Ramona, and Mrs Whaley sent a book for her to read.'

'Hi, Sara,' said Ramona with the weakest smile she could manage.

'Mrs Whaley said to tell you this book is not for DEAR. This one is for a book report,' Sara explained from the doorway.

Ramona groaned.

'She said to tell you,' Sara continued, 'that she wants us to stand up in front of the class and pretend we are selling the book. She doesn't want us to tell the whole story. She says she has already heard all the stories quite a few times.'

Ramona felt worse. Not only would she have to give a book report, she would have to listen to twenty-five book reports given by other people, another reason for wanting to stay home.

When Sara left, Ramona examined the big envelope she had brought. Mrs Whaley had written Ramona's name on the front with a floppy joined-up capital Q and beneath it in her big handwriting, 'Miss you!' followed by a picture of a whale and a *y*.

I bet she doesn't mean it, thought Ramona. She opened the envelope of the first letters anyone had ever written to her. 'Mother, they wrote joined-up!' she cried, delighted. Although all the letters said much the same thing—we are sorry you are sick and hope you get well soon—they made Ramona feel good. She knew they were written to teach letter writing and handwriting at the same time, but she didn't care.

One letter was different. Yard Ape had written, 'Dear Superfoot, Get well or I will eat your eraser.' Ramona smiled because his letter showed he liked her. She looked forward to the return of her father and sister so she could show off her mail.

Bored with television and cramped from lying still so she would not disturb Picky-picky, Ramona waited. How sorry they would be to see her so pale and thin. Surely her father would bring her a little present, something to entertain her while she had to stay in bed. A paperback book because she could now read books with chapters? New crayons? Her father understood the importance of sharp-pointed crayons to someone who liked to draw.

Beezus arrived first with an armload of books that she dropped on a chair. 'Homework!' she said and groaned. Now that she was in junior high school, she was always talking about all the work she had to do, as if Ramona did nothing in school. 'How do you feel?' she finally got around to asking.

'Sick,' said Ramona in a faint voice, 'but my whole class wrote to me.'

Beezus glanced at the sheaf of letters. 'They copied them off the blackboard,' she said.

'Writing a whole letter in joined-up writing is hard work for lots of people when they are in the third grade.' Ramona was hurt at having her letters belittled. She pushed Picky-picky off the couch so she could stretch her legs. The television droned on and on.

'I wonder what's keeping your father,' remarked Mrs Quimby, looking out of the front window.

Ramona knew why her father was late, but she did not say so. He was buying her a little present because she was sick. She could hardly wait. 'My class is giving book reports,' she informed Beezus, so her sister would know she had schoolwork to do too. 'We have to pretend to sell a book to someone.'

'We did that a couple of times,' said Beezus. 'Teachers always tell you not to tell the whole story, and half the kids finish by saying, "If you want to know what happens next, read the book," and somebody always says, "Read this book, or I'll punch you in the nose."'

Ramona knew who would say that in her class. Yard Ape, that was who.

'Here he comes now,' said Mrs Quimby, and she hurried to open the door for Ramona's father, who kissed her as he entered.

'Where's the car?' she asked.

'Bad news.' Mr Quimby sounded tired. 'It has to have a new transmission.'

'Oh, no!' Mrs Quimby was shocked. 'How much is that going to cost?'

Mr Quimby looked grim. 'Plenty. More than we can afford.'

'We'll have to afford it somehow,' said Mrs Quimby. 'We can't manage without a car.'

'The transmission people are letting us pay it off in instalments,' he explained, 'and I'll manage to get in some more hours as Santa's Little Helper at the warehouse.'

'I wish there were some other way . . .' Mrs Quimby looked sad as she went into the kitchen to attend to supper.

Only then did Mr Quimby turn his attention to Ramona. 'How's my little punkin?' he asked.

'Sick.' Ramona forgot to look pitiful, she was so disappointed that her father had not brought her a present.

'Cheer up,' Mr Quimby half smiled. 'At least you don't need a new transmission, and you'll feel better tomorrow.'

'What's a transmission?' asked Ramona.

'That's what makes the car go,' explained her father.

'Oh,' said Ramona. Then to show her father that her life was not so easy, she added, 'I have to give a book report at school.'

'Well, make it interesting,' said Mr Quimby, as he went off to wash for supper.

Ramona knew her father was worried, but she

could not help thinking he might have felt sorrier for his sick little girl. Anyone would think he loved the car more. She lay back genuinely weak, exhausted by television, and sorry her father would have to work more hours in the frozen-food warehouse where, no matter how many pairs of woollen socks he wore, his feet were always cold and he sometimes had to go outside until feeling came back into his cheeks.

When her mother, after serving the rest of the family, said the time had come for Ramona to get into her own bed and have a little supper on a tray, she was ready to go. The thought that her mother did not think she was a nuisance comforted her.

8

RaMONa's Book RePoRT

The Quimby family was full of worries. The parents were worried about managing without a car while a new transmission was installed and even more worried about paying for it. Beezus was worried about a party she had been invited to, because boys had also been invited. She was afraid it would turn out to be a dancing party, and she felt silly trying to dance. Besides, eighth-grade boys acted like a bunch of little kids at parties. Ramona, still feeling weak, moped around the house for another day worrying about her book report. If she made it interesting, Mrs Whaley would think she was showing off. If she did not make it interesting, her teacher would not like it.

On top of everything, Beezus happened to look at her father's head as he bent over his books at the dining-room table that evening. 'Daddy, you're getting thin on top!' she cried out, shocked.

Ramona rushed to look. 'Just a little thin,' she

said, because she did not want her father's feelings hurt. 'You aren't bald yet.'

Mrs Quimby also examined the top of her husband's head. 'It *is* a little thin,' she agreed, and kissed the spot. 'Never mind. I found a grey hair last week.'

'What is this? A conference about my hair?' asked Mr Quimby, and he grabbed his wife around the waist. 'Don't worry,' he told her. 'I'll still love you when you're old and grey.'

'Thanks a lot,' said Mrs Quimby, not wanting to think of herself as old and grey. They both laughed. Mr Quimby released his wife and gave her a playful slap on the bottom, an act that amused and shocked his daughters.

Ramona had two feelings about this conversation. She did not want her father's hair to grow thin or her mother's hair to grow grey. She wanted her parents to stay exactly as they were for ever and ever. But oh, how good it was to see them be so affectionate with one another.

She knew her mother and father loved one another, but sometimes, when they were tired and hurried, or when they had long, serious conversations after the girls had gone to bed, she wondered and worried, because she knew children whose parents had stopped loving one another. Now she knew everything was all right.

Suddenly Ramona felt so happy that a book report did not seem so difficult after all—if she could think of a way to make it interesting.

The book, *The Left-Behind Cat*, which Mrs Whaley had sent home for Ramona to read for her report, was divided into chapters but used babyish words. The story was about a cat that was left behind when a family moved away and about its adventures with a dog, another cat, and some children before it finally found a home with a nice old couple who gave it a saucer of cream and named it Lefty because its left paw was white and because it had been left behind. Medium-boring, thought Ramona, good enough to pass the time on the bus, but not good enough to read during Sustained Silent Reading.

Besides, cream cost too much to give to a cat. The most the old people would give a cat was half-and-half, she thought. Ramona required accuracy from books as well as from people.

'Daddy, how do you sell something?' Ramona interrupted her father, who was studying, even though she knew she should not. However, her need for an answer was urgent.

Mr Quimby did not look up from his book. 'You ought to know. You see enough commercials on television.'

Ramona considered his answer. She had always

looked upon commercials as entertainment, but now she thought about some of her favourites— the cats that danced back and forth, the dog that pushed away brand-X dog food with his paw, the man who ate a pizza, got indigestion, and groaned that he couldn't believe he ate the *whole* thing, the six horses that pulled the Wells Fargo bank's stagecoach across deserts and over mountains.

'Do you mean I should do a book report like a TV commercial?' Ramona asked.

'Why not?' Mr Quimby answered in an absentminded way.

'I don't want my teacher to say I'm a nuisance,' said Ramona, needing assurance from a grown-up.

This time Mr Quimby lifted his eyes from his book. 'Look,' he said, 'she told you to pretend you're selling the book, so sell it. What better way than a TV commercial? You aren't being a nuisance if you do what your teacher asks.' He looked at Ramona a moment and said, 'Why do you worry she'd think you're a nuisance?'

Ramona stared at the carpet, wiggled her toes inside her shoes, and finally said, 'I squeaked my shoes the first day of school.'

'That's not being much of a nuisance,' said Mr Quimby.

'And when I got egg in my hair, Mrs Whaley

said I was a nuisance,' confessed Ramona, 'and then I threw up in school.'

'But you didn't do those things on purpose,' her father pointed out. 'Now run along. I have studying to do.'

Ramona thought this answer over and decided that since her parents agreed, they must be right. Well, Mrs Whaley could just go jump in a lake, even though her teacher had written, without wasting words, that she missed her. Ramona was going to give her book report any way she wanted. So there, Mrs Whaley.

Ramona went to her room and looked at her table, which the family called 'Ramona's studio', because it was a clutter of crayons, different kinds of paper, Scotch tape, bits of yarn, and odds and ends that Ramona used for amusing herself. Then Ramona thought a moment, and suddenly, filled with inspiration, she went to work. She knew exactly what she wanted to do and set about doing it. She worked with paper, crayons, Scotch tape, and rubber bands. She worked so hard and with such pleasure that her cheeks grew pink. Nothing in the whole world felt as good as being able to make something from a sudden idea.

Finally, with a big sigh of relief, Ramona leaned back in her chair to admire her work: three cat masks with holes for eyes and mouths, masks that could be worn by hooking rubber bands over ears. But Ramona did not stop there. With pencil and paper, she began to write out what she would say. She was so full of ideas that she printed rather than waste time in joined-up writing. Next she phoned Sara and Janet, keeping her voice low and trying not to giggle so she wouldn't disturb her father any more than necessary, and explained her plan to them. Both her friends giggled and agreed to take part in the book report. Ramona spent the rest of the evening memorizing what she was going to say.

The next morning on the bus and at school, no one even mentioned Ramona's throwing up. She had braced herself for some remark from Yard Ape, but all he said was, 'Hi, Superfoot.' When school started, Ramona slipped cat masks to Sara and Janet, handed her written excuse for her absence to Mrs Whaley, and waited, fanning away escaped fruit flies, for book reports to begin.

After arithmetic, Mrs Whaley called on several people to come to the front of the room to pretend they were selling books to the class. Most of the reports began, 'This is a book about . . .' and many, as Beezus had predicted, ended with '. . . if you want to find out what happens next, read the book.'

Then Mrs Whaley said, 'We have time for

one more report before lunch. Who wants to be next?'

Ramona waved her hand, and Mrs Whaley nodded.

Ramona beckoned to Sara and Janet, who giggled in an embarrassed way but joined Ramona, standing behind her and off to one side. All three girls slipped on their cat masks and giggled again. Ramona took a deep breath as Sara and Janet began to chant. '*Meow*, meow, meow, meow. *Meow*, meow, meow, meow,' and danced back and forth like the cats they had seen in the cat-food commercial on television.

'*Left-Behind Cat* gives kids something to smile about,' said Ramona in a loud clear voice, while her chorus meowed softly behind her. She wasn't sure that what she said was exactly true, but neither were the commercials that showed cats eating dry cat food without making any noise. 'Kids who have tried *Left-Behind Cat* are all smiles, smiles, smiles. *Left-Behind Cat* is the book kids ask for by name. Kids can read it every day and thrive on it. The happiest kids read *Left-Behind Cat*. *Left-Behind Cat* contains cats, dogs, people—' Here Ramona caught sight of Yard Ape leaning back in his seat, grinning in the way that always flustered her. She could not help interrupting herself with a giggle, and after suppressing it she tried not to look at

Yard Ape and to take up where she had left off. '. . . cats, dogs, people—' The giggle came back, and Ramona was lost. She could not remember what came next. '. . . cats, dogs, people,' she repeated, trying to start and failing.

Mrs Whaley and the class waited. Yard Ape grinned. Ramona's loyal chorus meowed and danced. This performance could not go on all morning. Ramona had to say something, anything to end the waiting, the meowing, her book report. She tried desperately to recall a cat-food commercial, any cat-food commercial, and could not. All she could remember was the man on television who ate the pizza, and so she blurted out the only sentence she could think of, 'I can't believe I read the *whole* thing!'

Mrs Whaley's laugh rang out above the laughter of the class. Ramona felt her face turn red behind her mask, and her ears, visible to the class, turned red as well.

'Thank you, Ramona,' said Mrs Whaley. 'That was most entertaining. Class, you are excused for lunch.'

Ramona felt brave behind her cat mask. 'Mrs Whaley,' she said, as the class pushed back chairs and gathered up lunch boxes, 'that wasn't the way my report was supposed to end.'

'Did you like the book?' asked Mrs Whaley.

'Not really,' confessed Ramona.

'Then I think it was a good way to end your report,' said the teacher. 'Asking the class to sell books they really don't like isn't fair, now that I stop to think about it. I was only trying to make book reports a little livelier.'

Encouraged by this confession and still safe behind her mask, Ramona had the boldness to speak up. 'Mrs Whaley,' she said with her heart pounding, 'you told Mrs Larson that I'm a nuisance, and I don't think I am.'

Mrs Whaley looked astonished. 'When did I say that?'

'The day I got egg in my hair,' said Ramona. 'You called me a show-off and said I was a nuisance.'

Mrs Whaley frowned, thinking. 'Why, Ramona, I can recall saying something about my little show-off, but I meant it affectionately, and I'm sure I never called you a nuisance.'

'Yes, you did,' insisted Ramona. 'You said I was a show-off, and then you said, "What a nuisance."' Ramona could never forget those exact words.

Mrs Whaley, who had looked worried, smiled in relief. 'Oh, Ramona, you misunderstood,' she said. 'I meant that trying to wash egg out of your hair was a nuisance for Mrs Larson. I didn't mean that you personally were a nuisance.'

Ramona felt a little better, enough to come out

from under her mask to say, 'I wasn't showing off. I was just trying to crack an egg on my head like everyone else.'

Mrs Whaley's smile was mischievous. 'Tell me, Ramona,' she said, 'don't you ever try to show off?'

Ramona was embarrassed. 'Well . . . maybe . . . sometimes, a little,' she admitted. Then she added positively, 'But I wasn't showing off that day. How could I be showing off when I was doing what everyone else was doing?'

'You've convinced me,' said Mrs Whaley with a big smile. 'Now run along and eat your lunch.'

Ramona snatched up her lunch box and went jumping down the stairs to the cafeteria. She laughed to herself because she knew exactly what all the boys and girls from her class would say when they finished their lunches. She knew because she planned to say it herself. 'I can't believe I ate the *whole* thing!'

9

RAINY SUNDAY

Rainy Sunday afternoons in November were always dismal, but Ramona felt this Sunday was the most dismal of all. She pressed her nose against the living-room window, watching the ceaseless rain pelting down as bare black branches clawed at the electric wires in front of the house. Even lunch, leftovers Mrs Quimby had wanted to clear out of the refrigerator, had been dreary, with her parents, who seemed tired or discouraged or both, having little to say and Beezus mysteriously moody. Ramona longed for sunshine, sidewalks dry enough for roller-skating, a smiling, happy family.

'Ramona, you haven't cleaned up your room this weekend,' said Mrs Quimby, who was sitting on the couch, sorting through a stack of bills. 'And don't press your nose against the window. It leaves a smudge.'

Ramona felt as if everything she did was wrong. The whole family seemed cross today, even Picky-picky who meowed at the front door. With a sigh, Mrs Quimby got up to let him out. Beezus, carrying a towel and shampoo, stalked through the living room into the kitchen, where she began to wash her hair at the sink. Mr Quimby, studying at the dining-room table as usual, made his pencil scratch angrily across a pad of paper. The television set sat blank and mute, and in the fireplace a log sullenly refused to burn.

Mrs Quimby sat down and then got up again as Picky-picky, indignant at the wet world outdoors, yowled to come in. 'Ramona, clean up your room,' she ordered, as she let the cat and a gust of cold air into the house.

'Beezus hasn't cleaned up her room.' Ramona could not resist pointing this omission out to her mother.

'I'm not talking about Beezus,' said Mrs Quimby. 'I'm talking about you.'

Still Ramona did not move from the window. Cleaning up her room seemed such a boring thing to do, no fun at all on a rainy afternoon. She thought vaguely of all the exciting things she would like to do—learn to twirl a lariat, play a musical saw, flip around and over bars in a gymnastic competition while crowds cheered.

'Ramona, *clean up your room*!' Mrs Quimby raised her voice.

'Well, you don't have to yell at me.' Ramona's

feelings were hurt by the tone of her mother's voice. The log in the fireplace settled, sending a puff of smoke into the living room.

'Then do it,' snapped Mrs Quimby. 'Your room is a disaster area.'

Mr Quimby threw down his pencil. 'Young lady, you do what your mother says, and you do it now. She shouldn't have to tell you three times.'

'Well, all right, but you don't have to be so cross,' said Ramona. To herself she thought, Nag, nag, nag.

Sulkily Ramona took her hurt feelings off to her room, where she pulled a week's collection of dirty socks from under her bed. On her way to the bathroom hamper, she looked down the hall and saw her sister standing in the living room, rubbing her hair with a towel.

'Mother, I think you're mean,' said Beezus from under the towel.

Ramona stopped to listen.

'I don't care how mean you think I am,' answered Mrs Quimby. 'You are not going to go, and that is that.'

'But all the other girls are going,' protested Beezus.

'I don't care if they are,' said Mrs Quimby. 'You are not.'

Ramona heard the sound of a pencil being

slammed on the table and her father saying, 'Your mother is right. Now would you kindly give me a little peace and quiet so I can get on with my work.'

Beezus flounced past Ramona into her room and slammed the door. Sobs were heard, loud, angry sobs.

Where can't she go? Ramona wondered, as she dumped her socks into the hamper. Then, because she had been so good about picking up her room, Ramona returned to the living room, where Picky-picky, as cross and bored as the rest of the family, was once again meowing at the front door. 'Where can't Beezus go?' she asked.

Mrs Quimby opened the front door, and when Picky-picky hesitated, vexed by the cold wind that swept into the room, assisted him out with her toe. 'She can't sleep over at Mary Jane's house with a bunch of girls from her class.'

A year ago Ramona would have agreed with her mother so that her mother would love her more than Beezus, but this year she knew that she too might want to spend the night at someone's house someday. 'Why can't Beezus sleep at Mary Jane's?' she asked.

'Because she comes home exhausted and grouchy.' Mrs Quimby stood by the door, waiting. Picky-picky's yowl was twisted by the wind, and when she opened the door, another cold gust swept through the house.

'With the price of fuel oil being what it is, we can't afford to let the cat out,' remarked Mr Quimby.

'Would you like to take the responsibility if I don't let him out?' asked Mrs Quimby, before she continued with her answer to Ramona. 'There are four people in the family, and she has no right to make the whole day disagreeable for the rest of us because she has been up half the night giggling with a bunch of silly girls. Besides, a growing girl needs her rest.'

Ramona silently agreed with her mother about Beezus's coming home cross after such a party. At the same time, she wanted to make things easier for herself when she was in junior high school. 'Maybe this time they would go to sleep earlier,' she suggested.

'Fat chance,' said Mrs Quimby, who rarely spoke so rudely. 'And furthermore, Ramona, Mrs Kemp did not come right out and say so, but she did drop a hint that you are not playing as nicely with Willa Jean as you might.'

Ramona heaved a sigh that seemed to come from the soles of her feet. In the bedroom, Beezus, who had run out of real sobs, was working hard to force out fake sobs to show her parents how mean they were to her.

Mrs Quimby ignored the sighs and the sobs and continued. 'Ramona, you know that getting along at the Kemps' is your job in this family. I've told you that before.'

How could Ramona explain to her mother that Willa Jean had finally caught on that Sustained Silent Reading was just plain reading a book? For a while, Willa Jean wanted Ramona to read aloud a few boring books the Kemps owned, the sort of books people who did not know anything about children so often gave them. Willa Jean listened to them several times, grew bored, and now insisted on playing beauty shop. Ramona did not want her fingernails painted by Willa Jean and knew she would be blamed if Willa Jean spilled nail polish. Instead of Mrs Kemp's taking care of Ramona, Ramona was taking care of Willa Jean.

Ramona looked at the carpet, sighed again, and said, 'I try.' She felt sorry for herself, misunderstood and unappreciated. Nobody in the whole world understood how hard it was to go to the Kemps' house after school when she did not have a bicycle.

Mrs Quimby relented. 'I know it isn't easy,' she said with a half smile, 'but don't give up.' She gathered up the bills and chequebook and went into the kitchen, where she began to write cheques at the kitchen table.

Ramona wandered into the dining room to

seek comfort from her father. She laid her cheek against the sleeve of his plaid shirt and asked, 'Daddy, what are you studying?'

Once again Mr Quimby threw down his pencil. 'I am studying the cognitive processes of children,' he answered.

Ramona raised her head to look at him. 'What does that mean?' she asked.

'How kids think,' her father told her.

Ramona did not like the sound of this subject at all. 'Why are you studying *that*?' she demanded. Some things should be private, and how children thought was one of them. She did not like the idea of grown-ups snooping around in thick books trying to find out.

'That is exactly what I have been asking myself.' Mr Quimby was serious. 'Why am I studying this stuff when we have bills to pay?'

'Well, I don't think you should,' said Ramona. 'It's none of your business how kids think.' Then she quickly added, because she did not want her father to drop out of school and be a checker again. 'There are lots of other things you could study. Things like fruit flies.'

Mr Quimby smiled at Ramona and rumpled her hair. 'I doubt if anyone could figure out how you think,' he said, which made Ramona feel better, as if her secret thoughts were still safe.

Mr Quimby sat gnawing his pencil and staring out of the window at the rain. Beezus, who had run out of fake sobs, emerged from her room, red-eyed and damp-haired, to stalk about the house not speaking to anyone.

Ramona flopped down on the couch. She hated rainy Sundays, especially this one, and longed for Monday when she could escape to school. The Quimbys' house seemed to have grown smaller during the day until it was no longer big enough to hold her family and all its problems. She tried not to think of the half-overheard conversations of her parents after the girls had gone to bed, grown-up talk that Ramona understood just enough to know her parents were concerned about their future.

Ramona had deep, secret worries of her own. She worried that her father might accidentally be locked in the frozen-food warehouse, where it was so cold it sometimes snowed indoors. What if he was filling a big order, and the men who were lucky enough to get small orders to fill left work ahead of him and forgot and locked the warehouse, and he couldn't get out and froze to death? Of course that wouldn't happen. 'But it might,' insisted a tiny voice in the back of her mind. Don't be silly, she told the little voice. 'Yes, but—' began the little voice. And despite the worry that would not go away Ramona wanted her father to go on working so he could stay in school and someday get a job he liked.

While Ramona worried, the house was silent except for the sound of rain and the scratch of her father's pencil. The smoking log settled in the fireplace, sending up a few feeble sparks. The day grew darker, Ramona was beginning to feel hungry, but there was no comfortable bustle of cooking in the kitchen.

Suddenly Mr Quimby slammed shut his book and threw down his pencil so hard it bounced onto the floor. Ramona sat up. Now what was wrong?

'Come on, everybody,' said her father. 'Get cleaned up. Let's stop this grumping around. We are going out for dinner, and we are going to smile and be pleasant if it kills us. That's an order!'

The girls stared at their father and then at one another. What was going on? They had not gone out to dinner for months, so how could they afford to go now?

'To the Whopperburger?' asked Ramona.

'Sure,' said Mr Quimby, who appeared cheerful for the first time that day. 'Why not? The sky's the limit.'

Mrs Quimby came into the living room with a handful of stamped envelopes. 'But, Bob—' she began.

'Now don't worry,' her husband said. 'We'll manage. During Thanksgiving I'll be putting in more hours in the warehouse and getting more overtime. There's no reason why we can't have a treat once in a while. And the Whopperburger isn't exactly your four-star gourmet restaurant.'

Ramona was afraid her mother might give a lecture on the evils of junk food, but she did not. Gloom and anger were forgotten. Clothes were changed, hair combed, Picky-picky was shut in the basement, and the family was on its way in the old car with the new transmission that never baulked at backing down the driveway. Off the Quimbys sped to the nearest Whopperburger, where they discovered other families must have wanted to get out of the house on a rainy day, for the restaurant was crowded, and they had to wait for a table.

There were enough chairs for the grown-ups and Beezus, but Ramona, who had the youngest legs, had to stand up. She amused herself by punching the buttons on the cigarette machine in time to the Muzak, which was playing 'Tie a Yellow Ribbon Round the Old Oak Tree'. She even danced a little to the music, and, when the tune came to an end, she turned around and found herself face to face with an old man with neatly trimmed grey hair and a moustache that turned up at the ends. He was dressed as if everything he wore—a flowered shirt, striped tie, tweed coat, and plaid slacks—had come from different stores or from a rummage sale, except that the crease in his trousers was sharp and his shoes were shined.

The old man, whose back was very straight, saluted Ramona as if she were a soldier and said, 'Well, young lady, have you been good to your mother?'

Ramona was stunned. She felt her face turn red to the tips of her ears. She did not know how to answer such a question. Had she been good to her mother? Well . . . not always, but why was this stranger asking? It was none of his business. He had no right to ask such a question.

Ramona looked to her parents for help and discovered they were waiting with amusement for her answer. So were the rest of the people who were waiting for tables. Ramona scowled at the man. She did not have to answer him if she did not want to.

The hostess saved Ramona by calling out, 'Quimby, party of four,' and leading the family to a plastic-upholstered booth.

'Why didn't you answer the man?' Beezus was as amused as everyone else.

'I'm not supposed to talk to strangers,' was Ramona's dignified answer.

'But mother and Daddy are with us,' Beezus pointed out, rather meanly, Ramona thought.

'Remember,' said Mr Quimby, as he opened his menu, 'we are all going to smile and enjoy ourselves if it kills us.'

As Ramona picked up her menu, she was still seething inside. Maybe she hadn't always been good to her mother, but that man had no right to pry. When she discovered he was seated in a single booth across the aisle, she gave him an indignant look, which he answered with a merry wink. So he had been teasing. Well, Ramona didn't like it.

When Ramona opened her menu, she made an exciting discovery. She no longer had to depend on coloured pictures of hamburgers, French fries, chilli, and steak to help her make up her mind. She could now read what was offered. She studied carefully, and when she came to the bottom of the menu, she read the dreaded words, 'Child's Plate for Children Under Twelve'. Then came the list of choices: fish sticks, chicken drumsticks, hot dogs. None of them, to Ramona, food for a treat. They were food for a school cafeteria.

'Daddy,' Ramona whispered, 'do I have to have a child's plate?'

'Not if you don't want to.' Her father's smile

was understanding. Ramona ordered the smallest adult item on the menu.

Whopperburger was noted for fast service, and in a few minutes the waitress set down the Quimbys' dinners: a hamburger and French fries for Ramona, a cheeseburger and French fries for Beezus and her mother, and hamburgers with chilli for her father.

Ramona bit into her hamburger. Bliss. Warm, soft, juicy, tart with relish. Juice dribbled down her chin. She noticed her mother start to say something and change her mind. Ramona caught the dribble with her paper napkin before it reached her collar. The French fries—crisp on the outside, mealy on the inside—tasted better than anything Ramona had ever eaten.

The family ate in companionable silence for a few moments until the edge was taken off their hunger. 'A little change once in a while does make a difference,' said Mrs Quimby. 'It does us all good.'

'Especially after the way—' Ramona stopped herself from finishing with, '—after the way Beezus acted this afternoon.' Instead she sat up straight and smiled.

'Well, I wasn't the only one who—' Beezus also stopped in midsentence and smiled. The parents looked stern, but they managed to smile. Suddenly everyone relaxed and laughed.

The old man, Ramona noticed, was eating a steak. She wished her father could afford a steak.

As much as she enjoyed her hamburger, Ramona was unable to finish. It was too much. She was happy when her mother did not say, 'Someone's eyes are bigger than her stomach.' Her father, without commenting on the unfinished hamburger, included her in the orders of apple pie with hot cinnamon sauce and ice cream.

Ramona ate what she could, and after watching the ice cream melt into the cinnamon sauce, she glanced over at the old man, who was having a serious discussion with the waitress. She seemed surprised and upset about something. The Muzak, conversation of other customers, and rattle of dishes made eavesdropping impossible. The waitress left. Ramona saw her speak to the manager, who listened and then nodded. For a moment Ramona thought the man might not have enough money to pay for the steak he had eaten. Apparently he did, however, for after listening to what the waitress had to say, he left a tip under the edge of his plate and picked up his check. To Ramona's embarrassment, he stood up, winked, and saluted her again. Then he left. Ramona did not know what to make of him.

She turned back to her family, whose smiles were now genuine rather than determined. The sight of them gave her courage to ask the question that had been nibbling at the back of her mind, 'Daddy, you aren't going to be a college dropout, are you?'

Mr Quimby finished a mouthful of pie before he answered, 'Nope.'

Ramona wanted to make sure. 'And you won't ever be a checker and come home cross again?'

'Well,' said her father, 'I can't promise I won't come home cross, but if I do, it won't be from standing at the cash register trying to remember forty-two price changes in the produce section while a long line of customers, all in a hurry, wait to pay for their groceries.'

Ramona was reassured.

When the waitress descended on the Quimbys to offer the grown-ups a second cup of coffee, Mr Quimby said, 'Check, please.'

The waitress looked embarrassed. 'Well . . . a . . .' She hesitated. 'This has never happened before, but your meals have already been paid for.'

The Quimbys looked at her in astonishment. 'But who paid for them?' demanded Mr Quimby.

'A lonely gentleman who left a little while ago,' answered the waitress.

'He must have been the man who sat across the aisle,' said Mrs Quimby. 'But why would he pay for our dinners? We never saw him before in our lives.'

The waitress smiled. 'Because he said you are such a nice family, and because he misses his children and grandchildren.' She dashed off with her pot of coffee, leaving the Quimbys in surprised, even shocked, silence. A nice family? After the way they had behaved on a rainy Sunday.

'A mysterious stranger just like in a book,' said Beezus. 'I never thought I'd meet one.'

'Poor lonely man,' said Mrs Quimby at last, as Mr Quimby shoved a tip under his saucer. Still stunned into silence, the family struggled into their wraps and splashed across the parking lot to their car, which started promptly and backed obediently out of its parking space. As the windshield wipers began their rhythmic exercise, the family rode in silence, each thinking of the events of the day.

'You know,' said Mrs Quimby thoughtfully, as the car left the parking lot and headed down the street, 'I think he was right. We are a nice family.'

'Not all the time,' said Ramona, as usual demanding accuracy.

'Nobody is nice all the time,' answered her father. 'Or if they are, they are boring.'

'Not even your parents are nice all the time,' added Mrs Quimby.

Ramona secretly agreed, but she had not expected her parents to admit it. Deep down inside, she felt she herself was nice all the time, but sometimes on the outside her niceness sort of—well, curdled. Then people did not understand how nice she really was. Maybe other people curdled too.

'We have our ups and downs,' said Mrs Quimby, 'but we manage to get along, and we stick together.'

'We are nicer than some families I know,' said Beezus. 'Some families don't even eat dinner together.' After a moment she made a confession. 'I don't really like sleeping on someone's floor in a sleeping bag.'

'I didn't think you did.' Mrs Quimby reached back and patted Beezus on the knee. 'That's one reason I said you couldn't go. You didn't want to go, but didn't want to admit it.'

Ramona snuggled inside her car coat, feeling cosy enclosed in the car with the heater breathing warm air on her nice family. She was a member of a nice sticking-together family, and she was old enough to be depended upon, so she could ignore—or at least try to ignore—a lot of things. Willa Jean—she would try reading her Sustained Silent Reading books aloud because Willa Jean was old enough to understand most of them. That should work for a little while. Mrs Whaley—some things were nice about her and some were not. Ramona could get along.

'That man paying for our dinner was sort of like a happy ending,' remarked Beezus, as the family, snug in their car, drove through the rain and the dark towards Klickitat Street.

'A happy ending for today,' corrected Ramona. Tomorrow they would begin all over again.

RaMONa
FOReVeR

CONTENTS

Contents

I

THE RICH UNCLE

'Guess what?' Ramona Quimby asked one Friday evening when her Aunt Beatrice dropped by to show off her new ski clothes and to stay for supper. Ramona's mother, father, and big sister Beezus, whose real name was Beatrice, paid no attention and went on eating. Picky-picky, the cat, meowed through the basement door, asking to share the meal.

Aunt Beatrice, who taught third grade, knew how to behave towards her third-grade niece. 'What?' she asked, laying down her fork as if she expected to be astounded by Ramona's news.

Ramona took a deep breath and announced, 'Howie Kemp's rich uncle is coming to visit.' Except for Aunt Bea, her family was not as curious as Ramona had hoped. She plunged on anyway because she was happy for her friend. 'Howie's grandmother is really excited, and so are Howie and Willa Jean.' And so, to be truthful, was Ramona, who disliked having to go to the Kemps' house after school, where Howie's grandmother looked after her grandchildren and Ramona while the two mothers were at work. A rich uncle, even someone else's rich uncle, should make those long after-school hours more interesting.

'I didn't know Howie had a rich uncle,' said Mrs Quimby.

'He's Howie's father's little brother, only now he's big,' explained Ramona.

'Why, that must be Hobart Kemp,' said Aunt Beatrice. 'He was in my class in high school.'

'Oh, yes. I remember. That boy with the blond curly hair who played baseball.' Mrs Quimby motioned to her daughters to clear away the plates. 'All the girls said he was cute.'

'That's the one,' said Aunt Bea. 'He used to chew liquorice and spit on the grass to make the principal think he was chewing tobacco like a professional baseball player, which was what he wanted to be.'

'Where's this cute liquorice-chewing uncle coming from, and how did he get so rich?' asked Ramona's father, beginning to be interested. 'Playing baseball?'

'He's coming from—' Ramona frowned. 'I can't remember the name, but it sounds like a fairy tale and has camels.' Narnia? Never-never-land? No, those names weren't right.

'Saudi Arabia,' said Beezus, who also went to

the Kemps' after school. Being in junior high school, she could take her time getting there.

'Yes, that's it!' Ramona wished she had remembered first. 'Howie says he's bringing the whole family presents.' She imagined bags of gold like those in *The Arabian Nights*, which Beezus had read to her. Of course, nobody carried around bags of gold today, but she enjoyed imagining them.

'What's Howie's uncle doing in Saudi Arabia?' asked Mr Quimby. 'Besides spitting liquorice in the sand?'

'Daddy, don't be silly,' said Ramona. 'I don't know exactly.' Now that she was the centre of attention, she wished she had more information. 'Something about oil. Drills or rigs or something. Howie understands all about it. His uncle earned a lot of money.' The Quimbys were a family who had to worry about money.

'Oh, that kind of rich,' said Mr Quimby. 'I thought maybe a long-lost uncle had died and left him a castle full of servants, jewels, and rare old wines.'

'Daddy, that's so old-fashioned,' said Ramona. 'That's only in books.'

The conversation drifted off, leaving Ramona behind. Her father, who would earn his teaching credential in June, said he was enquiring around for schools that needed an art teacher, and he also told about the problems of the men who worked in the same frozen-food warehouse where he worked on weekends at below-freezing temperatures. Mrs Quimby told about two people who got into an argument over a parking space at the doctor's office where she worked. Aunt Bea talked about a man named Michael who had invited her to go skiing and was the reason she had bought new ski clothes. Beezus wondered aloud if Michael would ask Aunt Bea to marry him. Aunt Bea laughed at that, saying she had known him only two weeks, but since this was January, there were several months of skiing left and there was no telling what might happen.

No more was said about Howie's uncle that evening. Days went by. Uncle Hobart didn't come and didn't come. Every evening Mr Quimby asked, 'Has Old Moneybags arrived?' And Ramona had to say no.

Finally one morning, as Ramona and Howie were waiting for the school bus, Ramona said, 'I don't think you have a rich uncle at all. I think you made him up.'

Howie said he did too have a rich uncle. Even little Willa Jean, when Ramona went to the Kemps' after school, talked about Uncle Hobart and the presents he was bringing. Ramona informed Howie and Willa Jean rather crossly that her mother said it wasn't nice to talk about other people's money. They paid no attention—after all, he was their very own uncle, not Ramona's—and went right on talking about Uncle Hobart this and Uncle Hobart that. Uncle Hobart had landed in New York. He had actually telephoned, live and in person. Uncle Hobart was driving across the country. Uncle Hobart was delayed by a storm in the Rockies. Ramona wished she had never heard of Uncle Hobart.

Then, one day after school, Ramona and Howie saw a muddy van parked on the Kemps' driveway.

'It's Uncle Hobart!' Howie shouted, and began to run.

Ramona took her time. Somehow she had expected Uncle Hobart to arrive in a long black limousine, not a muddy van. She followed Howie into the house, where the famous uncle turned out to be a medium-young man who had not shaved for several days and who was wearing old jeans and a faded T-shirt. He was holding Willa Jean on his lap. The warm, sweet smell of apple pie filled the air.

'Down you go, Doll,' said Uncle Hobart, lifting Willa Jean to the floor and grabbing Howie in a bear hug. 'How's my favourite nephew?' he asked, and held Howie off to look at him while

Mrs Kemp hovered and Willa Jean embraced her Uncle Hobart's knee.

Ramona was embarrassed. She felt she was in the way because she was not related. She sat down on a chair, opened a book, but did not read. She studied Uncle Hobart, who didn't look rich to her. He looked like a plain man—a big disappointment.

Willa Jean let go of her uncle's knee. 'See what Uncle Hobart brought us,' she said, and pointed to a pair of objects that looked like two small sawhorses, each holding a red leather cushion. Willa Jean sat astride one. 'Giddyup, you old camel,' she said and informed Ramona, 'This is my camel saddle.'

'Hey, a camel saddle!' said Howie when he saw his present. He imitated Willa Jean. After a few more giddyups, there was nothing more to do with a camel saddle except sit on it.

Pooh, who wants a boring old camel saddle, Ramona wanted to say, at the same time wishing she had a saddle to sit on these winter days when she liked to read by the furnace outlet.

Finally Uncle Hobart noticed Ramona. 'Well, who's this young lady?' he asked. 'Howie, you didn't tell me you had a girlfriend.'

Both Ramona and Howie turned red and somehow felt ashamed.

252

'Aw, that's just old Ramona,' Howie muttered.

To Ramona's horror, Uncle Hobart began to strum an imaginary guitar and sing:

'Ramona, I hear the mission bells above.
Ramona, they're ringing out our song of love.
I press you, caress you,
And bless the day you taught me to care.'

Ramona knew right then that she did not like Uncle Hobart and never would. She had heard that song before. When Grandpa Day lived in Portland, he used to sing it to tease her, too. 'I'm not Howie's girlfriend,' she said in her most grown-up manner. 'I have to stay here until my mother is through work. It is'—could she get the words out right?—'strictly a business arrangement.'

Uncle Hobart found this very funny, which made Ramona dislike him even more.

'Cut it out, Uncle Hobart,' said Howie, a remark much appreciated by Ramona, who pretended to read her book while inside she churned with anger. She was *glad* she didn't have an Uncle Hobart. She was *glad* she didn't have any uncles at all, just Aunt Beatrice, who never embarrassed children and who always came when the family needed her.

'Did you bring us any more presents?' asked Willa Jean.

'Willa Jean, that isn't nice,' said Mrs Kemp, smiling because she was so happy to have her youngest son home at last.

'Willa Jean, how did you guess?' asked Uncle Hobart. 'Come on out to the van, and I'll show you.'

'Me, too?' Howie quickly forgot his annoyance.

'Sure.' As he went out of the door, Uncle Hobart said, 'It's great to be back in a country full of green grass and trees.'

Ramona heard Howie ask, 'What do camels eat if there isn't any grass?'

When they returned, Ramona lost her struggle to be interested in her book. Uncle Hobart was carrying a small accordion.

'Grandma, look!' Howie was wheeling what appeared to be part of a bicycle. 'It's a real unicycle!'

'Is it broken?' asked Willa Jean. 'It has only one wheel.'

'Hobart, whatever were you thinking of?' Mrs Kemp frowned at the unicycle.

'I was thinking of the unicycle you wouldn't let me have when I was Howie's age,' said Uncle Hobart. 'Now, Mom, don't you worry about a thing. I'll help him. He's not going to break any bones.' He set the accordion on the floor by Willa Jean. 'And this is for you,' he said.

Willa Jean eyed the accordion. 'What does it do?' she asked.

'You can play music on it,' answered her uncle. 'It's a Viennese accordion. I bought it from one of the men I worked with and even learned to play it a little.'

'Isn't that lovely, Willa Jean?' said Mrs Kemp. 'Your very own musical instrument. We'll put it away until you're old enough to learn to play it.'

'No!' Willa Jean put on her stubborn look. 'I want to play it now!'

Uncle Hobart took the accordion and began to play and sing:

'Ramona, I hear the mission bells above.
Ramona, they're ringing out our song of love.'

Ramona stared at her book as she thought mean, dark thoughts about Uncle Hobart. He stopped playing and said, 'What's the matter, Ramona? Don't you like my music?'

'No.' Ramona looked the uncle in the eye. 'You're teasing. I don't like grown-ups who tease.'

'Why, Ramona!' Mrs Kemp was most disapproving. 'That's no way to talk to Howie's uncle.'

'Now, Mom, don't get excited,' said Uncle

Hobart. 'Ramona has a point. I was teasing, but I'll reform. OK, Ramona?'

'OK,' agreed Ramona, suspecting he might still be teasing.

'Uncle Hobart, Uncle Hobart, let me play it,' begged Willa Jean.

The uncle placed Willa Jean's hands through the straps at each end of the accordion. 'You squeeze in and pull out while you press the little buttons,' he explained.

Before he could give any more instructions, Howie grabbed his uncle by the hand and dragged him outdoors. Mrs Kemp, sure that bones were about to be broken, followed. Ramona watched through the window. Uncle Hobart hopped on the unicycle and, waving to his audience, pedalled to the corner and back. 'See, nothing to it,' he said. 'Once you know how.'

'Hobart, where on earth did you learn to ride that thing?' his mother called out from the front steps.

'In college,' answered her son. 'Come on, Howie, it's your turn.' Holding the unicycle upright with one hand, he helped Howie mount the seat over the single wheel. 'Now pedal,' he directed. Howie pedalled; the unicycle tipped forward, setting Howie on the sidewalk.

Indoors, Willa Jean struggled with the accordion,

too heavy for her, and made it give out a loud groan, as if it were in pain.

'No, not that way,' Ramona heard Uncle Hobart say. 'It's like riding a bicycle, only instead of balancing sideways, you have to balance back and forth at the same time.'

With a flushed and determined face, Howie mounted the unicycle again. If he learns to ride it, maybe he'll let me ride his bicycle, thought Ramona, who longed for a bicycle, even a secondhand, three-speed bicycle. Howie tipped over backwards into his uncle's arms. The accordion squawked. Ramona felt rather lonely, left out and in the way.

'Hobart, do be careful,' shouted Mrs Kemp above the squawk and screech of Willa Jean's playing.

Ramona could see that learning to ride a unicycle was going to take time, so she turned her attention to Willa Jean and the accordion.

Willa Jean set her gift on the floor and sat down on her camel saddle with a scowl. 'It's too big and it won't play music.'

'Let me try.' Ramona was sure she could make music come out of the accordion. It looked so easy. She slipped her hands through the straps. The only song she could think of was, unfortunately, 'Ramona'. She pumped and pushed the buttons, only to produce the cry of a suffering accordion. She tried pushing different buttons while she pushed the bellows in and out. *Hee-haw, hee-haw.* This was not the music Ramona had in mind. 'Maybe your uncle can show you how when he has more time,' she told Willa Jean as she set the accordion down carefully on Howie's camel saddle.

From outside, Mrs Kemp's warnings continued. 'Hobart! Howie! Be careful!'

Ramona and Willa Jean stood by the window to watch Howie, protected by his uncle, actually ride a few feet before he pitched forward onto the sidewalk. 'I did it!' he shouted.

He's going to learn to ride it, thought Ramona, and then I'll get to ride his bicycle.

Willa Jean returned to the accordion as if it might have learned to play while she let it rest, but no, it went right on shrieking and groaning. 'I know how I'll make it play,' she said.

Ramona turned from the window in time to see Willa Jean set her accordion on one end on the floor. Holding it down with one foot through the strap, she used both hands to stretch it up as high as she could pull it. Then, as Ramona understood what she was about to do and tried to grab her, Willa Jean quickly took her foot out of the strap, turned, sat on the upended accordion, and lifted both feet from the floor. As she sank down, the accordion uttered one long screech, as if it were dying in agony.

'Willa Jean!' cried Ramona, horrified and delighted by the dreadful piercing noise that left her ears ringing. Willa Jean jumped up beaming. The accordion, Ramona could see, would never rise again. Its bellows had split, silencing it for ever. 'You broke it,' Ramona said, knowing she might have done the same thing at Willa Jean's age.

'I don't care,' said Willa Jean. 'I made a big noise, and now I don't want it any more.'

Mrs Kemp burst in to see what had happened. 'You naughty girls!' she cried when she saw the remains of Uncle Hobart's present.

'But I didn't do it,' protested Ramona. 'It's not my fault.'

'An expensive musical instrument ruined,' said Mrs Kemp. 'You're a big girl, Ramona. You should know better than to let Willa Jean break it.' She turned to her granddaughter. 'Aren't you ashamed of yourself?'

'No,' said Willa Jean. 'It's a dumb old thing that wouldn't play.'

'Willa Jean, go to your room,' ordered Mrs Kemp, who usually felt that anything Willa Jean did or said was cute, sweet, or adorable. 'I'm ashamed of you, spoiling your nice uncle's homecoming.'

Scowling, Willa Jean did as she was told.

Mrs Kemp turned to Ramona. 'As for you, young lady, you sit on that chair until your mother comes for you.'

Ramona sat, and Ramona seethed, angry at the unfairness of all that had happened. Why should she have to look after Willa Jean when her mother paid Mrs Kemp to look after Ramona? And Uncle Hobart was just plain stupid to give a little girl something she couldn't use until she was older, but then, grown-ups were often stupid about presents. Ramona knew. She had been given books 'to grow into', and by the time she had grown into them, they had lain around so long they no longer looked interesting. But an accordion—growing up to an accordion would take for ever.

Outside, other children had come to watch Howie learn to ride his unicycle. Ramona could hear shouts and laughing, and once in a while, a cheer. It isn't fair, Ramona told herself, even though grown-ups were always telling her life was not fair. It wasn't fair that life wasn't fair.

Ramona watched Mrs Kemp lovingly polish her new brass tray and coffee pot from Saudi Arabia. *Ping-ping-ping* went the timer on the kitchen stove. Howie burst in crying, one knee of his jeans bloody. Uncle Hobart followed with the unicycle. The afternoon was not fair, but neither was it boring.

'Oh, my goodness,' cried Mrs Kemp. 'I knew this would happen. I just knew he would get hurt on that contraption.'

Ramona could hear Willa Jean singing from her room:

> *'This old man, he is dumb.*
> *Knick-a-knack paddywhack,*
> *Give a dog a phone,*
> *This old man comes rolling home.'*

Ramona smiled. Willa Jean never got the words to songs right.

Ping-ping-ping insisted the timer. 'Hobart, turn off the oven and take out the pie while I attend to Howie,' directed harassed Mrs Kemp. Willa Jean stalked into the living room, picked up her camel saddle, and stalked out again. In spite of her bitterness, Ramona found the whole scene most entertaining to watch, better than TV because it was live.

When Howie limped back to the living room with one leg of his jeans rolled up and a bandage on his knee, he sat on the couch feeling sorry for himself. Ramona felt sorry for him, too.

'M-m-m.' Uncle Hobart inhaled. 'Smell Mom's apple pie. Just what I dreamed of every night when I was overseas.' He gave his mother a smacking kiss.

'You're not fooling me.' Mrs Kemp was delighted. 'You can't make me believe you dreamed of my apple pie every night. I know you better than that.'

Uncle Hobart noticed Ramona imprisoned on a chair. 'What's the matter with Howie's girlfriend?' he asked.

Of course, Ramona did not answer a man who did not play fair. He had promised to reform and not tease.

'Hobart, what do you think of a big girl who sits and watches while a little girl breaks her accordion?' Mrs Kemp, Ramona understood, did not want an answer. She wanted to shame Ramona.

Ramona was suddenly struck by a new and disquieting thought. *Mrs Kemp did not like her.* Until this minute she had thought all adults were supposed to like all children. She understood by now that misunderstandings were to be expected—she had had several with teachers—and often grown-ups and children did not agree, but things somehow worked out. For a grown-up to actually dislike a child and try to shame her, she was sure had to be wrong, very, very wrong. She longed for Beezus to come, so she could feel someone was on her side, but Beezus found more and more excuses to delay coming to the Kemps' after school.

Uncle Hobart apparently thought he was expected to answer his mother's question. 'What do I think of Ramona? Since she's Howie's girlfriend, I think she's a great kid. Don't you, Howie?'

'Oh, shut up, Uncle Hobart.' Howie scowled at the carpet.

Good for you, Howie, thought Ramona. You're on my side.

'Howie!' cried Mrs Kemp. 'That's no way to talk to your uncle.'

'I don't care,' said Howie. 'My knee hurts.'

'Really, I don't know what got into you children this afternoon.' Mrs Kemp was thoroughly provoked.

Ramona could have told her in one word: *grown-ups*. Instead, she stared at her book and thought, I am never going to come back here again. Never, never, never. She did not care what anyone said. She did not care what happened. She was not going to be looked after by someone who did not like her.

'Poor Mom,' said Uncle Hobart. 'How about a piece of your apple pie.'

Poor us. Ramona included Howie and Willa Jean in her pity as she wished that someday, just once, she too could sit on an accordion. She knew she never would, even if she had the chance. She had grown past Willa Jean's kind of behaviour, which had been fun while it lasted. Ramona smiled as she recalled the happy afternoon she had spent, when she was Willa Jean's age, boring holes in the garage wall with her father's brace and bit—until she was caught.

2

RaMoNa's PRoBLeM

At dinner the evening after the accordion incident, the members of the Quimby family were silent and thoughtful, as if they all had serious problems on their minds. They really were thinking about their problems, but they looked thoughtful because they were trying to avoid the bones in the fish they were having for supper. Eating fish with bones without looking thoughtful is impossible. Picky-picky, meowing for his turn, wove himself around their legs.

Ramona, who did not care for fish and was willing to let Picky-picky have her share, wished her mother would say, 'Ramona eats like a bird,' as if Ramona were unusually delicate and sensitive. Some mothers were like that, but not Mrs Quimby, who would only say cheerfully, 'Eat it anyway,' if Ramona complained that she did not like fish.

Since she could not get away with eating like a bird, Ramona poked her fork through her fish to remove every single bone before taking the first bite, and while she pushed, she worried. How was she going to inform her family that she was never going to stay with Mrs Kemp again? Never, and then what? If she did not stay at the Kemps' after school, her mother might not be able to work in the doctor's office, her father could not go to college, and the whole family would fall over like dominoes pushed by Ramona.

Mr Quimby laid a fishbone on the edge of his plate. 'Has Howie's rich uncle, Old Moneybags, turned up yet?' he said to Ramona. To the cat he said, 'Beat it, you furry nuisance.'

'Yes,' said Ramona, 'but he's just a plain man with whiskers and jeans. He doesn't look rich at all.'

Mr Quimby said, 'These days, you never can tell by clothes.'

'Is he nice?' asked Mrs Quimby.

'No,' said Ramona. 'He's the kind of grown-up who teases children and thinks he's funny.'

'You know the type,' said Beezus. 'When I got there, he said, "Who's this lovely little lady?" And I'm not lovely. I have three pimples, and I look terrible.' Beezus worried about her face lately, scrubbing it with medicated soap twice a day and refusing to eat chocolate.

'I'm never going back there after school,' Ramona burst out. 'I don't care what anybody says. I won't go there again! I'll come home and sit on the steps and freeze, but I will not let that awful Mrs Kemp look after me again.' Tears of anger spilled over her untasted fish.

The family was silent. When no one spoke, Ramona flared again. 'Well, I won't, and you can't make me. So there! Mrs Kemp hates me.'

There was a time when Mr Quimby would have said something such as, 'Pull yourself together, Ramona, and eat your dinner.' Instead, now that he was studying to be a teacher, he said calmly and quietly, 'Tell us about it, Ramona.'

This made Ramona feel worse. She did not want her father to be calm and quiet, as if she were sick in bed. She wanted him to be upset and excited, too. Her mother, also quiet, handed her a Kleenex. Ramona mopped her eyes, clutched the Kleenex in a ball, and began. She told about the uncle's presents, the song he sang, Howie's bloody knee, and how Willa Jean broke the accordion. Her parents laughed at that. 'That ought to make the neighbours happy,' said Mr Quimby. 'Now they're spared the racket.'

Ramona managed a shaky laugh, too. Now that she was safely in her own home, she could see the funny side to Uncle Hobart's visit—except her part.

'That must have been an interesting noise,' remarked Mrs Quimby.

'A wonderful noise,' agreed Ramona. 'A really terrible noise that hurt my ears—Picky-picky, you're tickling—but Mrs Kemp blamed me for not watching Willa Jean, and that isn't fair. And today I figured out something. Mrs Kemp doesn't like me. She's never nice and is always blaming me for something I didn't do. I don't care what you do to me. *I am not going back.*'

'Did you ever stop to think, Ramona,' said Mrs Quimby, 'that perhaps Mrs Kemp would rather not be a sitter for you or her grandchildren?'

No, Ramona had not thought of that.

'Women her age were brought up to keep house and take care of children,' explained Mrs Quimby. 'That's all they really know how to do. But now maybe she'd rather be doing something else.' She looked thoughtful, not fishbone thoughtful, but really thoughtful.

'She could like me a little bit.' Ramona now felt sulky instead of angry.

Beezus spoke up. 'Ramona is right. Mrs Kemp doesn't like either of us. That's why I try to go to Pamela's house after school, or to the library.'

'Ramona, what do you think you should do?' asked Mr Quimby.

Ramona did not want the responsibility of

thinking what she should do. She wanted help from a grown-up. Sometimes she thought learning to be a teacher had changed her father. 'Why can't I stay home and watch myself?' she asked. 'Lots of kids watch themselves when nobody is home.'

'And those are the kids who get into trouble— Picky-picky, take your claws out of my leg!— You're my daughter,' said Mr Quimby, 'and I don't like the idea of you staying alone.'

'Other kids don't watch themselves, they watch TV,' said Beezus as she cleared the table.

'I wouldn't watch TV,' was Ramona's reckless promise. She whisked her own plate to the kitchen and dumped her fish on Picky-picky's dish. 'I would sit on a chair and read a book. Cross my heart and hope to die and stew and fry.'

'I wouldn't go that far,' said her father, sounding more the way Ramona remembered him before he went back to college.

'I could watch her.' Beezus rose from the table to serve canned pears while Ramona followed with a plate of oatmeal cookies. 'Lots of girls in junior high baby-sit.'

'No dessert for me,' whispered Mrs Quimby.

'I'm not a baby.' Ramona wondered why Beezus was willing to give up going to Pamela's house. Pamela had everything—her own TV set, her own telephone. Pamela was popular. All the junior high girls wanted to be like Pamela.

Ramona thought fast. Beezus would act big. Beezus would be bossy. She and Beezus would quarrel with no one to stop them. Beezus might tattle. Sometimes she did, and sometimes she didn't. Of course, Ramona tattled, too, but somehow she felt that was different.

On the other hand, there was Mrs Kemp. As soon as her son left, she would go back to knitting and disliking Ramona. And there was Howie, her best friend, to think about. On sunny days, and even on damp days, he was off riding his bicycle with the boys in the neighbourhood, leaving her stuck with Willa Jean. 'Would Beezus get paid?' Ramona demanded.

Silence. 'Picky-picky, get *down*,' said Mrs Quimby. The cat, who had gobbled up Ramona's fish, wanted more.

'Well—' said Beezus, 'I guess I could sit for nothing. After all, I don't like going to the Kemps' myself. Mrs Kemp never makes me feel welcome, and their house always smells of old soup.'

'I'm sure Mrs Kemp would like to be with her son as much as possible while he is here,' said Mrs Quimby. 'I could suggest she take a week off. That way, you could try staying home without hurting her feelings, and we could see how it works out.'

'She'll be glad to get rid of me.' The raw, hurt feeling inside Ramona was beginning to heal now that her family was trying to help.

'You girls will have to come straight home from school,' said Mrs Quimby, 'and promise to behave yourselves. No fighting, and never, never, open the door to strangers.'

The sisters promised. 'Mother, will you phone Mrs Kemp now?' Ramona was anxious to have the matter settled before Mrs Kemp telephoned first to say Ramona was a bad influence on Willa Jean.

Howie's grandmother, as Mrs Quimby had predicted, was delighted to have more time to spend with her son. 'Whee!' cheered Ramona. She was free of Mrs Kemp for at least a week.

When the meal was over, Beezus went to her room to do her homework. Ramona followed and closed the door behind her. 'How come you are willing to stay with me instead of going to Pamela's or Mary Jane's after school?' She could not help feeling suspicious, so unexpected was Beezus's behaviour.

'Mary Jane is always practising the piano, and I'm not speaking to Pamela,' said Beezus.

'Why not?' Ramona often yelled at people, but never refused to speak. Nothing could happen if you didn't speak, and she liked things to happen.

Beezus explained. 'Pamela is always bragging that *her* father has a *real* job, and she's always asking when *my* father is going to stop fooling around and really go to work. So I don't go to her house any more, and I don't speak to her.'

'Pooh to old Pamela.' Ramona chewed a hangnail as painful as her thoughts. 'She doesn't have any right to say things like that about Daddy. I won't speak to her either.'

'And I heard something Aunt Bea said,' continued Beezus. 'She said schools are laying off teachers. How do we know Daddy will get a job?'

Ramona, who had imagined every school would want a man as nice as her father, now had a new worry. 'You don't think Daddy would go to Gaudy Arabia, do you? Even if it would be warmer than that awful frozen-food warehouse where he works?'

'*Saudi* Arabia,' corrected Beezus. 'No, I don't. He doesn't know anything about oil except it costs a lot, and do you know what I think?' Beezus did not wait for Ramona to answer. 'I think mother won't be working much longer, because she's going to have a baby.'

Ramona sat down on the bed with a thump. A damp, dribbly baby, another Quimby. 'Why would mother do a thing like that when she already has us?'

'Don't ask *me*,' said Beezus, 'but I'm pretty sure she is.'

'Why?' asked Ramona, hoping her sister was wrong.

'Well, you remember how Aunt Bea is always asking mother how she is feeling, as if she had a special reason for asking?'

Looking back, Ramona realized Beezus was right.

'And mother doesn't eat dessert any more,' continued Beezus, 'so she won't gain too much weight.'

'Maybe she just doesn't want to get fat.' Ramona was doubtful about this. Her mother had always been slender, never worrying about her weight like most mothers.

'And twice, back around Thanksgiving, mother threw up after breakfast.' Beezus added another reason.

'That's nothing,' scoffed Ramona. 'I've thrown up lots of times, and mince pie always makes me want to urp.'

'But ladies who are going to have babies sometimes throw up in the morning,' explained Beezus.

'They do?' This was news to Ramona. Beezus

might be right. She was interested in such things. 'Why don't we go ask mother?'

'When she wants us to know, she will tell us. And of course, I might be wrong . . .' Doubt crept into Beezus's voice before she said, 'Oh, I hope I'm right. I love babies. I'd love to help take care of one of our own. I just know it would be darling.'

Ramona sat on the bed thinking while Beezus opened her books. A little brother or sister? She did not like the idea, not one bit. If she had a little brother or sister, grown-ups would say in their knowing way, as if children could not understand, Somebody's nose is out of joint. Ramona had heard them say it many times about children who had new babies in the family. This was their way of talking about children behind their backs in front of them.

'But if it's true, I sure hope Daddy finds a teaching job fast,' said Beezus. 'Now go away. I have to study.'

Ramona wandered into the living room, where her mother was lying on the couch watching the evening news on TV with the sound turned low so it would not disturb her husband, who was studying at the dining room table. Ramona knew she was not supposed to interrupt when he was studying, but this time she decided he wasn't really working, just doodling on a piece of scratch paper with a worried look on his face. She slipped her head up between his ribs and arm.

'Hi,' said her father, as if Ramona had brought his thoughts back to the dining room.

'Hi,' answered Ramona as her father quickly turned over his page of doodles, but not before she had a glimpse of dollar signs and babies, doodles that must mean he was thinking about a baby.

'You have me to be your little girl,' Ramona reminded her father.

Her father rubbed his chin against the top of Ramona's head. 'That's right, and I'm mighty glad I do.'

'Then you wouldn't want another little girl would you?' Ramona had to find out.

'Oh, I don't know,' said Mr Quimby. 'I like little girls.'

3

BEING GOOD

On Monday, Howie looked troubled when Ramona hopped off the school bus and turned towards her house instead of his. 'Well—so long, Ramona,' he said. 'See you tomorrow.'

'Have fun with your uncle,' said Ramona, and walked down Klickitat Street to the Quimby house, where she found the hidden key, let herself in the back door, washed her hands, ate an apple, put the core in the garbage, changed from school clothes into old jeans and a T-shirt, and sat down on the couch to read. She felt grown-up and very, very good. How peaceful the Quimby house was compared to the Kemp house, where the television set was always tuned to soap operas and Willa Jean hopped around, yelling and insisting that Ramona play with her. Being good wasn't going to be hard after all.

Beezus came home a short time later. The sisters greeted one another with unusual courtesy, so determined were they to be good. Beezus took an apple into her room, where she settled down to do her homework.

Picky-picky meowed to be let out of the basement.

'Ramona, will you please let the cat out?' Ordinarily, Beezus would have shouted, Can't you hear Picky-picky? Let him out.

Another time, Ramona would have shouted back, Let him out yourself. He's more your cat than mine. I wasn't even born when we got him. Today she answered, 'Yes, Beezus,' as she opened the basement door.

Picky-picky immediately went to his dish to see if someone had surprised him with a choice titbit. Ramona returned to her book. Picky-picky, finding only leftover Puss-puddy, strolled out of the kitchen and went to the couch, where he waggled his rear end as if he were about to jump up beside Ramona. The effort was too great for his old age. Ramona, who was always pleased to receive attention from the cat, lifted him gently. He curled up beside her and purred as if his purring machinery had grown rusty and was wearing out.

Of course, the girls' parents, when they came home, were delighted to see what well-behaved daughters they had. The girls looked closely at their mother's waistline to see if she had gained weight since breakfast.

Tuesday afternoon was much the same as Monday. Beezus talked a long time on the telephone to a friend Ramona did not know. The conversation was about who said what to a new boy at school, and what was printed on someone's T-shirt, and how some girl said she had seen some boy looking at Beezus, because Beezus said, 'Do you think he looked at me, *really*?' and on and on. When the conversation, uninteresting to Ramona, finally ended, Beezus went into the bathroom and scrubbed her face with medicated soap.

'What good girls we have,' said Mrs Quimby when she returned from work with her waistline no larger than it had been the day before. However, she did look tired, and on the way home, had bought a pizza for dinner. Since pizzas were an extravagance in the Quimby household, this meant she did not feel like cooking dinner.

By Wednesday Ramona began to dread being good because being good was boring, so she was happy to see Howie coming down the street, wheeling his bicycle with his unicycle balanced across the seat and handlebars. She was even happier when he laid both on her driveway. Ramona met him at the door.

'Come on out, Ramona,' said Howie. 'Uncle Hobart helped me learn to ride my unicycle, so now you can ride my bicycle.'

Ramona's wish had come true. 'Hey, Beezus,' she shouted, 'I'm going out and ride Howie's bike.'

'You're supposed to ask first,' said Beezus. 'You can't go out unless I say so.'

Ramona felt that Beezus was showing off in front of Howie. 'How come you're so bossy all of a sudden?' she demanded.

'Mom and Dad left me in charge, and you have to mind,' answered Beezus.

'You talk the way you and Mary Jane used to talk when you played house and made me be the baby. Well, I'm not a baby now.' Ramona grew more determined and contrary. 'Mom always lets me go out and play with Howie.'

'Just the same, if you get hurt, I'm responsible,' said Beezus.

'You're just being mean,' said Ramona. 'So long, Pizzaface.' Just before she slammed the door, she was horrified to see Beezus's face crumple, as if she were about to burst into tears.

Howie cried out, 'Ramona, look at me!'

Ramona watched Howie mount his unicycle and ride it to the corner and back, but as she watched, she felt puzzled and uncomfortable. She had made Beezus unhappy, but why? She did not understand. She had called Beezus Pieface many times without upsetting her. What was so different about Pizzaface? She happened to think of it because they had eaten pizza the night before, and pizza was a sort of pie.

'Good work, Howie,' said Ramona when he had ridden to the corner and back a second time. But what about me? she thought, still worrying about Beezus. I can't spend the rest of my life sitting on a couch being good.

'Come on, ride my bike,' said Howie. 'Let's see if we can make it around the block.'

Ramona raised Howie's bicycle, made sure one pedal was high and the other low so she would have a good start, mounted, and rode wobbling down the sidewalk.

'Atta girl, Ramona,' said Howie, seating himself on his unicycle and pedalling ahead of her.

Ramona wobbled along after him, and as she wobbled, she worried. What was Beezus going to say to their mother and father? Would she have to go back to the Kemps'?

By the time Ramona reached the corner, she was less wobbly. She even managed to turn the corner without tipping over. She began to pedal faster. Now she was really riding, filled with joy, as if she were flying.

Ramona passed Howie. She stood up on the pedals to go faster. Ramona's mind was on speed, not balance, and at the next corner, as she turned, she lost control. Down she went, with the bicycle on top of her. Her left knee and elbow hurt; her breath was knocked out of her.

Howie dropped his unicycle and came running to lift his bicycle from Ramona. 'You OK?' he asked.

Ramona rose stiffly to her feet. 'I don't think anything's broken,' she said, struggling not to cry. Blood was running down her scraped elbow and soaking the knee of her jeans. Limping, she wheeled the bicycle, and Howie wheeled his unicycle, as far as her driveway.

'Come back again, Howie,' said Ramona. 'I love to ride your bicycle, even if I did take a spill.'

'Sure, Ramona,' agreed Howie. 'You better go mop up all that blood.'

When Ramona went to the back door so she wouldn't bleed on the living room carpet, she had to knock because the door was locked. When Beezus opened it, she ignored her sister's dripping blood and returned to her room without speaking.

Ramona limped to the bathroom. Maybe she could make Beezus speak if she let her know she had been right, that Ramona had hurt herself when she disobeyed. She said in her most pitiful voice, 'Beezus, I had a bad fall. Come and help me.'

'I don't care, you hateful little creep,' was her

sister's answer. 'Serves you right. I'm not speaking to you any more. It's not my fault my face is all red and blotchy like a pizza.'

What Ramona heard left her speechless, ashamed, and angry. She had hurt her sister's feelings accidentally; Beezus had hurt hers on purpose, and she didn't even care that Ramona was dripping blood. She was probably *glad*. Bossy old Beezus.

Ramona washed her own knee and elbow, sprayed them with disinfectant, plastered them with Band-Aids, and changed into clean jeans and a long-sleeved blouse to hide her wounds. She then lifted Picky-picky to the couch, sat down beside him to read and be good Ramona again.

Ramona, however, found she could not read, she felt so terrible, even though she was angry, about hurting her sister's feelings in a way she had not intended. The girls often called one another names—Beezus called Ramona Dribblepuss when her ice cream melted from a cone and trickled down her chin—but they never used really unkind names. Now Beezus called her a hateful little creep and meant it. And what if Beezus told their mother and father they had quarrelled? Then it would be back to the Kemps' for Ramona.

Good girl that she was, Ramona decided to set the table. She heard Beezus go into the bathroom and wash her face before coming into the kitchen.

Picky-picky managed to get down from the couch and follow her, in case she decided to feed him. Beezus scrubbed four potatoes and put them in the oven to bake. Then she picked up the cat, hugged and petted him. 'Nice Picky-picky,' she said so Ramona could hear. This, of course, meant that Ramona was not nice.

However, when their parents came home, Beezus acted as if nothing had happened, and so did Ramona—except they both talked to their mother and father but not to one another. Ramona thought maybe the white uniform her mother wore to work in the doctor's office looked tighter at the waist. Perhaps it had shrunk, or last night's pizza had been fattening, or maybe Beezus was right—she was going to have a baby.

As the family was about to sit down to dinner, the telephone rang, and since Mrs Quimby happened to be standing near it, she answered. 'Oh, I'm fine," she said.

Ramona wanted to look at Beezus. However, they were not only not speaking, they were not looking. She listened intently to their mother's side of the telephone conversation.

Mrs Quimby was smiling. 'Yes . . . yes, of course. I think that's a great idea . . . no, it doesn't hurt to try, so go ahead . . . it sounds like fun. Let me know how it turns out.'

'What sounds like fun?' demanded Ramona and Beezus at the same time.

'Oh—something,' said Mrs Quimby airily, and winked at her husband. 'I can't remember exactly what.'

'You winked at Daddy,' Ramona accused her mother, as if winking were somehow wicked.

'Mom! You're fibbing!' cried Beezus in exasperation. 'You can too remember.'

'It isn't nice to talk about things in front of people and not tell them what you are talking about.' Ramona suffered from curiosity as much as Beezus.

'Who called?' asked Mr Quimby.

Ha! thought Ramona, now we've got her. She won't fib to Dad.

'Howie's mother,' said Mrs Quimby. 'She needed some information.'

'Oh,' was all the girls' father had to say.

'Is it about a birthday party?' asked Ramona, because her mother had mentioned fun.

'Never mind, Ramona,' said her mother. 'Just eat your dinner.'

'Well, is it?' persisted Ramona.

'No, it isn't a birthday party,' said Mrs Quimby, 'and it doesn't concern you.'

Ramona hoped her mother was still fibbing. She wanted fun to concern herself.

The parents did not notice that the girls were not speaking—or if they did, they chose not to mention the matter.

After dinner, Mrs Quimby said she was a little tired and thought she would go to bed and read awhile. The girls avoided looking at one another, even though the remark was significant.

'I'll do the dishes,' volunteered Mr Quimby as the girls cleared the table. 'Then I'll work on my lesson plan for tomorrow's practice teaching.' He lowered his voice. 'And I want to make one thing clear to you girls. You are not to do anything to worry your mother. Do you understand?'

The girls nodded, avoiding one another's eyes. From the exasperation in their father's voice, they knew he understood they had quarrelled. Beezus went off to her room.

Ramona yearned to follow her sister, to say she was sorry, that she had not meant Pizzaface the way Beezus thought she meant it, to find out what Beezus thought of the mysterious telephone call, to ask when she thought her mother was going to have a baby—if she was. However, Ramona was not used to saying she was sorry, especially to someone who was bossy and called her a hateful little creep. Little creep she could overlook, but not hateful little creep.

4

PICKY-PICKY

Strangely, when Ramona's heart was heavy, so were her feet. She trudged to the school bus, plodded through the halls at school, and clumped home from the bus after school. The house felt lonely when she let herself in, so she turned on the television set for company. She sat on the couch and stared at one of the senseless soap operas Mrs Kemp watched. They were all about rich people—none of them looking like Howie's Uncle Hobart—who accused other people of doing something terrible; Ramona didn't understand exactly what, but it all was boring, boring, boring.

Beezus came home, left her books in her room, and hung up her jacket instead of throwing it on her bed. She then went to the basement door, her back saying silently to Ramona, *You* didn't let Picky-picky out. Ramona realized she had not let the cat out because she had not heard him meow.

When Beezus opened the door, no cat came out to investigate his dish. Beezus snapped on the basement light and descended the steps.

That's funny, thought Ramona.

'Ramona!' screamed Beezus. 'Come quick!'

At last! Beezus had spoken, but her voice told Ramona something dreadful must have happened. Frightened, Ramona ran down the basement steps, skipping the last two and jumping to the concrete floor. Her sister needed her.

Beezus, with her hands clasped to her chest, was standing over Picky-picky's basket. 'He's *dead*.' Beezus stared at the motionless cat in disbelief, tears in her eyes. 'Picky-picky is *dead*.'

'How can he be?' asked Ramona. 'He was alive this morning.' Both girls had forgotten, or at least put aside, their feelings towards one another.

'He just is,' said Beezus. 'I don't know why, unless he died of old age. I started to pick him up, and he's all limp and cold. Go ahead and touch him and you'll see.'

Ramona summoned courage to touch timidly with one finger the lifeless Picky-picky. He felt like cold, limp fur.

'What are we going to do?' asked distraught Beezus.

'Wait till mother and Daddy come home,' suggested Ramona.

'But Daddy said we weren't to worry mother,' Beezus reminded her. The sisters looked helplessly at one another. 'I know we didn't do anything to

Picky-picky, but I think coming home and finding a dead cat in the basement would upset her a lot.'

'Yes,' agreed Ramona. 'It sure would, especially at dinner time.' The two looked sadly at the remains of their pet. 'I guess we should bury him,' said Ramona, 'and have a funeral.'

'We'll have to hurry,' said Beezus, 'and I don't know if I can dig a grave.' She lifted her father's heavy shovel from the wall, where it hung upside down between two nails, and started up the steps. 'Come on, help me find a place.'

Ramona was glad to follow. Somehow she did not want to be alone with the ghost of Picky-picky. Silly, but that was the way she felt.

The girls walked across the wet grass to choose a spot in the corner of the backyard where their father had grubbed out an old laurel bush that had grown too large for the space. Beezus jabbed the shovel into the muddy soil, stepped on the top of the blade to push it further down, lifted out a shovelful of dirt, and laid it aside. 'What will we bury him in?' she asked, struggling with another shovelful of wet dirt.

'I'll find a box.' Now that Beezus was speaking to her, Ramona was eager to do her part. Besides, even though she felt sad and awed by her first experience with the death of someone she knew—birds didn't count—burying the cat was interesting. In the basement she picked up a cardboard carton and ran upstairs. In her room she found a doll's pillow and two doll's blankets. She lined the box with one blanket and placed the pillow at one end. She forced herself to return to the basement, where she found she could not bring herself to lift the lifeless Picky-picky. She would leave that to Beezus.

Out in the backyard, Ramona found Beezus panting as she wrestled with the shovel. 'Let me try,' she offered, but soon discovered the shovel was too long and unwieldy for her to manage. 'I'll get a trowel,' she said. Together, the girls worked, Ramona on her knees digging with the trowel and finally with her hands, until they had dug a small grave just right for a cat. 'Beezus, will you put Picky-picky in the box?' asked Ramona. 'I'm—not exactly scared, but I don't want to.'

Back in the basement, Beezus lifted Picky-picky into his cardboard coffin and laid his head on the pillow. Ramona tucked the second doll blanket around him, and together they set the lid in place.

Beezus carried the box out to the gravesite. 'It doesn't seem right just to bury him,' she said, 'and I don't remember much about Grandma Day's funeral except everyone whispered, there were lots of flowers, and I had to sit very still. You were just a baby then.'

Ramona knew about funerals. 'On TV when they bury somebody, they stand around the grave and pray,' she said. 'Then the wife of the dead person cries until someone leads her away.'

'I suppose we should pray.' Beezus sounded uncertain as to the proper way to pray for a cat.

Ramona had no doubts. She bowed her head and began, 'Now I lay me down to sleep—'

'That's not right,' interrupted Beezus. 'You're not the one who's being buried.'

'Oh. OK.' Ramona began again. 'Now we lay Picky-picky down to sleep. We pray thee, Lord, his soul to keep. Thy love stay with him through the night and wake him with the morning light. Amen.' When she finished the prayer, she said, 'There. That's that.'

Beezus frowned in thought. 'But he won't wake with the morning light. He isn't supposed to. He's dead.'

Ramona was not worried. 'Cats have nine lives, so tomorrow he will wake up someplace as somebody's kitten and start a new life.'

'I hadn't thought of that,' said Beezus, 'but it sounds logical. I hope his new owners give him melon rind. Picky-picky loved melon rind.' She picked up the shovel and began to fill in the grave. 'We should have some flowers for him, but there aren't any.'

'I wonder which of his lives we got him on,' said Ramona as she gathered damp brown leaves to strew on the grave. The girls stood looking sadly at the little mound left by Picky-picky's coffin. 'He was a good cat,' said Ramona, 'even if he didn't like me much when I was little.'

'I can barely remember when he was a little tiny kitten who climbed the curtains,' said Beezus.

'I'll make him a tombstone.' After sharing the sad experience, Ramona felt closer to her sister, close enough to speak of something other than their cat.

'Beezus—' she said with a gulp. 'I'm sorry about yesterday when I called you—you know—and I didn't mean it the way you took it.' She explained how she happened to change Pieface to Pizzaface. 'I didn't mean to hurt your feelings. I—I won't say it again, no matter how mad I get.'

'That's OK,' said Beezus with a big sigh. 'I shouldn't have been so cross with you. Mom says I'll outgrow skin problems, but it seems like for ever. Now maybe I better put something on these blisters on my hands.'

In spite of the funeral, Ramona felt light and happy. She and her sister had both apologized and forgiven one another. 'And we didn't worry mother,' Ramona pointed out as she skipped off to the basement to find a short board in a pile of scrap lumber.

By the time Beezus had changed out of her muddy clothes, scrubbed her hands, applied disinfectant, and covered her blisters with Band-Aids, the grave bore a marker made from a scrap of board. Printed in crayon were the words, 'Picky-picky Quimby. Aged 10 years. A good cat.'

Beneath the words, Ramona had drawn a picture of a yellow cat.

'But we'll have to tell mother and Daddy,' said Beezus. 'They're sure to miss him.'

'Won't that upset mother?' asked Ramona.

Beezus was filled with uncertainty. 'Well—I don't think our burying him will upset her as much as finding him dead in the basement.' She rearranged the Band-Aids on her hands. 'You'd better get into some clean clothes, or she'll really be upset. And don't forget to use the nailbrush on your fingernails.'

Before Ramona had time to change her clothes, her parents came home. As Mr Quimby set a bag of groceries on the kitchen counter, he looked at his younger daughter and remarked with a grin, 'Add water and get instant Ramona. You'd better add some soap, too.'

Mrs Quimby, used to seeing Ramona covered with dirt, only said, 'I found a bargain in cat food.'

Ramona exchanged an anguished look with her sister and went off to scrub her hands and change to clean clothes. What a waste of money, buying cat food now. The sisters exchanged another anguished look when Ramona returned to set the table. Beezus was washing lettuce with the tips of her fingers to keep her Band-Aid dry.

'Why, Beezus, what has happened to your hands?' asked her mother as she laid a bunch of carrots on the counter. 'You've hurt yourself.'

'It's nothing much,' said Beezus.

'Here, let me finish the lettuce,' said Mr Quimby as he took one of his daughter's hands to examine her wounds. 'Why, this is terrible,' he said. 'How did you get all those blisters?'

Beezus did not want to tell. She cast a look at Ramona that asked, What do I do now?

This is dumb, thought Ramona. Their parents had to know sometime. 'She blistered her hands digging a hole in the backyard,' she informed her parents and added in her saddest, most sorrowful voice, 'a little grave. We dug a little grave.' She really enjoyed the looks of astonishment the announcement produced.

Mr Quimby, who was first to recover, looked amused. 'And whom, may I ask, or what did you bury in a grave big enough to raise blisters on Beezus's hands?'

Ramona knew he was thinking of the little

graves they had dug for dead birds when they were younger. She sighed to make her announcement seem even more mournful. 'We buried Picky-picky. He passed away today.'

The parents' look of surprise and amusement turned to shock. They looked even more shocked than Ramona had expected. She began to feel frightened. Perhaps she had upset her mother after all.

'Why, you poor children—' said Mrs Quimby with tears in her eyes. 'Burying the cat all by yourselves.'

'Why didn't you wait for me?' asked their father. 'I could have taken care of him.'

'You said we shouldn't upset mother,' explained Beezus. 'And we didn't want her to come home and find Picky-picky dead.'

'We made a nice grave, with leaves and a marker,' said Ramona. 'And we remembered to say a prayer like they do on TV before somebody leads the dead person's wife away.'

Mrs Quimby brushed away a tear with the back of her hand. 'I'm a very lucky mother to have such dear girls,' she said.

'And I'm really proud of you,' said Mr Quimby. 'I hope we have such good luck the next time.'

The sisters stared at their mother's waistline. Her uniform was tight. It was not their imagination. They raised their eyes to her face. She was smiling.

'Then it's true!' Beezus was filled with excitement and joy.

'You're going to have a baby.' Although she had suspected the truth, Ramona was as disbelieving as if she were charging her mother with magic.

'When are you going to have it?' asked Beezus.

'In July,' confessed her mother.

'Correction,' said Mr Quimby. '*We* are going to have a baby. I'm going to be a proud father.'

'You just said you were proud of *us*,' Ramona reminded him.

'So I did,' said her father. 'But now I can be proud of three instead of two.'

'And I don't think we need worry about leaving the girls alone until I stop working,' said Mrs Quimby.

'Whee!' cried Ramona. 'No more Mrs Kemp!' At the same time she was thinking, a third Quimby child? Her mind was full of excited questions, but deep down inside where she hid her most secret thoughts, Ramona realized she would lose her favoured place as the baby of the family. She would become the middle child, neither big nor little. She thought maybe she would rather have another cat.

5

'IT'

Now that the news of the baby was out, Beezus and Ramona had no more trouble getting along with one another after school. Saying they were sorry and burying Picky-picky had brought them closer together. Their parents said nothing more about their returning to the Kemps' after school.

Ramona began to feel that life was humdrum. Even the weather was dreary—wet and cold, but not cold enough to snow. She tried wearing a Chiquita banana sticker plastered to her forehead when she went to school, to start a fad like the sticker fad in Aunt Beatrice's third grade. Her aunt said she sometimes felt as if she were teaching a bunch of bananas. Members of Ramona's class said, 'What are you wearing that for?' or 'That looks dumb.'

Then Ramona tried announcing, 'We're going to have a new baby at our house.' No one was interested. New babies were common in the families of her classmates. Because she had been to their homes, Ramona knew what new babies meant—a stroller in the hall, a playpen in the living room, a high chair in the kitchen, tiny clothes strewn around, plastic toys underfoot, zwieback crumbs sticking to chairs. Of course she could not expect her friends to get excited about the Quimbys' new baby.

Weeks went by. Aunt Beatrice telephoned almost every evening to ask how her sister was feeling. The conversation of the grown-up sisters was filled with laughter, which puzzled Ramona and Beezus, who failed to see why having a baby was funny. They hung around, trying to guess what the laughter was about from their mother's side of the mysterious conversations. They were able to guess that Aunt Bea was very busy, that she went skiing almost every weekend, but the ski season would soon be over. Their mother's remarks were meaningless. 'Why, Bea!' 'I don't believe it!' 'What did Michael say?' 'No. No, I won't tell the girls.'

Both Beezus and Ramona pounced on their mother when a conversation ended. 'What won't you tell us?' they demanded.

'If I told you, you would know,' answered their mother.

'Mother-er!' protested Ramona. 'You're just plain mean.'

'Yes, exasperating,' agreed Beezus.

'Me?' Mrs Quimby looked innocent. 'Mean? Exasperating? Wherever did you get that idea?'

'Did Michael ask Aunt Bea to marry him?' demanded Beezus, eager for romance.

'Not that I know of,' answered their provoking mother.

Ramona stamped her foot. 'Mother, you stop it! You're getting to be as bad as Howie's Uncle Hobart, always teasing.'

'Heaven forbid that I should be like Howie's Uncle Hobart,' answered Mrs Quimby, still teasing. 'I'll have to try to mend my ways.'

Ramona was strict with her mother. 'See that you do,' she said. 'I don't like mysteries, except in books.'

Mr Quimby, who was trying to study at the dining room table, frowned during all these conversations that disturbed his work. Something dreadful called a midterm was about to happen at the university. He was worried and nervous. The girls could tell because he made more jokes than usual. When he was worried, he always joked. When he saw Ramona lying on the floor looking at TV, he said, 'There's Ramona. Batteries not included.'

However, Mr Quimby's studies would be over by the middle of June, when he would receive his teaching credential a few weeks before the baby, known as It, was due. Then he would work during the summer as a checker at one of the Shop-rite markets to replace checkers who took vacations. By September, he would have found a place in a school, if not in Portland, at least in a suburb. Mrs Quimby would leave her job to take care of It, which pleased Ramona. The house always seemed so empty without her mother.

Of course, Beezus and Ramona were eager to know if It would be a boy or girl. Ramona wanted a boy. Beezus wanted a girl. Their parents said they would take whatever came along.

The girls were concerned with other questions. Whose room would It share? How long would their mother stay home to take care of It? Ramona wanted her mother home for keeps—babies weren't much work, they just lay around all day. Maybe her mother could find time to let down the hems of Ramona's skirts and pants and bake a few cookies. Beezus wished she could stay home from school to take care of It herself. However, she had the summer to look forward to. Mrs Quimby said that after the girls' father found a job and It was a few months old, she would like to take some evening courses at the university. 'And I'll take care of It while you study,' said Beezus.

'Enough of It,' said Mr Quimby. 'No child of ours is going to be called It Quimby. Think how everyone would laugh when the teacher called the roll. How would you feel introducing your new brother or sister by saying, "This is It"? And every time anyone said, "I don't like it," about bread pudding or stupid TV programmes, It's feelings would be hurt.'

The family agreed that of course the baby needed a real name. Robert Quimby, Junior? Maybe, if It turned out to be a boy. Mrs Quimby said the baby would not be named after herself because she had never liked being called Dorothy. Ramona thought Aston Martin would be good for a boy. She had heard the name someplace and thought it sounded nice. Beezus preferred Gary or Burt for a boy and thought April was a pretty name for a girl, except It would be born in July, which was not a name for a person.

Then Mr Quimby brought home a pamphlet from the drugstore, called *A Name for Your Baby*, which listed names and their meanings. Ramona immediately found her own name and discovered that Ramona meant 'wise helper'. How boring, she thought, and hoped this did not mean that she would be expected to change It's diapers or anything like that.

Beezus, on the other hand, laughed when she discovered Beatrice meant 'heavenly one'. 'Whee!' she said, twirling around the living room and flapping her arms like wings. Her complexion had improved, which made her happier about everything.

Together the girls studied the pamphlet. Many names would not do at all. Philbert, which meant 'superior', sounded good with Quimby, but at school, boys would call him a nut. Beezus thought Abelard might be a good name for a boy because it meant 'romantic hero', but Ramona pointed out that everyone at school would call him 'Lard'. Beezus also thought Lorelei, which meant 'romantic siren', was a pretty name for a girl until Ramona began to chant, 'Loreliar, Loreliar, pants on fire.'

Ramona preferred Gwendolyn for a girl because the name meant 'fair'. If she had to have another sister, she wanted one who always played fair.

Mr Quimby suggested names that were much too fancy—Alphonso Horatio, Clarinda Hepzibah, or Quentin Quincy Quimby. His daughters, however, did not take him seriously. This was more of his joking because he was worried.

'What if It is twins?' Ramona's thought presented a whole new problem. She studied the pamphlet once more. Paul and Pauline? Boris and Doris? Gerald and Geraldine?

'They could be two girls or two boys,' Beezus pointed out.

'Abby and Gabby,' said Mr Quimby. 'Peter and Mosquiter.'

'Daddy, you're just being silly.' Ramona was always stern with her father when she felt he had gone too far with his jokes.

Mrs Quimby asked what was wrong with plain names like Jane or John. Nothing, agreed her daughters, but fancy names were more fun to look up. They discovered that Hobart meant 'clever', but of course they weren't going to name their baby after Howie's uncle.

Finally It came to be known as Algie. When Mrs Quimby could no longer squeeze into her clothes and changed to maternity clothes, Mr Quimby recited:

> *'Algie went out walking.*
> *Algie met a bear.*
> *The bear was bulgy.*
> *The bulge was Algie.'*

Mrs Quimby said, 'You wouldn't think it was so funny if men had babies.' However, she laughed and referred to the new baby as Algie after that. The girls, when told that Algie was short for Algernon, looked up the name and discovered it meant 'courageous'.

'Of course, we couldn't really name it

Algernon,' said practical Beezus. 'Everyone at school would make fun of him. Nobody is named Algernon except in old-fashioned books.'

Besides the fun of finding names, Beezus and Mrs Quimby watched for sales of baby clothes. Ramona's diapers, inherited from Beezus, had long ago been used for dust cloths, much to Ramona's relief. She did not like to be reminded that she had ever worn diapers. 'On TV, babies wear disposable diapers,' she told her mother.

'Much too expensive,' said Mrs Quimby.

All the Quimbys' needs seemed too expensive. Still no letters arrived asking Mr Quimby to report for an interview. 'Maybe I should go to Saudi Arabia like Old Moneybags, work double shifts, and earn enough to pay off our bills and the mortgage, and buy a car that wouldn't eat us out of house and home in repair bills,' he said thoughtfully. This time his daughters were sure he was joking.

'Bob, please be practical,' said Mrs Quimby. 'You have no engineering experience.' Because she needed exercise, she left for her evening walk.

Ramona decided to go along because she wanted to talk privately to her mother. As they walked beneath the budding trees, she began by saying, 'When Algie comes, I won't be your baby any more.'

'That's right,' agreed her mother. 'You will be

my middle child, with a special place right in the middle of my heart. And when Algie comes, I will be home, so we can spend more time together. Daddy will have found a teaching job by then.'

Ramona was comforted. They walked in silence for a while before she asked another question that had been worrying her. 'Does Algie hurt you?'

Mrs Quimby's smile was reassuring. 'No, he doesn't hurt me, but he does kick.' She laid Ramona's hand on the bulge that was Algie, and sure enough, Ramona felt a kick so tiny it was almost a flutter. Ramona was stunned by the miracle of that little kick and was silent all the way home.

Mr Quimby began to work double shifts at weekends at the frozen-food warehouse. He looked so tired and discouraged that his daughters were frightened. Somewhere, someplace, there must be a school that wanted their father. Nothing in the world was worse than unhappy parents. Nothing. When parents were unhappy, the whole world seemed to go wrong. The weather even seemed rainier, although this was probably in Beezus's and Ramona's imaginations. Their part of Oregon was noted for rain.

Then one day a letter did arrive, offering Mr Quimby a teaching position in a one-room schoolhouse, grades one through eight, in a town no one had ever heard of, in south-eastern Oregon. Beezus ran out to the car for the road map. 'That's *miles* away,' she said when she had searched the map and found the town. 'It's miles from anyplace. It isn't even on a red line on the map. It's on a black and white line, almost in Idaho.'

'What's in that part of the country?' wondered Mrs Quimby who, along with her husband, had lived in Oregon all her life but never visited that corner of the state.

'Sagebrush, I guess.' Mr Quimby was vague. 'Juniper, lava rocks. I don't know.'

'Sheep. I learned that in school.' Beezus did not seem happy about her knowledge.

'Hooray for the Portland public schools.' Mr Quimby's hooray did not express excitement.

'Lambs are cute,' ventured Ramona, hoping to make her father feel better about his offer.

'But our house,' said Mrs Quimby, 'and a new baby.' No one had thought that the family might have to move.

'And Picky-picky's grave.' Ramona assumed her most sorrowful expression. 'We would have to leave his little grave.'

'If I were single,' Mr Quimby seemed to be thinking out loud, 'I might enjoy teaching in a one-room schoolhouse for a year or two.'

But you've got us, thought Ramona, and I don't want to leave Howie and my friends at school and Aunt Bea and all our nice neighbours.

'It sounds like Laura Ingalls Wilder,' said Beezus, 'only with sheep.'

'Bob—' Mrs Quimby hesitated. 'If you want to take the job, we could rent our house. A small town might be an interesting experience for the girls until you found a job in the city.'

Strangers in their house, some bratty child in her room, marking up her walls with crayons. Please, Daddy, thought Ramona with clenched fists, please, please say no.

Mr Quimby sat tapping the end of a ballpoint pen against his teeth. His family waited, each thinking of the changes that might be made in her life. 'No freeways,' he said, as if he were still thinking out loud. 'Blue skies, wide open spaces.'

'We have blue skies here,' said Ramona. 'Except when it rains.'

'No big library,' said Beezus. 'Maybe no library at all.'

Mrs Quimby kissed her husband on the forehead. 'Why don't we think it over a few days? Now that you've had one offer, another might come along.'

'Good idea,' announced Mr Quimby, 'but I need a steady income, and soon.' He patted the bulge that was Algie.

'Daddy,' ventured Ramona, 'if you don't teach in that school, promise you won't leave us and go to that Arabian Nights place. Please.'

'Not with Algie on the way.' Mr Quimby hugged Ramona. 'Anyway, I understand that camels spit.'

'Just like Howie's Uncle Hobart used to do,' said Ramona.

Somehow the whole family felt better knowing that one school wanted Mr Quimby, even if he was not sure he wanted the school.

6

A SURPRISE, SORT OF

Howie, who was beginning to wish his Uncle Hobart would go back to Saudi Arabia so he could sleep in his own room again, brought his bicycle and unicycle over to the Quimbys' every day after school. Beezus never again objected to Ramona's riding around the block.

Ramona thought how lonely she would be without Howie if she had to go and live in the land of sheep. 'Maybe we will move away to south-eastern Oregon,' she confided.

'Hey, that would be neat,' said Howie. 'They have wild horses down there. Maybe you could send me one.'

Ramona was offended. Howie wouldn't even miss her. 'I wouldn't send you one even if I could catch it,' she informed him.

Howie understood. 'I didn't mean I wouldn't miss you,' he said. 'I only meant if you have to leave and if catching a horse would be easy.'

Since no more offers of teaching positions arrived, no matter how often the family looked in the mailbox, Ramona saw that moving from Klickitat Street was a very real possibility.

One afternoon before Howie arrived, the telephone rang. Ramona beat Beezus to answering it.

'Ramona?' It was Willa Jean.

'Willa Jean!' Ramona was astonished. 'I didn't know you knew how to dial.'

'Uncle Hobart showed me,' explained Willa Jean. 'Ramona, come back and play with me. Please. It's lonesome here with Grandma.'

Ramona felt sad and guilty. 'I'm sorry, Willa Jean, I can't. Maybe your Uncle Hobart will play with you.'

'He's not around much,' said Willa Jean. 'He has a girlfriend, and anyway, he's a grown-up.'

'I know,' said Ramona, meaning she knew he was a grown-up, not that he had a girlfriend.

'Goodbye.' Willa Jean, who had nothing more to say, hung up.

Ramona sighed. She remembered what it was like to be the littlest child in the neighbourhood. She remembered all too well the days back in kindergarten when she was known as Ramona the Pest. Maybe she could ask Howie to bring Willa Jean over to play sometime when her mother stopped working. Nursery school had done Willa Jean a world of good, as all the grown-ups except

Mrs Kemp said. Mrs Kemp thought Willa Jean was perfect to begin with.

On the bus the next morning, Ramona sat beside Howie. 'Willa Jean says your Uncle Hobart has a girlfriend.'

'Yeah.' Howie wasn't much interested. 'Some teacher.'

A terrible suspicion crossed Ramona's mind. 'What teacher?' she asked.

'I don't know,' said Howie. 'He acts like it's a big secret. Maybe she has two heads or something.'

Ramona was silent all the way to school. She had that sinking feeling she always felt when she rode down in an elevator. She knew—she just *knew*—that Howie's uncle was seeing her aunt. She didn't know why she knew, but she knew.

After school, Ramona confided her fears to her sister, who said, 'Oh, I don't think that could be—Aunt Beatrice and Uncle Hobart.' She spoke so doubtfully that Ramona knew Beezus thought she might be right.

'Maybe that's what the big secret is. Mom doesn't want us to know because we don't like Uncle Hobart. She thinks we might say something to Aunt Beatrice.'

'Oh well,' said Ramona, 'he'll have to go back to Saudi Arabia sometime. Then we'll be rid of him.'

'I wonder what happened to Michael,' Beezus thought aloud.

Then one Sunday Mrs Quimby told the girls to set two extra places at the table for dinner.

'Who's coming?' asked Ramona.

'Your Aunt Bea and a friend.' Mrs Quimby was smiling.

'What friend?' demanded both girls.

'Oh, just a friend,' answered their maddening mother.

'A man?' asked Beezus.

'Girls, I really don't have time to play guessing games.' Mrs Quimby turned her attention to something on the stove.

'It's a man.' Ramona was positive. 'It's Howie's uncle.'

Mrs Quimby looked startled. 'How did you know?'

'Oh, a little bird told me.' Ramona tried to sound as annoying as any grown-up.

Beezus was indignant. 'You mean Aunt Bea is bringing that awful man *here*? How did she meet him?'

'He remembered her from high school and asked Howie's mother about her. She called to ask if I thought my sister remembered him, and I said she did, so he phoned her, and now they're coming to dinner.'

So that was what the mysterious telephone calls were all about, thought Ramona, but she said, 'Well, he better not spit around here.'

'You behave yourself,' said Mrs Quimby, and meant it.

Ramona made sure she answered the doorbell when the guests arrived. There they stood—Aunt Bea and Uncle Hobart.

'Good evening, Ramona.' Uncle Hobart, who had grown a neat beard and was wearing a jacket and tie, spoke to Ramona as if they were the same age.

Ramona was blunt. 'Mr Kemp, how come you're still here?' Nobody would catch her calling him Uncle Hobart even though, because of Howie, this was the way she thought of him.

'Ramona!' Mrs Quimby's voice was a warning. 'Come on in,' she said to the couple. 'Don't pay any attention to Ramona.'

Aunt Bea laughed and said to Ramona, 'Hobart and I have renewed our high school friendship.'

'Does he still spit?' Ramona asked under her breath, hoping her mother wouldn't hear.

'Not on the carpet,' answered Uncle Hobart under his breath.

Mrs Quimby had heard. 'Ramona, do you want to go to your room?'

'No.' Ramona sulked. Aunt Bea would be

sorry if the family moved off to the land of sheep. Where would she go for Thanksgiving and Christmas? Her imagination spun a sad picture of Aunt Bea alone in her apartment, eating a frozen chicken pie.

When dinner was served, Ramona was seated across from Uncle Hobart. While the adults talked and laughed, she stared at her plate until a lull came in the conversation, when she asked as politely as she could under the circumstances, 'Mr Kemp, I expect you'll be going back to Saudi Arabia soon.'

He smiled a very nice smile. 'What's the matter, Ramona? Are you trying to get rid of me?'

Ramona looked down at her plate.

'As a matter of fact, I'm not going to Saudi Arabia at all,' Uncle Hobart informed Ramona. 'I'm going to Alaska.'

At least he was going someplace.

'That's why I grew a beard,' he explained. 'Alaska is cold in winter and full of mosquitoes in summer.'

'Oh,' said Ramona.

'Of course, women can't grow beards, so they scratch a lot in summer,' said Uncle Hobart.

Ramona refused to laugh.

When dessert had been eaten by everyone except Mrs Quimby, who was careful about calories, and the adults were drinking coffee, Ramona was about to ask to be excused when Uncle Hobart spoke directly to her. 'Ramona,' he said, 'how would you like to have me for an uncle?'

Ramona felt her face grow red. She was surprised and puzzled by his question. She wanted to say, No, thank you. Of course, grown-ups would think her rude, so she said, 'You're already Howie and Willa Jean's uncle.'

'I would like to have a couple of ready-made nieces,' said Uncle Hobart.

Ramona had not caught on. 'But how could you be our uncle?' she asked.

'Nothing to it,' said Uncle Hobart. 'All I have to do is marry your Aunt Beatrice.'

Ramona sank back in her chair and thought, How dumb can I get? Aunt Bea was trying to hide her laughter, which did not make Ramona feel any better.

'You mean—' began Beezus.

Aunt Bea burst out laughing. 'Hobart and I are getting married in two weeks, before we leave for Alaska. There is oil in Alaska, too, you know.'

Ramona frowned at Uncle Hobart. Why didn't he come right out and say he and Aunt Bea were going to marry? Her parents were smiling. They already knew and hadn't said a word. Traitors!

Ramona felt as if her world were falling apart—Aunt Bea in Alaska, the Quimbys among strangers, sagebrush, and sheep.

'But, Aunt Bea, what will you do in Alaska?' asked Beezus.

'Fish through the ice,' said Uncle Hobart. 'Build us an igloo.'

'Don't listen to him,' said Aunt Bea. 'I plan to teach. I sent off an application and received a telegram accepting me.'

Suddenly Ramona saw the solution to all her family's problems. 'Aunt Bea,' she said, bursting with excitement. 'If you aren't going to teach in Portland, Daddy can have your job.'

Sudden silence at the table. 'I'm afraid not,' said Aunt Bea gently. 'I'm not going to be replaced. My school is not expecting as many pupils next fall and is not hiring any teachers.'

'Oh,' said Ramona. There was nothing more to say. Her happy plan had come to nothing.

The silence was broken by Beezus. 'Oh, Aunt Bea!' She was ecstatic. 'A wedding!'

'We aren't planning a wedding,' said Aunt Bea. 'There isn't time. We're going to be married at the City Hall.'

'Bea, you can't.' Mrs Quimby was distressed. 'A wedding should be a happy occasion, a gift from the bride's family.'

'But there isn't time for a real wedding,' insisted Aunt Bea. 'Dad can't plan a wedding from his mobile home in Southern California. With a baby due so soon, you can't possibly take on a wedding.'

'Aunt Bea,' wailed Beezus. 'There must be a way. It isn't fair for Mom to have had a wedding and you to get married at City Hall without any bridesmaids or anything.'

Mrs Quimby's voice was gentle. 'Don't forget— your Grandma Day was living when I was married. She arranged it all.'

'Don't men count in this event?' asked Uncle Hobart. 'I don't like the idea of a City Hall wedding myself. There's no reason why we can't throw together some kind of wedding.'

Pooh to you, thought Ramona with a scowl. You'd just mess things up.

'But weddings aren't that simple.' Mrs Quimby pushed her chair back from the table to rest her arms on the bulge that was Algie. 'You can't throw together a wedding.'

'Nonsense,' said Uncle Hobart. 'Women just make them complicated. Watch me take charge.'

'You could wear mother's wedding dress,' Beezus suggested to her aunt. She and Ramona had often lifted their mother's wedding dress from its tissue-paper-lined box to admire. Beezus always held it up and tried on the veil in front of the mirror.

'There you are,' said Uncle Hobart. 'The wedding dress is taken care of.'

'But you won't catch me being matron of honour, not in my shape,' said Mrs Quimby.

'Beezus and Ramona can be bridesmaids, and I won't have a matron of honour.' Aunt Beatrice was beginning to like the new plan.

Ramona perked up at the thought of being a bridesmaid. A wedding might be interesting after all.

'Willa Jean can be a flower girl.' Aunt Bea stopped and frowned. 'Oh, what am I thinking about? I have to write out performance reports for twenty-nine third-graders, we both have to buy cold weather clothes for Alaskan winters, I have to sell my car, Hobart has to trade in the van for a four-wheel-drive truck, and—'

'You have a great new ski outfit,' interrupted Uncle Hobart, who probably did not know that a man named Michael had been the reason for the ski clothes. Whatever happened to Michael? Only Aunt Bea knew.

Uncle Hobart went on. 'And all you have to write on those twenty-nine performance reports is, "You have a great kid who will turn out OK." That's what parents want to hear, and most of the time it's true.'

Ramona looked at Uncle Hobart with real respect. He understood about performance reports. Perhaps he would not make such a bad uncle after all.

Mr Quimby, who had been quiet, spoke up. 'I'll donate my frozen-food warehouse socks to cut down on shopping. As soon as school is out, I am leaving the frozen-food warehouse for ever. The temperature in there is about the same as Alaska in winter, and you are welcome to my socks. If the market hadn't furnished the rest of my cold-weather gear, I'd give that to you, too.'

This news produced silence, broken by Ramona. 'Daddy, did you hear from another school that wants you to teach?'

'No, baby, I didn't,' he confessed, 'but I was offered a job managing one of the Shop-rite markets. The pay and fringe benefits are good. I accepted, and start as soon as school is out.'

'Daddy!' cried Beezus. 'You mean you're going back to that market and won't teach art after all? But you don't like working in the market.'

'We can't always do what we want in life,' answered her father, 'so we do the best we can.'

'That's right,' said Mrs Quimby. 'We do the best we can.'

'It's not the end of the world, Beezus. Being

manager is better than being a checker and much better than filling orders in the frozen-food warehouse.' Mr Quimby's smile could not hide the discouraged look in his eyes. 'Now let's get on with plans for the wedding.'

Relief flowed through Ramona. No strange child would mark her walls with crayons. She would not have to leave Howie, her school, her friends. Only Aunt Bea would be missing.

Uncle Hobart broke the silence that followed Mr Quimby's news by saying, 'Yes, about our wedding. Women get all worked up and exhausted when there's a wedding in the family, but not this time. You invite your friends by telephone, and I'll take care of the rest. There's nothing to it.'

The adult sisters looked at one another with amused 'he'll-see' smiles. 'Great!' said Aunt Bea. 'I'll be perfectly happy with any wedding you plan. Now all I have to do is persuade Dad to leave his shuffleboard, bingo, and sunshine and come up from Southern California to give me away.' The family had seen little of Grandpa Day since he had retired and moved away from Oregon's rainy winters.

'He'll come,' said Ramona, who loved her grandfather. 'He's got to come.'

'First thing Saturday morning,' said Uncle Hobart, 'I'll gather up you girls, along with Willa

Jean, and we'll go shopping for your dresses while Bea dashes off those progress reports.'

'It sounds like the fastest wedding in the West,' said Mr Quimby.

Ramona and her sister exchanged a look that said each was wondering what shopping with a bachelor petroleum engineer would be like.

7

THE CHAIN OF COMMAND

Saturday morning, Willa Jean and a very cross-looking Howie arrived with Uncle Hobart in his van to collect Beezus and Ramona to go shopping for wedding clothes.

'How come you're going shopping with us?' Ramona demanded of Howie.

Howie did not answer Ramona, but instead complained to his uncle, 'I've said a million times I don't want to be a ring bearer. I don't care what Grandma says. I'm too big. That stuff is for little kids. Carrying a ring on a pillow is dumb. Besides, it will fall off.'

'I'm on your side, kid,' said Uncle Hobart. 'But let's humour your grandmother. She's busy making a fancy pillow for the ring, and says she will fasten the ring in place with a couple of loose stitches. And don't blame me if my favourite nephew's a big kid instead of a little kid.'

'I'm not your favourite nephew,' said Howie. 'I'm your only nephew.'

'You may have competition when Algie arrives,' said Uncle Hobart. 'Now, Beezus, where do we go for girl things?'

'Well . . . there's a bridal shop in the mall of the shopping centre.' Beezus was shy about directing Uncle Hobart. 'But I'm not sure they have our sizes.'

'Heigh ho, off we go!' Uncle Hobart backed his van out of the driveway and headed for the shopping centre, where they found the parking lot crowded. 'Now what we need is a chain of command,' said Uncle Hobart when he had finally found a parking space. 'I'll keep an eye on Beezus, who keeps an eye on Howie, who keeps an eye on Ramona, who watches out for Willa Jean. Each makes sure that the next person behaves and doesn't get lost.'

'I don't need Beezus to keep an eye on me,' grumbled Howie. 'And Beezus always behaves.' Willa Jean slipped her fingers into Ramona's hand, an act that Ramona found touching and made her feel protective, even though the little girl's fingers were sticky. The chain of command proceeded into the mall, where they found the bridal shop filled with pale, floating dresses, wedding veils, and thin, floppy hats.

'Oh—' breathed Beezus.

'Yuck,' said Howie.

The three-way mirror tempted Ramona to look at herself, but she resisted. She must set a good example for Willa Jean. Howie flopped down on a couch and scowled at his feet. The saleswoman looked as if she wished they would all go away.

'Bridesmaid dresses for two, and one flower-girl dress.' Uncle Hobart sounded as casual as if he were ordering hamburgers.

Dresses were produced. Beezus and Ramona were bashful about spending so much of Uncle Hobart's money and were uncertain about choosing. Willa Jean was not. 'I like that one,' she said, pointing to a ruffled pink dress in her size.

'OK, girls?' asked Uncle Hobart. The sisters, who would have preferred yellow, nodded. The correct sizes for Beezus and Ramona, it turned out, would have to be ordered from other outlets in the chain of bridal shops. Yes, they would arrive in time for the wedding. The saleswoman promised. While Uncle Hobart paid for all three dresses, Ramona whispered to Willa Jean to sit beside Howie. Willa Jean actually minded.

Ramona slipped over for a glimpse of herself in the three-way mirror, which reflected her back and forth from every angle. She began to dance, to watch all the Ramonas. Obediently, they imitated her, dancing on and on into the distance, tinier and tinier until they could no longer be seen. For ever me, thought Ramona. I go on for ever.

'Now, what about our ring bearer?' Uncle Hobart looked at Howie, who slid down on the couch and scowled.

Ramona was aware that the saleswoman eyed Howie as if he did not belong on her couch. She danced on, twirling to make the myriad Ramonas twirl.

'To dress properly,' said the saleswoman, 'a boy in a wedding party should wear short pants, knee socks, a white shirt, and a jacket; but ring bearers are usually little boys. Four- or five-year-olds.'

'See, what did I tell you?' Howie said to his uncle.

Uncle Hobart ignored his nephew. 'Come, Beezus,' he said, holding the box with Willa Jean's dress under his arm. As the next link she said, 'Come on, Howie,' who said. 'Come on, Ramona,' who said, 'Come on, Willa Jean. Thank you for being such a good girl.' Willa Jean beamed. The saleswoman looked happy to see them go.

Uncle Hobart led his chain of command to a boys' shop where, much against Howie's wishes, he bought short navy blue pants, a white shirt, and a pale blue jacket. 'Everybody will make fun of me,' said Howie. The salesman said the shop did not carry knee socks for boys.

Beezus felt responsible for Howie. 'Girls' shops have knee socks,' she suggested.

'You shut up,' said Howie.

Uncle Hobart's good nature was not disturbed. 'Shut up yourself,' was his cheerful order as he led his troops into a girls' shop, where he bought a pair of navy blue knee socks for Howie. 'Now, Beezus, what else do we need for a wedding?'

'Flowers,' was the answer.

On the way to the florist, the shoppers came to a ski goods store that was having a sale. 'Just what your aunt and I need,' said Uncle Hobart, leading the way among the racks of ski clothing, where he quickly bought quilted down jackets for himself and his bride, waterproof pants, fur-lined gloves, heavy socks, and boots, all great bargains. Fortunately, Beezus knew her aunt's sizes.

'You don't suppose he would wear any of this stuff at the wedding, do you?' Ramona whispered to Beezus as she pulled a man-sized jacket off Willa Jean.

'Who knows?' said Beezus. There was no telling what Uncle Hobart might do.

The troops carried all the bags and boxes across the hot parking lot to the van. On the way back to the mall, Willa Jean, who spotted the ice-cream store that sold fifty-two flavours, told her uncle she needed an ice-cream cone.

Uncle Hobart agreed that ice-cream cones were needed by all.

Inside the busy shop, customers had to take numbers and wait turns. Ramona, responsible for Willa Jean, who could not read, was faced with the embarrassing task of reading aloud the list of fifty-two flavours while all the customers listened. 'Strawberry, German chocolate, vanilla, ginger-peachy, red-white-and-blueberry, black walnut, Mississippi mud, green bubble gum, baseball nut.' Grimly, Ramona read on, skipping pistachio because she wasn't sure how to pronounce it, and stumbling over nectarine and macadamia nut. 'Avocado (avocado ice cream?), fudge brownie—' She thought Uncle Hobart's number would never come, but of course it did.

'Five double scoops of chocolate mandarin-orange dipped in nuts,' was Uncle Hobart's order.

Double scoops with nuts. Beezus and Ramona were impressed.

As ice-cream cones were handed around and the group walked out into the sunbaked parking lot, Uncle Hobart said, 'In the heat and dust of Saudi Arabia, I lay on my bunk at night listening to the wolves howl and longing for chocolate mandarin-orange double-scoop ice-cream cones dipped in nuts.'

Ramona licked a drip of ice cream. 'I thought

you said you dreamed of your mother's apple pie.'

'That too,' said Uncle Hobart. 'A man can have more than one dream in life.'

'They don't have wolves in Saudi Arabia,' said Howie.

'OK, listening to camels howl.' Uncle Hobart led the way to a flower shop in the mall, where they were told they could not enter with ice-cream cones. This did not bother Uncle Hobart, who pulled a list from his pocket, stood in the doorway, and ordered one bouquet of white flowers for the bride, three wreaths of little flowers for girls—here he pointed to the girls—and two bridesmaids' bouquets, not too big. 'What colour?' he asked Beezus, and took a big bite of ice cream.

'Mostly pink, to go with our dresses,' said Beezus, daintily nibbling into her ice cream instead of licking.

'Pink,' ordered Uncle Hobart, 'and a little bunch of flowers for the flower girl. We can't have a flower girl without flowers, can we, Willa Jean?' Willa Jean was too busy trying to keep ahead of her melting ice cream to answer. 'And whatever one groom, one best man, and two ushers wear in their buttonholes. Oh, yes, and a flower for my ring bearer here.'

'Aw, Uncle Hobart,' grumbled Howie as his uncle

handed over a credit card to the astonished florist and gave the time the flowers were to be delivered to the Quimbys' address. Willa Jean's flowers and the men's flowers were to go to the Kemps'.

'Come on, troops, let's go home,' said Uncle Hobart. 'Like I told you. There's nothing to planning a wedding.'

Ramona hoped the dresses really would arrive in time as she licked the ice cream running down her arm. She knew Beezus was wishing the same thing.

'Uncle Hobart, I don't think camels howl,' said Howie. 'I think they sort of snort.' Anyone could see Howie had no interest in the wedding.

Beezus, who had managed to eat her cone neatly, asked, 'What about the church and minister?' She could not entirely trust Howie's uncle to remember.

Uncle Hobart crunched the last bite of his cone. 'All taken care of, along with the wedding ring and the caterer, who will supply the food. But thanks for keeping track. I might forget something.'

He probably will, thought Ramona, and wished she had a three-way mirror in her room at home so that when her bridesmaid dress was delivered, she could watch herself twirling for ever.

8

THE FAMILIES GET TOGETHER

Life at the Quimby home soon became busy
and confused. Mr Quimby now went to work
regularly every morning, but Aunt Bea, to save
paying a whole month's rent on an apartment she
would leave before the end of the month, had
moved in with the Quimbys. She stored most of
her belongings in the Quimbys' basement, and
the rest she piled in Ramona's room to be packed
for shipment to Alaska.

Ramona slept on the floor in Beezus's room in the
sleeping bag Beezus had taken to camp one summer.
The telephone rang constantly—neighbours offering
to help with the wedding, people enquiring about
Aunt Bea's little sports car that she had advertised
for sale, friends returning calls to say yes, they would
be delighted to attend the wedding.

Teachers at Aunt Bea's school gave her a bridal
shower. Most of the gifts were flat and easy to
pack—bath towels, cheese boards, place mats.
Aunt Bea's class gave her a coffee maker. Boxes
piled up in Ramona's room.

Willa Jean's old bassinette was moved into the Quimbys' house and placed in the parents' bedroom. Neighbours gave Mrs Quimby a baby shower, which meant more boxes. Beezus and Ramona hoped Algie would stay where he belonged until after the wedding. Their mother seemed to grow larger every day—or perhaps the maternity clothes she was wearing made her look bigger than she really was.

Wedding presents, mostly sets of bath towels, began to arrive. Ramona had never seen such beautiful towels—big, thick, fluffy, and in soft, pretty colours. She stroked them, laid her cheek against them, traced her finger along the designs. They were truly towels to marry for. The Quimbys' thin, faded towels had frayed edges.

The afternoon before the wedding rehearsal, Grandpa Day was arriving by plane so he could practise giving the bride away. Aunt Bea, whose car had been sold, borrowed Uncle Hobart's van, and with her nieces, drove to the airport to meet her father. Grandpa Day seemed older and thinner than the girls had remembered. He hugged his granddaughters, said they had grown, and announced he wanted to stay in a motel— no couch in a living room for him with a bunch of women fussing about a wedding. 'At my age, I need a little peace and quiet,' he informed his daughters. Leaving his carryon bag at the nearest motel, Aunt Bea drove her father to the Quimbys', where more boxes had arrived, none of them containing the bridesmaid dresses. 'You can count on it,' said Grandpa Day. 'Something always goes wrong when there's a wedding.' The sisters exchanged looks of anguish.

Uncle Hobart walked over to the Quimbys' to see the newest wedding presents—loot, he called them—and to pick up his van, which he was about to trade in for a four-wheel-drive truck for Alaska. A snowplough could be attached to the front.

Mrs Quimby, looking tired and very big around the middle, was preparing a huge tossed salad because the two families were getting together before the rehearsal. Beezus was buttering stacks of French bread. Mr Quimby arrived home late from work because a checker at the market had caught a shoplifter; the police had to be called, and questions answered. Even Aunt Bea looked tired.

When Uncle Hobart returned, desperate Beezus whispered to him that the bridesmaid dresses had not been delivered. 'We'll see about that,' he said and telephoned the shop, which promised the dresses first thing in the morning. 'This evening. You will deliver those dresses this evening,' ordered Uncle Hobart, as if he were speaking to a crew in the oil fields.

The Kemps arrived with two casseroles and dessert. Because the dining room was too small to seat so many people, the food was set out on the dining room table. Everyone picked up a plate and helped himself. Ramona was happy that she was no longer responsible for Willa Jean, who had trouble serving herself and was helped by her grandmother.

When everyone was seated in the living room enjoying chicken with noodles, a casserole of mixed vegetables, and salad, Aunt Bea, sitting on the floor beside Uncle Hobart, asked, 'What kind of flowers did you order for the church and reception hall?'

Uncle Hobart dropped his fork and slapped his forehead with his palm. 'Flowers for the church! I completely forgot.'

'Hobart, you didn't! I had them on the list.' Aunt Bea was not sure he meant what he said. Her groom was a great kidder.

'I did,' confessed Uncle Hobart. 'We were all so busy eating ice-cream cones. I'll call the florist the first thing in the morning.'

'Are you crazy?' cried Aunt Bea. 'The day of the wedding, when florists are swamped with June weddings? Where would they find more flowers, especially so soon after the Rose Festival?' Worn out from progress reports, moving, and excitement, she turned to her fiancé and said, 'I thought you said there was nothing to planning a wedding. Well, that just shows how wrong you can be.'

'If I can be so wrong, why are you marrying me?' demanded Uncle Hobart. He looked tense, which was unusual for him.

Both families tried to act as if they were not listening—except, of course, the older children, who were fascinated. Willa Jean looked as if she might cry.

'That's a good question,' said Aunt Bea.

'That's a good question! That's a good question! All the years I was in school, teachers were always telling me I had asked a good question. Half the time they didn't even answer. They just asked me what I thought the answer should be, or asked some other kid to answer. Now you're telling me I asked a good question. You sound just like a teacher.'

'I am a teacher.' Aunt Bea's voice was cold.

Beezus and Ramona exchanged a 'there-goes-the-wedding' look. Now the bridesmaid dresses no longer mattered. Howie looked hopeful, as if he thought he might escape carrying that ring on the pillow after all.

Uncle Hobart raised his voice. 'Just once I would like to hear a teacher answer a question. Why are you marrying me—if you still plan to marry me?'

Aunt Bea began by sounding like a teacher. 'Hobart has asked a good question,' she said with a pleasant smile before she turned and shouted, 'Because I love you, you cootie!' She then burst into tears.

Ramona was stunned. Third- and fourth-graders called people cooties. Grown-ups did not.

Mr Quimby put his arms around his wife, who looked as if she wished everyone would go away. 'Feeling OK?' he whispered.

'I feel great.' Mrs Quimby's voice was unusually sharp. 'Why shouldn't I feel OK when I'm having a baby? It's all perfectly natural. Stop fussing.' Mr Quimby looked hurt.

Uncle Hobart calmed down and looked ashamed. Aunt Bea wiped her eyes on the corner of one of her new bath towels.

'Why can't we just pick some flowers?' asked Ramona.

'What flowers?' demanded Beezus. 'Those buggy pansies in the backyard?'

'Now, now,' said Grandpa Day. 'Just a case of pre-wedding jitters. Relax, everybody. I lived in this neighbourhood for forty years, and I know how the women enjoy a challenge. Make a few phone calls, and you will have all the flowers you need.'

Grandpa Day was right. Two neighbours had

peonies in bloom, bushels of them; several had bumper crops of roses they would be happy to share. Another had plenty of laurel, which made a nice background and needed pruning anyway.

When the matter of the flowers was settled. Aunt Bea said with a wicked smile, 'I forgot something, too. I forgot to tell you that I had invited all my third-graders. They wanted so much to come.'

Oh, no, thought Ramona. Third-graders would gobble up all the food at the wedding reception and run around bumping into people and spilling things. Still, she looked forward to seeing the class she had heard so much about from Aunt Bea.

'Great!' said Uncle Hobart. 'I'll order champagne for twenty-nine more guests.'

Ramona was horrified. Twenty-nine third-graders sloshing around with champagne.

'Hobart!' Mrs Kemp spoke severely to her youngest son. 'Settle down and do be sensible. You can't serve champagne to children. Order some punch for them.'

'Sure, Mom.' Uncle Hobart glanced at his watch. 'Speaking of forgetting, let's not forget the rehearsal.'

The members of the wedding party whisked their dishes into the kitchen—they would eat Mrs Kemp's homemade cheesecake later—then they climbed into the truck and the Kemps' car to go to the church. Ramona, Beezus, and Howie squeezed into the truck with Uncle Hobart and his bride. This was their only chance to ride in it.

'Swell, just swell,' muttered Howie. 'Twenty-nine kids laughing at me in girls' socks carrying a stupid little pillow.'

'The dresses still haven't come,' worried Beezus.

Uncle Hobart was reassuring. 'Don't worry. You girls would look pretty even if you had to walk down the aisle in gym suits.'

As the truck pulled away from the kerb, a car pulled up. A man jumped out with a big box and ran up the Quimbys' driveway. Ramona glimpsed the word BRIDAL on the box. 'Our dresses!' she shrieked.

'Whew, what a relief,' said Beezus. 'Now, if they will just fit.'

'Uncle Hobart,' said Howie, 'you never did say what kind of noise a camel makes.' Ramona wished Howie would forget about camels and pay attention to the wedding.

Uncle Hobart whinnied like a horse. 'How's that?'

'I'm not sure it's right,' said Howie.

Ramona, who was not worried about the fit of her dress—safety pins could take care of that—or the sound of camels, wondered if twenty-nine third-graders, now promoted to the fourth-grade, would arrive at the wedding with banana stickers on their foreheads and if Algie would stay where he belonged until it was all over. July was coming closer every day.

9

Ramona Saves The Day

The day of the wedding!

The bridesmaids' dresses were too long. 'Pins!' cried Aunt Bea. 'Get me some pins!' Algie made kneeling on the floor too difficult for Mrs Quimby.

While Aunt Bea pinned up the hems, two for each because the dresses came with matching slips, the girls tried to stand very still, but how could they? The florist had delivered flowers that they couldn't wait to see. The girls fidgeted. 'Beezus, just baste up the hems,' said Aunt Bea when she had pushed the last pin in place. 'They'll hold until after the wedding.' She hurried off to press the wedding dress.

With flushed cheeks, Beezus basted as fast as she could. Ramona did not trust her sister's stitches and reinforced her hem with Scotch tape.

Everyone's hair had to be washed; everyone had to take a shower. By Ramona's turn for a shower, all the hot water had been used. Why, oh why, did the youngest always have to be last?

Mr Quimby, who was taking the afternoon off from the market, was delayed. Would he never come? But he did come, and Ramona was sure she heard him say a bad word when he turned on the shower.

Where was Grandpa Day? 'Bob, weren't you supposed to pick up Dad?' Mrs Quimby called through the bathroom door.

'He said he wasn't ready and not to worry. He would get here on his own,' answered Mr Quimby between splutters. The family busied itself doing nothing—picking up wedding presents, putting them down, fussing with their hair, making sandwiches no one felt like eating.

Time to dress! Aunt Bea disappeared into Ramona's room while the girls dressed in Beezus's room. Ramona pulled on white socks while Beezus tugged at panty hose. Pink slips slid over their heads, then the dresses, the prettiest they had ever owned. They shoved their feet into their best white slippers. Beezus brushed her shining hair and Ramona's, too.

Feeling like princesses, the girls went to show off to their mother, who said they looked lovely. Except for Algie, the girls had never seen their mother look so beautiful. She was wearing a soft, airy dress borrowed from a neighbour who had already had a baby. That dress had been passed around among the women of Klickitat Street for several years. 'A neighbourhood needs only one dress-up maternity dress,' explained Mrs Quimby.

And then Aunt Bea appeared in her sister's wedding dress and veil. 'Oh, Aunt Bea,' sighed Beezus, 'you're beautiful.' Ramona was too stunned to speak.

Mrs Quimby kissed her sister and said, 'I hope that dress will be as lucky for you as it has been for me.'

Ramona began to have an uneasy feeling that she had outgrown her white slippers, which she had not worn for at least a year. She would have died rather than complain.

'Where on earth is Dad?' the anxious bride wanted to know. 'I don't want to keep Hobart waiting at the church.'

Yes, where was Grandpa Day? Everyone worried, everyone fussed. His motel was called. No, his room did not answer. More worrying until Ramona, posted at the window, screamed, 'Look!' There was Grandpa Day, arriving in a long black limousine driven by a real chauffeur wearing a real chauffeur's cap, just like chauffeurs on television.

'Why, Dad,' cried Aunt Bea. 'You didn't have to rent—'

'Say no more,' said Grandpa Day. 'I want to give my youngest daughter away in style.'

'Wow!' exclaimed Ramona, forgetting her shoes. 'And we get to ride in it!' Wait till Aunt Bea's third—now fourth—graders saw this.

Mrs Quimby lifted wreaths of tiny pink roses from the florist's box, anchored them firmly to her daughters' hair with bobby pins before she handed them their nosegays. Both girls inhaled the fragrance of their flowers. 'Ah-h.'

Aunt Bea lifted out her bouquet of white blossoms. 'Come along,' ordered Grandpa Day. 'The groom might get tired of waiting and leave.' The family climbed into the limousine, Mr Quimby sitting with the chauffeur and Beezus and Ramona sitting on fold-down seats facing the bride, their mother, and their grandfather. Under her long dress, Ramona slipped her feet out of her pinching slippers so she could enjoy every second of the ride.

'Now remember, girls,' said Mrs Quimby, 'after you take your places at the front of the church, *stand still.*'

As the limousine glided up to the church, Aunt Bea's class, arriving in car pools, was properly awed. They climbed quietly out of their ordinary cars and walked in pairs into the church. Most of the boys were wearing stiff new jeans and clean shirts. A couple wore suits. The girls were dressed in their best. Ramona could see that many heads of hair had been washed in Portland that morning and that Aunt Bea had instructed her class in wedding behaviour. Then she discovered she had to squeeze hard to get her feet back into her shoes.

The wedding party entered a small room behind the church reception room, where all the Kemps except Uncle Hobart and Howie's father, who was the best man, were waiting. Ramona was surprised to see how pretty Willa Jean looked with the wreath of roses resting on her fair curls. Howie leaned against the wall in his short pants and knee socks. Except for his grumpy expression, Ramona thought he actually looked handsome, until he began to sing, very, very softly:

> 'Here comes the bride,
> Fair, fat, and wide.
> Here comes the groom,
> Skinny as a broom.
> Here comes the usher,
> The old toilet-flusher.'

'Howie, you shut up!' ordered Ramona with all the ferocity she could summon in a whisper. What if the bride heard? The bride did hear, and laughed. She knew what to expect from boys Howie's age. Mrs Kemp handed her grandson a small lace pillow with the wedding ring fastened in place with basting stitches.

'It will probably fall off,' he predicted.

'No, it won't,' said his grandmother. 'I've made sure of that.'

'Beezus, my feet are killing me,' whispered Ramona with tears in her eyes. 'My shoes are way too short.'

'So are mine,' agreed Beezus. 'I'll never make it down the aisle.'

Grandmother Kemp was lining up the wedding party in the order in which they were to enter the church. 'Once you reach your place at the front of the church, *don't move*,' she ordered.

'Quick,' whispered Beezus to Ramona. 'Give me your shoes.' Astonished, Ramona obeyed. As the wedding party proceeded through the reception room to the vestibule of the church, Beezus dropped the two pairs of slippers into a large bouquet of rhododendron blossoms. When the organ burst forth with the processional, the girls stiffled their giggles. Uncle Hobart's friends, the bearded ushers splendid in their rented clothes, grinned at the girls and, after escorting Howie's mother and grandmother and Mrs Quimby to the front pew, returned to walk slowly down the aisle together.

Ramona and Beezus counted to four. With

the carpet tickling the bottoms of their feet and their nosegays quivering from nervousness, they followed, slowly and with dignity. Ramona could hear Willa Jean counting to four, and knew that she was following, and behind her, four counts later, Howie. Uncle Hobart and Howie's father, surprisingly handsome, were waiting with the minister at the end of what seemed like a long, long aisle.

Suddenly all the guests rose to their feet. Aunt Bea, on the arm of her father, had entered the church. Her class strained for a glimpse of their teacher.

From her place at the front of the church, Ramona could see her aunt, almost floating on the arm of Grandpa Day. Then they, too, took their places. The ceremony began. Grandpa Day gaveth this woman, as the minister called Aunt Bea, to be married and stepped back to the front pew. So much for the father of the bride.

All went well, with Ramona happily wiggling her toes inside her socks, until Howie's father tried to lift the wedding ring from the pillow. Unfortunately, Howie's grandmother, not trusting her grandson, had fastened the ring with such tight stitches it would not lift. Mr Kemp tugged. The ring remained in place. Howie clutched the pillow in a good tight grip while his father yanked.

The ring came off the pillow, slipped through his fingers, flew through the air, and disappeared.

The guests gasped. The children in the wedding party, instructed not to move, stood like statues. The wedding had come to a standstill. The men in the party began to look around for the ring. Even Aunt Bea took a step back to see if it had rolled under her skirt. The men leaned forward, searching. In a minute, they might even be on their knees, feeling around on the carpet with their hands. Ramona prayed that Aunt Bea's class would not giggle.

Then, as Aunt Bea bent over, Ramona caught a glimpse of something shiny.

The wedding ring was around the heel of the bride's sandal. How did it get there? It must have rolled under Aunt Bea's dress, and when she stepped back, she stepped into it. A rustle went through the church, the sound of restless, uneasy guests. Something must be done, and now.

What should Ramona do? She was under strict orders not to move, but she was the only one who knew where the ring had landed. She thought fast. Why should she obey Mrs Kemp, who had sewn the ring too tight and been the cause of its disappearance? In a minute someone would snicker and set off the whole congregation. Ramona could not bear to have her aunt's wedding laughed at. She decided to act, even if it meant showing her white socks. Laying her nosegay on the carpet, Ramona got down on her hands and knees, prayed her wreath wouldn't slip, crawled over to her aunt, reached under her skirt, took hold of her ankle, and when the surprised bride looked down, raised her foot and pulled the ring off her heel. Ramona then crawled backwards, picked up her nosegay, handed the ring to the best man, and took her place once more, standing like a statue with her wreath still in place. Aunt Bea flashed Ramona a smile while her lips silently formed the words 'thank you'.

Everyone in the church relaxed, the wedding proceeded as if nothing had happened. Oh, that romantic moment when the minister pronounced the couple husband and wife, Uncle Hobart kissed Aunt Bea, and the organ sounded notes of joy! The wedding party sped up the aisle and into the reception hall where, under Howie's grandmother's direction, they formed a receiving line.

Guests trickled in, kissed the bride, congratulated the groom, and told Beezus and Ramona they looked sweet, pretty, charming, and like flowers—a new experience for Ramona. Some said, 'So this is the girl who saved the day,' or 'It's a good thing you found the ring.' One said, 'You were a real little heroine.' Ramona smiled modestly. One old gentleman told her she looked 'as pretty as a speckled pup'. Ramona had never been so filled with joy.

Aunt Bea's class was shy about kissing the bride, so the bride kissed every one of them. Some said hi to Ramona; others told her they had heard about her from Miss Day, or said it was a good thing she found the ring. Some girls wistfully told her they thought her dress was pretty. Several boys said, 'How come you're not wearing shoes?' Ramona did not mind. She was so happy she felt as if she could stand in the receiving line for ever, but of course it came to an end, and when it did, Howie's grandmother actually thanked Ramona for finding the ring, smiled a real smile, and told her she looked pretty.

Waiters passed trays of tiny sandwiches, punch, and champagne. Ramona noticed each member of her aunt's class was careful to take only two sandwiches, which showed Aunt Bea had told them how to behave. No one spilled punch; nobody threw up.

Ramona helped herself to three sandwiches. As a member of the wedding party, she felt she deserved them. Besides, she was hungry. As she nibbled to make the sandwiches last, she had an idea that she whispered to Beezus. 'If we had some string, we could tie our slippers to the bumper of Uncle Hobart's truck. We can't wear them any more.'

Beezus, usually so proper, was delighted with the idea. 'There must be some string someplace,' she said.

'I'll ask Howie,' said Ramona.

Howie, who was leaning against the wall stuffing himself with what Ramona considered more than his share of sandwiches, and looking embarrassed because the girls from Aunt Bea's class stared at him with admiration, liked the idea. 'I don't carry string in these pants,' he said, 'but I bet I can find some.' He began to ask around among the boys from Aunt Bea's class, and sure enough, string was found in several pockets. When Ramona pulled the slippers from the flowers, she discovered she did not want to leave the reception. Neither did Beezus. They liked being paid compliments one after another, and Beezus had noticed a boy her age looking at her as if he wanted to talk to her. Besides, the bride was about to cut the wedding cake.

'You do it.' Ramona shoved the shoes at Howie.

'Sure,' agreed Howie, glad to escape. The donors of the string went with him and, by the time the cake was cut, returned looking pleased with themselves and ready for their share of cake.

Uncle Hobart, whom Ramona had been avoiding because she felt ashamed that she had not been nicer to him, cornered her. 'I want to thank my new niece for saving the day by finding the ring,' he said and kissed her. His beard was not as scratchy as she had expected.

'Thank you, Uncle Hobart,' she said, shy about calling him uncle for the first time. 'It's nice, sort of, having an uncle. And thank you for our dresses.'

'You're welcome. And I like having another spunky niece.' Uncle Hobart and Ramona were friends. Peace at last!

The bride threw her bouquet, aiming it, Ramona suspected, at Beezus, who caught it, which meant she would be the next bride. The newlyweds, both laughing, ran out to Uncle Hobart's truck in a shower of rice and birdseed and drove off. Two pairs of white slippers danced from the rear bumper. The wedding was over.

The Quimbys climbed into Grandpa Day's rented limousine and sank back into the rich upholstery with happy sighs. You could make teddy bears out of these seats, they are so soft and furry, thought Ramona.

'Funny about those white shoes on the back of the truck,' remarked Mr Quimby. 'They look familiar.'

The girls burst into giggles. 'They hurt,' confessed Ramona. 'They were too tight.'

Mrs Quimby, resting her arms on Algie, smiled. 'I had forgotten how long you girls had had those shoes,' she said. 'I should have thought.'

Ramona marvelled that neither of her parents said the girls should have saved Beezus's slippers for Ramona to grow into.

'I'm starved,' announced Grandpa Day. 'Giving away a bride is hard work, and that dainty little wedding food doesn't fill me up. When we get home, I'll send out for pizza.'

Pizza! thought Ramona. A limousine and a pizza! The end of a perfect day.

IO

ANOTHER BiG EVENT

After the wedding, everyone felt let down, the
way they always felt the day after Christmas, only
worse. Nothing seemed interesting after so much
excitement. Grandpa Day had flown back to his
sunshine and shuffleboard. Mr Quimby was at
work all day. Friends had gone off to camp, to the
mountains, or the beach. Howie and Willa Jean
had gone to visit their other grandmother.

'Girls, please stop moping around,' said Mrs
Quimby.

'We can't find anything to do,' said Beezus.

Ramona was silent. If she complained, her
mother would tell her to clean out her closet.

'Read a book,' said Mrs Quimby. 'Both of you,
read a book.'

'I've read all my books a million times,' said
Ramona, who usually enjoyed rereading her
favourites.

'Then go to the library.' Mrs Quimby was
beginning to sound irritable.

'It's too hot,' complained Ramona.

Mrs Quimby glanced at her watch.

'Mother, are you expecting someone?' asked Ramona. 'You keep looking at your watch.'

'I certainly am,' said her mother. 'A stranger.' With a big sigh, Mrs Quimby sank heavily to the couch, glanced at her watch again, and closed her eyes. The girls exchanged guilty looks. Their poor mother, worn out by Algie kicking her when there was so much of her to feel hot.

'Mother, are you all right?' Beezus sounded worried.

'I'm fine,' snapped Mrs Quimby, which surprised the girls into behaving.

That evening, the sisters helped their mother put together a cold supper of tuna fish salad and sliced tomatoes. While the family was eating, Mr Quimby told them that now that the 'Hawaiian Holidays' sale with bargains in fresh pineapple and papaya had come to an end, all the Shop-rite markets were preparing for 'Western Bar-b-q Week' with specials on steak, baked beans, tomato sauce, and chilli. He planned to paint bucking broncos on the front windows.

Mrs Quimby nibbled at her salad and glanced at her watch.

'And everybody will see your paintings,' said Ramona, happy that her father was now an artist as well as a market manager.

'Not quite the same as an exhibit in a museum,' said Mr Quimby, who did not sound as happy as Ramona expected.

Mrs Quimby pushed her chair further from the table and glanced at her watch. All eyes were on her.

'Shall I call the doctor?' asked Mr Quimby.

'Please,' said Mrs Quimby as she rose from the table, hugged Algie, and breathed, 'Oo-oo.'

Ramona and Beezus, excited and frightened, looked at one another. At last! The fifth Quimby would soon be here. Nothing would be the same again, ever. Mr Quimby reported that the doctor would meet them at the hospital. Without being asked, Beezus ran for the bag her mother had packed several weeks ago.

Mrs Quimby kissed her daughters. 'Don't look so frightened,' she said. 'Everything is going to be all right. Be good girls, and Daddy will be home as soon as he can.' She bent forward and hugged Algie again.

The house suddenly seemed empty. The girls listened to the car back out of the driveway. The sound of the motor became lost in traffic.

'Well,' said Beezus, 'I suppose we might as well do the dishes.'

'I suppose so.' Ramona tested all the doors, including the door to the basement, to make sure they were locked.

'Too bad Picky-picky isn't here to eat all this tuna salad no one felt like eating.' Beezus scraped the plates into the garbage.

To her own surprise, Ramona burst into tears and buried her face in a dish towel. 'I just want mother to come home,' she wept.

Beezus wiped her soapy hands on the seat of her cut-off jeans. Then she put her arms around Ramona, something she had never done before. 'Don't worry, Ramona. Everything will be all right. Mother said so, and I remember when you came.'

Ramona felt better. A big sister could be a comfort if she wanted to.

'You got born and mother was fine.' Beezus handed Ramona a clean dish towel.

Minutes crawled by. The long Oregon dusk turned into night. The girls turned on the television set to a programme about people in a hospital, running, shouting, giving orders. Quickly they turned it off. 'I hope Aunt Bea and Uncle Hobart are all right,' said Ramona. The girls longed for their loving aunt, who was cheerful in times of trouble and who was always there when the family needed her. Now she was in a truck, riding along the Canadian Highway to Alaska. Ramona thought about bears, mean bears. She wondered if two pairs of white shoes still danced from the bumper of the truck.

The ring of the telephone made Ramona feel as if arrows of electricity had shot through her stomach as Beezus ran to answer.

'Oh.' There was disappointment in Beezus's voice. 'All right, Daddy. No. No, we don't mind.' When the conversation ended, she turned to Ramona, who was wild for news, and said, 'Algie is taking his time. Daddy wants to stay with Mom and wanted to be sure we didn't mind staying alone. I said we didn't, and he said we were brave girls.'

'Oh,' said Ramona, who longed for her father's return. 'Well, I'm brave, I guess.' Even though the evening was unusually warm, she closed all the windows.

'I suppose we should go to bed,' said Beezus. 'If you want, you can get in bed with me.'

'We better leave lights on for Daddy.' Ramona turned on the porch light, as well as all the lights in the living room and hall, before she climbed into her sister's bed. 'So Daddy won't fall over anything,' she explained.

'Good idea,' agreed Beezus. Each sister knew the other felt safer with the lights on.

'I hope Algie will hurry,' said Ramona.

'So do I,' agreed Beezus.

The girls slept lightly until the sound of a key in the door awoke them. 'Daddy?' Beezus called out.

'Yes.' Mr Quimby came down the hall to the door of Beezus's room. 'Great news. Roberta Day Quimby, six pounds, four ounces, arrived safe and sound. Your mother is fine.'

Barely awake, Ramona asked, 'Who's Roberta?'

'Your new sister,' answered her father, 'and my namesake.'

'*Sister.*' Now Ramona was wide-awake. The family had referred to the baby as Algie so long she had assumed that of course she would have a brother.

'Yes, a beautiful little sister,' said her father. 'Now, go back to sleep. It's four o'clock in the morning, and I've got to get up at seven-thirty.'

The next morning, Mr Quimby overslept and ate his breakfast standing up. He was halfway out of the door when he called back, 'When I get off work, we'll have dinner at the Whopperburger, and then we'll all go see Roberta and your mother.'

The day was long and lonely. Even a swimming lesson at the park and a trip to the library did little to make time pass. 'I wonder what Roberta looks like?' said Beezus.

'And whose room she will share when she outgrows the bassinette?' worried Ramona.

The one happy moment in the day for the girls was a telephone call from their mother, who reported that Roberta was a beautiful, healthy little sister. She couldn't wait to bring her home, and she was proud of her daughters for being so good about staying alone. This pleased Beezus and Ramona so much they ran the vacuum cleaner and dusted, which made time pass faster until their father, looking exhausted, came home to take them out for hamburgers and a visit to the fifth Quimby.

Ramona could feel her heart pounding as she finally climbed the steps to the hospital. Visitors, some carrying flowers and others looking careworn, walked towards the elevators. Nurses hurried, a doctor was paged over the loudspeaker. Ramona could scarcely bear her own excitement. The rising of the elevator made her stomach feel as if it had stayed behind on the first floor. When the elevator stopped, Mr Quimby led the way down the hall.

'Excuse me,' called a nurse.

Surprised, the family stopped and turned.

'Children under twelve are not allowed to visit the maternity ward,' said the nurse. 'Little girl, you will have to go down and wait in the lobby.'

'Why is that?' asked Mr Quimby.

'Children under twelve might have contagious diseases,' explained the nurse. 'We have to protect the babies.'

'I'm sorry, Ramona,' said Mr Quimby. 'I didn't

know. I am afraid you will have to do as the nurse says.'

'Does she mean I'm *germy*?' Ramona was humiliated. 'I took a shower this morning and washed my hands at the Whopperburger so I would be extra clean.'

'Sometimes children are coming down with something and don't know it,' explained Mr Quimby. 'Now, be a big girl and go downstairs and wait for us.'

Ramona's eyes filled with tears of disappointment, but she found some pleasure in riding in the elevator alone. By the time she reached the lobby, she felt worse. The nurse called her a little girl. Her father called her a big girl. What was she? A germy girl.

Ramona sat gingerly on the edge of a Naugahyde couch. If she leaned back, she might get germs on it, or it might get germs on her. She swallowed hard. Was her throat a little bit sore? She thought maybe it was, way down at the back. She put her hand to her forehead the way her mother did when she thought Ramona might have a fever. Her forehead was warm, maybe too warm.

As Ramona waited, she began to itch the way she itched when she had chickenpox. Her head itched, her back itched, her legs itched. Ramona scratched. A woman sat down on the couch, looked at Ramona, got up, and moved to another couch.

Ramona felt worse. She itched more and scratched harder. She swallowed often to see how her sore throat was coming along. She peeked down the neck of her blouse to see if she might have a rash and was surprised that she did not. She sniffed from time to time to see if she had a runny nose.

Now Ramona was angry. It would serve everybody right if she came down with some horrible disease, right there in their old hospital. That would show everybody how germfree the place was. Ramona squirmed and gave that hard-to-reach place between her shoulder blades a good hard scratch. Then she scratched her head with both hands. People stopped to stare.

A man in a white coat, with a stethoscope hanging out of his pocket, came hurrying through the lobby, glanced at Ramona, stopped, and took a good look at her. 'How do you feel?' he asked.

'Awful,' she admitted. 'A nurse said I was too germy to go see my mother and new sister, but I think I caught some disease right here.'

'I see,' said the doctor. 'Open your mouth and say "ah".'

Ramona *ahhed* until she gagged.

'Mh-hm,' murmured the doctor. He looked so

serious Ramona was alarmed. Then he pulled out his stethoscope and listened to her front and back, thumping as he did so. What was he hearing? Was there something wrong with her insides? Why didn't her father come?

The doctor nodded as if his worst suspicions had been confirmed. 'Just as I thought,' he said, pulling out his prescription pad.

Medicine, ugh. Ramona's twitching stopped. Her nose and throat felt fine. 'I feel much better,' she assured the doctor as she eyed that prescription pad with distrust.

'An acute case of siblingitis. Not at all unusual around here, but it shouldn't last long.' He tore off the prescription he had written, instructed Ramona to give it to her father, and hurried on down the hall.

Ramona could not remember the name of her illness. She tried to read the doctor's scribbly joined-up writing, but she could not. She could only read neat writing, the sort her teacher wrote on the blackboard.

Itching again, she was still staring at the slip of paper when Mr Quimby and Beezus stepped out of the elevator. 'Roberta is so tiny.' Beezus was radiant with joy. 'And she is perfectly darling. She has a little round nose and—oh, when you see her, you'll love her.'

'I'm sick.' Ramona tried to sound pitiful. 'I've got something awful. A doctor said so.'

Beezus paid no attention. 'And Roberta has brown hair—'

Mr Quimby interrupted. 'What's this all about, Ramona?'

'A doctor said I had something, some kind of *itis*, and I have to have this right away.' She handed her father her prescription and scratched one shoulder. 'If I don't, I might get sicker.'

Mr Quimby read the scribbly writing, and then he did a strange thing. He lifted Ramona and gave her a big hug and a kiss, right there in the lobby. The itching stopped. Ramona felt much better. 'You have acute siblingitis,' explained her father. '*Itis* means inflammation.'

Ramona already knew the meaning of sibling. Since her father had studied to be a teacher, brothers and sisters had become siblings to him.

'He understood you were worried and angry because you weren't allowed to see your new sibling, and prescribed attention,' explained Mr Quimby. 'Now let's all go buy ice-cream cones before I fall asleep standing up.'

Beezus said Roberta was too darling to be called a dumb word like sibling. Ramona felt silly, but she also felt better.

For the next three nights, Ramona took a book

to the hospital and sat in the lobby, not reading, but sulking about the injustice of having to wait to see the strange new Roberta.

On the fourth day, Mr Quimby took an hour off from the Shop-rite Market, picked up Beezus and Ramona, who were waiting in clean clothes, and drove to the hospital to bring home his wife and new daughter.

Ramona moved closer to Beezus when she saw her mother, holding a pink bundle, emerge from the elevator in a wheelchair pushed by a nurse and followed by Mr Quimby carrying her bag. 'Can't mother walk?' she whispered.

'Of course she can walk,' answered Beezus. 'The hospital wants to make sure people get out without falling down and suing for a million dollars.'

Mrs Quimby waved to the girls. Roberta's face was hidden by a corner of a pink blanket, but the nurse had no time for a little girl eager to see a new baby. She pushed the wheelchair through the automatic door to the waiting car.

'*Now* can I see her?' begged Ramona when her mother and Roberta were settled in the front, and the girls had climbed into the back seat.

'Dear heart, of course you may.' Mrs Quimby then spoke the most beautiful words Ramona had ever heard, 'Oh, Ramona, how I've missed you,' as she turned back the blanket.

Ramona, leaning over the front seat for her first glimpse of the new baby sister, tried to hold her breath so she wouldn't breathe germs on Roberta, who did not look at all like the picture on the cover of *A Name for Your Baby*. Her face was bright pink, almost red, and her hair, unlike the smooth pale hair of the baby on the cover of the pamphlet, was dark and wild. Ramona did not know what to say. She did not feel that words like darling or adorable fitted this baby.

'She looks exactly like you looked when you were born,' Mrs Quimby told Ramona.

'She does?' Ramona found this hard to believe. She could not imagine that she had once looked like this red, frowning little creature.

'Well, what do you think of your new sister?' asked Mrs Quimby.

'She's so—so *little*,' Ramona answered truthfully.

Roberta opened her blue-grey eyes.

'Mother!' cried Ramona. 'She's cross-eyed.'

Mrs Quimby laughed. 'All babies look cross-eyed sometimes. They outgrow it when they learn to focus.' Sure enough, Roberta's eyes straightened out for a moment and then crossed again. She worked her mouth as if she didn't know what to do with it. She made little snuffling noises and lifted one arm as if she didn't know what it was for.

'Why does her nightie have those little pockets at the ends of the sleeves?' asked Ramona. 'They cover up her hands.'

'They keep her from scratching herself,' explained Mrs Quimby. 'She's too little to understand that fingernails scratch.'

Ramona sat back and buckled her seat belt. She had once looked like Roberta. Amazing! She had once been that tiny, but she had grown, her hair had calmed down when she remembered to comb it, and she had learned to use her eyes and hands. 'You know what I think?' she asked and did not wait for an answer. 'I think it is hard work to be a baby.' Ramona spoke as if she had discovered something unknown to the rest of the world. With her words came unexpected love and sympathy for the tiny person in her mother's arms.

'I hadn't thought of it that way,' said Mrs Quimby, 'but I think you're right.'

'Growing up is hard work,' said Mr Quimby as he drove away from the hospital. 'Sometimes being grown-up is hard work.'

'I know,' said Ramona and thought some more. She thought about loose teeth, real sore throats, quarrels, misunderstandings with her teachers, longing for a bicycle her family could not afford, worrying when her parents bickered, how terrible she had felt when she hurt Beezus's feelings without meaning to, and all the long afternoons when Mrs Kemp looked after her until her mother came from work. She had survived it all. 'Isn't it funny?' she remarked as her father steered the car into their driveway.

'Isn't what funny?' asked her mother.

'That I used to be little and funny-looking and cross-eyed like Roberta,' said Ramona. 'And now look at me. I'm wonderful me!'

'Except when you're blunderful you,' said Beezus.

Ramona did not mind when her family, except Roberta, who was too little, laughed. 'Yup, wonderful, blunderful me,' she said and was happy. She was winning at growing up.

RaMONa's WORLD

CONTENTS

Contents

I

RaMONa SPReaDS THe NeWS

Ramona Quimby was nine years old. She had brown hair, brown eyes, and no cavities. She had a mother, a father, a big sister named Beatrice who was called Beezus by the family, and—this was the exciting part—a baby sister named Roberta after her father, Robert Quimby.

'Look at her tiny fingernails,' Ramona marvelled as she looked at the sleeping Roberta, 'and her little eyebrows. She is already a whole person, only little.' Ramona couldn't wait for the first day of school so she could spread the news about her baby sister.

That day finally came. It was a warm September day, and Ramona, neat and clean, with lunch bag in hand, half skipped, half hopped, scrunching through dry leaves on the sidewalk. She was early, she knew, but Ramona was the sort of girl who was always early because something might happen that she didn't want to miss. The fourth grade was going to be the best year of her life, so far.

Ramona was first to arrive at the bus stop in front of Mrs Pitt's house. Mrs Pitt came out of the front door and began sweeping her front steps.

'Hi, Mrs Pitt,' Ramona called out. 'Guess what! My baby sister is two months old.'

'Good for her,' said Mrs Pitt, agreeable to a baby in the neighbourhood. Babies did not scatter candy wrappers or old spelling papers on the lawn in front of her house.

Ramona pretended she was playing hopscotch until her friend Howie, who was already familiar with Roberta, joined her along with other children, some with their mothers, who were excited about the first day of school. 'Hi, Ramona,' he said, and leaned against a tree in the strip of grass between the sidewalk and the street. He opened his lunch bag and began to eat his sandwich. Ramona knew he was doing this so he wouldn't be bothered carrying his lunch.

'Little boy!' Mrs Pitts called out. 'Little boy, don't you drop any papers or orange peels in front of my house. And stay off my grass!'

'OK.' Howie took another bite of his sandwich as he moved to the sidewalk. Howie was not easily excited, which Ramona sometimes found annoying. She was often excited. She *liked* to be excited.

When the yellow bus stopped, Ramona was

first on board. She plunked herself down on a seat across the aisle from another fourth grader, a boy named Danny who was wearing a white T-shirt with *Trail Blazers* printed on it. Ramona called him Yard Ape because she thought he acted like an ape on the playground. She was glad he had not moved away during the summer. 'I have a new baby sister,' she informed him.

Yard Ape closed his eyes and hit his forehead with the palm of his hand. 'Another Ramona,' he said, and groaned.

Ramona refused to smile. 'You have a little brother,' she reminded him.

'I know,' answered Yard Ape, 'but we just keep him for a pet.'

Ramona made a face at him so he wouldn't know she liked him.

When Ramona jumped off the bus at Cedarhurst School, she greeted old friends, most of them in new, or at least clean, clothes for starting the fourth grade. When she saw Janet, whom she had often seen in the park during the summer, the two girls compared calluses on the palms of their hands. 'Your calluses are really big,' said Janet, impressed.

It was true. Ramona's calluses were hard and yellow because she lived close to the park, where she often went with Beezus and her mother and

Roberta on warm sunny days. She worked hard at the rings—*pump, pump, swing, pump, pump, swing*—and by the end of summer she was able to travel down the line of rings and back again.

'There's Susan,' cried Janet, and ran to join her. Reluctantly Ramona followed. 'Hi, Susan,' she said, eyeing Susan's short blonde curls.

'Hi, Ramona,' answered Susan. Neither girl smiled. The trouble was the grown-up Quimbys and Susan's parents, the Kushners, were friends. Ramona did not know what Mrs Kushner said, but her own parents often said things like, 'Now, you be nice to Susan', 'Susan is such a well-behaved little girl', or 'Susan's mother says Susan always sets the table without being asked'. Such remarks did not endear Susan to Ramona. There was more. In kindergarten Susan did not like Ramona, who could not resist pulling the long curls she had at that time and saying, '*Boing!*' as she released them. In first grade, when the class was making owls out of paper bags, Susan copied Ramona's owl. The teacher held up Susan's owl to show the class what a splendid owl Susan had made. This seemed so unfair to Ramona that she crunched Susan's owl and found herself in trouble, big trouble. So how could anyone expect the two girls to be friends? As Ramona expected, the calluses on Susan's hands were so small they could scarcely be seen.

Then Ramona saw a new girl who was standing alone. A new fourth grader, Ramona decided, and because she admired the girl's long fair hair she went over to her and asked, 'What's your name?'

'Daisy,' answered the girl. 'Daisy Kidd.' When she smiled, Ramona saw that she was wearing braces on her teeth. 'What's your name?' Daisy asked. As Ramona told her, the bell rang, ending their conversation.

On her way to the fourth grade Ramona passed her former classroom, where the teacher was standing outside the door welcoming her new class. When she saw Ramona, she waved and said, 'How's bright-eyed, bushy-tailed Ramona?' People often called Ramona bright-eyed and bushy-tailed. When she was younger, she blinked her eyes, held up her hands like paws, and wiggled her bottom as if she were wagging a tail. Now that she was a fourth grader, she was too grown-up for such babyishness, so she waved and said, 'Hi, Mrs Whaley.'

Ramona's fourth-grade teacher was Mrs Meacham, a plump, cheerful woman in a green trouser suit and blouse printed with flowers, a good sign. Ramona liked teachers who wore bright cheerful clothes. Mrs Meacham, Ramona decided, must be very old, because Howie's father had gone to school with her when he was a boy.

After inspecting her new teacher, Ramona looked at the blackboard for spelling words. The board was blank, another good sign. Mrs Meacham passed out name tags and made a little speech about how learning was fun in the fourth grade and everyone should work together to make this a great year. She then passed out papers with borders of dinosaurs, another hopeful sign, Ramona thought, even though dinosaurs were more for third graders than fourth graders. Mrs Meacham said, 'So I will get to know you better, I want each of you to write a paragraph telling me about yourself.'

Ramona tapped her pencil on her nose and noticed that Yard Ape, who sat across the aisle, was already writing, apparently without having to think. Susan, in front of Ramona, leaned her head on her fist. A boy went to the pencil sharpener. Someone sighed. Feet shuffled. Ramona began to write. She enjoyed joined-up writing because her third-grade teacher once said, 'Ramona, your joined-up writing is better than mine.' Now she wrote fast because she had so much to say: 'My name is Ramona Quimby. I have a baby sister. She is cute. She screems if she is hunrgy.' Ramona paused. *Screems* looked peculiar. Maybe it was spelled with *ea* instead of *ee*. Oh, well. Anyone would know what she meant. She had so much to say she did not want to waste time spelling. 'Sometimes I sit on the coach and hold her.'

Ramona enjoyed writing. Her face grew flushed as she wrote faster and faster towards the dinosaurs at the bottom of the page. Her last lines, not as neat as her first, were written across the dinosaur heads. 'She can grab my figner. Mother says I used to look like her. She says I can be her roll modle.' Ramona squeezed a tiny sketch of a baby's sleeping face between a brontosaurus and a tyrannosaurus.

Ramona was proud of her work. She glanced around to see what her classmates had written about themselves. She leaned forward to look over Susan's shoulder. Susan had written half a page in neat joined-up writing and was busy colouring dinosaurs, neatly of course, with crayons. Ramona read, 'My name is Susan. My favourite colour is blue. My favourite food is . . .' Ramona did not need to read any further. She half rose from her seat to look across the aisle towards Yard Ape and read in his neat uphill writing, 'My name is Daniel. Call me Yard Ape. I am nine years old. I am not married. I am a kid and proud of it.'

Me too, thought Ramona, filled with admiration for Yard Ape, a smart boy who always earned stars or Good Work! at the top of his papers and looked as if he was about to get into trouble. Somehow he never did, not in the classroom. On the playground he ran faster, yelled louder, and kicked balls further than any of the other boys.

'All right, class,' said Mrs Meacham, 'pass your papers to the front.' Ramona was so pleased with her work she was almost sorry to part with it.

At lunchtime when the class went to the multi-purpose room, Daisy sat down beside Ramona. 'OK if I sit here?' she asked.

'Sure,' said Ramona. Together the girls tore open their lunch bags. They shared Ramona's corn chips and each ate half of Daisy's brownie. Ramona told Daisy about Roberta; Daisy wished she had a little sister. She only had a big brother. Ramona admired Daisy's long blonde hair; Daisy admired Ramona's short hair and said she was lucky to have hair that didn't get tangled when it was washed. It was a good beginning.

After lunch Mrs Meacham said, 'I've had time to look over what you have written. There is one description I would like to read to you.'

Mine! Mine! Ramona silently prayed, and sure enough, it was Ramona's description of Roberta that her teacher chose to read. Mrs Meacham did not seem to notice a few misspelled words, because she knew what Ramona meant. The class seemed to enjoy it, and Ramona was ecstatic. She couldn't wait to tell her mother.

The rest of the day passed quickly. Ramona ran all the way home from the bus and found her mother sitting on the couch drinking tea and reading a book for her book club, which met once a month. 'Guess what!' Ramona burst out. 'I wrote a composition about Roberta.'

'Sh-h-h. Roberta's asleep.' Mrs Quimby placed a marker in her book and closed it. 'Sounds interesting,' she said, and took a sip of tea.

'It was,' whispered Ramona. 'It was so interesting that Mrs Meacham read it to the whole class. Mrs Meacham is about a million years old, but she's nice.'

'I can't wait to read your composition,' said her mother.

Ramona frowned thoughtfully. 'I suppose I could have said Roberta spits up sometimes.'

'We don't have to tell the whole world our little secrets.' Mrs Quimby looked amused, which Ramona found pleasant, not like being laughed at. Mrs Quimby sipped her tea.

It was a moment for confidences. Ramona told her mother, 'There's a new girl named Daisy Kidd with braces on her teeth and long golden hair like a fairy princess and a brownie in her lunch. I know I am going to like her a lot.'

'Good. She sounds nice,' said Mrs Quimby.

Ramona picked up her mother's book. *Moby Dick*. 'What's this about?' she asked.

'A whale that bit off a man's leg,' said Mrs Quimby. 'Our book club decided to read a book we had all heard about all our lives but had never actually read.'

'Sounds exciting.' Ramona opened the book, which turned out not to look exciting at all. The print was small, the lines were close together, and there were almost no quotation marks. She closed the book. She liked her own writing better. That wasn't all she liked. She liked Mrs Meacham, she liked Daisy, she liked Yard Ape, she liked fourth grade. It was going to be a great year.

2

THE ROLE MODEL

The next morning Ramona was excited and happy when she entered her classroom, that is, until she saw—she might have known—spelling words on the blackboard. She mentally groaned. Why did nice Mrs Meacham have to do this? She soon found out.

Mrs Meacham explained. 'Today we are going to study words we use. When we wrote about ourselves, we discovered words we need to learn how to spell.'

Ramona looked more closely at the words on the blackboard. Among them she saw *scream, hungry, couch, finger, role, model.* They looked familiar. They were familiar. They were her words. She scowled.

'Is something the matter, Ramona?' asked Mrs Meacham, who had been quick to learn names.

Ramona decided to speak up. 'What difference does spelling make if people know what you mean?' she asked.

'You wouldn't want people to think you sat

on a coach instead of a couch, would you?' Mrs Meacham asked.

The class found this funny, but Ramona did not, not when the class laughed. She felt her face grow hot. She slid down in her seat and shook her head. Mrs Meacham knew the answer. Why did she bother to ask?

Mrs Meacham continued, 'And before lunch are you hungry or hunrgy?'

The class laughed, harder this time. The warm day suddenly seemed warmer. Ramona decided right then that she *did not like Mrs Meacham*, and this was only the second day of school. Mrs Meacham did not tell the truth. She said learning was fun, and it wasn't. At least not all the time. Not when it came to spelling.

The fourth grade suddenly began to stretch ahead, long and dreary and full of spelling. Before long, rain would begin to fall, day after day. The school bus would smell like old boots. Then, with luck, snow might fall. Ramona imagined herself making snow angels in the front yard.

'Ramona, please join the class.' Mrs Meacham spoke sharply. The class laughed a third time.

Ramona sat up and stared glumly at the spelling words on the blackboard. She did not really want to be a bad speller. She simply did not want to bother being a good speller. She had more interesting things to do, although at the moment she couldn't think what. She frowned and studied the words based on her own misspellings as well as those of others and disliked every minute. Mrs Meacham gave a little talk on not confusing *h* with *k* in joined-up writing and pointed to *muck* on the blackboard. Ramona knew *much* was not her word but that of some babyish person in the class. Imagine spelling it *muck*. How silly.

When recess came, Yard Ape stopped chasing a ball to ask, 'What kind of coach did you sit on? Baseball or football?'

'You keep quiet.' Ramona saw no reason to be polite, especially when the day was so warm. Then she had an inspiration. 'I sat on a coach like a stagecoach,' she informed him. She could tell he didn't believe her.

Susan smiled that superior smile of hers and said nothing.

'Everybody makes mistakes,' Janet reminded Ramona.

'I'm a rotten speller, too,' said Howie, as if that would help.

Daisy smiled, showing the braces on her teeth, and said, 'I don't think Mrs Meacham was very nice to you.' Ramona felt better.

When the long day finally ended, Ramona sat as far as she could from Yard Ape on the bus. She gave ever-sweeping Mrs Pitt a tiny smile and did not bother to wave. At home she found her mother sitting on the couch, not coach, still reading *Moby Dick*.

'Sh-h-h,' said Mrs Quimby. 'Don't wake Roberta. She was fussy last night and the heat makes her cross.' She laid her book aside. 'What happened in school today?'

Ramona was in no mood to be hushed. 'Oh— nothing much. Same old stuff. Spelling and multiplication facts and stuff.' Then, because her mother often told her to look on the bright side, she added, 'Daisy gave me half of her chocolate-chip cookie.'

'That's good.' Mrs Quimby spoke as if she was thinking of something else. 'Ramona,' she said in that quiet voice that meant Ramona was about to get a little talking to, 'you've been using the word *stuff* entirely too much. Surely you can find a better word to say what you mean.'

Ramona felt picked on, first by her teacher and now by her mother. *Stuff* was a perfectly good, handy, multipurpose word and easy to spell, too. She flopped into a chair and scowled. If she had written, 'My sister is cute and stuff', or 'I like to hold her and stuff', she wouldn't have misspelled so many words, and Mrs Meacham wouldn't have had a chance to be so mean.

Before the discussion could continue, Beezus came home from school, dumped an armload of books on the dining room table, and gave her mother and sister a cheerful 'Hi.'

Ramona returned it with a grumpy 'Hi.'

Beezus, smiling and full of enthusiasm, perched on the arm of the couch. 'I love high school. I didn't get lost in the halls even once today. I think I made a new friend. My French teacher makes French seem easy, and I have the nicest man teacher for English, and—'

Ramona interrupted. 'And I suppose you spelled every single word right.'

'Well, aren't you Miss Grouchypuss?' Beezus said. 'Yes, I did, and in French, too.'

'Smartypuss,' countered Ramona, feeling that everyone picked on her.

'Girls!' Mrs Quimby's voice was weary. The afternoon was too warm for this sort of disagreement. From the bedroom came the sound of fussing, crying, and finally screaming.

S-c-r-e-a-m, thought Ramona, mentally spelling the word in spite of herself.

'I'll get her,' Beezus offered.

Good old Beezus, thought Ramona, sliding further down in the chair.

'Ramona, *please*,' said Mrs Quimby. 'Try to be agreeable.'

'I am agreeable,' said Ramona with an even darker scowl.

Beezus returned with sobbing Roberta in her arms. Because of the heat the baby was wearing only a nappy. 'What's the matter with Roberta?' Beezus crooned, and kissed the baby's hair.

Mrs Quimby held out her arms for Roberta, who snuggled against her mother's shoulder. 'Sh-h-h,' whispered her mother. Roberta stopped crying with one last hiccuping sob. 'That's my good girl,' whispered Mrs Quimby, and she too kissed the baby's hair.

All this made Ramona feel worse than ever—unloved, left out, and a rotten speller with the whole horrible fourth grade ahead of her. Nobody kissed her hair, at least today, and it was clean, too. She pulled herself out of the chair, found the remote control, and turned on the television to a rerun of her favourite after-school programme, *Big Hospital*. She wanted to forget her troubles and lose herself in the corridors of the hospital where people in green pyjamas fell in love if they weren't too busy saving lives or comforting the lost and lonely.

'Ramona, please turn that off.' Mrs Quimby looked over Roberta's head at her middle daughter. 'I wish you'd tell me what's bothering you.'

'Nothing's bothering me,' grumped Ramona as she pushed the button on the remote control without finding out what Handsome Doctor and Blonde Nurse would say next. She waited for her mother to coax her problems out of her, to soothe her, to tell her things would be better tomorrow, and maybe even kiss her hair. She picked at a callus but did not pull it off. Calluses were one thing she had to be proud of. Right now she felt they were the only thing.

Before Mrs Quimby could coax, the telephone rang. 'I'll get it!' Beezus shouted. She and Ramona usually tried to beat each other to the telephone in the hall.

Of course, Ramona eavesdropped. She heard Beezus say, sounding surprised, 'Yes, I'd love to, but I'll have to ask mother. Just a minute—'

Beezus, her eyes shining and her face alight with joy, came back into the room and said, 'Mother, guess what! Mrs Lucas wants me to baby-sit with Benjamin Saturday evening. They won't be out late, and they'll pay me and everything!'

And stuff, thought Ramona.

Beezus continued. 'And Mrs Lucas says she wants me because she knows I'm responsible. Oh, please, *please*—'

'I don't see why not,' said Mrs Quimby. 'We'll be

home, so we could help if there is an emergency, which I'm sure there won't be.'

Not with good old Beezus being so responsible all over the place, thought Ramona as Beezus danced off to the telephone. After she had accepted the offer, she returned, gathered up her books, and started down the hall to the room the sisters had shared since Roberta was born. The baby now occupied Ramona's old room.

Beezus paused and said, '*Au revoir.*'

'What does that mean?' asked Ramona, annoyed with Beezus for using words she did not understand.

'It means goodbye in French,' answered Beezus, and went off to the room the sisters shared. Probably to be responsible about her homework, thought Ramona.

Mrs Quimby shifted Roberta to her lap and patted the couch beside her. 'Ramona, come sit by me,' she coaxed.

Reluctantly Ramona moved to the couch, staying as far away as she could from her mother. She balanced the heel of one sandal on the toe of the other and longed to lean against her mother and confide her troubles. Life was hard enough, and now Beezus would be showing off by speaking French. She picked at a callus.

'Can you tell me what's bothering you?' Mrs

Quimby's voice was gentle. Roberta stared at Ramona as if she were giving her serious thought.

'Nothing.' Ramona sighed.

'Now, Ramona,' her mother said in her soothing voice, 'I know something's bothering you. You'll feel better if you tell me.'

Ramona knew her mother was right, but she sighed again before she burst out, 'My spelling is rotten and Mrs Meacham doesn't like me and makes me feel stupid in front of the whole class and they laughed at me and made me feel super-stupid and everybody says Beezus is responsible and nobody says I'm responsible and everybody fusses over Roberta and says she is cute and adorable and stuff and nobody pays any attention to me and I'm not supposed to say "stuff" and—and—stuff.'

Roberta looked worried.

Mrs Quimby ignored the stuffs. 'Has anybody ever said you weren't responsible?' she asked.

Ramona thought. 'Well—no,' she admitted, 'but Mrs Meacham probably will. She only likes people who can spell. She *loves* good spellers. She *adores* good spellers.'

Mrs Quimby smiled. 'Ramona, I think you are exaggerating.'

Ramona knew her mother was right, but that was the way she felt. Exaggerating felt *good*.

our spelling words home, and we'll help
rs Quimby was comforting, but Ramona
t ready to be comforted. 'And don't forget,'
nother went on, 'this is only the second day
of school, and Mrs Meacham is there to teach you.
You'll feel differently when you get to know her
better and when your spelling improves.'

Ramona felt calmer after spilling out her
troubles, but she wasn't ready to admit it. How did
she know her spelling would improve? It might
get worse. Roberta stared as if she were trying to
understand. Ramona stared back, still engulfed in
self-pity, and thought, I wish somebody would call
me darling and adorable like Roberta. But no, I'm
just plain old messy Ramona. She stuck her tongue
out at Roberta and immediately felt ashamed of
herself. Her sweet innocent baby sister—

Then, to Ramona's astonishment, Roberta stuck
her tongue out at Ramona. Ramona couldn't
believe it. Roberta was too little to understand. It
must have been a coincidence. As an experiment
Ramona stuck *her* tongue out again. Roberta
smiled a real smile and stuck *her* tongue out again.
It was a game. Ramona could scarcely believe
what she had seen. 'Mother, did you see that?'
she asked in wonder. 'Roberta stuck her tongue
out when I stuck my tongue out, and she smiled,
really smiled, like it was some kind of game.'

Mrs Quimby laughed. 'I told you Roberta would take after you.'

'But she's so awfully little,' said Ramona, still marvelling.

'Babies are more observant than we realize,' said Mrs Quimby.

Ramona's troubles seemed to vanish. She had taught her baby sister to stick out her tongue. She could teach her other things when she was older, things like playing noughts and crosses and roller-skating. As for spelling—pooh! Mrs Meacham was just another teacher. Ramona had survived others, liked them, and even loved her kindergarten teacher. She would survive Mrs Meacham, maybe get to like her, even though at the moment this seemed doubtful. Ramona didn't care. Suddenly the sun was shining—it had shone all day, but Ramona hadn't noticed, since she had gone to school—and now Roberta had copied her by sticking out her tongue.

Ramona felt so good she held up her finger to Roberta, who grasped it in her tiny perfect hand. 'See,' Ramona said to her mother, 'I really am Roberta's role model.' Then, in spite of herself, Ramona thought, *r-o-l-e m-o-d-e-l.*

3

AT DaisY's House

As September sunshine changed to autumn clouds, life at the Quimbys' house settled into a peaceful routine. Mr Quimby, who managed the Shop-rite Market, came home from work looking cheerful. Groceries had been delivered on time, no shoplifters were spotted, and no one had slipped on bits of lettuce dropped by careless produce customers.

Mrs Quimby found more time to read *Moby Dick*, a book with so many pages that members of the book club, most of them mothers or women who worked outside their homes or both, had difficulty finishing it. They postponed their meeting for another month. Ramona wondered why they didn't just skip the hard parts.

Roberta was a happy baby, busy enjoying her hands and feet. She could even put her toes in her mouth. So could Ramona, just barely, but no one else in the family even tried.

Beezus was still filled with enthusiasm for high school. She liked all her teachers, and she had made a new friend, Abby Alexander, whose real name was Abigail. At dinnertime the Quimbys heard a lot about Abby: Abby wanted to be a maths teacher or a dietician someday, Abby's mother got her contact lenses, Abby got an A on her maths test, Abby this and Abby that.

All this left Ramona full of wishes. She sighed a lot and wished she had long hair like Daisy, and even though she had no need for them she wished she had braces on her teeth. She unfolded a paper clip, held the wire in front of her mouth, and smiled at herself in the mirror to see what she would look like if she wore braces. She wished she were a better speller without having to work at it, she wished Yard Ape would pay as much attention to her in school as on the bus, but most of all she wished there were girls her age on Klickitat Street. She wanted girls to play with. She wanted a best friend. That was why she ran all the way home from the bus stop one afternoon. She had news. A wish might be about to come true.

'Guess what!' she cried as she burst through the door and found her mother folding nappies on the living room couch. They were nappies Ramona had worn, but she didn't like to think about that. Disposable nappies were expensive, she knew.

'What am I to guess?' Mrs Quimby was

interested but not excited. After all, she had known Ramona for nine years.

Ramona was glad Roberta was still napping, so she could have her mother all to herself. She took a deep breath and began, 'Daisy Kidd, the new girl in my class I told you about—you know, the one with long hair and braces on her teeth—wants me to come home with her on the bus after school tomorrow! Her mother will bring me home after dinner.'

Mrs Quimby pulled a nappy out of the jumble beside her and flapped it to shake out the wrinkles, but before she could answer, Ramona went on, 'Please, please, mother. I never get to play with a girl because there aren't any girls around here except Willa Jean, who doesn't count because she is only in kindergarten and besides, she's a nuisance, and Daisy is lots of fun and she's a good speller and is a really, really nice girl, so she must have really, really nice parents and—'

Mrs Quimby calmly folded the nappy as she interrupted. 'Of course you may go, dear. I already know about Daisy's family because one of the book club members' cousins lives next door to her family and says they are fine people. Daisy's father was transferred here during the summer, and her mother works mornings as a school nurse.' Obviously the conversation of the book club was not limited to books.

Somehow Ramona felt let down. She had expected to argue, to have to persuade her mother of the niceness of Daisy and the importance of their playing together.

'You could have asked Daisy to come here,' Mrs Quimby said.

'Oh. I didn't think about it,' admitted Ramona. 'I guess because we ride different buses.'

Mrs Quimby laid down the nappy she was folding to look thoughtfully at Ramona before she said, 'Don't you think you should play with Susan once in a while?'

Ramona picked at the one callus that had not peeled off since school started before she said, 'Do I have to? I see her at Sunday school.'

Mrs Quimby said, 'You could ask her to come here or you could go to Susan's house. Her mother was saying just the other day that you girls should get together more often.'

Ramona made a face. She wished grown-ups would stay out of their children's affairs.

Mrs Quimby was curious. 'Don't you like Susan?' she asked.

'Well—not really,' confessed Ramona. 'She's the kind of girl who gets mad, really mad, when boys call her Snoozin' Susan. When boys call you a name, you are just supposed to get a little bit mad and not go telling the teacher.' Ramona found her reason for disliking Susan difficult to explain. 'And I don't like to go to her house because—well, it is too clean, I guess.'

Mrs Quimby looked surprised. 'You can't say that about our house.'

Ramona was loyal to her house. 'Our house isn't dirty,' she said. 'There are magazines and stu—things on the coffee table, but everything isn't all nicey-nice and just so, and you don't hang around talking when someone comes over. You mind your own business.'

'Thank you, dear.' Mrs Quimby's mouth was serious, but her eyes were smiling. 'I'm glad to know.'

The evening could not pass fast enough for Ramona. The next afternoon she was filled with excitement as she climbed with Daisy onto the bus. After showing her permission note to the driver, the girls found seats together. Ramona felt as if she were about to have an adventure. Although she was familiar with the streets they rode through, somehow they seemed different when seen from someone else's school bus. 'I feel like I'm really going someplace,' she told Daisy. She had never been so far from home without an adult before.

'You are going someplace,' said Daisy. 'To my house.' Both girls found this funny.

Daisy's house turned out to be an old two-storey

house on the other side of the high school. The girls were greeted by a friendly tail-wagging dog, a sort of collie. Daisy patted and introduced him. 'This is Mutley. My brother Jeremy found him abandoned in the park.'

'Hi, Mutley,' said Ramona. The dog seemed pleased.

Daisy's house had a pleasant fragrance, something like cookies, and was comfortably untidy. There were still packing boxes in the corner of the living room, and a vacuum cleaner and its attachments lay nearby. A cat dozed in a patch of sunlight and opened one eye to look at Ramona.

Daisy's mother, who was plump, looked younger than her hair, which was grey, long, and held back with a clasp. 'Welcome, Ramona,' she said as she looked up from a box filled with dishes, crumpled newspaper, and bubble wrap. 'What nice shoes you're wearing.'

Ramona looked down at her shoes, surprised by their niceness.

Mrs Kidd continued, 'Daisy needs new shoes, but we're not familiar with stores around here. Where do you buy your shoes?'

Ramona knew right away that she liked Mrs Kidd. Not every mother who asked questions really wanted to know the answer. Mrs Kidd plainly was not a person who asked children how they liked school or what they wanted to be when they grew up. 'Fix yourselves a snack,' she said, and pulled a platter out of a carton. 'I hope I can get all these packing boxes out of the living room before Daisy goes to high school.' Obviously she was a mother who knew how to mind her own business.

Daisy picked up the large, limp cat that was almost too heavy for her. 'This is Clawed,' she said. 'C-l-a-w-e-d,' she spelled. 'Not like a man's name. My brother named him Clawed because he had been clawed by another cat when he found him hiding in a gutter. Daddy says he hopes Jeremy never finds a wounded skunk.'

Ramona stroked Clawed's fur. He was such a nice comfortable cat, unlike Picky-picky, the cat the Quimbys had once had. Daisy returned him to his patch of sunshine before she led the way to the kitchen, where she found juice bars in the refrigerator, another good sign, Ramona thought. Susan's mother provided apples or a glass of milk and crackers for an after-school snack. While the girls were busy licking their juice bars, Daisy's brother came in the back door, dropped his book bag on the floor, and said, 'Hi, Fence Face,' to Daisy as he opened the refrigerator. 'And you must be the Ramona we've heard too much about.' He began to throw together a sandwich.

'That's my brother Germy,' said Daisy. 'He thinks he's a genius because he's in high school.'

'Jeremy,' corrected the brother to Ramona and added, 'Tinsel Teeth,' to his sister. With that he took his sloppy sandwich and a dill pickle into the living room, where he turned on the television to a sports channel.

Daisy made a face. 'I wanted to watch *Big Hospital*. That's my favourite programme.'

'Mine too,' said Ramona. Sharing a favourite made her feel closer to Daisy.

When the girls had finished their juice bars, Daisy said, 'Come on, let's vacuum Clawed. He loves to be vacuumed.' Jeremy, who had picked up the cat, was sitting on the couch with his feet on the coffee table. Mrs Kidd, busy unpacking dishes, did not seem to mind. Daisy seized the vacuum cleaner and pulled it towards Clawed, who jumped off Jeremy's lap as if he expected it. 'Here, you do it,' Daisy said, and thrust the vacuum cleaner hose at Ramona as she turned on the vacuum cleaner. 'He likes the upholstery attachments. I guess you could say he is upholstered in fur.'

Clawed did not run as Ramona expected, but stood bracing himself with his chin raised as if he was enjoying the feel of the attachment Ramona was running down his back. 'Some cat,' said Ramona.

'Here, let me have a turn,' said Daisy, taking the vacuum cleaner from Ramona. Clawed rolled over on his back to allow her to vacuum his soft underneath fur. Ramona was amazed. Picky-picky would never have stood for such a thing. She said so.

'Clawed is a smart cat,' Daisy explained. 'He knows he won't have to scratch fleas if we run the vacuum cleaner over him.' When she finished, Clawed went back to his patch of sunshine. The girls entertained themselves by popping bubbles in the bubble wrap while Mrs Kidd carried cartons to the basement. Mutley went to the door and whimpered. Jeremy picked up a leash by the front door and took his dog outside.

'Quick!' directed Daisy. 'Before he gets back.' She seized the remote control and switched the television from the sports channel to *Big Hospital*. 'Pretend we've been watching it all along.' The girls settled themselves on the couch and tried to look as if they had been there for some time. When Jeremy returned, Daisy looked up from the screen and, pretending to be surprised to see her brother said, 'Oh, hi, Jeremy.'

'OK, Fence Face, you win,' said Jeremy, and went thumping up the stairs to his room. Mutley flattened himself, his nose on his paws, in front of the television set. When Daisy was sure the coast was clear and the girls had suppressed their giggles, she went to the refrigerator for a second helping of juice bars.

Ramona and Daisy contentedly licked their juice bars as they watched Handsome Doctor and Blonde Nurse and a number of other people in green pyjamas save the life of a little boy who had been hit by a car while playing in the street. His weeping mother, holding the ball he had been chasing, watched through a window on the swinging door.

Ramona's thoughts strayed from the hospital to Daisy, her house, and her family. Everything seemed so calm and so comfortable. Even Clawed and Mutley liked each other. Ramona wished she had a big brother who teased her a little bit. On the television Not-quite-so-handsome Doctor who was secretly married to Blonde Nurse joined the mother to watch through the window in the swinging door, but Ramona was thinking about Daisy.

Ramona had never had a girl best friend, only Howie, and now that they were in the fourth grade they did not play together as often as they used to. Howie was always banging around with a hammer, building things. Ramona used to enjoy this, too, but lately, as her mother said, she was at loose ends. She was tired of pounding nails with Howie. She wasn't bored exactly. She could always find something to do, but lately something was missing from her life. She wished she were old enough to baby-sit like Beezus, who was busy every weekend. Now she knew what had been missing—a best friend, a girl best friend.

Big Hospital and Ramona's thoughts were interrupted by a commercial for pills to cure aches and pains followed by another for a spray to relieve stuffy noses. Neither girl was interested.

'Let's be best friends.' Daisy spoke suddenly, as if she had just thought of it.

'That's what I was thinking.' Ramona, who did not usually feel shy, reached out to pet Mutley with her foot.

'I've been sort of—lonesome, I guess you'd call it—starting a new school,' confided Daisy.

'I've always wanted a best friend,' Ramona admitted. 'My neighbourhood is mostly boys. They're OK, but—well, you know.'

'I know,' agreed Daisy. 'Boys can be pretty awful, like Danny on the playground.'

Ramona was silent. Yard Ape never did anything bad. He was just smart and lively and liked to tease. She did not want anyone, not even her best friend, to know how much she liked him.

The girls watched television in contented silence. Men in green pyjamas ran down the hall wheeling a woman groaning in pain. Her faithful dog followed. 'Get that dog out of here!' shouted Handsome Doctor. Mutley looked up, startled, saw he wasn't threatened, and laid his nose on his paws again.

Ramona and Daisy smothered their giggles over Mutley's confusion. A spicy fragrance came from the kitchen. Ramona hoped it meant they would have lasagna for dinner. Lasagna would make her day perfect. She couldn't wait to tell her family all about it. Her thoughts drifted to what she would say: Daisy's mother lets her have juice bars after school, Daisy has a big brother who calls her Fence Face, Daisy vacuums the cat . . . Now Beezus wasn't the only one with a best friend to talk about. Ramona hoped she could be Daisy's best friend for ever.

4

THE INVITATION

One chilly day late in October when rain was
beginning to clog the gutters with leaves, Ramona
came home alone because it was Daisy's day to see
her orthodontist to have the braces on her teeth
adjusted. She found her mother sitting on the
chair holding Roberta to her shoulder and patting
her on the back. An almost empty bottle of baby
milk stood on the lamp table. As Ramona pulled
off her raincoat, she inspected a small bald spot
on the back of Roberta's head, which at first had
frightened Ramona because she thought Roberta
was going bald like their father. Mrs Quimby had
explained that many babies wore off their first
hair and that it would soon grow back. And it was,
to Ramona's relief.

With her inspection out of the way, Ramona
said, as if she were making an important
announcement, 'Boys are just awful.'

'How so?' asked her mother as she patted the
baby's back.

'A couple of girls wore knitted caps—their

mothers made them wear them—and the boys grabbed them and threw them into the boys' bathroom.' Boys, at this moment, were very much disapproved of by Ramona, who promised herself she would never, never wear a knitted cap to school.

'All boys?' Mrs Quimby had the look of someone trying to hide a smile. 'I can't imagine Howie doing such a dreadful thing.'

'Well, maybe not Howie.' Ramona backed down but soon flared up again. 'Mother,' she said sternly. 'It is not funny. Boys *are* just awful.'

'If you say so, dear,' was Mrs Quimby's mild answer. 'How was spelling?'

Ramona was a tiny bit annoyed with her mother for not getting upset over the awfulness of boys and for bringing up spelling. 'I missed one word, *project*. I spelled it *p-r-o-d-j-e-c-t*, which is the way it sounds.'

Discussion of Ramona's spelling came to an end because Beezus returned from school, dumped her armload of books on a chair, waved an envelope, obviously happy with whatever was in it, and said without bothering to take off her rain jacket, 'Guess what?'

'I can't imagine,' said Mrs Quimby.

'You won a million dollars,' said Ramona, glad to forget her spelling.

'No, silly. Abby is giving a party two weeks from tomorrow. She passed out the invitations today.'

'That's nice.' Mrs Quimby was still patting Roberta's back. 'I don't think I know where Abby lives.'

'In one of those nice big houses the other side of high school,' Beezus explained.

'Will her parents be home?' asked Mrs Quimby.

'Oh, *Mom!*' Beezus was annoyed even though she was used to her mother's concern. 'Yes, they will be home and all that stuff. I asked because I know how old-fashioned you are.'

Mrs Quimby said, 'Funny, I used to think my parents were old-fashioned, too.'

Stuff, thought Ramona. Beezus said 'stuff' and mother didn't say anything. Then, to avoid arguments between her mother and sister, she said, 'I hope you don't have to play pin-the-tail-on-the-donkey.'

'Of course not, silly. That's a game for little kids.' Beezus spoke as if Ramona were still in kindergarten. 'Abby is inviting boys and we're going to dance!'

'Wow!' said Ramona. 'But you don't know how to dance.'

Beezus seemed to wilt. At that moment Roberta startled them with a noise, the sort of noise Mrs Quimby called a bubble, Beezus and Ramona called a burp, and Mr Quimby, when he was being funny, a belch, a word his daughters disapproved of because it sounded too ugly for such a sweet baby.

'Good girl,' crooned Mrs Quimby. Roberta's sisters paid no attention. By now they were used to Roberta.

'How can you dance if you don't know how?' persisted Ramona.

'That's what's bothering me,' admitted Beezus. 'Abby's mother made her take ballroom dancing lessons to help her be popular, and now she's giving this party to get her going on being popular. Maybe Abby can show me.'

'Dancing can't be that hard.' Ramona tried to cheer Beezus. 'I've seen it on TV. Kids just sort of wiggle around and wave their arms.'

'Don't worry. Your father will show you how,' reassured Mrs Quimby.

Ramona thought about Howie and Yard Ape. She could not imagine them dancing.

After the party invitation, telephone calls that were not about baby-sitting began to come for Beezus. Of course, Ramona listened to Beezus's half of the conversations, which involved which boys were invited, which boys might actually come, what to wear, and who said what to whose locker partner in the hall at school. Ramona wished she had a locker at school instead of a coat hook at the back of the classroom. Beezus even got to have a padlock on her locker.

On Saturday afternoon Beezus took her baby-sitting money out of the mug on her study table and in spite of drizzling rain set off to meet some friends at the shopping centre. '*Au revoir*,' she said as she went out of the door.

Ramona was annoyed with her sister for not speaking plain English and for not asking her to come along. She tried to pass the time reading Mother Goose rhymes to Roberta, because their mother had read a book that said babies should be read to as soon as they were born so they would grow up to be good readers. Ramona wasn't sure how this would work, but she enjoyed the rhymes and read with expression and dramatic gestures. Roberta seemed fascinated, especially with 'The Three Little Kittens', which Ramona recited over and over until the baby fell asleep and Mrs Quimby carried her off to her crib.

Not as much time had passed as Ramona hoped. Late in the day, when Mrs Quimby was still trying to finish *Moby Dick*, Beezus came home carrying a plastic shopping bag and wearing a head scarf tied under her chin.

That's funny, thought Ramona. Beezus always said head scarves were for old ladies or the Queen of England.

'Successful shopping trip?' Mrs Quimby barely raised her eyes from her book. The book club meeting was not far away.

'Mm-hm.' Beezus beckoned Ramona into their room and shut the door.

'Why are you wearing that dumb scarf?' Ramona demanded. 'It isn't that wet outside.'

'Sh-h-h.' Beezus looked worried. 'What am I going to say?' she whispered.

'About what?' asked Ramona.

'My ears.' Beezus pulled off her scarf. She was wearing a tiny gold ball in the lobe of each ear.

Ramona was so surprised it took her a moment before she whispered, 'Earrings! What will Mommy and Daddy say?'

'That's what's bothering me.' Beezus carefully felt her ears as if to make sure her earrings were still there.

'Well . . .' Ramona was dubious. 'I'm glad they're your ears, not mine.' Then, because she really wanted to know, she asked, 'Did it hurt a lot?'

'Just for a minute, but it was scary,' admitted Beezus. 'They shoot the earrings into your lobes with a thing that looks like a staple gun.'

Ramona winced as Beezus picked up her hairbrush and tried to brush her hair over her ears. At the same time she admired her sister's courage. 'Why don't you show mother and get it over before Daddy comes home.' Ramona was eager to find out what would happen. Besides, she couldn't wait to tell Daisy what Beezus had done.

When the girls advanced cautiously into the living room, Mrs Quimby glanced up from her book, took a second look, and laid the book down. 'Why, Beezus—' she said.

Ramona, ashamed of her curiosity, tried to help her sister. 'Some girls in kindergarten have their ears pierced. I've even seen babies with teeny little earrings.'

Mrs Quimby paid no attention to Ramona but said, 'Beezus, why didn't you ask?'

Beezus looked both unhappy and defiant. 'They are my ears, and I used my baby-sitting money. If I asked, you might not let me.'

'Yes, but—' began Mrs Quimby.

Beezus interrupted. 'I'm tired of being plain old responsible Beezus. I'm tired of people saying how sensible I am. I want to be glamorous for a change. People are always asking me to do things because they know I will do them right. Well, I want to wear earrings and lipstick and be somebody different. I want to look nice for the party. I want to have fun!'

Ramona was shocked. She had never heard her sister speak this way in her whole life.

'Oh, Beezus—' Mrs Quimby had tears in her eyes. 'I had no idea— You always seemed so contented.'

'Not on the inside,' said Beezus in despair. 'Just on the outside.'

'Oh, Beezus—' repeated Mrs Quimby as if she could not find words to express her sympathy for her daughter.

Roberta seemed to understand that her home at the moment was not as happy as she wanted it to be. First she looked worried. Then she began to whimper.

'Sh-h-h,' soothed Mrs Quimby, trying to distract the baby before she spoke to Beezus. 'You are pretty. You have lovely eyes and shining hair.'

'Nobody ever says so.' Beezus's anger melted, leaving her wilted and tearful. 'And sometimes my face breaks out in spots.'

'I think you're sort of pretty, even with spots.' Ramona, loyal to her sister, wanted her to be happy. If Beezus was happy, Ramona could look forward to being happy when she reached high school. Not that Ramona wasn't happy now. She was, except sometimes.

Beezus did not seem comforted. She sniffed and blew her nose. 'I'm sorry for being such a—I don't know what.'

'Don't be.' Mrs Quimby wiped her own eyes. 'Everyone has to let off a little steam now and then. I'm glad to know how you feel. I don't know what your father will say, but cheer up. What's done is done. Next Saturday we'll go shopping for some pretty earrings and something to wear to the party.'

'Thank you,' said Beezus with a watery smile as her mother carried Roberta off to the bedroom to change her.

'One down, one to go,' said Ramona as if life were a football game on television. Beezus picked up a magazine and sat turning the pages without really looking at them. Ramona could tell she was trying to think what to say when she faced her father.

When Mr Quimby came home from work, he left an armload of groceries in the kitchen before he came into the living room. 'Hi, kids,' he said, and when he looked at Beezus said, 'Well, well, what have we here?'

Beezus dropped the magazine to face her father, ready to defend her ears. 'They are my ears and I used my own money,' she informed him. 'I don't care what you say.'

'Relax, Beezus.' Mr Quimby kissed the top of her head and said, 'So our little girl is growing up. I'm surprised you didn't have your nose pierced while you were at it.' He rumpled her hair affectionately.

'Dad, don't be silly,' said Beezus, obviously relieved. 'You know I wouldn't do a thing like that.'

'You never can tell,' said Mr Quimby. 'Kids today . . .' He left to change out of his supermarket clothes.

Beezus fell back in her chair and said, 'Whew. That's over.'

Ramona felt the same way. Now, if she ever wanted her ears pierced, which was hard to imagine, but if she ever should, all she would have to say was, Beezus had her ears pierced. And then when Roberta's turn came—Ramona did not even want to think of Roberta's tender little ears being shot with a thing that looked like a staple gun.

'Ramona, time to set the table,' Mrs Quimby called out.

'OK,' said Ramona, but she was thinking about Beezus growing up and about what it would be like to grow up herself. She felt the way she felt when she was reading a good book. She wanted to know what would happen next.

5

THE PRINCESS AND THE WITCH

Ramona was impatient to go to Daisy's house again, especially now that Beezus was talking so much about the upcoming party. She liked the Kidds' big untidy house with a dog, a cat, and a big brother. She also liked licking juice bars while watching *Big Hospital*. When the next visit was arranged, Ramona and Daisy ran from the school bus to Daisy's house. Jeremy was already lounging in front of the television set watching an ice hockey game.

The girls exchanged looks. 'Germy, aren't you going to walk Mutley?' Daisy asked as if the dog were all she had on her mind. On hearing his name, Mutley raised his head, decided Daisy's words were not important, and rested his nose on his paws once more.

'Nope.' Jeremy was definite. 'And no, I'm not going to let you have the TV this time.'

'Oh, well.' Daisy was used to her big brother. 'Come on, Ramona, let's go upstairs to my room and play dress-up.'

'Nice try,' said Jeremy.

As the girls climbed the stairs, Ramona could not help thinking that if the Quimbys' house had a second storey they would have more bedrooms, and she and Beezus would not always be arguing over whose turn it was to dust the crowded space they now had to share because Roberta had Ramona's old room. Daisy, Ramona could see, was not neat at all.

Daisy pulled a carton to the centre of her room and began to pull out clothes: satins, velvets, hats with flowers and veils, a long black cape, high-heeled shoes.

'Wow!' breathed Ramona. 'Where did you get all this?'

'Oh—around,' said Daisy. 'Mom collected most of it for me, because she loved to dress up when she was my age, only she couldn't find much to dress up in.'

Nice mom, thought Ramona as she chose a long red dress with a flounce around the bottom and slipped it over her head.

Daisy pulled out a long yellow dress trimmed with little things that glittered, but before she poked her head into it she pulled off her slacks. 'Dresses don't look good over trousers, and besides, I like the swishy feeling against my legs,' she explained.

Ramona, deciding she was right, pulled her trousers off, too. Her dress felt smooth and silky against her bare legs. She snatched up a hat trimmed with some battered roses and set it on her head. Then she pulled off her shoes (her nice shoes!) and stuck her feet into high-heeled sandals, which made her glamorous, she felt, even if they were too big. 'Look! I'm a star!' Ramona lifted her arms as if she were a dancer before she clonked across the room to look at herself in the mirror. 'I'm gorgeous,' she announced, pretending she had long blonde hair. 'I'm beautiful. I'm me, gorgeous, beautiful me!'

'I'm Miss America.' Daisy twirled around. 'I'm so beautiful all the other girls in the competition went home.'

Both girls clonked around, turning and swishing as if they were in a television fashion show. When they both turned their ankles and fell off their shoes, they collapsed on the bed in a fit of giggles.

Then Ramona discovered a long pink dress and because she was already gorgeous and beautiful decided to promote herself to princess. She quickly changed while Daisy switched from Miss America to a witch in a long black velvet gown and a small green hat with only three small holes in the veil. 'I'm wicked!' cried Daisy.

'Great,' said Ramona. 'I never liked books with nice witches.'

'I'm going to shut the beautiful princess in a dungeon!' Daisy made a witch face.

'Where are you going to find a dungeon to shut me in?' Ramona was a defiant princess.

'That's easy.' The wicked witch pushed aside the clothes in her closet to reveal a small door, which she opened. Behind it was a dark space under the eaves, which was the attic.

Inside, in the half-light, Ramona saw a few boards laid across the joists to make a place for storing luggage. Beyond, Ramona could see, barely, the lath and plaster that made the ceilings of the rooms downstairs.

'See!' cried Daisy. 'The wicked witch is going to shut the beautiful princess in the dark dungeon full of rats and feed her bread and water.' She grabbed Ramona and pushed her towards the closet within a closet.

'No, she isn't!' cried Ramona, twisting away from Daisy. 'The princess is going to throw the witch in the dungeon and feed her cold oatmeal!'

'Yuck,' gagged Daisy. She shoved Ramona. Ramona shoved back. One shoe fell off. Daisy pushed harder and shoved Ramona through the little door into the dim space beyond. Ramona, in one shoe, stepped on her pink dress, lost her balance, turned, grabbed at nothing, and stepped off the boards onto the lath and plaster. There was an ominous cracking sound beneath her feet.

'Oh no!' cried Daisy.

'Help!' shouted Ramona as the lath began to break beneath her weight, and she found herself sinking. Daisy screamed. The lath made snapping sounds. The pink dress ripped. Ramona heard bits of plaster hitting something below and felt her legs being scratched as the pink dress bunched up around her waist. Her other shoe fell off and hit something downstairs with a thump. She heard Mrs Kidd cry out, 'Oh my!'

Jeremy yelled, 'Hey!' Mutley barked.

Desperate, Ramona bent forward over the joist to stop her fall and searched frantically with her feet to find something to stand on. There was nothing, only air. Above her, rain pattered on the roof.

'Ramona, hang on!' Daisy called out. 'Jeremy, come quick!'

'I'm hanging.' Ramona was terrified. The sharp edge of the joist was pressing into her waist and her legs were cold. She wondered how much longer she could hang on. What if there really were rats in the attic? Dust was everywhere. Ramona sneezed. Below, Mutley barked harder, as if he were warning off an intruder. 'Hurry,' she wailed. On the television a referee blew a whistle and a crowd roared.

'They're coming,' cried equally terrified Daisy, grabbing at the back of the pink dress. Thumping feet were heard on the stairs.

In a moment Jeremy pushed his sister aside and, standing on the boards, seized Ramona under the arms and tugged. 'Dumb kids' was his comment.

'Ow,' said Ramona. Jeremy tugged harder and managed to pull her out of the hole she had made. 'Yow!' escaped from Ramona even though she was grateful to be rescued. As she was pulled out of the hole, she had a glimpse below of the dining room table covered with rubble.

'Oh, you poor child.' Mrs Kidd was filled with sympathy, concern, and relief.

Ramona was so glad to be standing on the hard floor with the remains of the pink dress heaped around her feet that she began to cry.

Mrs Kidd hugged her and murmured, 'There, there. You're safe now. Everything is all right.'

'No, it isn't,' wept Ramona. 'I made a big hole in the floor—ceiling—'

'Whatever,' said Jeremy, and left the room to clump down to the television set.

'Thank you,' sniffled Ramona, remembering her manners even though Jeremy had left. 'You saved my life.' She began to cry harder. She had broken the ceiling and could never come to the Kidds' house again and she and Daisy couldn't be best friends and she would be left with Howie and messy old Willa Jean to play with and—

'Daisy, find Ramona some Kleenex,' said Mrs Kidd. Daisy produced a box from her dresser. Ramona mopped her nose and eyes as Mrs Kidd helped her down the stairs.

'I'll get her trousers,' said Daisy.

Downstairs, in the bathroom, Mrs Kidd pulled off the pink dress. 'Oh, my dear—' she said when she saw Ramona's legs. She began to clean the scratches with cotton wool and stinging liquid from a bottle. Then she covered them with Band-Aids, all sizes. When she had finished, Ramona gave a final sniff. Mrs Kidd washed her face, kissed her, and said, 'There. You're as good as new.'

A fresh worry, paying for the damage, crept into Ramona's mind. Payday, the cheques her mother wrote to pay bills, taxes, and all those grown-up things whirled around in her mind.

'That was some hole you made,' said Jeremy as she and Mrs Kidd went into the living room, where Clawed was peeking out from under the couch. Mutley, his tail drooping, looked anxious.

Ramona suddenly had a new thought. If Daisy hadn't been trying to shut her in a dungeon, none of this would have happened. Maybe it was Daisy's fault. Maybe she should be angry with Daisy. She was confused. She didn't want to be angry with her best friend. Still . . . she didn't know what to think.

Only then did Ramona gather her courage to look towards the dining room, where she saw in the ceiling a dark hole edged with broken lath and bits of plaster. The dining room table was covered with dust, rubble, and, in the midst of the mess, one high-heeled sandal. And the table had been set for—this made Ramona feel really bad—five places, one for her. Suddenly, she didn't want to stay for dinner. She wanted to go home. She wanted to be home with her own mother comforting her for her scratches and for the loss of her best friend. She looked at Daisy, wanting to say, It was all your fault for pushing me, but she did not say it, not in front of Mrs Kidd. She would wait until school on Monday and then she would—

Mrs Kidd put her arm around Ramona. 'Would you rather not stay for dinner?' she asked. Ramona nodded. 'Then come along,' said Mrs Kidd. 'I'll have you home in a jiffy.'

'Ramona—' Daisy was blinking back tears. 'It was all my fault. I—I shouldn't have pushed.'

Ramona instantly felt both ashamed and much better. So often things that went wrong turned out to be her mistake. She should have known Daisy wasn't the kind of girl to blame people. 'No, it wasn't your fault. It was both our faults, I guess.' Ramona hesitated. 'Promise you won't tell the kids at school.'

Daisy crossed her heart, smiled shakily, and said, 'Of course, if the beautiful princess had gone peacefully to the dungeon—'

Ramona interrupted, 'And if the witch had been a nice witch—'

Daisy finished for her. 'The kind you don't like to read about.'

Ramona managed to smile back over her shoulder as she followed Mrs Kidd out of the door. On the way home she ventured a question that had been hovering in the back of her mind. 'Will—will it cost a lot of money to fix the ceiling?' she asked Mrs Kidd.

Mrs Kidd patted Ramona's knee. 'Don't worry about it. It was an accident, and I'm sure our insurance will take care of it. And you know something? Even before we moved in, I didn't like the colour of the dining room. Now we have an excuse to repaint it.'

Ramona felt so much better, except for the scratches and stiffness in her legs, that she began to consider the drama of the afternoon.

When Mrs Kidd delivered her to the Quimbys'

door, she merely said to Mrs Quimby, 'Ramona had a little accident. She will tell you about it.'

It was a big accident, thought Ramona, pleased that Mrs Kidd did not spoil her chance to tell. She really was a nice mother, the nicest she had ever known, next to her own, of course.

Mrs Quimby immediately wanted to know what had happened but was distracted by Roberta. Ramona stalled for time by going to the bathroom and by darting into her room. When she came out, the family was seated at the dinner table. She then had the attention of her entire family, even Roberta, who was lying in her playpen nearby. Mrs Quimby said, 'Ramona, I thought you were going to have dinner at Daisy's house. And what did her mother mean about a little accident?'

Ramona assumed a sorrowful expression. 'I was going to stay, but a terrible thing happened.' Her family stopped eating. Ramona paused dramatically. Here was her chance to keep Beezus from talking so much about Abby and the party.

'Yes. Go on,' said Mr Quimby.

Ramona took a deep breath. 'I broke the ceiling'—another dramatic pause—'I broke it all to smithereens and it's going to cost a bazillion dollars to fix and it fell all over the dining room and made a terrible mess, so I decided not to stay for dinner.'

Mr Quimby became more impatient. 'Ramona, get to the point. What on earth are you talking about?'

Ramona basked in the attention. 'I was a princess trying to escape from a wicked witch who was shutting me in a dungeon, and there I was all alone in the dark with spiders and bats—well, maybe not bats'—Ramona felt if she exaggerated too much her family would not believe her—'and I was terrified because the wicked witch was about to break down the door'—maybe she was stretching the truth a tiny bit, but perhaps no one would notice—'and I was terrified because I felt something bump against my leg, something big, something evil and crawly'—of course, suitcases weren't evil and crawly, but by then Ramona did not want to spoil her story with the truth—'and I was so terrified all alone in the creepy dark full of cobwebs that I tried to flee—'

'Eeee!' crowed Roberta.

'Ramona.' Mrs Quimby spoke quietly. 'I think you're getting carried away.'

Beezus, who had been quiet until now, spoke up. 'So you stepped back on the unfinished part of the attic and fell through the ceiling. I know all about those attics because mothers were always telling us to stay off the lath and plaster, and I know someone who really did fall through.'

Of course, Ramona was annoyed with Beezus for spoiling her story. 'Sort of like that,' she admitted with a scowl.

Mrs Quimby was shocked. 'Why, Ramona— Did you fall all the way through? You might have been seriously hurt.'

'I hung on, but I was wounded.' Ramona tried to regain her family's sympathy. 'My legs got all scratched and scraped and it hurt a lot. I was in agony.' There, take that, Beezus, she thought. 'And then a handsome prince, I mean Daisy's brother, rescued me.'

'Jeremy Kidd?' Beezus began to laugh. 'He's in my maths class. Wait till I tell him you called him a handsome prince!'

'Don't you dare!' Ramona was furious.

'Girls!' warned Mr Quimby. 'Beezus, there are some things we keep in the family.'

Beezus stopped laughing. Finally she asked, 'Weren't you wearing trousers?'

Ramona said in her most dignified way, 'Princesses don't wear trousers.' She paused and added, 'Unless they are in disguise.'

The family found this funny. Beezus recovered enough to say, 'You must have looked weird, just your bare legs hanging down from the ceiling.'

And my underpants, thought Ramona in horror, not having pictured the scene from below until this moment. Did I fall far enough for them to show? What if Jeremy saw them? She could never face him again. She could see that her family were hiding their smiles at the picture of Ramona's bare legs hanging from the ceiling. This made Ramona sulky. 'It really did hurt, because I was wounded. I bled.' That ought to impress her family.

Her father patted her hand. 'I know it was painful and you could have been badly hurt.'

'But I was brave.' Ramona held her head high. 'I hung on with all my might and main.' She wasn't quite sure what that meant. She had read it in a book someplace and it sounded right.

'Maybe you have a fairy godmother,' suggested Mrs Quimby.

A best friend is better, thought Ramona.

'Maybe,' agreed Mr Quimby, 'but I think she has been reading fairy tales.'

'I like fairy tales,' said Ramona. 'Fairy tales always have happy endings.' She paused before she added, 'And so does mine, I guess.' Her family had paid attention to her and she still had a best friend. Then she thought to herself, A happy ending except for my underpants showing.

6

THe PaRTY

Before Ramona's scratches healed and her Band-Aids were pulled off, Ramona had grown bored with her sister's party invitation, the shopping, and most of all with the telephone calls. Beezus seemed always to be talking on the telephone. Boredom did not prevent Ramona from listening to her sister's half of the conversations: 'I'm sorry. I won't be able to baby-sit that evening. I'm going to a party.' 'If George won't come, maybe you could ask Randy. He's only a semi-creep.' 'I just love my new skirt. We found it on sale. Have you bought yours yet?'

Then there were dancing lessons given by Mr Quimby with much twirling and *step, slide, step, step, slide, step.* One evening when the lesson was finished and Beezus went off to do her homework, Mr Quimby held out his hand to Ramona. 'Let's give it a try,' he said. Ramona shook her head. It all looked so silly.

Silliness did not stop Ramona from telling Daisy about the dancing lesson or from giving her a demonstration when she came to the Quimbys' after school. The girls stepped and slid, getting in the way of each other's feet, until, laughing, they fell over on the couch.

Another evening when Beezus was talking on the telephone, Ramona heard her father say to her mother, 'I'll be glad when this party is over and we can all settle down again.'

Mrs Quimby lowered her voice, which of course made Ramona listen harder. 'I'm glad Beezus is finally coming out of her shell. She has always been such a quiet girl. I do hope she has a good time. It could be a terrible letdown.'

This conversation was a surprise to Ramona. She had assumed Beezus would have a good time twirling and gliding and eating good things. Maybe not. Maybe their mother was right.

Mrs Quimby was not the only one concerned. When the girls were in bed, Beezus confided, 'I hope Daddy's dancing isn't too old-fashioned.'

'Daddy's a good dancer,' said Ramona, loyal to their father even though his dancing did not look like some of the dancing she had seen on television.

Finally, to the relief of everyone, the day of the party arrived. Beezus washed her hair in the afternoon and was so nervous and excited she could scarcely eat her dinner. Afterwards she lingered in the bath. 'Whew!' said Ramona as perfume from bubble bath wafted down the hall.

At last Beezus appeared, ready for the party. 'Ta-dah!' she announced as she came into the living room. 'Do I really look all right?' She was wearing her new long skirt, a pretty blouse, small gold hoops in her ears, and her hiking shoes that laced above her ankles. Her hair was shining, her cheeks pink.

'You look lovely, dear,' said Mrs Quimby, 'but— ah—don't you think you should change your shoes?'

'Oh, Mom, nobody wears party shoes any more these days.' She gave her mother a pitying look.

'Oh,' said her mother. 'I didn't know.'

'I think you look great.' Ramona was impressed by the change in Beezus but somehow missed her plain big sister. Oh, well, at least her feet still looked sensible. Will I look like that someday? she wondered as she put her hand to her own hair and decided maybe she should brush it more often, the way her mother was always telling her.

Mrs Quimby kissed Beezus and said, 'Have a good time, dear. But don't you think you should wear a coat? This is November, you know.'

'Oh, mo-*ther*,' said Beezus. 'I don't want to wrinkle my new blouse. Besides, it's not like it's snowing or anything.'

'I'll turn on the car heater,' reassured Mr Quimby. 'We can't wrinkle that blouse.'

Ramona suddenly did not want to let go of her sister. 'Can I come, too?' she asked.

'Sure. Come along,' Mr Quimby said. The ride was made in silence with Beezus sitting up straight in the backseat and unwrinkled. In spite of the car heater she hugged her arms to keep warm. When they pulled up in front of Abby's house, Beezus said in anguish, 'Dad, what do I do? My hands are all clammy.'

'Don't worry, you'll do fine,' said her father, 'and it will all be over by eleven o'clock.' After he dropped Beezus off among the arriving guests, he said, almost as if he were speaking to himself, 'Well, there goes our little girl.'

Ramona moved as close to her father as her seat belt would permit. 'You still have me,' she reminded him.

'That's right.' Her father patted her knee. 'And Roberta.'

'Yes,' whispered Ramona with a tiny sigh. She loved her baby sister, but sometimes she wished her father did not have quite so many daughters.

When the two returned home, Mrs Quimby looked up from her book (she did not have many pages left) and said, as if her thoughts were far away, 'I'll never forget my first dance. It was in the school gym, and the only boy who asked me to dance I didn't want to dance with. He was a weird little fellow who grew up to be an interesting man, but at the time I wanted to dance with a tall, handsome boy. Silly me. I was a real wallflower and spent most of the evening hiding in the girls' bathroom with a couple of other miserable wallflowers.'

Ramona was indignant. Stupid boys, not asking her nice mother to dance. She hoped Beezus wasn't hiding in the bathroom, even though the Alexanders' bathroom was sure to be nicer than a school bathroom. Their bathroom wouldn't have scratchy tan paper towels.

When her father told her to stop stalling and go to bed, Ramona lay awake thinking. She would never hide in a bathroom. She would march right up and ask a boy to dance if she ever wanted to do such a silly thing as dance.

Even though Ramona thought that dancing was silly, she wanted her sister to have a good time. She even said a little prayer as she lay awake, waiting, full of hope and curiosity. The minute she heard her father drive off to bring Beezus home, Ramona bounced out of bed and went into the living room, where her mother was finally finishing *Moby Dick*. Of course Mrs Quimby said,

'Ramona, you should be in bed asleep.' Parents always did that.

Ramona ignored this remark and snuggled up under her mother's arm. She loved moments alone with her mother, which made her feel cosy and protected. She must have nodded off, for suddenly there was Beezus, her eyes still shining, her cheeks still pink. The rest of her face was unrecognizable. She was wearing dark red lipstick and green eye shadow.

'Wow!' was Ramona's comment. 'What happened to you?'

Beezus dropped into a chair and laughed.

Mrs Quimby laughed as well, distracted from Beezus's new make-up by her relief at seeing her happy.

Ramona spoke up before Beezus could answer. 'What's so funny?' she asked.

'Boys,' said Beezus. 'Boys are funny.'

'Who says boys are funny?' Mr Quimby had come in from the garage. 'I was a boy once. I wasn't funny.'

'I say boys are funny,' said Beezus. 'So do all the girls.'

Mrs Quimby asked, 'What do boys do that is so funny?'

Beezus explained. 'Except for one boy, they wouldn't even come in the house. One boy brought a miniature chess set and he and another boy played chess under the porch light. The others just sort of flopped around or tried standing on their hands in the wet grass. Some boys who weren't even invited joined in. There was a lot of whooping and yelling and neighbours coming out to see what was going on. One boy pulled a night crawler out of the lawn and chased another boy around with it. You know the stuff boys do. Mrs Alexander got all upset because she wants Abby to be popular, and she wasn't being popular with all the boys sitting outside acting like a bunch of little kids. Somebody must have called the police, because we saw them drive by, but they kept on going.'

'What about the boy in the house?' asked Mr Quimby.

'He watched TV,' Beezus explained. 'Nobody paid any attention to him. The other boys said they had just come for the food.'

Sounds like Yard Ape, Ramona thought, and Howie might bring a chess set.

'Poor hungry boys,' said Mr Quimby. 'I hope somebody fed them.'

'Oh, sure,' said Beezus as if this was not important. 'The girls had fun experimenting with free samples of lipstick and all the other free samples Mrs Alexander gets when she buys cosmetics.'

'I wondered what happened to your face,' said Mrs Quimby with a smile, 'but I was afraid to ask.'

'Mrs Alexander wears lots of make-up,' Beezus continued, 'and her hair is a funny colour. She wears it all fluffed up and it looks something like those coppery things we scour pans with.'

'You look weird, like a vampire or something,' was Ramona's comment. 'What about the dancing?'

'That's the best part. We didn't have to dance,' said Beezus. 'Some girls were disappointed, but we sort of played Monopoly and Scrabble. Mostly we talked about—oh, you know—and had a good time anyway, and then the boys began to yell that they were hungry. Mrs Alexander just about had a fit after paying for Abby's dancing lessons and everything, but we took sandwiches and punch and cookies out to them. Mrs Alexander had old-fashioned food instead of pizza and stuff. They quieted down after that.'

'What a relief,' said Mr Quimby. 'I was worried about those poor hungry kids out there in the cold.'

'Dad, you're just being silly.' Beezus giggled and continued, 'I didn't really want to dance anyway. At least not yet, not until boys get over being such little kids.'

'Well, how do you like that?' said Mr Quimby. 'My dancing lessons wasted. Those boys had probably shined their shoes and didn't want girls stepping all over them.'

Ramona could see her sister was so happy she didn't mind being teased. 'But what about the night crawler?' she asked.

'When we brought out the food, they threw it back in the grass,' Beezus explained.

Ramona was only slightly disappointed. 'Did you get anything to eat?' What was the point of a party without food?

'Of course,' said Beezus. 'You don't think we'd let the boys have everything, do you? We ate the salad and the ice cream.'

'I'm so glad you had a good time, dear,' said Mrs Quimby. 'Now wash your face *good* with soap and run along to bed. It's almost midnight.'

Beezus paused in the doorway. 'You know something?' she asked. 'I don't think Abby and I are the popular type. And you know something else? I don't care.'

'I'm glad you feel that way,' said Mrs Quimby with a tender smile. 'I wish I had been that sensible when I was your age.'

'*C'est la vie*,' said Beezus and, as she headed to the bedroom, added to Ramona, 'That's French for "That's life".'

Ramona made a face. '*Au revoir*.' She had picked up a word or two of French herself.

'You, too, kiddo,' said Mrs Quimby to Ramona.

Ramona snuggled against her mother, stalling for time, and said, 'I'm glad I have a nice plain mother instead of a mother with hair you could scour pans with.' If she could postpone going to bed, she might get to hear what her parents would say about Beezus.

'Thank you.' Mrs Quimby smiled affectionately and rumpled Ramona's hair. 'But compliments won't keep you out of bed. Now run along.'

Ramona pattered on light feet down the hall and climbed into bed. Her next-to-last thought, before she fell asleep, was, I can't wait to tell Daisy. Her last thought was, I'm glad Beezus is still sensible on the inside.

7

THE GROWN-UP LETTER

It was almost Thanksgiving when Ramona decided that she liked Mrs Meacham most of the time. Not that Mrs Meacham did not have flaws. She did, in Ramona's opinion. Mrs Meacham was enthusiastic about spelling and especially enjoyed words with silent letters such as *knit* and *wrist*. She was also a stickler for pronunciation and corrected anyone who said 'gonna' or 'shoulda'. 'If you don't pronounce correctly, you can't spell,' she said much too often, Ramona thought.

Most of the fourth grade thought Mrs Meacham had another flaw. She confiscated any notes written by her class that were thrown, passed, or dropped on desks. She then read them for misspelled words and, if she found one, added it to the list on the blackboard: Words We Need to Work On. She then tore up the notes and threw the pieces in the wastebasket.

The fourth grade thought this was unfair, but Ramona was not much concerned. By the fourth grade she had learned to put up with teachers. She was not concerned, that is, until one day when Yard Ape, on his way to the pencil sharpener, dropped a note on her desk. She picked it up and was about to read it when Mrs Meacham said, 'Ramona, bring the note to me.' Trapped, Ramona obeyed.

Mrs Meacham read it, smiled, and turned to the blackboard, where she added one word to the list of Words We Need to Work On. That word was 'Ramona'. She then tore up the note and gave a little talk about not confusing *n* with *m*. Ramona along with the rest of the class, then knew Yard Ape had written 'Ranoma' instead of 'Ramona'. She glanced at him. He was looking straight ahead and even his ears were red. She had never seen Yard Ape embarrassed before. What could he have written in the note?

At recess all the boys chanted, 'Danny loves Ramona! Danny loves Ramona!'

Daisy asked, 'Didn't you get to read any of it?' Ramona shook her head, more curious than ever. She decided to ask Yard Ape, but he was so busy kicking a ball that he acted as if he had never met her. Oh, well. Now her class would have to study her name in spelling. Ramona liked that.

Yard Ape continued to avoid Ramona. When he wasn't paying attention in class, he was busy drawing a wristwatch in ink on his arm. On the bus he sat with the rowdy boys in the last seats.

As the winter rains beat against the classroom windows, Ramona plodded along with spelling, day after day, spelling most words right if she had worked hard, something she did not often do. On tests, if she spelled them all right, Mrs Meacham wrote, 'Keep up the good work!' on her paper. Ramona sometimes wondered if spelling correctly was worthwhile, because those who spelled all their words right were given what Mrs Meacham called Reward Words to work on. These were really hard words, some with three syllables; Ramona did not feel rewarded.

At home Ramona's parents and sometimes Beezus sat beside her on the couch and went over spelling words with Ramona, who squirmed, unfastened and refastened the Velcro on her shoes, or tried to put one foot behind her head. Her parents sighed. Beezus said, 'Oh, grow up, Ramona.'

'I am a potential grown-up,' Ramona said with dignity, pleased to have used a Reward Word. She looked at Roberta lying in her playpen with her chewed-up bear and felt a moment of pity for her baby sister and what lay ahead of her in growing up, especially spelling.

All this made Ramona feel surrounded by words. There were words everyplace she looked: in books and newspapers, on signs and television, on cereal boxes and milk cartons. The world, Ramona decided, was full of people who used their dictionary skills and probably weren't any fun.

Then one day when Ramona was riding on the school bus going to Daisy's house, she glanced out of the window and happened to notice a licence plate on a car in the next lane. Instead of numbers it had letters: LIBARY. 'Daisy, look!' she said. 'They left out a letter.' Ramona was sure of the spelling of *library* because she went to the branch library once a week and saw the word above the door every time she entered.

'You'd better tell Mrs Meacham,' said Daisy.

The next morning Ramona approached Mrs Meacham, planted herself squarely in front of her teacher, and said, 'I saw a licence plate with *library* spelled with only one *r*, and that is wrong.'

'Good for you, Ramona,' said Mrs Meacham. 'I know that licence plate. It belongs to the county librarian.'

Ramona was indignant. 'If she can't spell, why is she a librarian? Librarians should know how to spell.'

Mrs Meacham laughed and said, 'I'm glad you think so, Ramona, but the state of Oregon allows only six letters on personalized licence plates. I am sure the librarian is really an excellent speller.'

'Oh,' said Ramona, disappointed. She wanted a grown-up to be wrong for a change. She was tired of the rightness of grown-ups.

That same day, late in the afternoon, when Ramona was grouchy because her mother had turned off *Big Hospital*, she was reading when she came across a strange word: *asinine*. She did not want to spoil the pleasure of reading by looking it up, so she called out to anyone listening, 'What does *as-i-nine* mean?'

Beezus answered, 'Stupid, dumb, silly, acting like a mule.' She was cross because she was having trouble with French verbs.

Ramona scowled, annoyed by her sister's superiority. 'I didn't ask to have my vocabulary built. I just wanted to know what it meant.'

'Like I said. Stupid, dumb, foolish, mulish,' said Beezus. 'Like you.'

That was too much for Ramona. She threw down her book and called out, 'Mother, Beezus called me a bad name.'

'Well, you are,' said Beezus. 'You are stupid, dumb, foolish, mulish, and asinine. Everybody has to learn how to spell.'

'I wasn't asking about spelling, and just because you're in high school, you think you're so big!' countered Ramona. 'Well, I think you're mean.'

'At least I keep my half of our room neat,' said Beezus.

Mrs Quimby came into the room. 'Girls! Stop it this minute. I've had enough of this nonsense. Ramona, you are being foolish, yes, asinine about learning to spell, and Beezus, you are being stupid when you call your sister names. This sort of thing will only escalate into more name-calling. This is no example to set for Roberta.'

The girls were startled. Their mother rarely spoke so sharply. They looked at each other with looks that said, Stupid? Foolish? Us?

'And furthermore,' said Mrs Quimby, 'I don't want to hear any more bickering about whose turn it is to clean up your room.' With that she stalked out of the room to look after fussing Roberta, who was feverish. The pediatrician had given her a shot to prevent her from getting whooping cough.

'We're nice most of the time.' Beezus regretted name-calling. 'We wouldn't be normal if we didn't forget sometimes.'

'I don't suppose Roberta will be one of those people who grows up just naturally knowing how to spell.' Ramona sighed, defeated. 'Not with me for a role model.'

'Spelling is just one of those things you have to *do*,' said Beezus, 'and there's always the dictionary.'

'Boring,' said Ramona, and thought fondly of Daisy, herself a good speller, who never criticized Ramona's spelling, because she could tell what she meant.

After that, Ramona and Beezus stopped bickering so much, and Ramona continued, with tiresome help from her family, to muddle along with spelling. When progress report time came, she delivered her envelope to her mother without peeking. Mrs Quimby read the report, smiled, kissed Ramona, and said, 'Good work. I'm proud of you.' Then she turned the report over to the Habits and Attitudes section, frowned, and read aloud, 'Ramona's spelling will improve when she decides she wants it to improve.' Mrs Quimby looked at Ramona, but all she said was 'Well?'

'Mrs Meacham is *mean*,' Ramona explained. 'If we get all the spelling words right, she gives us hard words and calls them Reward Words as if they were some kind of treat. They aren't. They are really, really hard words like *foreign* and *quarantine*, the kind of words where you don't know which letter comes first. I think you should go talk to Mrs Meacham and tell her she's mean.'

'And what do you think she would say to that?' Mrs Quimby asked.

Ramona thought a moment. 'She'd say I am a

horrible, stupid child with bad habits and attitudes, the worst fourth grader she's ever had,
and she can't wait to get rid of me and she never
wants to see me again as long as she lives.'

Mrs Quimby did not seem upset. 'Do you really
think Mrs Meacham would say that?'

Once more Ramona thought before she
answered in a small voice, 'No, but I'm tired of
spelling.'

Mrs Quimby said, 'So am I. So is your whole
family.'

'Except Roberta,' Ramona reminded her
mother.

Mrs Quimby ignored the interruption. 'From
now on, you're on your own.' She meant it, because
after that no one said, 'Come on, Ramona, let's
go over your spelling words.' Nobody said, 'How
about a little spelling before bedtime?' Nobody
cared about Ramona's spelling.

Ramona began to feel that no one cared about
her, either. Her mother was busy reading a new
book for her book club or comforting drooly
Roberta, who was teething, Beezus was either
talking on the telephone or doing her homework,
and Mr Quimby was in the basement refinishing
his grandmother's chest of drawers for Roberta's
room.

That left Daisy, who had no trouble spelling.

One afternoon when she had come to Ramona's house, the girls were looking for something to do. Daisy picked up the sports section of the newspaper, which was lying on the coffee table, and began to read aloud as if she were an excited television announcer, '"Crash! Splash! $25 Cash Back! No down payments for six months!"'

Ramona picked up another part of the paper and read in a stern voice, '"Stop sneezing! Get rid of dust, mould, and fungus with our duct clean-up system"'—here, a dramatic pause— '"and keep it clean!"'

Both girls found this funny.

'Sounds like what Jeremy's room needs,' remarked Daisy before she read in a dreamy voice, '"Planning a romantic wedding?"'

'Not right away,' said Ramona, scanning the newspaper. 'Here's a funny letter somebody wrote to some people who do income tax stuff. They put it in their ad.'

'Boring,' said Daisy.

Ramona ignored her and read, '"You J. K. Barker people really know your stuff. I shoulda come here last year, and I'm gonna come here next year."' She frowned her disapproval.

Daisy was indignant. 'They shouldn't put words like *gonna* and *shoulda* in the newspaper. Mrs Meacham wouldn't like it.'

'Or maybe we should show it to Mrs Meacham,' suggested Ramona, 'so she would know it is OK to use them because they are in the newspaper.'

Daisy was doubtful. 'You know Mrs Meacham. She'll march right down to the newspaper with her red pencil and—'

'I know!' Ramona was inspired. 'Let's write to the tax people. I bet they made up the letter themselves.'

Daisy was enthusiastic. Ramona found paper and an envelope, and the girls went to work composing their letter. 'Dear Tax People,' Ramona wrote, because her joined-up writing was better than Daisy's. 'There are no such words as gonna and shoulda which you put in your ad. You set a bad example for children who are learning to spell. We think you made up the letter yourself.' Ramona added the last sentence. 'There are better words than stuff.' Daisy read the letter carefully to make sure they had not misspelled words. They both signed it, including their ages. Ramona addressed the envelope and included the Quimbys' return address. Then they ran to the corner mailbox, mailed it, and forgot about it. They had other things to think about.

That was why Ramona was surprised a week later when she came home from school and her mother handed her a long envelope addressed to Miss Ramona Quimby. Nobody had ever called her 'Miss' except when they were joking or were cross with her. This looked serious. The return address read, 'J. K. Barker. Certified Public Accountant'.

'Ramona, are you having problems with your income tax?' Mrs Quimby asked, behaving as if she were serious even though she was joking.

'Oh, mother. You know my allowance isn't that big.' Ramona tore open the envelope and pulled out a crisp sheet of paper, a real grown-up business letter addressed to her and to Daisy. Only then did Ramona remember the letter they had written, a letter they did not expect to be answered. This letter read: 'Dear Ramona and Daisy: I goofed and you caught me! I did make up the letter in the newspaper, and I promise never to do it again, not when two sharp-eyed nine-year-olds read my advertisements. You must do good work in school and are sure to do well in life. When you earn millions of dollars, please bring your income tax work to my office. Cordially, J. K. Barker.'

Ramona was so impressed she reread the letter. Grown-ups almost never admitted they goofed.

'May I see?' asked Mrs Quimby. When she had read the letter, she said, 'This is great. Mrs Meacham should be proud of you.'

Ramona ran to the telephone. Daisy, as she had

expected, was every bit as excited as she was. Like Ramona, she could not wait to show Mrs Meacham their real grown-up letter.

The next morning Daisy met Ramona as she got off the school bus. Together they accosted Mrs Meacham and held out J. K. Barker's letter. Mrs Meacham read it and said, 'Good for you! This world needs more people like you to keep things in order. May I read this to the class?' Of course the girls agreed, and while she read it they tried to look modest. Then their teacher fastened it with drawing pins to the bulletin board for all to behold.

Everyone was impressed, even Susan. Yard Ape, looking straight ahead, smiled, but Ramona noticed that out of the corner of his eye he was looking at her.

Ramona felt good, better than she had felt since the first day of fourth grade.

8

Peas

The rainy winter days passed quickly. Thanksgiving came and not long afterwards Christmas vacation. Ramona missed Daisy, who went with her family to visit her grandparents. When she returned, the girls spent an afternoon dressing up Roberta in the clothes she had received for Christmas. Roberta was agreeable to having a dress pulled over her head, her arms stuffed into a sweater, her head shoved into caps. She enjoyed the girls' admiration. She was not so happy about a pair of crocheted slippers with ears and tails that looked like rabbits, a gift from Howie's grandmother, who enjoyed crocheting. Roberta did not care for the slippers. She puckered up, ready to cry.

'Come on, Roberta,' coaxed Ramona. 'You'll have bunnies for feet. See.'

Bunny feet did not interest Roberta, especially when she was beginning to feel tired. She began to fuss.

'Maybe the bunnies tickle her feet,' suggested Daisy.

'Roberta, feel how nice and soft the bunny is.'
Ramona pulled a slipper over Roberta's curling toes.
Roberta began to howl. She was not going to wear
those slippers, and Ramona could not make her.

'OK, OK,' said Ramona, giving in. Roberta, she
could see, was no longer the happy, cooing baby
she had been except when teething or when the
pediatrician had given her a shot to keep her from
getting sick. She now had a will of her own. She's
growing up, thought Ramona, like me.

Not long after this, when Ramona splashed
home from the bus in the icy rain, her mother
called out as she opened the back door, 'Don't
step on Roberta.'

After the wind and rain, the kitchen felt warm
and cosy. Mm-m. Ramona inhaled. Meat loaf for
dinner. She would not have to struggle to cut it
with a knife. Roberta was sitting in the middle
of the floor pounding on a pan with a wooden
spoon. Ramona sat down on the floor beside her
to pull off her wet boots. 'Mother, guess what?'
she began.

Mrs Quimby, too busy to guess what, did not
answer. Instead she said, 'Would you please give
me a hand with Roberta? This is your father's
bowling night, and I want to have dinner early. I'm
behind because Roberta pushed a jar of tomato
sauce onto the floor in the market.' Moving

quickly, she picked up Roberta, said, 'Upsy-daisy,' set her in her high chair, scooped up the pan and wooden spoon, and tossed them into the sink. She placed a plastic dish of Roberta's dinner and a cup with a spout on the high-chair tray, and handed Ramona a spoon.

Ramona examined Roberta's dinner. 'What's this green stuff?' she asked as she tied a bib around Roberta's neck. Roberta, in a happy mood, squealed and patted her hands on the tray.

'Peas,' answered their mother, busy rolling wet lettuce in a towel. 'I was in a hurry and I found an old jar of baby food. I know Roberta has outgrown strained peas, but I didn't want to waste them.'

'Yuck,' said Ramona. The peas were unappetizing, and Roberta looked so innocent and trusting. Oh well, Roberta was the one who had to eat them. Spooning food into the baby's rosy mouth or guiding her little hand clutching her spoon made Ramona feel grown-up and responsible, a big sister for a change.

The telephone rang in the hall. Mrs Quimby answered. 'Oh, hello, Sally,' she said.

A book club lady, Ramona thought. That meant a long, boring conversation. Maybe if she hurried she could see part of *Big Hospital* before her mother finished her conversation and told her to turn it off. Curly-haired Doctor had fallen in love with Blonde Nurse, who was secretly married . . . Ramona couldn't wait to see what happened next. She decided to hold the spoon herself to feed Roberta more quickly.

Mrs Quimby was saying, 'Let's read a shorter book this time. I thought I would never finish *Moby Dick.*'

Ramona dipped up a spoonful of cottage cheese. 'Open wide,' she said to Roberta. 'Down the little red lane.' That was what her mother said when she fed Roberta. Ramona opened her own mouth, because she was Roberta's role model. Roberta obediently imitated her and accepted the cottage cheese. 'Good girl,' said Ramona. Roberta smiled a messy smile and pounded her heels against the high chair.

Mrs Quimby was saying, 'I really enjoy our book club. Now that I am no longer working—not that looking after my daughters isn't work—I enjoy exercising my brain.'

Ramona was surprised and a little hurt that her mother found her daughters work. Roberta reached for the spoon. Ramona held on to it because Roberta would finish faster if she was fed. Ramona tried strained peas next. 'Come on, Roberta. Down the hatch,' she said, using her father's words.

The hatch remained closed. Ramona tried to

poke the spoon between Roberta's lips. Roberta did not care to be poked. She began to look stubborn. Ramona was growing impatient to get to the television. If the husband of Blonde Nurse found out about Curly-haired Doctor—

Roberta kept her lips tightly closed. 'Look, Roberta. Watch your big sister.' Ramona opened her mouth wide, and after thinking it over, Roberta did the same. Ramona popped the peas into her mouth. Roberta frowned but accepted another spoonful. Then she leaned out of her chair, opened her mouth, and let peas dribble out onto the linoleum.

'Roberta!' cried Ramona. When Roberta looked worried, she changed the tone of her voice and said, 'Yum-yum. Nice peas full of vitamins and good things.' She smiled as she held a generous spoonful to Roberta's lips and thought, Horrid, nasty peas, before she said, 'Open wide.' When Roberta did as she was told, Ramona spooned in the peas.

With her mouth full of peas, Roberta looked both surprised and disappointed, as if her sister had betrayed her. Then she blew hard, spraying mushy, squishy, smelly green peas all over Ramona.

'Roberta!' cried Ramona, dropping the spoon on the high-chair tray and wiping her face on her sleeve. Roberta picked up the spoon, beat it in her food, and crowed. Then, filled with glee at what she had done, she threw the spoon on the floor. Why bother with it when she had hands? She patted her food and rubbed her hair.

'Mother!' cried Ramona. 'Roberta's making a mess.'

'Cope, dear. I'm busy,' answered Mrs Quimby from the hall. 'Just do the best you can.'

'E-e-e!' squealed Roberta as she threw her cup on the floor. Before Ramona could unfurl a banner of paper towels to wipe Roberta's face, her hair, her high chair, everything, Roberta tried to pick up her dish, which was held fast by the suction cup. She scowled, picked up a handful of food instead, and let it plop out of her hand onto the floor. This pleased her so much she squealed again.

'Roberta! Naughty girl!' cried Ramona, wiping peas off her own face. She never wanted to smell peas again. Roberta looked as if her feelings were hurt.

This time Mrs Quimby said, 'Sorry, Sally. I hear a damsel in distress.' And ended her book club conversation. When she saw the mess in the kitchen, she sighed, reached for a sponge, and said, 'Well, this really has been one of those days.'

Ramona tried to scrub peas out of Roberta's hair with a paper towel. She no longer felt like a big sister. She felt like a cross sister, even if Roberta was just a baby. Roberta smiled a peas-and-cottage-cheese-smeared smile.

'Don't worry about it, Ramona,' said Mrs Quimby. She sounded tired. 'Messes are a part of being a mother. A big part, now that I think about it. What was it you started to tell me before the telephone rang?'

Ramona hesitated. Somehow her news no longer seemed important. 'Oh, nothing much,' she said as Mr Quimby and Beezus came dripping through the back door. 'Only that a photographer is coming to take our school pictures tomorrow, and Mrs Meacham says we are going to have a Valentine box in our room.'

'Good,' said Mrs Quimby. 'Grandpa Day and Aunt Bea always like to have your picture.'

'Remember to say cheese,' said Mr Quimby as he stepped over peas and cottage cheese.

'Photographers always tell you to say that,' said Beezus, the experienced older sister. She pulled off her raincoat and dropped it on a chair before she picked up Roberta's cup from the floor.

Mr Quimby did not bother to take off his raincoat. He dampened a towel and began to wipe Roberta's hands and face. 'I see that Third Daughter has a mind of her own,' he remarked.

'E-e-e,' squealed Roberta, happy to have her

family waiting on her. That was the advantage of being a baby sister.

Feeling somewhat dejected because she had not been able to feed Roberta neatly, Ramona went off to her room to see what she could find to wear for her class picture.

The next morning Ramona put on a red plaid pinafore dress and a white blouse with a ruffle around the collar. The shoulders and armholes were a little tight, but she loved the twirly pleated skirt, even if it had once belonged to Beezus. Under the skirt she wore a pair of play shorts so no boy could see her underpants if she happened to bend over. She brushed the back of her hair, although it wouldn't show in the picture.

'Isn't your dress a little too—' began Mrs Quimby as Ramona picked up her lunch bag. She must have changed her mind because she finished with 'You look very nice today, dear.'

'Don't choke in that blouse,' said Beezus. 'It looks awfully tight.'

Ramona ignored her sister and walked off to the bus stop feeling neat, clean, and beautiful. The rain had stopped, and even though the day was cold, she left her raincoat unfastened because, like Beezus, she wanted to arrive unwrinkled. She walked instead of skipped so her hair would stay flat. She resisted stomping in puddles.

Mrs Pitt, busy picking up advertising circulars from her porch, said, 'My, don't you look nice this morning?' Ramona smiled modestly. This was the sort of grown-up question that did not demand an answer.

'What are you all dressed up for?' asked Howie, who was eating his sandwich in the middle of the sidewalk.

'My picture,' said Ramona.

'Big deal,' said Howie.

'Are you drethed up for a party?' asked a little girl Ramona could tell was in the second grade because she had lost her two front teeth.

When Ramona reached her classroom, Mrs Meacham, whose hair was freshly curled, smiled and said, 'You look very nice today, Ramona.'

'I know,' answered Ramona modestly. She felt a shoulder seam in her blouse split.

'You're all dressed up like you think you're somebody,' said Susan.

'I am somebody,' said Ramona with a toss of her head. She managed to stay neat until just before spelling time, when the school secretary opened the door and beckoned to Mrs Meacham, who said, 'All right, boys and girls. Picture time. Line up and walk *quietly* to the library, where we will all wait *quietly* for our turn. And remember to smile. At our school learning is fun. Let's show our parents by smiling.'

Ramona was glad to escape working on ôr, ôr, and yŏŏr words for a little while.

In the library a screen had been set up. On it was a picture of nothing in particular—clouds maybe, or shadows. The photographer was a young man with a lock of hair sticking straight up from the back of his head. 'Hi, kids,' he said. 'My name is Bill.' He pointed to a box of paper combs. 'Make yourselves pretty.' Some children took combs; others smoothed their hair with their hands. Bill motioned to the first girl in line, who as usual was Susan. Being first was important to Susan. He positioned her in front of the camera and said, 'Say cheese,' just as Beezus had predicted.

Susan said cheese. The camera clicked.

'Next!' said Bill as Susan stepped aside. A boy took her place. 'Say cheese,' ordered Bill. This went on over and over until it was Yard Ape's turn. He stood up straight, grinned, and after saying cheese did not step aside. 'How come you always tell us to say cheese?' he asked. 'Don't you get tired of it?'

'As a matter of fact I do, now that you mention it,' answered Bill. 'Next!'

It was Ramona's turn to step in front of the screen for 'cheese'.

Bill surprised her. 'Say peas,' he said.

Instantly Ramona thought of Roberta's spitting gooshy, smelly peas in her face. Ee-yew. Without thinking she scowled, wrinkled her nose as if smelling something bad, and pulled down the corners of her mouth. The camera clicked, the class laughed, and Bill said, 'Next!' Ramona hesitated. 'Move along,' ordered Bill. 'I have a gazillion kids waiting.' Ramona moved. She began to feel as if the neck of her blouse was choking her, so she unbuttoned the top button. She wondered what her family would say when they saw her picture.

Gradually, as the day went on and the class became engrossed in the study of pioneers crossing the plains in their covered wagons, Ramona began to feel that perhaps her picture was not as bad as she thought it was. Maybe Bill had snapped her picture a millionth of a second before she made a face. Of course. That was what had happened. Of course it was. Ramona spent the rest of the day feeling cute and perky even if her clothes were too tight.

9

RAMONA SITS

Ramona put her class picture out of her mind
entirely. She had other things to think about. 'I
wish I would hurry up and be old enough to baby-
sit,' she confided to Beezus one cold, wet morning,
as she watched her sister put on a new T-shirt she
had bought with money she had earned. 'I've had
a lot of practice with Roberta when mother is
busy. I know I could do it.'

Beezus looked thoughtful. 'Maybe . . .' She was
not so sure. She looked at her sister, who was
pulling on her socks as she lay on her bed with her
feet in the air. 'You're really more of a cheerleader
type.'

'I am?' Ramona sat up, startled at this insight
into her character. 'How come?'

'Oh, you know—' Beezus airily waved her
hand. 'You're always jumping around and waving
things.'

Ramona did not know what to say, so she said,
'I don't care. I still want to baby-sit.'

That was why, one afternoon shortly before

semester break, Ramona came home from school and faced her mother with a question: 'If I'm not old enough to baby-sit, am I old enough to cat-sit?'

Mrs Quimby thought a moment before she asked, 'Are you asking about cats in general or about one specific cat?'

'Daisy's brother's cat, Clawed,' explained Ramona. 'The family is going down to Roseburg to be with Daisy's grandparents during semester break. They take their dog in the car, but they have to take Clawed to the Kitty Corner and Clawed will be unhappy because he will be shut up in a cage and nobody will pet him.'

'Oh,' said Mrs Quimby.

'Mo-*ther*.' Ramona was impatient. 'Clawed is a really *nice* cat. He doesn't claw furniture or anything. Daisy said when he stayed at the Kitty Corner at Christmas he came home all grouchy. Besides, Daisy's mother will pay me for cat-sitting.'

'Oh?' Mrs Quimby smiled. 'It sounds to me as if you and Daisy have this all figured out.'

Ramona pressed on. 'If Beezus can baby-sit, I don't see why—'

'Ramona,' Mrs Quimby, no longer smiling, interrupted. 'I really can't drive you to Daisy's house every day to feed a cat. With Roberta it would be too much.'

Ramona was not a girl to give up easily. 'We
could bring Clawed here. We used to have a cat.'
She took a deep breath and prepared for major
pleading. If necessary she would even whine. 'Pu-
leeze, pu-*leeze*. I'll take care of him and everything.
You wouldn't have to do a thing. And I just know
Roberta would love to pet him.'

Mrs Quimby sighed. 'Well—as long as you agree
to be entirely responsible for him. How long did
you say they would be gone?'

'Just a week,' said Ramona. 'Just a teeny tiny
short week.'

Mrs Quimby's smile returned. 'There is no
such thing as a short week. A week is seven days,
no more, no less. All right. You may look after
Clawed for a week if Daisy's family can bring him
here. But remember, he is your responsibility and
no one else's.'

Delighted to have a chance to be responsible,
Ramona ran to the telephone to tell Daisy the
good news.

Several days later Mrs Kidd, Daisy, and Jeremy
delivered yowling, angry Clawed in his carrier
along with his litter box, a bag of litter, a brush,
canned and dried cat food, two dishes, and a square
carpet-covered construction with two holes, one
above the other, each big enough for Clawed to
hide in. 'Jeremy built Clawed's scratching post

himself.' Daisy was proud of her brother. 'We call it Clawed's kitty condo.'

Ramona had not thought of Clawed's equipment. She had expected an unencumbered cat.

Mrs Kidd unfastened the latch on the carrier. 'This will be much better for Clawed,' she said. 'He will settle down as soon as he has a chance to look around. We can't thank you enough.'

'That's perfectly all right,' said Mrs Quimby. 'Ramona is eager to take care of him.'

Clawed sat down and began to use his rough tongue to smooth his rumpled fur and to wash away the taint of his cage.

Ramona eyed the litter box. She had pictured herself holding and petting Clawed while she looked at television or read a book.

At that point Beezus came into the room, looked at Clawed, and said, 'Don't expect *me* to empty his litter box. I am not the one who is responsible.' Then she noticed Jeremy, quickly changed the tone of her voice, and said, 'Oh— hello, Jeremy.'

'Hello, Beatrice.' Jeremy turned red.

'Come on, kids. We have a zillion things to do.' Mrs Kidd hugged Ramona and said, 'I thank you, Clawed thanks you, we all thank you. Oh—and don't forget to brush him every day. That way he won't throw up so many hair balls.'

'You're welcome,' said Ramona with as much enthusiasm as she could muster. She disliked the smell of canned cat food, and she did not want to think about hair balls.

Jeremy bent over to stroke Clawed. 'So long, you old rascal. I'll miss you.' Clawed rubbed against Jeremy's legs, and the family departed with the carrier, leaving Ramona in charge of the cat.

'Nice kitty.' Ramona tried to mean it. Clawed paused in licking his paw to look at her. Then he continued washing as if he did not care to associate with her.

'Ramona, take the litter box to the basement.' Mrs Quimby spoke in a brisk, no-nonsense voice. Ramona knew she had no choice but to do as she was told. When she returned, Beezus was holding Roberta and saying, 'See the kitty? See the nice kitty?' Roberta's thoughts did not show. She had not made up her mind about Clawed, who ignored everything but his own paw and fur.

'You might put out some food and water for him so he will feel more at home,' suggested Ramona's mother.

Ramona spread newspapers on the floor in the corner of the kitchen, set out Clawed's dishes, and with the electric can opener opened a can of Puss-puddy. *Pee-yew.*

One whiff and she tried not to breathe.

Clawed, recognizing the sound of a can opener, came running to investigate. 'There, Your Royal Highness.' Ramona spoke crossly. Clawed chose to ignore her. She tried to make up for speaking so disagreeably by stroking him, but Clawed merely turned his head long enough to give her a look that said, You are not my friend. After eating, he explored the house before he curled up in a hole in his kitty condo and stared balefully out at the Quimbys' living room. Then he went to sleep.

Later that evening Mrs Quimby said to Ramona, 'Bedtime for your boarder. You'd better shut him in the basement.'

Clawed had different ideas. 'Here, kitty, kitty,' coaxed Ramona. Clawed glared from the hole in the post.

'Come on, puss-puss,' wheedled Beezus, trying to help. After all, she really liked cats. Clawed ignored her, his chin still resting on his paws.

Mrs Quimby reached into the hole and stroked the cat's head. 'Good kitty,' she whispered. Clawed closed his eyes.

'I'll show you how to deal with an old tomcat.' Mr Quimby picked up the carpeted post, turned it on its side, and dumped Clawed onto the carpet. 'Catch him!' he directed.

Ramona tackled Clawed and picked him up. Clawed went limp. 'Nice kitty-cat,' she said, trying to make up for the indignity of his being dumped. He was heavier than she expected.

Mr Quimby scratched Clawed's ear. 'Into the basement, old boy,' he said.

Ramona lugged the cat to the basement door, set him down on the top step, and closed the door quickly. She thought better of this unkindness, opened the door a crack, and said, 'Nighty-night, Clawed.'

The cat was silent. He was silent, that is, until the family was in bed asleep. He then began to protest. He yowled at the basement door, he meowed pitifully, and yowled some more. Except for Roberta, who always slept soundly, the whole family was awake.

'Ramona,' Mr Quimby called out. 'Do something about that cat.'

'What am I supposed to do?' asked Ramona, only half-awake.

'Just cope,' said her father. This annoyed Ramona. Now that she was in the fourth grade, her parents often told her to cope when she wanted help.

Without bothering with slippers, she stumbled sleepily down the hall, faintly illuminated by the tiny green light on the electric toothbrush in the bathroom. The kitchen linoleum felt cold to her feet as she opened the basement door.

'Come on, you old cat,' she said, and felt Clawed brush against her nightgown. 'See if I care what you do.'

What Clawed did was sleep on the living room couch. He had won. In the morning, when the Quimbys were getting out of bed, he yawned, stretched, went to his water dish, decided he didn't care for it, strolled into the bathroom, and drank out of the toilet. 'You old scoundrel,' muttered Mr Quimby through the sound of his electric razor.

Now that Clawed had made it clear to the family that he was going to set the rules for his treatment, he turned into a mostly agreeable cat, and as Ramona had predicted, Roberta was fascinated by a creature smaller than she was. She crawled after him, patted his fur, squealed with pleasure. Clawed did not seem to mind. If she was too rough or pulled his tail, he simply retired to the hole in his kitty condo.

Ramona, who had hoped someone would go with her to the park so she could work on a new set of calluses, now felt her life was full of chores. She washed Clawed's dish, changed his water even though he drank from the toilet, served his meals, brushed his hair off the couch, brushed Clawed himself so he wouldn't shed so much, watched him when Roberta was crawling around on the floor. She began to look forward to Clawed's going home.

Then late one afternoon when Beezus was at Abby's house and Ramona was sitting on the floor keeping one eye on Roberta and Clawed and her other eye on a book, Mrs Quimby said, 'Do you think you could watch Roberta while I drive over and pick up Beezus? I'll only be gone a few minutes.'

'Sure, Mom.' Ramona felt a ripple of pleasure. She had been promoted from cat-sitter to baby-sitter. She was proud that her mother finally trusted her.

'You're sure?' asked Mrs Quimby.

'Of course I'm sure. I watch her all the time,' said Ramona, and added words she had heard Beezus speak so often. 'Mom, you worry too much.'

'That's what mothers are for,' said Mrs Quimby as she went out of the door.

'Now, you be a good girl,' Ramona instructed her baby sister, who was sitting on the floor holding her precious little blanket against her face.

Roberta looked agreeable to being a good girl. She pulled a magazine off the coffee table, tearing the cover off as it fell to the carpet. 'E-e-e,' squealed Roberta, so delighted with her accomplishment she dropped her blanket. With both hands she rumpled a few pages, a sound that disturbed Clawed, who was napping under the window.

'No-no, Roberta,' said Ramona. 'Don't hurt the nice magazine.'

Roberta had seen her mother leave. She gave Ramona a you're-not-my-mother-and-I'm-not-going-to-stop look and rumpled a few more pages. She did not intend to mind her sister, not when she had invented a new game. She tore off another page and took a bite.

'No-no, Roberta,' cried Ramona. 'Icky. Nasty. 'Pit it in Ramona's hand.'

Roberta's game was getting better. She opened her mouth and let soggy paper fall into Ramona's hand.

'Ick,' said Ramona. 'Good girl.' She pulled the magazine away from Roberta and tossed it on the coffee table. Then she threw the wet, chewed-up paper into the cold fireplace.

While Ramona was doing this, Clawed began to cough, a hacking, gagging cough. Hair balls, thought Ramona, stricken. She hadn't brushed him enough. He was going to throw up, right there on the carpet, and she would have to clean it up. Ugh. Ick. Clawed hacked harder. There was the ripping sound of Roberta tearing up more paper. She had managed to pull the magazine off the coffee table again. At least tearing up a magazine would keep her busy for a while.

'Hang on, Clawed,' cried Ramona as she opened the front door. She seized the cat around his heaving middle and, in spite of his weight, managed to carry him outside, down the steps, and set him on the shaggy winter grass. She started back to Roberta. But what if Clawed ran off? What would she do if she lost Jeremy's cat? She decided that Roberta, busy with the magazine, was safe for a few seconds. She returned to Clawed, hung on to him to make sure he wouldn't get away, and ordered, 'Spit it out, Clawed,' while she worried about what her mother and Beezus—they were due any minute—would say if they found her outside with the cat instead of inside with Roberta.

With one last cough Clawed freed himself of the hair ball.

'Thanks,' muttered Ramona as she started to lug him into the house. Clawed had a different idea. He struggled out of her grasp and ran back into the house without any help from her. 'Stupid cat,' said Ramona. 'If you didn't wash so much, you wouldn't get hair balls.' She found Clawed sitting on the carpet washing just as Roberta, leaving her blanket behind, crawled towards his uninhabited kitty condo. Before Ramona could reach her, she stuck her head inside the lower hole to see what was inside.

'Roberta!' cried Ramona. What if her mother and Beezus walked in now?

Roberta sneezed and began to cry. The inside of the kitty condo was dark, scary, and full of cat hair. She did not like it one bit. Ramona grasped her little sister around the waist and pulled. Roberta, frightened at being tugged, screamed harder. Clawed stopped washing long enough to look over his shoulder with disapproval. Clawed did not care for noise.

'It's all right, Roberta.' Ramona tried to sound soothing as she pulled. Roberta screamed harder, her cries muffled by the walls of the scratching post. Ramona held her breath when she heard a car and let it out when the car did not turn into the Quimbys' driveway. She did not want her mother and Beezus to find Roberta breathing cat hair with her head stuck in a hole.

What do I do now? Ramona thought desperately as she gently stroked Roberta's back to calm her. 'There, there. Ramona will get you out.' But how? Screaming, Roberta frantically beat her little feet on the carpet and pushed at the scratching post with her hands.

What if she suffocates? thought equally frantic Ramona. Should I call 911? Firemen would come and save her, wouldn't they? They often saved people on television. She started for the telephone. But she isn't going to smother, Ramona suddenly realized, not if she's screaming. She has to breathe to scream, and she must be breathing hard from all the noise she's making. Once more Clawed paused in his washing to disapprove. A cat needed peace and quiet, especially when his fur had been rumpled.

I've got to think, Ramona told herself. Fast, before mother comes home. If Roberta's head went into the hole, it should come out. What was different? Roberta was not crying when she stuck her head in the hole—that was what was different. Her mouth was closed. Now it was open. Her chin was in the way. All Ramona had to do was get Roberta to stop crying. How? Then Ramona had an inspiration. She said as cheerfully as she could manage when she was so frightened, 'Whe-e-ere's Roberta?' Her sister always enjoyed the peekaboo game.

Roberta's answer was to beat her feet harder and go on screaming. Ramona could see her idea was not going to work. She would have to think of something else. She heard another car. Was it? No, it wasn't the Quimby car. She tried to think what else amused Roberta. Then it came to her. Mother Goose rhymes! Ramona gently rubbed her sister's back, put her mouth close to her shoulder, and began softly, 'Three little kittens . . .'

Roberta's feet stopped pounding on the carpet. Encouraged, Ramona continued '. . . lost their mittens . . .' Roberta stopped crying. She must be listening. Ramona went on reciting as she gently tugged at Roberta's shoulders. 'Lost your mittens, you naughty kittens! Then you shall have no pie. Mee-ow, mee-ow . . .' That was Roberta's favourite part of the rhyme. Ramona carefully pulled her sister's head out of the hole and went limp with relief. Then she hugged the baby, who was, at the moment, the most precious person in the whole world. Roberta snuggled against Ramona, who finished the rhyme, 'No, you shall have no pie.' Roberta was pleased. 'Mo-mo,' she said.

Ramona kissed her sister. 'Mo-mo' was Roberta's way of saying 'Ramona'. She set Roberta down, handed her the little blanket, ran for a Kleenex, wiped her nose, and threw all the torn pages in the fireplace. Then, as she heard the Quimby car pull into the driveway, she picked up her book. Roberta was holding her blanket against her face with one hand while she sucked the thumb of her other hand and watched Clawed carefully wash the tip of his tail. I did it, thought Ramona. I baby-sat. I was responsible. Worn-out by her responsibility, she opened her book and pretended she had been reading all along, but she was thinking, One more day and Clawed will go home.

'I can see that the three of you got along just fine,' commented Mrs Quimby as she came into the room.

'Yes, and you were gone a long time,' answered Ramona.

Mrs Quimby glanced at her watch. 'Only fifteen minutes. There was more traffic than I expected.'

Only fifteen minutes. It had seemed like hours to Ramona.

'Roberta looks ready for a nap,' said Mrs Quimby as she picked up the baby—'oopsy-daisy'—and carried her off to her room.

Ramona laid down her book and watched Beezus take off her jacket and unwind her scarf. 'I was just thinking . . .' she said, and paused.

'Good for you,' said Beezus.

Ramona ignored this and said, 'I was just thinking—how do you get to be a cheerleader?'

10

THE VALENTINE BOX

Early in February the weather changed to wind and snow. Mrs Pitt managed to shovel a path on the sidewalk in front of her house. Then schools were closed for almost a week. Ramona and Daisy were too busy coasting on the Thirty-seventh Street hill on Mr Quimby's old sled, 'a real antique,' Beezus called it, to think about anything that had happened at school.

That was why Ramona was surprised when school reopened and grey envelopes of class pictures were handed out. Feeling sure that Bill had snapped her picture a second before she made a face, she opened her envelope expecting to see herself cute and perky, maybe a little bit pretty. But no. She wasn't cute. She wasn't perky or the least bit pretty. She was a plain, ordinary girl making an ugly face. Ashamed, she shoved her envelope into her book bag.

Unfortunately, everyone in the class had, in addition to a big picture and several smaller pictures, a sheet of pictures of each member shown slightly larger than a postage stamp. Everyone pointed to Ramona's picture and snickered.

Susan said much too nicely, 'It's too bad about your picture, Ramona.'

Daisy, who was always kind, said, 'Don't worry about it, Ramona. We all know you don't really look like that.'

Yard Ape was silent. Ramona was suddenly cross with him for not paying attention to her, not even on the bus. It wasn't her fault Mrs Meacham confiscated his note and embarrassed him in front of the class.

Ramona tossed her hair to show her class she didn't care what they thought. When she returned home that day, she hid her pictures and hoped her family would never find them.

This lasted for about a week until one evening at dinner Mrs Quimby asked, 'Ramona, what happened to your school pictures? Howie's grandmother says he has his.' There were no secrets in this neighbourhood.

Ramona took a big bite of potato. She wasn't supposed to talk with her mouth full.

'You don't like your picture,' guessed Beezus.

Ramona chewed her potato more than potato needed to be chewed.

'Come on, Ramona,' said her father. 'We love you no matter how you look. Go get them.'

Ramona swallowed, sighed, and fetched the grey envelope, which she thrust at her father. He pulled out the individual pictures and passed them around to the family, who, as Ramona expected, laughed. She put on her you-hurt-my-feelings expression and said, 'You're being horrid to me.'

'I think this is a great picture.' Mr Quimby smiled at his middle daughter. 'It captures the real Ramona.'

'It does not!' contradicted Ramona.

'Your Grandpa Day is going to love this,' said Mrs Quimby, 'and so will your Aunt Bea.'

'Mom, that's *mean*! That picture is awful. I hate it.' Ramona wondered if this was all worth a tantrum and decided it wasn't. Maybe she was outgrowing tantrums. Instead she explained about Roberta and the peas. She concluded with, 'If Roberta had eaten her peas, I would have had a nice picture. At least I don't spit on the floor like Roberta.'

Mrs Quimby reached over and patted Ramona's hand. 'We all know you are nicer than your picture,' she said.

'Except sometimes,' said Beezus.

Ramona ignored her sister. 'All the kids at school except Daisy laughed at me,' she went on, 'and now our relatives will, too.' She was beginning to run out of reasons to feel sorry for herself.

Beezus spoke up. 'What difference does it make? When we take our family picture for our next Christmas card, you can smile twice as hard to make up for your school picture.'

This led to a discussion of how the family should pose for their Christmas-card picture even though Christmas was months away. After that no more was said about Ramona's picture. At school everyone seemed to have forgotten it, too, perhaps because Mrs Meacham brought out a box decorated with hearts that Ramona could see had been used in the many classes Mrs Meacham had taught in years past. Mrs Meacham made a little speech about not hurting anyone's feelings. Everyone must give a valentine to everyone else in the class. Ramona had heard this speech from previous teachers and knew the problem could be solved by buying kits that held enough valentines for an entire class, silly valentines with words such as 'Bee my valentine' with a picture of a bee, or 'I choo-choose you for my valentine' with a bear driving a train. For special friends some people might enclose a candy heart with 'Be my valentine' or 'I love you' printed on it. For extra-special friends fourth graders, usually girls, made valentines decorated with heart stickers and paper lace. This was the part of Valentine's Day Ramona liked best.

That week after dinner Ramona worked on her valentines. Of course she made Daisy's first, with a big pink heart surrounded by yellow daisies, which she drew with the coloured pencils her father had bought her. She made another with pink and red hearts for Janet and another, a plain valentine with just one heart, for Howie. It looked too plain, so she drew a hammer, a saw, and some nails around the heart. Howie would like that.

The evening before Valentine's Day she addressed her store-bought valentines, leaving Yard Ape to the last because she wasn't sure she should even give him one, no matter what Mrs Meacham said. Then she discovered she had no more valentines left. Would Mrs Meacham notice if she skipped Yard Ape? Yes. Mrs Meacham never missed a thing. Eagle-eyed Mrs Meacham might even stay after school, open the box, and go through the valentines to make sure everyone remembered everyone else.

Ramona tapped her nose with her red pencil while she tried to think. Roses are red, violets blue—no, that wouldn't do. Everyone said that. Roses are pink, you sti— No. She was cross with Yard Ape but not that cross.

'Bedtime, Ramona,' said Mr Quimby.

The third time her father spoke to her, Ramona was still trying to think of a valentine for Yard

Ape, something not too icky-sweet but not really mean. She found Beezus propped up on her bed studying. Ramona sat down on her bed, kicked off her shoes, and began to pull off her socks by the toes. She sighed noisily to get her sister's attention which was not the same as interrupting her when she was studying.

Beezus looked up from her book. 'Something bothering you?' she asked.

Ramona explained her dilemma, which Beezus did not see as a problem. 'Just give him one of your school pictures with the funny face you made. That way he won't know if you gave it to him because you like him or because you don't like him.'

Sensible Beezus. Ramona wished she had thought of this herself. She found a picture, stuffed it in an envelope, printed DANNY on the front, brushed her teeth, and went to bed hoping the class would have chocolate-chip cookies at the Valentine's Day party the next day.

The next afternoon, after the bell rang for the last period, the room mother of Mrs Meacham's class arrived with a tray of cookies (peanut-butter, Ramona's next-to-favourite) and cartons of pink punch. Mrs Meacham opened the valentine box and asked the valentine monitors to distribute the envelopes.

As Ramona ate her cookies, she sorted through her valentines. Several looked interesting and a couple were lumpy, which meant they had candy hearts inside. Then she found the one she had been looking for, an envelope addressed in Yard Ape's uphill scrawl. She felt uneasy. Had she made a mistake in giving him her picture? She bit into a cookie and glanced across the aisle in time to see Yard Ape pull her photograph out of the envelope. She stopped chewing. He looked at her picture, grinned, and put the picture in his shirt pocket.

Ramona quickly looked away and tore open his envelope. She pulled out, not a valentine, but a sheet of paper without a single heart. Printed in big letters that ignored lines were the words:

IF YOU ARE EATING PEAS
THINK OF ME BEFORE YOU SNEEZE

Signed,
Yard Ape
PRESIDENT

An original poem! A poem Mrs Meacham didn't have a chance to read. Ramona looked at

Yard Ape and smiled. He smiled back. Then she carefully folded his valentine smaller and smaller until it was small enough to fit into the little box in which she kept her baby teeth at home. She would keep it forever.

11

BIRTHDAY GIRL

Spring finally came. Rain no longer fell every day.
Lawn mowers whirred through the shaggy winter
grass. People went to the park again. Everyone,
especially Ramona, felt good. One evening, late
in May, the Quimby family was enjoying an
unusually quiet dinner. The telephone did not ring.
Roberta had been fed and, worn-out from pulling
herself to her feet by hanging on to chairs, was
asleep. Beezus and her father were talking about
something—Ramona wasn't paying attention
because she was busy examining the new calluses
beginning to form on the palms of her hands. The
girls at school, those who enjoyed swinging on the
rings, were once more comparing calluses. This
thought gave Ramona an idea.

'You know what I would like to do on my
birthday?' she asked, and did not wait for an
answer. 'Have a birthday party in the park. We
can play on the rings and skip playing pin-the-
tail-on-the-donkey and all those babyish games.'

'I think we can manage that if Beezus will help

491

with Roberta,' agreed Mrs Quimby, and added, 'If it doesn't rain.'

'Sure. I'll help,' said Beezus. 'The park is a good idea. That way the house doesn't get messed up.'

Although she knew what Beezus said was true, Ramona ignored her sister and said dreamily, 'Just think. I'll be a teenager.'

'Aren't you getting ahead of yourself?' asked Mr Quimby.

'No, you won't,' said Beezus. 'You will be ten years old.

'That's a teenager, sort of,' said Ramona. 'Zeroteen. That's a double-digit number.' *Double-digit* sounded serious and important. 'And next year I'll be oneteen and the year after twoteen, then thirteen and fourteen.' Her family looked amused, but Ramona did not care. She was too busy with her plans. 'And I don't want a birthday cake,' she continued. 'I want a big bowl of whipped cream.' Ramona liked thick, soft, fluffy, sweet whipped cream much more than she liked cake, which was sometimes dry and with thin frosting.

'Think of the calories,' said Mrs Quimby, who thought a lot about calories since Roberta was born.

'And the cholesterol,' said Mr Quimby, who sometimes said he should begin to watch his diet.

'Whipped cream will make your face break

out in spots,' said Beezus, who spent a lot of time looking at herself in the mirror.

Ramona considered all these worries ridiculous, so she ignored them. She leaned back in her chair, closed her eyes, and thought of a big bowl of whipped cream. On a table in the park. Surrounded by birthday presents. With the sun shining through the fir trees.

'But where would you put the candles?' asked Beezus.

Ramona opened her eyes. She had forgotten about candles. 'Just—stick them around in the whipped cream' was the best answer she could come up with.

Of course Beezus found something wrong with this. 'If you blow hard enough to blow out the candles, whipped cream will fly all over the place.'

Ramona was silent. She liked the picture of whipped cream flying across the table with her friends ducking and squealing, but then she wouldn't get to eat the whipped cream. Beezus was right, which Ramona found a tiny bit annoying.

Mrs Quimby, sensing trouble, quickly said, 'I could bake a cake with whipped cream for icing.'

'OK,' said Ramona. 'Chocolate cake and thick whipped cream.' That evening she sat at the kitchen table to work on her guest list: three girls who were her good friends, four others who had invited Ramona to their birthday parties. She read her list to her mother.

'What about Susan?' asked Mrs Quimby. 'You went to her birthday party.'

Ramona made a face. 'Yes, but I didn't have a good time.'

'That has nothing to do with it,' said Mrs Quimby. 'And I think it is time you and Susan learned to get along.'

Reluctantly, in less than perfect writing, Ramona added Susan's name to her list. She did try, medium hard, to get along with Susan, who always waved around her papers on which Mrs Meacham had written Excellent! Good Work! or Prize Speller! at the top. She hoped Susan would not come. She did not want to hear her mother tell her to play nicely with Susan or her father tell her to cut out this nonsense about Susan.

As it turned out, everyone accepted, even Susan. When Ramona's birthday—the most important day of the year, next to Christmas—finally came, the sky held only a few unimportant clouds. Ramona opened family presents at breakfast. After waffles served with blueberries, Ramona sang, 'O frabjous day! Callooh! Callay!'—happy words from a book about a girl named Alice.

Then the telephone rang. Beezus got to it before Ramona. The call turned out to be from a neighbour who had an emergency and needed a baby-sitter right away. 'Please, please, Mom, can I take it?' Beezus begged. 'These are *nice* people who always have the right change.'

'But this is Ramona's birthday,' Mrs Quimby reminded her.

'It's OK with me,' said Ramona, who enjoyed having her mother to herself. Along with Roberta, of course. She also liked feeling she was being kind to Beezus.

'Please, Mom,' begged Beezus. 'I don't want someone else to get their business.'

Mrs Quimby, who was sliding layer cake pans into the oven, reluctantly agreed.

Then telephone calls came for Ramona: Grandpa Day from his mobile home park in California, where he was table-tennis champion; Aunt Bea and Uncle Hobart all the way from Alaska, where Ramona pictured them surrounded by the seals and polar bears she had seen on television. A lovely chocolate smell of baking cake filled the house, and the few clouds in the blue sky remained as fluffy as whipped cream. It was the beginning of a great day.

Finally, *finally*, Roberta was bathed and dressed in her red corduroy overalls. Ramona stuffed her into her little sweater and wondered if she would ever learn to hold her thumbs in so her hands would slip through the sleeves without a struggle. The cake was iced with swirls of whipped cream, and the car was loaded with the picnic, along with Roberta in her car seat, her nappy bag, and her teddy bear. Ramona buckled her seat belt in happy anticipation. 'Whew!' said Mrs Quimby as she turned the key in the ignition. 'We're on our way.'

Fortunately, the picnic table Ramona wanted, the one between the wading pool and the playground, was vacant. Mrs Quimby lifted Roberta out, car seat and all, and set her on the grass where Ramona could keep an eye on her. Roberta waved her hands and feet, fussing, until Ramona released her and, holding her by the hands, helped her walk on the grass. The teeter-totter thumped, rings clanged, little children in the wading pool splashed, tennis balls bounced.

The great day was about to get better. Ramona's guests, all of them carrying interesting packages, came running across the grass. Of course Susan was among them, the only one wearing a dress instead of play clothes. Roberta, crawling fast, started towards the wading pool while the girls piled their presents on a bench. Ramona caught her and brought her back.

'Hello, girls,' Mrs Quimby called out as she laid out plastic forks and spoons on the checkered tablecloth and poured punch into paper cups.

Without a word about Happy Birthday, the guests hovered over Roberta, cooing, squealing, and admiring. 'Look at her tiny fingers with those teeny-weeny fingernails!' 'She's so *sweet*!' 'I wish I had a baby sister.' 'Look at her little teeth when she smiles!' Smiling, Roberta crawled away. The girls caught her and brought her back. Roberta had invented a new game that the girls played, catching her and bringing her back.

Ramona felt forgotten. She knew all about Roberta's tiny hands and feet. All babies had them. She knew about her teeth, too. She had listened to Roberta fret and wiped up her drool when she was teething. She marvelled at Roberta's growth, but not today. This was her birthday, her very own day, not Roberta's. Ramona sat beside her pile of presents and scowled.

'Ramona!' whispered Mrs Quimby as she dealt out tuna-fish sandwiches and carrot sticks. 'Behave yourself. Smile.' Ramona turned up the corners of her mouth, hardly a real smile. Roberta tired of excitement and began to fuss until Mrs Quimby picked her up.

Ramona's friends then remembered to say Happy Birthday as they gathered around to watch her open her presents. This is more like it, Ramona thought as she untied bows, read cards, and tore fancy wrappings off paperback books, hair bands, stationery, a big box of crayons, and a floppy stuffed frog, while her mother, with Roberta balanced on her hip, poked candles into the whipped cream icing.

Then, as the girls were eating their sandwiches and carrot sticks, one of them said, 'Look! There's Danny!' Everyone looked to see Yard Ape and two other boys climbing up the slides. Ramona knew they felt too old to slide down, so they had to show off by climbing up. 'Ee-yew! Boys!' the girls squealed.

On hearing this, Yard Ape and his friends came running and whooping. Ramona's squealing guests all disappeared under the table, hidden by the tablecloth. Roberta howled. Mrs Quimby tried to comfort her, but she only cried louder, her face puckered, tears streaming down her face.

'Yard Ape, you go away!' ordered Ramona, annoyed at Yard Ape's taking away her birthday. 'You're scaring my baby sister.' The boys, still whooping, ran back to the playground.

'You can come out now,' Ramona ordered her less-than-perfect guests. Roberta stopped howling and looked surprised to see girls crawl out from under the table. She was old enough to know girls did not belong under tables. Mrs Quimby returned the baby to her car seat on the grass, where, worn-out by excitement, she fell asleep. Somehow, with Ramona helping, Mrs Quimby managed to serve everyone ice cream, light the candles, and say, 'Make a wish.' Ramona closed her eyes, unsure of what to wish for. New skates? Susan transferred to another room at school? She settled on an all-purpose wish: I wish all my wishes would come true. Then she blew out all her candles with one breath.

'No cake for me, please,' said Susan. 'I brought an apple.'

The girls looked at her in surprise as she pulled an apple out of her pocket. Not eat birthday cake? Everyone ate birthday cake.

'There might be spit on the cake from blowing out the candles,' explained Susan.

Ramona was shocked. 'I did *not* spit on my birthday cake,' she informed Susan, while her mother continued to serve cake as if nothing terrible had been said.

Susan was very sure of herself. 'You could have. Little bits of spit so tiny you couldn't see them.' The girls began to giggle. Susan looked superior in that annoying way of hers and said, 'My mother says blowing out candles is unsanitary and cake can give you cavities.' She crunched into her apple. The girls stopped giggling and looked thoughtfully at their cake.

'You ate cake at other people's birthday parties,' said an indignant Ramona. 'I saw you.'

Susan had an explanation. 'Yes, but that was before mother read a book on how to stay healthy.'

Now Daisy spoke up. 'I think that's silly. I'm going to eat my cake. I've eaten birthday cake all my life and I'm still alive.' Ramona was glad she had Daisy for a best friend.

Susan went on crunching her apple. She frowned. Obviously she did not like to hear her mother and the book called silly.

'All right, girls,' said Mrs Quimby, smiling brightly. 'You don't have to eat your cake if you don't want to.' Used to Quimby spit, she took a bite of her own cake.

'I hope your apple has a worm in it,' Ramona whispered to Susan.

Three girls carefully scraped their whipped cream aside. Two did not touch their cake but ate their ice cream. The rest ate as if nothing had happened. 'I think you are all being stupid,' Daisy said to the non-eaters. 'If you can't see spit, maybe it isn't there.'

'You can't see germs, and they can make you sick,' someone pointed out. Two girls laid down their plastic forks.

'I don't have germs!' Ramona insisted.

'Of course you do,' someone said. 'Everyone has germs. You can't see them, but they are there.' This set off an argument about germs—how small they were, did they stick together, could they jump.

Even though she suspected her mother of being amused, Ramona spoke sternly to her guests. 'You aren't supposed to talk about germs at someone's birthday party.'

Daisy spoke up once more. 'Who cares about a few teeny germs. It's not like we picked something up off the sidewalk or bit into something someone else was eating.'

All the guests except Susan began to eat their cake, which, after all, looked delicious. 'So there, Susan,' said one of the girls before she took a big bite.

'See what you're missing,' another said. Everyone except Susan agreed that whipped cream was better than icing. They all wanted whipped cream on their birthday cakes, too.

To everyone's surprise Susan threw her apple across the lawn without even trying to hit the trash can. Her face crumpled as if she were about to burst into tears. Ramona was stunned. People didn't cry at birthday parties unless they were little and missed their mothers. The rest of the girls were shocked into silence.

'Why, Susan.' Mrs Quimby put a comforting arm around her shoulders. 'Whatever is the matter, dear?'

'Everything,' said Susan through her tears. 'Nobody likes me and everybody likes Ramona.'

'You are supposed to like people on their birthdays,' Ramona tried to explain to make things better.

'I don't mean just on your birthday,' said Susan with a tearful gulp. 'I mean every day. People even make valentines for you. All mine were store-bought. You aren't perfect and nobody cares.'

Ramona wasn't so sure about the part about nobody caring. Take Mrs Meacham and spelling—

'I'm supposed to be perfect every single minute,' said Susan, her chin quivering.

How awful, thought Ramona, beginning to feel sorry for Susan.

'Nobody's perfect,' Mrs Quimby reminded Susan. 'I could tell you a few things about Ramona. Like the time she was playing at Daisy's house—'

'Mother!' cried Ramona. The guests were immediately alert to a dark secret about to be revealed. Having distracted the guests, Mrs Quimby did not continue.

Susan was too engrossed in her troubles to be

curious. She sniffed and said, 'Even Yard Ape likes Ramona.'

Here Ramona modestly lowered her eyes. Other girls giggled. Mrs Quimby hugged Susan and said, 'Cheer up. Things are often not as bad as they seem.'

'That's right,' agreed Ramona. 'I survived spelling.'

These words seemed to comfort Susan.

'Maybe I could eat a little piece of cake,' she ventured with a sniff. 'I don't think mother would mind if I don't eat the whipped cream and if I brush my teeth as soon as I get home.'

Ramona was relieved that the other girls did not laugh at Susan. It must be terrible, always having to be perfect when everyone else was messy and full of faults part of the time, maybe even most of the time. She discovered she really felt sorry for Susan.

The other girls' attention had been diverted from Susan. 'Mrs Quimby, tell us about what happened when Ramona was playing at Daisy's house,' one of the girls requested.

Fortunately, at that moment Roberta woke up, felt wet and neglected, and began to cry. Mrs Quimby, having comforted Susan, went off to change and soothe Roberta.

Daisy, eager that the question not be answered

when Mrs Quimby returned, said, 'Let's see who has the biggest calluses.' Hands were held out, calluses felt, and it was agreed that those who lived closest to the park were lucky. Ramona felt secure. By the end of summer she would have super calluses.

Mrs Quimby finished changing Roberta's nappy and returned to the table with the smiling baby in her arms. Before anyone could ask again what had happened at her house, Daisy spoke up. 'Let's go play on the rings.'

The girls, even Susan, scrambled from the table, remembered their manners, and chorused, 'Thank you for the party,' before they ran off to the rings. Mrs Quimby started to clear the table with her free hand, and even though she wasn't sure a birthday girl should have to clean up after her own party, Ramona felt obliged to help. After all, she lived near the park and would have plenty of time to swing on the rings when school was out.

'You know, Ramona,' said Mrs Quimby, 'Susan's mother isn't the only one who has read a book. The book I read said ten is the nicest age of growing up. It said ten year olds are pleasant and agreeable.'

'That's me,' said Ramona, suddenly at her pleasant and agreeable best.

Mrs Quimby dropped a kiss on Ramona's hair

before she changed the subject. 'I wonder what we should do with the rest of this cake,' she said. 'Whipped cream doesn't keep very long.'

Ramona saw Yard Ape and his merry band of two running across the grass. 'Feed it to the boys,' she said to her mother, and called out, 'Hey, Yard Ape! Want some birthday cake?'

'Sure.' Danny picked up a tennis ball a beginning player had batted over the fence and threw it back. Then he and his friends came running.

Ramona seized the knife and clumsily divided the leftover cake into three pieces. The boys picked up their cake with their fingers and sang, led by Yard Ape, 'Happy Birthday to you . . . happy birthday, dear Ramona. You belong in a zoo.'

Ramona could ignore the part about the zoo because she was secretly pleased that Yard Ape had called her dear Ramona even if the words were part of a song everyone knew.

The boys finished their cake, licked their germy fingers, and wiped them on the seats of their germy jeans. 'Thank you for the birthday cake,' said Yard Ape, who must have been taught manners, even if they did not show in school. 'Happy tenth birthday.'

'Zeroteenth,' corrected Ramona. 'I'm a teenager now.'

Yard Ape stopped. 'I never thought of it that way.' He started off across the grass.

'And I'm a potential grown-up!' Ramona called after him.

'Me too!' Yard Ape shouted back.

'Come on, Ramona,' one of the girls called out. 'It's your birthday.'

'Run along,' said Mrs Quimby as she returned Roberta to her car seat.

'I'm coming,' Ramona answered. Her sticky fingers would help keep her hands from sliding off the rings. The sky was blue, little children still laughed and splashed in the wading pool, the rings clanged. She felt better about Susan. Yard Ape liked her. The day was perfect—well, not really, but close enough.

Beverly Cleary is one of America's most
popular authors and her many successful stories,
including the best-selling *Ramona* series,
have delighted children all over the world
for many years.

Beverley Cleary's books have earned her many
prestigious awards, including the American
Library Association's Laura Ingalls Wilder
Award, presented in recognition of her lasting
contribution to children's literature. She lives in
California and is the mother of grown-up twins.